Liz Byrski was born and brought up in England and has lived in Western Australia since 1981. She is the author of a number of non-fiction books, and has worked as a staff and freelance journalist, a broadcaster with ABC Radio and an adviser to a minister in the WA Government. Liz now lectures in professional writing at Curtin University. She is also the author of *Gang of Four*; *Food, Sex & Money* and *Belly Dancing for Beginners*.

www.lizbyrski.com.au

Also by Liz Byrski

Gang of Four
Food, Sex & Money
Belly Dancing for Beginners

TRIP OF A LIFETIME

Liz Byrski

MACMILLAN
Pan Macmillan Australia

First published 2008 in Macmillan by Pan Macmillan Australia Pty Limited
1 Market Street, Sydney

National Library of Australia
cataloguing-in-publication data:

Byrski, Liz.
Trip of a lifetime.

ISBN 978 1 4050 3827 0 (pbk.).

I. Title.

A823.3

Typeset in 11/14pt Palatino by Post Pre-press Group
Printed in Australia by McPherson's Printing Group

Papers used by Pan Macmillan Australia Pty Ltd are natural, recyclable
products made from wood grown in sustainable forests. The manufacturing
processes conform to the environmental regulations of the country of origin.

ONE

Later, even when she'd had time to think about it, she still couldn't remember anything unusual about that evening; no sense of foreboding, no warning signal, not even a feeling of unease. The meeting ran late, it was dark and wet as they came out of the office and she was fiddling with her umbrella while she waited for Shaun to set the alarm and lock the door. But as she turned to go down the steps to the street, she tripped and grabbed his arm and that was when it happened. Something hit her shoulder with tremendous force, propelling her forward as her neck was thrown back, the noise a sharp explosion as she hurtled down the steps. The next thing she remembered was the ambulance, the wail of the siren, a mask over her face, and Shaun urging her to hang on, before everything went blank again. When she finally regained consciousness, it was in the harsh light of the emergency ward.

'I can't have been shot,' she insisted, closing her eyes again.

'Try to keep your eyes open, Miss Delaney,' someone said. 'Can you talk to me, please?'

She forced her eyelids open, aware now of pain, a lot of pain in her left shoulder and her head.

'Can you see me?' She nodded in the direction of a white coat. 'How many fingers am I holding up?'

'Three.'

'Yes, good. Someone took a shot at you. They got you in the shoulder but you're going to be fine.'

'My head . . . '

'You hit your head. It's not serious but it'll need a few stitches, and an x-ray will show us where the bullet is. I'm going to give you something for the pain. This'll sting a bit.'

'Shaun?' she asked.

'I'm here, Heather.' His drawn face appeared above her. 'I'm going to stay with you.'

'Are *you* okay?'

'Fine, and you're going to be okay too, just hang in there. This is Detective Roussos.'

The room lurched drunkenly and a new face emerged.

'Sorry, Miss Delaney, but time's important. Do you have any idea who might have done this? Who might want to . . . want to kill you?'

'Kill me?'

'A grudge, perhaps? Something political, past or present?'

'Of course not . . .'

His faced blurred and then clarified. 'You're sure? Not a constituent or some protest group?'

She tried to shake her head but it hurt too much.

'Any threats? An old boyfriend, an ex-husband?'

'Christ,' she murmured, 'it's a wonder I've lived so long with all those people wanting to kill me,' and she closed her eyes against the glare of the lights.

Barbara heard about it as she was driving home from her book club. It was the lead story on the eleven o'clock news and she swerved onto the verge, reaching for her mobile before remembering she'd left it plugged into the charger in the kitchen. Her stomach churned with anxiety as she accelerated back onto the road, wheels spinning on the wet Tarmac, and drove home as fast as she could through the rain. There was a message from Shaun on the answering machine and another from Adam, left some time later, asking her to call him when she got in. Her hand shook so much she misdialled and had to start again.

'Heather's okay,' Jill said when she answered the phone. 'She was hit in the shoulder. Adam was going to go up to Newcastle tonight, but they told him she needs to rest. So he's getting a flight in the morning. Here, I'll put him on.'

Barbara took a deep breath and dropped into a chair. 'I can't believe it. Who'd want to shoot Heather? It doesn't seem possible.'

'Apparently that's what she keeps saying,' Adam said. 'Shaun was with her. Someone in a car shot at her as they left the office. Heather was hit and fell down the steps. She *is* okay, though.'

'But shot! What about Shaun?'

'Shocked but okay. He's going to stay with her until they take her up to the ward.'

'But *why*?' Barbara persisted. 'She's only a backbencher, it's not like she's a minister, or even particularly controversial.'

'Not to us, perhaps, but there's the abortion stuff, the refugees, and Jill just reminded me that she led that protest about the high-rise development, so . . . '

'But no one would shoot her for that, surely? Not for any of those things.'

'People *have* been shot over abortion,' Adam said.

'In the US, but this is Australia,' Barbara protested, 'and it's not even Sydney, just provincial Newcastle, for heaven's sake.'

'I can barely believe it either, Barb,' Adam said wearily. 'But it's happened. I'm getting a flight out just before six thirty so I'll call you from the hospital.'

'No. I'll see you there,' she said. 'I'll meet you, we can go to the hospital together. And, Adam, sorry for interrogating you. You must be feeling terrible.'

'Not the best,' he said, 'but I'll see you tomorrow. Maybe we'll know more by then. Flight gets in at seven twenty-five.'

Barbara stared at the smouldering embers in the woodstove and shivered with shock. Perhaps she should get straight back into the car and drive there now. A quarter to midnight, it was only forty minutes from Morpeth to Newcastle, less at this time of night. She could be at the hospital by half past twelve. But then, if they'd told Adam not to fly up from Sydney until the morning . . . She dialled the hospital and asked for emergency. Miss Delaney was fine, the nurse told her, she'd just been transferred to the ward. 'Best to wait until morning,' she said. 'Come in after eight o'clock. You get a good night's sleep now and try not to worry.'

Propped up on pillows, Heather watched archival footage of herself on the midday news. There were grabs of her speech in state parliament about asylum seekers, and some sound bites taken outside her office during the protest about the high-rise development on the coast. The final fifteen seconds came from a speech she'd made at a pro-choice meeting.

'Obviously I'm just a troublemaker,' she said in a weak attempt at humour. 'Heaps of people want to kill me.'

'Well, we don't *know* that,' the doctor said, looking up from her chart to stare at the screen. 'Just that *one* person *might* have wanted to. I guess most of us could think of at least one person who might like to take a shot at us, and that's without going outside our immediate families.' She smiled and returned the chart to its rack. 'I think my ex would be first in line with an AK47. Now, you take it easy, you're doing fine. There's a mob of journalists outside. Shall I send them away?'

'Please.' Heather rested her head back on the pillows, contemplating her own detachment. Shouldn't she be worrying about who had done this and whether they might try again? But it seemed enough to be in a safe place where everyone knew what they were doing; enough to be alive when she could, so easily, have been dead.

'You're still in shock,' Barbara had said earlier. 'It'll take a while.'

'Shock and drugs,' Adam suggested, with a break in his voice, and Heather, thinking that they both looked terrible, had urged them to get some breakfast in the hospital café.

'It is not an assassination,' said the Premier, his hawk-like face filling the screen as he corrected the breathless reporter. 'Heather Delaney was shot and wounded, and I want to assure the people of New South Wales that the perpetrator of this horrible crime will be found and brought to justice.' He looked around at the cameras, pausing for effect. 'Law and order and public safety top my government's list of priorities. We're working right now on a new initiative to make our streets safer. And yes, I'm flying up to Newcastle to visit Ms Delaney later today.'

'Remind me to be painting my toenails,' Heather said aloud, and the doctor gave her a wry smile.

'I'll be back this afternoon,' she said. 'Try to stay out of trouble.'

There were pictures now of her electorate office where people had left messages, flowers and hastily made signs and placards: '*RU 486, the fight goes on!*' read one. '*Stop the high rise! We will not be moved.*' '*Stop the Pacific solution.*' And the camera homed in on a chilling note of dissent. '*Better shot next time.*' Had someone really tried to kill her for any of those reasons? A woman for whom Heather had fought a couple of battles with Centrelink wept as she tried to tear it down and was calmed by a police officer who took the sign away.

Heather wished *she* could cry, shout or even smash something, but her emotions had deserted her. And the painkiller that she could pump through her veins at the touch of a button had scrambled her ability to think straight. They were running a story from the US now, George Bush and Tony Blair walking up to a podium, the Stars and Stripes and the Union Jack in the background. Heather sighed and hit the mute button.

'Risky job, politics,' Detective Roussos had said when he came back this morning. 'Being in the public eye, sticking your neck out. Risky.'

'Not as risky as yours.'

He raised his eyebrows. 'No? At least we know who our enemies are.'

Heather started to muster an argument about rogue elements recently uncovered in the police force making that hard to believe, but she was exhausted after the first two sentences and gave up. She had never thought of politics as risky; hard, yes, frequently frustrating, always challenging and often rewarding but never risky, at least not in the sense of her physical safety. Fifteen years in parliament and, in the split second it took to pull a trigger, everything had changed. Everything she knew and thought she knew about the job, about herself, about the future, was thrown into chaos. She closed her eyes and wondered how she could be so coolly aware of the significance of what had happened but still feel no emotion.

While Heather contemplated her own lack of emotion, the Prime Minister and the leaders of the federal and state Oppositions were expressing theirs to the nearest available microphones. And political allies and opponents who, in the past, had spoken less than kindly of Heather now issued statements laced with outrage and dripping with affection. Meanwhile, the talkback lines were running hot with callers upset, angry and shocked, and blaming, variously, the government, the opposition, illegal immigrants, terrorists, Christian or Muslim fundamentalists, teenagers and junkies. And one shock jock took time to point out that as a feminazi from a now outdated women's movement, Heather had probably only got what was coming to her.

In the hospital café, Barbara was feeling weak and nauseous. She had barely slept and at four o'clock had given up trying, got out of bed, revived the fire, made tea and waited impatiently for it to be time to drive to Newcastle. When she'd called the hospital the night before, the nurse had asked if she was Heather's mother and she had been tempted to lie, because she felt as though she were.

'Her aunt,' she'd said. 'Her mother's dead, we're very close.'

She was the younger sister of Roy, Heather and Adam's father, and had been at school with Dorothy, his wife. When Roy contracted polio in the fifties, she moved in to help with his care and, when he died, Barbara stayed on with Dorothy and the children. Long after Heather and Adam had grown up and left home, the two women shared the house in a friendship that lasted until Dorothy died of cancer in the eighties. In the bleak morning light of the hospital café, against the background clatter of crockery and cutlery and the steady hum of conversation, Barbara felt bloated with a lifetime of love not fully expressed and tears not openly shed; tears that now threatened to burst the dam of her usual self-control. On the table in front of her, Adam's clasped hands were shaking. She pushed aside the remains of a rubbery croissant and reached out, putting her own hands over his. He grasped them and looked up. He seemed to have aged ten years overnight.

'She's going to be okay, they said so, and you can see she *is* okay,' Barbara said.

'I know, but what do we do now? How's she going to be when the shock wears off? That maniac is still out there and presumably still out to get her.'

'Perhaps it was meant as a warning . . . or maybe it was an accident. Did they say if there was another crime there last night?'

Adam shook his head and fidgeted in his chair. He'd drunk far too many cups of bad coffee and was feeling jittery and confused. 'The police reckon it was deliberate.' He paused and ran a hand through his hair, and Barbara noticed that it was greyer than she'd remembered, and thinning. 'I don't know what to do next,' Adam went on. 'Maybe Shaun will know. He texted me to say he's on his way. And I guess we'll have to talk to the media.'

Barbara gave him a weak smile. 'Did you call Jill?'

'Yes. I told her I'd be staying on for a few days. She's fine. Toby thinks it's terribly exciting, can't wait to get to school to tell his friends.'

'He'll be a hero for a day with this story,' Barbara said. 'His aunty being shot; how wonderful to be young enough not to know what it all means.'

'I wish,' Adam said. 'I don't know how to deal with any of this. It's something you only expect to happen to other people.' He thought longingly of Sydney, of home, of Jill and the kids, the chaos of family breakfast, and the safe monotony of the orchestra with whom he should by now have been rehearsing Brahms' 1st Symphony on his beloved cello.

Jill was in the kitchen drinking her second mug of coffee and watching the news.

'But who *did* it?' Daisy persisted, her mouth full of banana. 'Who shot Aunty Heather?'

'Shut up, dumbo,' Toby said. 'Mum's already told you, they

don't know. It's a mystery. Like on *The Bill* or *Blue Heelers*. Don't you know *anything*? This is so cool. I bet no one else at school has anyone in their family that got shot.'

'*You* shut up,' Daisy retorted. 'You're mean. You don't even care about Aunty Heather. She might die.'

'She won't die, will she, Mum? Dad said –'

'Stop squabbling,' Jill cut in. 'Aunty Heather's not going to die. Daddy says she's going to be fine. You can call him this afternoon and he'll tell us more about it. Now, get a move on or we'll all be late.'

She stared at the screen as the kids gathered up their school things. It was weird that something life-threatening could happen to someone close to you, and you could sit at home watching it on television and then head off to work as if nothing had happened. But Jill knew that something important *had* happened, something more than a bullet in Heather's shoulder, something more than all the crap the politicians were talking. Something had happened to her family, to their private world; something that would change them all. She didn't know how she knew it but as she flicked the remote to off and picked up her bag, she felt quite dizzy with the knowledge that nothing would ever be quite the same again.

News of Heather's shooting was almost four days old when Diane heard about it in an email from her daughter. She was getting bored with the poolside chat of her travel companions and had walked into Ubud to browse through the market and the jewellery shops. She bargained ruthlessly over some silver bangles and a ring set with a large turquoise, and waited with satisfaction while the vendor wrapped them. The bargains were some sort of compensation for her disappointment with the holiday. It had seemed like a good idea when the women from the tennis club had suggested going to Bali, but you never really knew people until you went on holiday with them and, away from the familiar surroundings of the club, Diane felt hopelessly out of place. She slipped her new jewellery into her bag, headed for a nearby bar and decided to check her email while she waited for her banana and mango lassi.

It bugged her that Shaun hadn't let her know personally and she considered sending him a curt message. After all the work she did for them in the electorate office it was the least she would have expected. It was awful, of course, and frightening. She closed the email and went onto a news site to read some of the reports. 'It could have been me,' she murmured. 'It could so easily have been me.' She was always at the electorate office, stuffing envelopes, photocopying, making coffee and running errands. 'I often come out of there in the dark. They could have confused me with Heather.'

'Sorry, ma'am?' said the large American backpacker at the adjacent computer. 'You say something?'

She shook her head. 'Just talking to myself.'

'First sign, they say . . . '

Diane gave him a forced smile, switched on her mobile and dialled her daughter's number but Charlene's phone was diverted to message bank, as was Shaun's, and all four lines to the electorate office were busy. Tense with shock and resentment, she moved to a small table under a sunshade of palm fronds and sipped her lassi, the creamy sweetness soothing the bitterness of the insult. Had they even given a thought to calling her? Bugger them, bugger the lot of them, she had better things to do than bother about selfish politicians and their ridiculously ambitious staff. But she didn't like this feeling of being on the outer, just a volunteer, not sufficiently important to merit a call or an email.

Diane finished her drink and made her way back up the hill in the heat to the hotel. Her room was pleasantly cool and newly serviced. She loved the feeling of being looked after by staff; she was so sick of looking after herself. Peeling off her dress, she stared at herself in the mirror wondering if she could pass for less than her age. Fifty-three, perhaps; fifty, even? No, that was kidding herself. But she looked fit. Three times a week at the circuit gym, frequent games of tennis and watching her diet did pay off. She had a small frame and she'd never tended to put on weight, unlike Heather, who, as was obvious from early photos, had certainly stacked on the kilos.

Diane stepped closer to the mirror. Her hair was good – as

thick as ever, and the grey had merged quite attractively with the natural blonde. But her face seemed to be disappearing, the features becoming smaller, less defined, her eyes less bright. It made her feel colourless and insignificant, and although she was onto the latest beauty products in a flash, they didn't seem to make much difference. Sometimes she wondered if all these tiny but hugely expensive pots of special oils and serums and creams were just a con. She'd read somewhere that a five-dollar jar of sorbolene from the local pharmacy was just as effective. She looked like a woman of a certain age, whatever that meant, and she wasn't sure whether it was just age or being a divorcée of a certain age that made her feel so faded and nondescript.

With a sigh of resignation, Diane turned away from the mirror, pulled on her bathers and a sarong and wandered back down to the pool. There was hardly anyone around, and the line of banana lounges where she had left the other women was completely empty.

'Excuse me!' Diane called to a waiter who was on his way to the pool bar with a tray of empty glasses. 'Do you know where the other ladies are? The ones I was with earlier?'

He paused for a moment. 'Yes, ma'am,' he said. 'They go for massage. Special price before four o'clock. Too late now; you pay full price, I think.'

Diane shook her head and sat down. 'I'll stay here,' she said quietly. 'Just bring me a sparkling mineral water, would you? And some of those little dry salted nuts.'

With a slight bow he turned and hurried away, and Diane, feeling more on the outer than ever, stretched out in the sun and put on her Dior sunglasses and a hat with a big brim. If she were to be alone, at least she would look stylish.

Several days later, Adam took a cab home from Sydney airport high on the relief that had flooded his veins since they took off from Newcastle. From the moment of Shaun's first shattering call from the hospital, he had been living a nightmare; as if Heather's injuries weren't enough to cope with, there was the full-scale drama of a serious crime. The police everywhere, journalists shoving microphones in front of him when he stepped outside, and Heather's parliamentary colleagues pumping his hand and promising that justice would be done. And, on top of it all, there was the feeling that as her next-of-kin he ought to take charge, make decisions and know what to do.

'It's okay,' Shaun had said. 'We'll do it together; crisis management is part of my job.'

Adam clung to his guidance, marvelling that Shaun seemed to know exactly what to do and could assertively send pesky journalists and members of parliament packing, while he, who was old enough to be Shaun's father, didn't know where to start.

Detective Roussos had asked them to search their files and their memories for clues as to who might have a grudge against Heather, and Adam had been profoundly shaken when Shaun produced a file of hate mail. It had never occurred to him that people would write to his sister with such vitriol. The police had taken the file and urged them to consider the personal as well as the political, to reflect on whether someone from the past might feel they had a score to settle. They had also taken away all the cards and letters whose senders Heather couldn't identify.

'They're just constituents,' Heather had protested, but Roussos had been adamant.

'There may be something useful here,' he said. 'We have to make sure.'

'But you can't think the gunman would send a get-well card?' Adam said. He found the prospect almost laughable.

Roussos shrugged. 'Stranger things have happened, we can't rule it out. But are you sure there's no one from your sister's past? Someone she dumped, maybe, or who was jealous?'

'No.' Adam was unequivocal. 'Heather hasn't had many partners and none of them is a potential gunman. Are you sure she hasn't been caught in the flak from something else?'

Alex Roussos shrugged again. 'I'm not saying it's impossible, but so far there's nothing to suggest it. It's very quiet around there after hours, not a place for gang wars or drive-by shootings.'

And in the ensuing days there was no further progress, the only evidence being the bullet, which had, apparently, been shot from an old .38 Smith & Wesson revolver.

A police psychologist who specialised in post-traumatic stress had been sent to counsel Heather, and advised her to give herself time to recover.

'I want to go home,' she'd insisted. 'And I need to get back to work.' But eventually she had been persuaded that when she was discharged she would go to Barbara's place in a government car with a police escort and stay there until she was fit to return to work. Meanwhile, there were constant questions from police; discussions about protection at Barbara's house; plans for new security systems at her own home, the office, and the unit she rented in Sydney for the times when parliament was sitting.

Adam's sense of incompetence had dogged him all week. He longed to talk meaningfully with Heather, but she was operating on a superficial plane and her attention span was minimal. He wanted to find out how she was really feeling, and to tell her about his guilt, the guilt he felt for having failed to protect her. He knew that she would consider the latter perfectly ridiculous, but to him it was real and painful, as though he had failed to do his older-brother job.

Now, as he walked up the path and let himself into his own house, Adam sighed with the satisfaction of being home. The kitchen was filled with the familiar smell of cold toast and coffee, remnants of which were still on the kitchen table. He smiled affectionately at the evidence of his family's typically chaotic departure for work and school, and began to stack the crockery in the dishwasher. Jill had left her scarf over the back of a chair and he picked it up and buried his face in it, breathing in the scent of her skin, her hair, closing his eyes and visualising the perfect creamy oval of her face under the short dark hair, the strength in her wide-set eyes, and the pure energy and fortitude he felt when he held her. He thought of going out again, of going to her office – perhaps she'd have time for coffee or lunch – but then he remembered that she'd told him on the phone that she was going to be out most of the day at a seminar. Holding on to the scarf,

Adam glanced quickly at the mail and then made his way upstairs to the spare bedroom, which doubled as his music room.

The score of Rachmaninov's Second Symphony lay on his desk, a reminder that he needed to mark up the cello parts, and make overdue phone calls about rehearsals. Taking off his jacket he stretched his arms above his head, luxuriating in the silence and the prospect of a few hours of solitude. His favourite baroque cello stood in its open case beckoning him back to peace and normality. He lifted it out and settled into his chair, reassured by the comforting intimacy of the instrument against his body; he tightened his bow and tuned to a perfect A. The first notes of the Bach prelude soothed him, drawing him, as he had known it would, out of anxiety and into his own musical universe. Once more the cello was an extension of himself, its unique voice transforming the turmoil of the past week into beauty and logic, until the final chord faded away and he put down his bow, sank his head into his hands and wept.

Diane was not the last person to hear about Heather's shooting. Lots of people heard later, and thousands never heard at all and didn't care. Ellis didn't hear about it until he emerged from a six-day retreat in the Blue Mountains and read the feature story in the *Weekend Australian*. Along with meditation and total silence, the retreat had included withdrawal from stimulants, including alcohol, tobacco, caffeine, sugar and the print and electronic media.

Ellis drove a diplomatic distance from the retreat centre, bought the papers, stopped at a café, and ordered a strong coffee and a large double-chocolate muffin. He peered at the file photographs that accompanied the lengthy feature, particularly the one taken as Heather left hospital. It was several decades since he'd seen her in person, although he'd caught the end of a TV interview a few years earlier, and, apart from putting on weight, she seemed to have worn well.

Ellis studied the images more closely. What would it feel like to be shot at, to know someone wanted to kill you, that they might be out there waiting, hiding behind a bush or a building, crouched behind a parked car or masked by shadows? Six days of silence and meditation were great for clearing the mind and reviving the senses and Ellis shivered at the feeling of threat he had managed to conjure up for himself. He closed his eyes to savour the feeling but it was dispelled by images of the past: a lithe body moving towards him across a room hazy with dust particles floating in the summer light, clasped hands, the brush of skin on skin, the sounds of sighs and laughter, all so long ago.

'Anything else?' a waiter asked suddenly, jolting him back to the present. Ellis shook his head, and the man took his plate and cup and disappeared behind the counter.

The papers had made a big thing of her being single, some using it to make her appear more vulnerable, others to imply that women who failed to demonstrate their credentials as wives and mothers were a little odd and possibly even threatening. How would Heather cope with being dissected in opinion columns and the letters pages, with being middle-aged, single and under threat? Was she still as tenacious as ever, still worrying terrier-like at things until she got what she wanted?

Ellis tipped his chair backwards, locking his hands behind his head, and contemplated the sort of changes that an event as traumatic as a shooting might trigger. One thing was for sure, Heather would be feeling the chill of being ultimately alone in a time of crisis: the lack of a patient ear to hear the oft-repeated fears, a hand to hold when words were not enough. Ellis had had plenty of experience with people in despair; with those who resorted to brashness and false confidence, with those who slipped constantly back and forth between panic and optimism, and those who carried on, seemingly coping with everything that was thrown at them. He knew that independence, spirit and strength of character were small consolation when one looked into the dark pit of fear.

TWO

Barbara's move from a smart little townhouse in Sydney to a damp cottage with an overgrown garden in the Hunter Valley had surprised most of her friends. It had signalled a complete change of lifestyle they had never envisaged for the smartly dressed and successful publisher of academic books who had worked fifty-hour weeks for as long as they could remember. And while the prospect of Barbara in a country cottage, pruning roses and going for long walks, was weird enough, the reality of the dilapidated property and her almost overnight change of appearance had been an even greater shock.

Ten years on, the cottage had been tastefully, if modestly, restored: dried out, heated, air conditioned, replumbed and rewired, and the garden thoughtfully pruned, replanted, fertilised and fenced. While the house had smartened up, Barbara had loosened up. She had delivered her tailored business suits, neat blouses and court shoes to the op shop and abandoned herself to the comfort of loose pants, shirts and sweaters. Her thick, silver-grey hair, worn for years in a smart bob, was now more often bundled into an unruly knot; sometimes she could even be caught wearing thick woolly socks with leather sandals, and an old pair of spectacles repaired with a Band-Aid. Only a very small handful of her friends had really registered the depth of change represented by her new life and appearance. They assumed such eccentricity was an unfortunate side effect of ageing, and that slacker standards of dress were the result of living alone. They seemed to have forgotten that Barbara had lived alone and well-dressed for many years in Sydney.

Adam, Jill and the children visited for long weekends and Heather, too, spent occasional weekends there, arriving on a Friday afternoon longing for peace and quiet, and by Monday morning itching to get back to her own hectic existence. She had noticed the changes in Barbara's appearance, but was too preoccupied with her own life to question them. Sitting now in the thin winter sunshine on the back verandah, she watched as Barbara clambered over a cluster of mossy rocks to talk to her friend George through the fence. She looked all of her seventy-five years, but for the first time Heather noticed how agile she was, and how energetic. Meanwhile, her own body felt as though it were fragmenting, falling apart, as if the bullet had penetrated not just her shoulder but shattered all the muscles and tendons that held her together.

'This emotional numbness will wear off,' the trauma counsellor had told her, 'and when it does it's going to be hard, but remember that it's really the start of healing.'

In the brightly lit comfort and security of the hospital with staff always on hand, Barbara, Adam and Shaun in and out all the time, colleagues and constituents visiting and a police officer on duty outside the door, it had seemed eminently sensible advice. Now, in a small cottage in the heart of the country surrounded by unfamiliar noises and with waves of emotion threatening to drown her, it seemed woefully inadequate. Heather closed her eyes and breathed deeply in an attempt to calm herself.

'Let yourself feel, but don't abandon yourself to it,' the counsellor had said. 'It *will* pass and despite the awfulness it's actually a good thing.' And she'd handed Heather a card. 'Call the after-hours number if you need me. I'll come as soon as I can or we can talk on the phone.'

Sometime before leaving hospital, Heather had binned the card. She'd never needed a counsellor in her life and the advice she'd been given would be more than adequate.

'It might be a good idea . . . ' Adam had begun, but she'd silenced him with a look that could have slashed a tyre at twenty paces. Now she wished she had the card, just as she had wished for it in the middle of the last two nights when she'd woken in terror, convinced that the gunman was hiding in the shadows outside her window. The knowledge that the house was under guard day and night was only partially reassuring; a guard could only be in one place at a time – if he were checking the rear garden, he was not outside her window; if he were taking a pee, his eyes were not on the path to the house.

Focus on being alive, she told herself, you're a survivor. But she still felt suffocated by fear, and by grief for the sense of security that she had taken for granted and which was now gone, probably forever. Salty tears ran down her face, and she flicked them away with her good hand and licked them off her lips. The counsellor had given her a booklet about the effects of being shot and she'd read about the tearing of muscle and tissue, the release of stress hormones and the visceral memory of penetration by a bullet. Heather remembered that in her mother's struggle to gain control of her cancer, Dorothy had attempted visualisation, the channelling of creative energy towards healing. She had imagined white cells as white knights laying intruders to waste, and pictured her tumour breaking up into fragments and being expelled by natural bodily functions. At the time, Heather had thought it fanciful; twenty years on and with her own body in trauma, she grasped at it. Focusing the dual forces of creativity and energy on visualising her own recovery now seemed entirely logical and potentially powerful.

Closing her eyes she tried to visualise her body healing itself, the chaotic battle of the hormones, the struggle of the red and white blood cells, the toil of microscopic fibres engaged in the process of repair. But she couldn't sustain it, haunted as she was by fear. What if she weren't concentrating hard enough? What if her body gave up? What if the sniper tried again? Terror reared like great waves of water threatening to dash a lone swimmer on the rocks.

'Herbal tea,' Barbara called, and Heather forced her eyes open and tried to rearrange her face. 'George sent this,' Barbara said, walking back up the garden with a handful of lemon balm twigs.

'He says it's very healthy and soothing . . . you've gone grey in the face, Heather, are you all right?'

Heather forced a weak smile. 'Crying again,' she said ruefully.

Barbara paused at the top of the verandah steps and rested a hand on Heather's good shoulder. 'It's better than storing it up. You cry, and I'll make this into tea and come and sit with you.'

Heather closed her eyes and wondered if healthy, soothing tea could possibly make any difference or whether it was just some-one who loved you making it that mattered. She thought it was the latter. Each day in hospital the cards and letters from strangers had bathed her in goodwill. Now, on reflection, she could see that they represented not a personal connection, but a universal horror at something so entirely removed from most people's experience. The cards and letters were not about her, they were about out-rage at the act itself, about a communal sense of shock and anger. The number of people who really cared was small, so small that it shocked her. It must surely say something about her, about the sort of person she had become.

Sometimes when Jill looked at Adam, she was so overwhelmed by tenderness that it seemed to melt her insides. At other times, like right now, she only needed to see him sitting there, reaching out blindly from behind the newspaper for his coffee mug, to be con-sumed by anger and resentment. That this was totally unfair and irrational didn't make it any easier to bear. Having someone else on whom to project blame was a partial relief, and she could hardly blame Toby or Daisy. Jill wiped the breadboard and slammed it down with a satisfyingly loud thud; the newspaper didn't twitch.

'Why can you bang stuff in the kitchen but I get yelled at for slamming doors?' Toby asked in the bored, adults-are-so-stupid tone that he'd adopted since his twelfth birthday.

'Toby, go right now and find your boots or you'll be late for footy practice,' Jill said, with what felt like remarkable self-control. 'And, Daisy, if you want to come shopping with me, you'd better wash the yoghurt off your face. You really are the messiest eater in the entire world.'

'Not the *entire* world, Mum,' Daisy said, scrubbing her face with her sleeve. 'I mean, you can't actually *know* that, because Miss Rahjeen comes from India and she says there are hundreds of millions of people there and in China, so how can you –'

'What about the doors, then?' Toby cut in.

Adam lowered the paper. 'Not now, Tobes. Get your gear and I'll run you down to the oval.'

Toby made a muttering exit, slamming the kitchen door behind him.

'He slammed the door –' Daisy began.

'Mum told you to go and wash your face, Daisy, so go and do it,' Adam said. 'Properly. And hang the towel on the rail, not the floor.'

'Daaad, you can't hang something on the floor –'

'Just go!' He got up from the table, went over to where Jill stood at the sink and slipped his arms around her waist.

'Stay calm, you know what they say – all will be well and all manner of things will be well,' he whispered against her ear.

'You know that it was a nun who wrote that, not a mother?' Jill said, turning to him and burying her face in his neck, comforted by his familiar smell and the way their bodies fitted together. 'When will all be well? Sorry I'm such a grump. I know you're worried about Heather, but the kids are getting on my nerves this morning, this week . . . this life! I'm too *old* for all this.'

He kissed her lightly. 'We both are,' he said. 'Only eight more years and we're off the hook.'

Jill sighed, stepping back, seeking more comfort in the familiarity of his lean face and the steady eyes that seemed to grow more blue as his hair turned grey. 'You reckon? Kirsty's older than that and shows no sign of leaving.'

'But at least she can eat breakfast without splattering everyone with yoghurt,' he said, wiping some of Daisy's off his shirtsleeve with the dish cloth. 'We make it too comfortable. Let's try cruelty, and maybe they'll report us to the authorities.'

'Who gets taken into protective custody, us or them?'

'Us, hopefully, a nice rest home somewhere with comfy chairs, kindly staff, crocheted knee rugs . . . '

'And a Bach prelude playing in the background, I suppose?'

'Exactly. Look, let's see if Kirsty'll babysit tonight and we'll go out for dinner.'

Jill pulled a face. 'Who wants to babysit her half-siblings on a Saturday night?'

Adam grinned. 'Possibly an impecunious university student whose evening only begins around the time we're ready to go to bed. I'll ask her later, when she surfaces; bribe her, if necessary.' He picked up his jacket and headed for the door. 'Have fun shopping, darling. Toby . . . ' he called from the doorway, 'get a wriggle on. I'll meet you at the car.'

Occasionally, in moments of pure frustration, Jill gave credence to the idea that it might have been easier if Adam weren't so thoroughly nice, then she could legitimately rage against his insensitivity. As it was, each time she fired her frustration at him it ricocheted back, repelled by his essential goodness. This morning, though, she was duly appreciative of the fact that she didn't have to face the oval and the battery of footy mums with their bright eyes and bouncy ponytails. It exhausted her just to look at them marshalling kids into teams, jogging to warm up the little ones, and cutting oranges into quarters for half-time, while a motley collection of dads with clipboards stood around chatting about the real footy on the television. How could she ever have thought that it would be okay to be fifty-five with a ten-year-old and a twelve-year-old? Why hadn't she realised that when her women friends were enjoying the freedom of empty nests, she would still be washing footy strip and discussing Barbie's possible new career in the finance sector?

'*I'm* old too,' Adam had said the previous evening, 'older than you.'

'Only four years. Besides, it's different for you. Older men are cool; sexy, even.'

'Sexy?' he'd said, yawning widely. 'What's that?'

How could she ever have thought that a late second marriage and having a baby at forty-three made any sense? But they had wanted a family together and at the time lots of women seemed to be getting pregnant in their forties. So, along came Toby, planned and welcome, and then, two years later, Daisy: unplanned, antici-pated with caution and then universally adored. And they'd never imagined that Adam's daughter, Kirsty, would eventually choose to live with them. Adam's first wife, Yvette, had drifted into an affair with her boss and left to live with him in Glebe, taking Kirsty with her. But a few years later, when Yvette was married and her partner was offered a job in Perth, Kirsty refused to go. Jill loved Kirsty dearly but it was another person in the house, another mouth to feed . . .

Jill sighed. Where were all those older mothers now, twelve, thirteen years later? In psychiatric hospitals? Dead? They cer-tainly weren't outside the Hadley Road Primary School when Jill dropped Daisy off, or Woodstone High, where Toby had just started, or at footy practice. Had they just been figments of her imagination?

'You could give up work for a while,' Adam had said recently. 'Take a few years off. Go back when Daisy's sixteen, it'll be easier then.'

'And I'll be over sixty and unemployable,' she said. But it was more complicated than that. Right now, having a professional, grown-up other life was the only thing that was keeping Jill sane.

Heather hadn't helped, of course, not that she could be blamed for getting shot, but once again she was the centre of everyone's attention and, not for the first time, Jill was niggled by the fact that her single, successful sister-in-law was everybody's priority. Jealousy was an ugly emotion, almost as ugly as the *Schadenfreude* that she hadn't completely managed to shake off. She knew it was despicable to feel like this, just as it was despicable to envy the fact that Heather probably earned almost as much as she and Adam put together and only had herself to spend it on. But the real bot-tom line of Jill's resentment was Heather's freedom; freedom at a time of life when Jill felt so acutely in need of it, but was so firmly shackled by love and responsibility.

'You should leave,' Charlene said. 'It's dangerous. You might get killed because of her.'

'It's not dangerous,' Shaun said, pouring her a glass of wine. 'Statistically I'm more likely to be killed or injured driving to work than I am to get shot.'

'Statistics! A week ago you were next to her and she was shot. It could've been you.'

'Sure, but it wasn't. Not many people are shot in Australia, and how often do you hear of politicians being shot here? Name one.'

'Well, there was that bloke in Cabramatta, they said on *A Current Affair*.'

Shaun sighed. 'Yes, okay, John Newman *was* shot. And everyone was horrified and shocked and that was not just because it was so awful but because it was so unusual. But no electorate officer ever got shot in the course of their work. It's not as though it rates anywhere on the list of high-risk occupations.'

Charlene sniffed and took the glass from him.

'Look,' Shaun went on, 'I like Heather, I like my job and there's no way I'm going to leave, so don't even go there.' He took his glass and sat down on the couch, kicking off his shoes.

This was a conversation he really didn't need. It had been a dreadful week and he was exhausted. On top of the shock and the sheer terror of that night, Heather unconscious and bleeding, what seemed like an endless wait for the ambulance, and the chaos at the hospital, managing the rest of the crisis had been a nightmare. It was especially hard as all the time he was struggling to silence the niggling inner voice that kept reminding him that it could so easily have been him. Another step, a slight move in the wrong direction, and he would have been the one who ended up wounded or dead. After the mental effort he'd made to cast the experience as escape and survival for himself rather than obsessing about what might have been, he did not want to have to do that for Charlene too.

Maybe he should have agreed to see the trauma counsellor but he'd been juggling far too many balls to make time for that. Now, at last, the party had drafted in a retired electorate officer to help out and he felt he could relax a little. With Heather now safely out of the way in Morpeth, this was the first day he'd felt things might begin to return to normal. He leaned back and put his feet up on the ottoman that Charlene had bought two weeks earlier in Freedom.

'Besides,' he said, 'I don't think anyone *does* want to shoot Heather.'

Charlene straightened up from the oven and turned to stare at him. 'Of course they do, they *did* shoot her!'

'Yes, but I don't think someone was actually *trying* to shoot *her.*'

'Who, then? You? You just said it wasn't dangerous.'

Shaun shook his head. Sometimes Charlene was really hard work, especially when she'd had a few glasses of wine. Conversations like this fuelled his anxiety about their living together. Her incremental colonisation of his territory was a persistent stress factor that made him short-tempered and resentful. 'I think it was an accident, or a mistake,' he said. 'She was just unlucky. I don't think it was about Heather, either personally or politically. That's all. Instinctively it doesn't work for me.'

'Instinct,' Charlene scoffed. 'The last time you trusted your instinct you lost fifty bucks on the Melbourne Cup. Instinct!'

Shaun watched her stirring something in a saucepan, while also checking out her own fuzzy reflection in the stainless-steel trim of the range hood. He was a strong believer in instinct, especially his own, and usually it served him well. His political instincts were particularly good. Years earlier, while he was still at uni, he'd got an internship in Heather's office, and when he graduated she'd offered him a job. He'd been with her ever since.

'Are you thinking of a political career?' she'd asked him. 'State? Federal?'

'Not sure right now,' he'd replied. 'I know I want to work in politics but probably behind the scenes.'

'Where the real power lies,' she'd said with a smile. And he'd felt they understood each other perfectly.

Shaun was both smart and ambitious and he'd had other offers, but he liked working for Heather; it was good to feel valued and competent. And if she got a ministry after the next election he'd be first in line as chief-of-staff. He was young still, there was plenty of time. His father liked him having this job too – he was always keen to chew over the state of public transport, fuel prices in the bush, or states' rights. His mother, on the other hand, couldn't have given a toss and sometimes Charlene reminded him of her, which wasn't necessarily a good thing; although maybe it was better than reminding him of her own mother.

Shaun sipped his wine, closed his eyes and listened to the sulky silence punctuated by the clatter of cutlery. Since moving in, Charlene had conducted an insidious campaign of domestication: new bed linen, even His and Hers towels had suddenly appeared in the bathroom, and hurried meals or takeaway eaten on the sofa had been more or less banished in favour of proper meals at the table. Shaun felt he'd been ambushed. What had begun as a light-hearted, no-strings arrangement had turned into an extended audition for the position of wife. There were constant references to settling down, friends getting engaged or married, people at work thinking she must be engaged to him because they were living together.

Realisation had crept up on him slowly; after all, until they met, Charlene had spent most of her time in nightclubs psyched up on speed or eccies and then sleeping it off. While Shaun felt some satisfaction in having steered her away from drugs, and from the particularly unpleasant boyfriend who dealt them, domesticity and her unsubtle hints about the future were starting to bug him. He hoped they weren't in for another engagement conversation tonight because he just wasn't in the mood. He needed another drink, food, some really crap television and then bed.

'It's ready,' Charlene said. 'Thai chicken curry, your favourite. You can't say I don't look after you. Did I tell you that Tina at work picked up her engagement ring today? It's mega gorgeous, a one-carat diamond in a rose gold setting. Can you pour me another glass of wine, please?'

'You're not worried about leaving her on her own, then?' George asked. He was chopping vegetables for soup and nodded towards a stool.

Barbara hoisted herself onto it, shaking her head. 'She's not alone. Shaun from the office is there. He drove up this morning with a stack of work and they're ploughing through it on the back verandah.'

'So how is she?'

'Not good, but through the worst, I think. The last few days have been pretty awful, and the nights are worse. But it had to come and it's better than having her sitting there with a frozen smile on her face behaving as though nothing's happened.'

'Maybe I'll pop in later and see her?'

'Do, she'd like that. Come for dinner?'

George peered at her over the top of his glasses. 'Okay, but only if I can bring this soup. You look done in.'

'I'm starting to feel that way,' Barbara admitted. 'I think I was running on adrenaline for a while, now I'm stuffed. Getting old.'

'Tell me about it,' George said. He straightened up from the chopping board. 'Cup of tea?'

Barbara nodded, watching him move slowly around the kitchen. His former city life and the things that went with it had, like her own, been abandoned in favour of the peace and quiet of the Valley. This morning he had clearly been gardening; the knees of his old jeans were stained with damp earth, and a few fragments of twig were caught in his grey hair.

'Damn,' he said, putting down the kettle at the sound of the phone. 'Could you do the tea while I get that?'

Barbara filled the kettle and walked out onto the deck, enjoying the silence. Her cherished solitude had been in short supply over the last few weeks. Heather was counting on going back to work soon, and while Barbara worried that it might be too early, she also welcomed the prospect of getting her life back.

Moving out of the city had not been simply about *where* to live, but *how*. There had been a time when she had thought she would die in harness if she got the chance, and as she had passed her sixty-fourth and then her sixty-fifth birthdays with no one mentioning retirement, she enjoyed the sense of having beaten the system. But a few months later she lost an old school friend, a fit, energetic woman who died suddenly from a heart attack. Barbara took a few days off to go to the funeral in Adelaide and realised that, for the first time ever, she wasn't keen to get back to work. In fact, as she walked into the office the following Monday, she knew without a shadow of a doubt that she didn't want to be there.

'Are you absolutely sure?' Adam had asked on the evening she had turned up on the doorstep, saying she needed to talk. Jill, just pregnant with Daisy and nauseous throughout her waking hours, had gone to bed early, and Barbara and Adam had sat at the kitchen table with a bottle of red. 'It's a big decision. No going back,' he'd said.

Barbara remembered how her stomach had lurched at the prospect. 'I know, but why would I want to? I could get a place in the country, do the things I never have time to do. Read things I want to read instead of academic manuscripts. Write the book I've been threatening to write for years. Be part of a community –'

'Listen to music,' Adam cut in. 'It was you who introduced me to it, on the piano, and your old gramophone. Remember?'

Adam had been eight years old when he'd started to show an interest and she had grasped the opportunity of introducing him to the great composers, and the instruments of the orchestra. Roy and Dorothy had been mildly disapproving at first, although they soon began to realise that the boy showed some talent. But it was Barbara who had paid for his lessons when he showed an aptitude for the cello, and who had bought him his first instrument.

'As long as it doesn't distract him from his schoolwork,' Roy had wheezed from his chair in a corner of the lounge, struggling to breathe with lungs irreparably damaged by polio. 'He's got to do well, get a good job, a proper job.'

Barbara smiled remembering Adam's determination and the energy he had invested in balancing his love of music with his efforts to meets his father's expectations.

'Yes,' she said now, 'listen to music. In fact, I could have a piano again, like we had in Balmain. That's it, that's what I want.'

And now, here she was with the cottage that Adam and Jill had helped her find, the garden, the piano, half a manuscript, and life so pleasant and satisfying that she could barely believe she had ever considered dying at her desk in the city.

Barbara stared out beyond George's garden, wondering about Heather; her seemingly tireless commitment to the job, her patience with belligerent constituents and colleagues, the endless struggle to do her best.

'Don't you think it could be time to move on?' Barbara had urged her on several occasions. 'Get a life – a different life, I mean. Have some time for yourself.'

'Maybe,' Heather had said. 'Sometimes I think that but I'm not sure what that life would be. What I'd be without the job; a pain in the bum to everyone, probably, with all that time on my hands.'

'You'd be surprised,' Barbara said. 'No one thought I'd ever retire, including me, but it's the best decision I've ever made; wish I'd done it earlier.'

'I'll think about it,' Heather had said. But, of course, she hadn't. Or if she had, she'd clearly rejected the idea because here she was, just over a year out from another election, with a bullet wound in her shoulder and facing the aftermath of a brush with death.

The kettle switched itself off and Barbara turned back into the kitchen to make the tea, listening to the low rumble of George's voice on the phone. They had met as neighbours and become friends, and Barbara couldn't begin to measure the ways that friendship had enriched her retirement. She felt completely at home in this house, which was meticulously maintained to the standards established by George's late wife.

'Can't let things slip,' he always said, 'might never get them back together again.'

'Tea up?' George asked now, coming back into the kitchen. 'Good. Trying to sort out delivery of some manure for the garden.' He peered at her. 'You've got to look after yourself through this business, you know, Barbara. No sense knocking yourself out, you're no good to anyone then.'

Barbara sipped her tea. 'I know. It's just the worry. She's like my daughter, but I'm *not* her mother, I don't want to interfere too much.'

'Rubbish,' George said brusquely. 'You're her best friend and her mother's best friend, that's why she's there with you now. Where else would she go? Tell her what you think.'

'Who do you think did it?' Barbara asked.

George shrugged. 'Hard to say, but my money's on that nasty little mob of neo-Nazis that got done for trying to set fire to the mosque. What about you?'

Barbara shook her head. 'I don't know. I can't make sense of it. It's like Shaun said just now, if it's someone trying to make a political point you'd think they'd be claiming responsibility; otherwise, what *is* the point? I just know we'll all feel a whole lot better when they catch whoever it is and lock him up.' She paused, leaning forward as George started chopping vegetables again. 'Don't you think it must be horrible to be in a job that people hate and despise?'

'Yes. But I don't think Heather is. People are cynical about politics and politicians, but I'll bet if you talk to them most would say that they like, or at least respect, their own local member. And look at all the support she's had over this nasty business, the affection. A lot of people think very highly of her. Don't feel sorry for her, she likes her job and she does it well.'

Barbara laughed. 'I suppose you're right. But Heather's talking about "getting back to normal" as though it's simply a matter of going back to her office, her house and parliament. I don't think she has any idea what a trial of strength that's going to be.'

George stopped chopping and looked up. 'And you can't protect her from that,' he said. 'All you can do is warn her, and then be there for her when it happens. You shouldn't be trying to live her life for her. Now, have a look in the wine rack and pick us out a nice bottle for tonight's dinner.'

'So, now that Barbara's not around to hear, how do you really feel?' Shaun asked.

Heather leaned back in her chair and took off her glasses. 'Honestly?'

'Honestly.'

'Awful. But more like me again. The drugs blunt and confuse everything and now I've got a bit more clarity, but that isn't very comfortable.'

Shaun poured coffee from the plunger Barbara had left for them. 'What do you mean?' he asked pushing a mug towards her.

'Clarity seems to be an invitation to fear – paranoia, even. Everything seems threatening and the nights are the worst. I'm not sleeping well and I imagine I hear something, people outside or in the house, see shadows. I mean, I *know* they've put a guard on the place, I *know* we've got the panic-button thing they gave me, but even in the day I'm jumpy all the time, sort of hyper-alert, everything seems suspicious. Just a car door slamming, the phone ringing, every tiny sound seems threatening.'

Shaun nodded. 'I can imagine. I'm a bit the same. It's the heightened awareness of things we usually don't notice. It's like what they say about rats – you're never more than six feet away from one. Something like this makes you feel that all sorts of terrible things must be just behind you waiting to pounce.'

'I'm so sorry you're going through this because of me,' Heather said. 'But why, Shaun? Why was it me? I'm sure the police must have asked you this heaps of times, but you don't remember anything, you didn't see anything?'

He shook his head. 'Nothing. I wasn't aware of anything until it happened. There was the noise, you went flying off the steps, and all I can remember is hearing a car engine revving and then the screech of tyres. But I'm sure they were waiting for us, parked like that without the lights on, tucked away down the side of the building.'

'They? There was more than one person?'

'A figure of speech, Heather. I couldn't see anything, not who was in the car, what sort it was, numberplate, nothing, it was all so fast, and I was in a panic. I thought you were dead –'

'I'm sorry,' she cut in. 'I know you've been through it over and over again but it's a relief to talk about it. I don't like to say too much to Barbara and Adam because they're both already so worried about me.'

'It's fine,' Shaun said, 'you should talk about it, we both should.'

'Do you . . . well, do you think how it could so easily have been you that got hit?'

Shaun blushed. It seemed selfish in view of the fact that he was unharmed but it was a relief to admit it. 'Yes,' he said, 'I do, constantly, and I try to stop myself thinking that. I'm not over it by any means, Heather. It's just that I've been so busy I've had to get on with things. I suppose that's helped. And I wasn't the target.'

'I thought you weren't convinced that I was either,' Heather said, looking at him in surprise. 'You said you thought it was random –'

'I did at first. But then I thought it had to be you because otherwise why would they be sitting there waiting?'

She nodded. 'The hate file did it for me. Those letters are pretty scary and most of it I hadn't seen.'

'You've worked on some pretty contentious stuff.'

'And, you know, that's the other awful thing about all this,' she said, 'realising all that vitriol and abuse is directed at me, for things I believe in.'

'But you've always known that. You're not naive enough to think that it didn't exist.'

'Of course not, but this makes it more real, and very personal. Before this I could ignore it, now it's in my face.' She sighed. 'Surely the police will arrest someone soon, so I can stop seeing gunmen everywhere. Apart from feeling safer, I might be able to stop questioning the value of everything I've ever done.'

Shaun leaned forward in his chair. 'Heather, you've made a hell of a difference to a lot of people over the years, and often at some cost to yourself. And obviously you've changed things. If not, why would someone be trying to shoot you?'

'That's the problem,' Heather said. 'I don't know about any of it anymore.' She got up and wandered to the edge of the verandah. 'Hopefully, getting back to work will help me get things in perspective again.'

'You don't really look as though you're ready to come back,' Shaun said. It had shaken him to see how much worse she looked since she'd left the hospital. Coming out of that cocoon and coping with the delayed shock had taken a toll. She was pale and drawn, with purple shadows under her eyes, and he sensed that some fundamental change had taken place in her. 'You really don't need to yet.'

'Yes I do,' Heather said. 'I'll take it slowly, a few hours each day. But it's only four weeks until the end of the recess. I want to break myself in before parliament sits again.'

'I guess there's not much point arguing with you if you've made up your mind,' he said. 'If you're really sure . . . '

'The only thing I'm sure about is that the longer I stay away the harder it's going to be and the more frightened I'll get.'

Shaun nodded and began to tidy papers into his briefcase. Heather watched him with affection; in the eight years he'd worked for her he'd proved loyal and hardworking, he'd developed excellent political judgment and diplomacy in handling colleagues and constituents. His only blind spot seemed to be in relation to her and his belief that she would get a ministry at the next election. Heather knew it would never happen. She was far too much of a loose cannon to get promoted to cabinet, and she really didn't care. But Shaun cared, for her and for himself, and it surprised her that with his otherwise sound political judgment he couldn't, or wouldn't, see it. At some point she would have to talk to him about it. He needed to think strategically about his own career.

'You've got a new haircut,' she said with a smile. 'It looks good.'

Shaun straightened up, grinning, and ran his hand over his head. 'It's a number two,' he said. 'Never had it this short before. I quite like the look of it but I wish I'd waited till summer. I've had to start wearing a beanie these cold mornings, sometimes even in bed.'

Heather laughed. 'Very sexy! And how's everything else at the office?'

'Calming down,' he said. 'Fred Williams is great value, he's been an enormous help, and the staff and volunteers have been terrific. Oh, and Diane's back.'

'Really back, like, helping us again?'

'Really back.'

'I rather hoped she might find some rich and amiable expat and stay in Bali.'

Shaun shook his head. ''fraid not. She's back and she's very sulky.'

'Sulky?'

'She didn't receive official communication about the shooting from me.'

'Didn't Charlene let her know?' Heather asked.

'Of course, but by email a few days later, and as far as Diane's concerned that's not good enough. She thinks I should have called her. So I'm in the doghouse.'

Heather laughed. 'She can't make her mind up about you. You straightened out her daughter, but you also encouraged her to move out of home. She seems such an angry woman, I think she must be very unhappy. How *is* Charlene, by the way? Is it working out with you two?'

Shaun put his head into his hands. 'Letting her move in was not the smartest thing I've ever done. The thing I liked about Charlene was that she was fun, a total antidote to my work life; shiftless, funny, sexy, out for a good time. Then she moves in and starts buying linen and making nesting noises.'

Heather smiled. 'I did warn you. She's her mother's daughter.'

'I know. I wish I'd listened because right now she's driving me round the twist.' He stood up. 'I'd best get back and you look as though you could do with a rest.'

Heather walked with him to the door, catching his arm as he turned to leave.

'Shaun. I haven't thanked you, for that night. For staying with me and all you did then and since. I'm very, very grateful.'

He smiled. 'I'm thankful I was there, but I must say I don't want to do all that again in a hurry.'

She nodded. 'Me neither. Take care of yourself. Take a couple of days off now, before Fred goes. You need a break too.'

'Maybe,' he said, walking out to his car. 'I'll see you next week.'

Heather stood watching until the car reached the end of the laneway and turned out into the road, then she walked back through the house to the verandah. The work Shaun had left for her lay on the table and she shuffled the papers with her good hand, thinking back over their conversation. It had been a relief to talk to him in ways she couldn't to Barbara and Adam, who worried so much. But she couldn't articulate, even to Shaun, how profoundly this had affected her. She couldn't describe the battle to stop thinking like a victim, not just a victim of crime but of a lifetime of events and decisions that now left her alone, without anyone to share the intimate terrors of the night, or in whom to confide the barrage of strange emotions and mood swings that clattered through her days.

The pain in her shoulder, even the possibility of losing some sensation in her hand and arm, were minor compared with the emotional impact of what had happened. And recovery was releasing more than her own fear and insecurity. The constant attention from the police here in Barbara's home had brought the realisation that the way she lived her public life had put everyone she loved at risk. Shaun was right, she *had* always known; politics was rough, parliament a bear pit, the media ruthless, the compromises often heartbreaking, all par for the course. But this – this was different.

Jill was conducting a brutal cull of the paperwork on her desk. Her usual system, based on trays marked 'in', 'out', 'action' and 'leave it there long enough and it'll go away', had let her down. On the other hand, she mused, maybe *she* had let *it* down. In the weeks since Heather's shooting she'd found it unusually difficult to concentrate, and the present onslaught was a diversionary tactic: tidying, sorting and dumping seemed like a possible route back to normality. Jill did not believe in the causal relationship between local government and heaps of paperwork. Usually things ran smoothly, efficiently and with a minimal amount of unnecessary correspondence; the present problem was of her own making. It was like the great backlog of stuff that needed doing at home – it seemed to be growing into a monster challenging her to do something to remove it. But work was easier than home. Her mother would definitely turn in her grave.

Jill had never expected to be a bureaucrat, which is what she supposed she now was. Armed with an arts degree in the seventies

she had fancied herself working in a gallery, but for want of opportunities she'd drifted into a temporary job in local government
and discovered that she liked the fact that it dealt with real issues
that could improve people's lives. By the time she reached her
forties and married Adam, she'd built a résumé packed with useful
experience, and as community development became an increas-
ingly important part of the municipal agenda, she found she was
in demand. Two periods of maternity leave came and went, and
the second time she returned to a promotion. Now she had a job
that kept her sane when the demands of motherhood undermined
her spirit and her stamina, but in the last few weeks even work
had begun to feel like just another form of drudgery.

Earlier that morning, incapable of working through the draft of
the new community arts policy, she had called services and asked
for a paper recycling bin. Now she was ruthlessly clearing up and
chucking out in the belief that mess, and the concern that something
vital might be lurking beneath it, was compounding her mood.

'Impressive,' Renée said from the doorway. 'What's prompted
this?'

'Stuff,' Jill said, dumping the complete contents of the 'leave
it there' tray into the bin. 'Loads of stuff threatening to take over
my life.'

'Hmm. Lunch?' Renée asked. 'Looks like you need it.'

Jill glanced at a pile of brochures and press kits that had been
sitting on the corner of her desk for weeks. 'I do, desperately. Preferably something sinful like chips or chocolate mousse with cream.'

'Or both?'

'Yes, both.' She picked up the pile. 'You're the boss, tell me it's
okay to dump these.'

'It's okay,' Renée said. 'Dump 'em and let's get going.'

Jill tossed the brochures in the bin and closed the lid. 'That feels
a whole lot better,' she said, grabbing her bag from the top of the
filing cabinet.

'So what's bugging you?' Renée asked when they had found a
table at their favourite café. 'You've been all over the place for the
last couple of weeks.'

'Have you brought me here to counsel me?' Jill asked.

'I'm concerned about you, that's all. Concerned as a friend and a colleague.'

'And as the CEO? Sorry, my inner bitch is on high alert at present. My sister-in-law getting herself shot has had a very strange effect on me.'

Renée raised her eyebrows. 'She didn't actually *get herself* shot, Jill, it's hardly her fault. It's not as though she organised it as a photo op.'

'I know, I know,' Jill agreed. 'It really *is* awful, and the fact that the police don't seem to be any closer to solving it just prolongs the agony. Part of my problem is that I feel uneasy about *us*. It must seem really selfish, but if someone hates Heather enough to want to kill her, it seems like a threat to all of us – Adam, me, the kids, Barbara. Does that sound a bit far-fetched?'

'It does, but at the same time it's understandable,' Renée said. 'I guess I'd feel the same. It's the horrible sort of awareness of danger, and the feeling that it was always there before but you never thought about it. Like we don't think about the risk of getting killed on the road, until it happens to someone we know.'

Jill nodded. 'That's it exactly. But . . . ' she paused and realised she was glancing around to see if anyone could overhear her, 'I'll say this to you, Renée, but no one else: this has brought out the worst of my feelings towards Heather.'

'I thought you two got on like a house on fire,' Renée said, signalling to a waiter to take their order.

'We do, but it's on the surface. I don't think we've ever really gotten to know each other, but there's a part of me that's always resented her. It's not fair, it's not logical, but it's there.'

'Why?' Renée asked. 'Heather's really nice, and she's done great stuff for women, the environment . . . I don't understand.'

'That's the thing, nobody does, nobody could. It's totally petty and unreasonable and it's been worse than ever since the shooting.'

'But you can't blame her for getting shot?'

'Of course not. I don't, but . . . it's hard to explain.'

'I suppose,' Renée said, 'something like this happening is bound to open up some cracks in a relationship.'

'Maybe,' Jill said. 'It goes back a long way and I know Heather's a really good person, but there's something unreachable about her. And, if you really want to know about the baser side of my nature, it's probably about all the things she's got that I haven't.'

'Like what?'

'Prestige, respect, money, energy and, most of all, freedom – oh, and everyone's attention every time she crooks her little finger.'

'But you've got prestige and respect, you have a great reputation and a good job, and you've got Adam and the kids, a nice home . . . '

'I said it wasn't fair or logical. I don't like this part of myself, especially now that it seems to be taking a firmer grip on me, but I can't seem to shake it off.'

'We'll have the grilled snapper with salad and a huge bowl of fries,' Renée said. 'Maybe you should see a counsellor.'

'Huh?' said the waiter, who was still writing 'fries'.

'Not you, I'm talking to my friend.' She turned her attention back to Jill. 'This isn't something trivial. It's affecting your work and presumably things at home too.'

'Nobody's noticed at home,' Jill said. 'Kirsty's the only one who *might* notice and she's working on her honours thesis so she doesn't even know what day it is. But I know it's been showing at work – I'll get myself back on track in a few days, I promise.'

'It's not that, Jill,' Renée said. 'You always get things together, but this doesn't sound like you. Really, I mean it, I think you should get some help. You look tense and worn out.'

Jill was shocked to feel a sob rising in her throat and her eyes filling with tears. 'Maybe,' she nodded, looking out of the café window. 'There's other stuff too. Being responsible for everything is getting me down.'

'How d'you mean?'

'Well, Adam, everyone thinks he's a saint, right? And he almost is but he's so . . . so passive. Loathes taking decisions, leaves it all to me.'

'And then complains about it?'

Jill shook her head. 'Never.'

'Well, then . . . ?'

'But, in a way, *that's* the problem. He thrives on being out of touch with everything, almost not in the world, disappearing into his music when things get tough.'

'But he's great with the kids.'

'Yes, he does his share. He does whatever I ask, but it's as though he's helping out because he loves me.'

'What's wrong with that?'

'All the responsibility is mine. I hold everything together and it's wearing me down.' She watched as the waiter set clean cutlery and a basket of bread on the table. 'I know that no one else sees this, and they'd think it's all in my head. Trouble is, it's taking over my head. Sometimes living with a saint has its drawbacks. You feel guilty because you're feeling exhausted or frustrated or bored or jealous or *anything* other than grateful. And that's when the inner bitch becomes an inner python and rears up ready to strike.'

Renée helped herself to bread. 'So is this about Heather or Adam?'

Jill shrugged and looked away again, determined to control the threatening tears. 'Who knows? Either, both, whatever.'

'Meaning what exactly?'

'Meaning I don't know *exactly*, Renée,' she said, irritated now. 'I just don't know.'

Later that afternoon, sitting at a desk liberated from every unnecessary piece of paper, folder, file, magazine and report, Jill waited for the purge to take effect at a deeper level. But clarity of the desktop failed to translate into clarity of mind. Shortly after they'd got back from lunch, Renée had sent her an email with the contact details of the counselling service provided by the council for its executive staff. Revealing her vulnerability and her irrational emotions to the boss had been the ultimate stupidity. Renée was an old friend, and she was professional, supportive and discreet. Jill knew that the subject would only be discussed again if she raised it herself, but by blurting it out she had not only created the elephant in the room that they would both now struggle to ignore, she had destroyed the comfort zone that work had afforded her as the only place where she felt competent and, until now, absolutely clear about her own boundaries.

*

In the cosmetics section of David Jones, Diane tried the new Dior lipstick on the back of her hand.

'Nice,' she said, moving it around to catch the colour in a different light. 'What d'you think?'

'Yeah, it's okay but a bit crimsony for you,' Charlene said.

'I like dark lipstick,' Diane said, twirling the tester down into its case. 'I need something to make my features stand out more now I'm older.'

'I know, but women over fifty shouldn't wear those very strong colours. You need something more subtle.'

Diane stared at her. 'Says who?'

'Everybody. All the magazines. I read it the other day. They said dark colours and dark reds are out for the over-fifties. You don't want to look older than you are. Subtle browns and golds are the thing.'

'What, and I should wear beige too? How come you're reading about the over-fifties? You usually think embalming fluid is the only thing I should be using.'

Charlene slipped her arm through her mother's. 'I don't. You look great, Mum, you always do. I'm just telling you what I read. C'mon, let's get out of here. I want to go in to Skin Deep before I go back to work.'

The city centre was busy with lunchtime shoppers and the two women weaved their way through the mall where a young man, coated from head to foot in silver paint, stood on a small platform moving like a puppet.

'That's what I need,' Diane said. 'A nice, quiet, well-behaved boy to be my puppet.'

Charlene stifled a laugh. 'You *do not*! You'd hate it. You need a nice, quiet, well-behaved man to make a big fuss and take care of you. Big Daddy protective thingo.'

Diane nodded. 'True, but most men my age seem to want someone to look after *them*, to replace their mothers or their wives. Or they're sitting on stools in pubs getting drunk.'

'Someone'll turn up someday,' Charlene said. 'You should get out more.'

'You speak with the confidence of youth, naturally straight

blonde hair and newly capped teeth,' Diane said. 'It's not so easy at my age, especially the getting out bit – like, where should I get out *to*?'

'You could try Internet dating,' Charlene said. 'Lots of people are doing it. That's how Lauren's mum met that guy she's been seeing.'

'Really?'

'Yep, and they're getting married at Christmas.'

'Married? She's actually marrying him? Didn't she only just get divorced?'

'Six months ago,' Charlene replied.

'I thought he seemed a bit . . . well . . . sleazy.'

'Lauren thinks so too, but she says her mum wants the security. Apparently he owns a vineyard.'

Diane took a deep breath. Security was something else she had lost when Gerry left, security and a sense of the future, but the sleazy vigneron was a high price to pay – there were worse things than being alone and insecure. 'Oh well, good luck to her if that's what she wants. By the way, I gather Shaun's off visiting Heather today. Taken her some work. I don't know why he couldn't have sorted it over the phone instead of leaving us to cope with the office.'

'Isn't that Fred person still there?' Charlene asked, stopping to look in the window of a shoe shop.

'Just the same, there's plenty to do. They've got me stuffing envelopes again.'

'Well, if you don't like it, don't go there,' Charlene said. 'It's not as if they're paying you, and you're always complaining about it. Get a proper job.'

'I don't *want* a job,' Diane said irritably. 'I don't need one, and I like my freedom. And I shouldn't have to be working at all at my age.'

Charlene broke away to pick up a leaflet on the benefits of wheatgrass from the stand outside the health food shop. 'You're only fifty-six. Heather's older than you and she's still working.'

'I don't need to,' Diane said.

'Only because Dad pays a load of money into your account every month to stop him feeling guilty for buggering off.'

Diane halted in her tracks, tugging on her daughter's arm to make her face her. 'Are you saying I'm not entitled?'

Charlene rolled her eyes and tipped her head to one side. 'No, Mum, I'm saying it's stupid to volunteer for something you're always grumbling about when you could get a job you'd enjoy. But you won't do that because you want to make Dad keep paying.'

'He *should* pay,' Diane said. 'I've got more right to it than that little tart he lives with. She's only a few years older than you.'

In the wake of Gerry's desertion, Diane had made up her mind to hurt him in the only way she now knew how – through his wallet. She resisted all his efforts to get her to sell the house, insisted on maintenance and refused to get a job. She was not going to give him the satisfaction of her earning her own living and, anyway, she had been out of hairdressing for too long. Going back would mean retraining and there was no way that she, who had once been a senior stylist, was going to sign up as a junior to someone the age of Gerry's girlfriend.

She found herself a lawyer who had recently dealt with the divorce of a prominent AFL hero and won him a huge settlement from his equally famous soapie-star wife. 'Take him to the cleaners,' she had instructed in those dark early days when life as she knew it seemed to be over. 'Get me everything you possibly can, no holds barred.'

These days she blushed to think how mercenary she must have seemed, how clichéd she must have sounded, how much like a wronged wife in a B-grade fifties movie. But it was her only revenge – at least, that is, until she had thought of volunteering in Heather's office. It was a year after the break-up and Heather was leading a protest against a high-rise development a little further up the coast. Gerry was part of the consortium, his first involvement in anything outside the housing market, and it was sweet satisfaction to work (at Gerry's expense) with the person who was instrumental in ensuring that the project never got off the ground. Despite some occasional unease over her uncharacteristic ruthlessness, Diane's anger burned on. It kept her going, kept her turning up at Heather's office, kept her struggling to maintain a youthful, attractive appearance.

'Anyway,' she said now, grabbing Charlene's arm, '*you* shouldn't grumble. You get plenty from what your father pays.'

'I'm not grumbling, Mum, I'm just saying –'

'What about you and Shaun, anyway?' Diane said, changing the subject. 'I thought you might have some good news waiting for me when I got home.'

'Like what?'

'Like getting engaged.'

Charlene sighed. 'I'm sure he's getting round to it, but he's worried about all this stuff happening with Heather. When it calms down, I'm sure he'll ask me. Come on,' she said, steering Diane towards the beauty salon, 'my lunch break's nearly over and I want to find out the price of their tanning and Botox.'

Diane peered at her daughter's face. 'What for?'

'The lines on my forehead,' Charlene said, lifting the hair from her brow and pointing. 'They're really horrendous.'

'I can't even see them,' Diane said. ' I'll wait outside.' She hated that salon. All the girls were about twelve and looked as though they'd been cloned from the same host: long, straight blonde hair; perfect teeth; and all-over tans that bordered on orange. Was this the ideal that Charlene was aiming for? Why did young women all want to look the same? The place made Diane feel like a fossil. It was bad enough in David Jones's cosmetics department, where she felt she shouldn't trespass with less than perfect make-up and newly styled hair. Not that Diane would ever dream of going outside the house looking less than her best anyway, but these days her best just didn't seem good enough. Facing the mirror was becoming a torture, noting the bits that seemed to have dropped further overnight, noticing new lines every day. From here on it would just be a daily process of crumbling and flaking, but then, what did it matter? There was no one around to notice. She could grow mildew, rust and hairy warts and no one would blink an eyelid because she was, essentially, invisible.

THREE

Ellis woke to the sound of a pair of parrots scrabbling about in the tree outside his bedroom window. It was a perfect awakening – indeed, this was why he had designed a house built on stilts and nestling in the tree tops. Here he could wake daily to the sound of birds and the rustle of twigs and leaves. He had dreamed of a house like this since the fifties, when he had seen a Movietone newsreel of the Kenyan hunting lodge where Princess Elizabeth received the news of the death of her father, King George. Ellis didn't hold any special brief for Princess Elizabeth, or the royals generally, but the hunting lodge remained engraved on his memory.

In the News Cinema at London's Victoria Station, where he sat with his mother killing time before they caught the train back to Brighton, he stared at the lodge on its high stilts and vowed that he would, one day, live in a house just like it. At twelve it seemed to Ellis to be reasonably easy to achieve; he simply had to persuade his parents to move from the three-storey terrace in Hove to a hunting lodge. It wasn't necessary for it to be in Kenya – anywhere in Sussex would be fine. Strangely enough, neither of his parents took to the idea, but while his mother told him he was being silly and to get on and eat his tea, his father commended him on an admirable plan and built him a tree house in the branches of the oak tree at the bottom of their narrow garden.

'There you are, lad,' he'd said proudly, snapping his son with the Brownie camera as Ellis made his inaugural climb up the rope ladder. 'There's your tree house, you'll never find one better than that.'

Delighted though he was with this new hideaway, Ellis was absolutely sure that he *would* find a better one, that one day he would have the real thing, and it would be as good as, or better than, the one in which the Princess had spent her holiday. It took several decades, by which time he'd long since moved to the other side of the world, before his dream became reality. When he decided he was done with the law and planned his transition from city to coast, from legal rat race to spiritual life-coaching, he drew his dream and handed it over to an architect. Before long the dream was alive in seasoned timber, on solid brick piers, nestled among the eucalypts and palms on a steep hill overlooking a glorious beach just outside Byron Bay. It had an open living area, two bedrooms and a bathroom and, unlike the Princess's lodge, deep shaded balconies on three sides. Ellis was confident that if the Queen, now in her eighties, ever saw it, she would confirm his excellent taste.

Living in the tree tops did, however, have some disadvantages. Branches constantly needed to be cut back to prevent them pounding the roof loudly enough to wake the dead; possums found their way too easily into the roof space and peed with abandon; and squirrels, and the occasional rat, scampered noisily across the corrugated metal. None of this, however, detracted from Ellis's enjoyment of his property. Not only was it a glorious place but it contributed considerably to his image of himself.

On this particular Sunday morning he was happy to be woken by the parrots, to get up and watch the mist lifting, and to drive down into town for his morning coffee. Sipping a large macchiato and gazing out across the calm waters of the Bay, he reflected on the admirable balance of his life: he ate well, exercised regularly, drank lots of water, got plenty of sleep and was about to embark on a business venture that would put him at the cutting edge of the lifestyle industry. All that was missing was love. True love. The sort of love he had watched between his grandparents in their cottage at the foot of the Sussex Downs. 'They were passionately in love all their lives, even in their nineties,' he told anyone who would listen. 'In all those years together it was perfect, never a cross word between them.'

'Don't be so ridiculous,' Wendy, his first ex-wife, had said on a number of occasions. 'Of course they had cross words, they must have done, they wouldn't have been human if they didn't. It's just that you were a small child and you didn't see it.'

Wendy had become even more outspoken on the subject when Ellis's mother let slip that his grandfather had had a brief affair with the village postmistress in the thirties. 'So, of course, there would have been more than a few cross words,' Wendy had said triumphantly. 'And apparently your grandmother cleared off and left him for several weeks just after the war because he'd also been having it off with a woman in the Women's Voluntary Service.'

But Ellis retained his faith in the power of love. It all depended on finding the right woman, and so far he simply hadn't managed that. 'I'm the world's greatest romantic,' he would say, believing it and also believing that it made him more attractive. 'Men are simply more romantic than women.'

'Because women know the high price of romance,' Wendy had said snippily.

The second time around, Ellis had decided that perhaps romance was not, after all, the ideal condition for marriage. Julia, his second wife, was a highly desirable companion: intelligent, well-connected, and always looking as though she had stepped out of the pages of *Vogue*. They had fun together but neither had fooled themselves that they were in love. It was a marriage of convenience, of shared interests, rather than a romance made in heaven, but that too ran aground, reaffirming Ellis's belief that romantic love was all. But now here he was, a survivor of two marriages and several other romantic attachments, alone again, and he had been for some years.

Several weeks had passed since Ellis read the news about Heather, and he had been watching for subsequent reports. It distressed him that the police hadn't even produced a suspect. He was intrigued too by all the talk of a 'gunman'. Wasn't it possible, he suggested to acquaintances in the coffee shop, that the shot was fired by a woman? The women at the table dismissed the idea; even the men weren't willing to give it much credibility.

'Perhaps a woman jealous of her success,' he persisted, 'or even a jealous wife?'

'You should have been a novelist, Ellis,' one woman said. 'You've always got some weird theory. This is so obviously political.'

'Probably,' said another. 'But on the other hand, Ellis, you know Heather Delaney personally. Is she likely to be having an affair with someone else's husband?'

Ellis shrugged. 'No idea. It's almost forty years since I saw her. All I know about her these days is what I read in the paper.'

Knowing Heather had certainly done something for Ellis's street cred. He'd only mentioned it to a few people but the news had spread through his circle like wildfire and seemed to confer an interesting status on him. He contemplated the idea of building on this by admitting to having known Heather in the biblical sense, but on weighing it up decided that it was a declaration that could work against him – too much information. But it all combined to keep Heather in the forefront of his mind just as she had been all those years ago: copper-haired, slim and sexy with exceptionally shapely legs. And apart from her looks and her obvious intelligence she had something else: a girlish softness combined with strength of character.

Moistening a fingertip to collect up the slivers of almond croissant from his plate, Ellis saw Heather and himself together, blurred into flattering soft focus like the dream sequences of a French film, luminous with meaning. She, delicate, loving and just a little in awe, and himself lean and muscled, his hair brushing the collar of his Cambridge blue shirt, standing hand in hand in a field of long grass. Had they ever stood together in a field of long grass? Well, it didn't really matter because the more Ellis thought about it, the image acquired, as imagination so easily can, the veracity of memory; it became entirely real, a piece of their shared history. It convinced him that in some extraordinary way this terrible attack on Heather had a purpose, that he could provide a resolution to the confusion and conflict she must now be facing. And this would, in turn, resolve the past, bringing them back finally to where they should always have been – together.

Kirsty loathed getting up early and for each semester of her journalism degree she had planned her university timetable around ten o'clock starts, aiming to reach Ultimo at nine forty-five and race up to UTS in time for her first tutorial. Sometimes, if Adam had a rehearsal call nearby, she could get a lift with him, which gave her an extra fifteen minutes in bed. On other days she took the train. The one day on which she voluntarily rose early, however, was Fridays, the day she and Adam would struggle into their cycling gear, strap on their helmets and set off at six to ride a route they'd devised for themselves several years earlier. It was a ritual which they only varied if one of them was sick or away: a familiar, comforting and energetic ride through quiet streets, around the lake and along the cycle track through two parks until, an hour later, they ended up at the coffee shop two blocks from home.

Along with rising early, Kirsty also loathed sport and any sort of organised exercise, but there were two things she loved about cycling. The first was the way that, once encased in Lycra and wearing a helmet, she felt insulated from the rest of the world; the second was the bond it created with Adam, the companionable silence of the ride, and the special time in the coffee shop when she didn't have to compete with Jill, Daisy or Toby or, worst of all, the wretched cello, for his undivided attention.

On this particular Friday morning, sitting at an outside table while Adam went in to order their usual coffee and muffins – blueberry for her, banana and raisin for himself – Kirsty contemplated how she would break the news that would freak her father out entirely.

'Thanks,' she said, as he unloaded the tray and dumped it on a nearby table. 'Great ride.'

Adam nodded, and put his helmet with hers on the spare chair.

'Beautiful, best moment of the week.'

Kirsty knew that this was a lie. She knew that although he loved the weekly cycle ride as much as she did and for the same reasons, for him it could never be better than time spent communing with Bach or Brahms or perhaps Dvořák, but she appreciated the sentiment.

'I'd miss it if we couldn't do it,' she said. 'Like, I really miss it when you go on tour or something.'

He nodded, breaking his warm muffin in half and spreading butter on it. 'Me too.'

'The thing is,' she began, suddenly finding that her heart was starting to beat really fast, 'the thing is that I was thinking that if I didn't actually live at home, as long as I was somewhere nearby we could still do it.'

Adam sipped his coffee. 'Mmm. If and when that time comes, we'll have to find a way,' he said.

'Well . . . ' she hesitated briefly, 'that time might have come.' She swallowed hard, seeing his change of expression.

'What do you mean?'

'The time might have . . . actually, *has* come for me to move out of home. But I wouldn't be far away,' she rushed on. 'Ten minutes, really. Just ten minutes on the bike.'

Adam put down his cup. 'Leave home?'

She nodded, trying to swallow a piece of muffin.

'To go where?'

'Woodstone Road, with Nick. I'm going to move in with him.'

Adam choked on some muffin crumbs. 'Move in with Nick,' he spluttered. 'Since when?'

'Since as soon as possible,' she said. 'Like, probably the end of the month, when I've submitted my thesis.' She felt his shock like a physical pain.

'But why?'

'Why not? We love each other. You like him and so does Jill. Even Mum liked him last time she was here. Why not?'

Adam seemed to be having trouble catching his breath. 'Well . . . ' he stammered, 'well . . . but I mean, are you sure? It's such a big step, living together. Wouldn't it be best to stay at home for a while at least?'

'Dad, Nick and I have been going out for more than two years, we've known each other for yonks, and I'm twenty-two.'

'But lots of people live at home these days. It's cheaper for you and . . . and . . .'

'And you can keep an eye on me.'

'Yes. No! That's not what I meant, it's just a bit of a shock, that's all, the idea of not having you there.'

'One less person to worry about.'

'Not really.'

'I thought you might be relieved. More space for you and Jill. It can't be easy . . . for her, anyway . . .'

'No,' he said. 'It's not like that. We're together, a family, that's what I feel, Jill too, she feels the same, we all belong together.' He picked up his cup and downed the short black in one gulp.

'Dad, I'm grown up now. I have to go sometime. I have to get my own life.'

Adam sighed and rubbed both hands over his eyes. 'Yes, of course. I know you do. But right now?'

'Not today, but the end of the month. Like I said, it's as good a time as any.'

'I suppose so,' he said, and Kirsty ached hearing the sadness in his voice. 'I suppose you're right. It had to happen sometime but I don't like it, and I don't suppose I'd like it any better if you were forty.'

'But you *do* like Nick?'

'Very much, it isn't that. It's just that you still seem like my little girl but, as you rightly said, you've grown up. I've been trying not to think about that but I'll have to get used to it. Have you told Jill?'

'No, I wanted to tell you first.'

Adam cleared his throat. 'Yes, yes, I'm glad you did.' He gave a strange, strangled sort of gulp. 'I might never get used to it, of course, it only seems like yesterday . . .' He stopped himself and stood up. 'Sorry. I need a glass of water. You?'

'Please,' she said, 'and, Dad, I'm sorry.'

'No,' Adam cut in quickly. 'No, you mustn't be. You're right, you have to have your own life.' He put his hand on her hair letting it linger there briefly, and she reached up and squeezed it. 'You'll always be with me, Kirsty, wherever you are. You know that, don't you?'

Kirsty watched him make his way into the café and up to the counter. He was doing the funny crab-like walk that you did in bike shoes, and there was a droop to his shoulders that was very familiar. She knew he had gone to get water to give him time to reorganise his face. When they got home he would head for the music room, close the door and that was where he'd stay for several hours. She felt like crying for him but she also felt the relief of having leapt a huge emotional hurdle. Telling Jill would be easier. Kirsty loved Jill, as much as she loved her own mother. Yvette was more pedantic and controlling than Jill, and much harder to live with. Sometimes Kirsty wondered how Jill coped with Adam, the obsession with his music, the way he ran for cover whenever things got difficult. She thought Jill had been looking a bit strained recently, probably work and the littlies, or all the drama around Heather.

'So you'll tell Jill when we get back?' Adam said, returning with the water.

'Yes. Is she okay, by the way?'

'Jill? Fine, why wouldn't she be?'

Kirsty shrugged. 'Oh, nothing. Just thought she was looking a bit stressed out.'

Adam shrugged. 'Don't think so. Well, not any more than usual . . . you know, Daisy, Toby, work . . . '

Kirsty nodded, considered saying something further and then changed her mind. This wasn't the time to start him worrying about Jill. She skimmed the foam from her cappuccino with a spoon. 'Okay then,' she said. 'I'll tell her when we get home. And, Dad? . . . Thanks, thanks for understanding.'

Adam nodded and stared bleakly down into his empty coffee cup.

Diane had missed Heather's first two days back at the office but, by all accounts, they hadn't been an overwhelming success.

According to Patsy, the other staff member and Shaun's second-in-command, Heather had arrived about nine thirty and Shaun had had to take her home again within a couple of hours.

'I think it's the anxiety as much as anything,' Patsy said. 'We've got panic buttons everywhere now, even in the loo, and I guess you saw that guard on the door – he's the size of a commercial refrigerator – but since Heather came back the whole place feels like a target lit up with neon signs.'

'Well, we have to keep going,' Diane said briskly. 'The police are bound to tie it up soon; meanwhile, we just need to hang in till then.' Everything was irritating her today and she hadn't yet gotten over her resentment for not having been kept in the loop when it was all going on. She gathered up a mailing list and switched on one of the spare computers just as Shaun came out of his office.

'Diane, I didn't really expect to see you,' he said. 'The other volunteers felt it was too stressful worrying about security now Heather's back. They're staying away until things are sorted out.'

Diane shrugged. 'Business as usual. You can't let the bastards win,' she said. 'I thought I'd start updating this mailing list unless there's something else you want me to do.'

'That'd be good,' Shaun said. 'I'm going across the road to get some real coffee. Can I get you one?'

She looked up in surprise. The coffee run was usually dumped on her. 'Thanks,' she said. 'I'll have a strong latte.'

Diane genuinely believed it was important not to give in to the fear. It was a matter of principle, like not bargaining with terrorists; giving in went against everything she believed in. That belief had overridden the urge to stay away and look for something to do where she might really be appreciated.

She watched Shaun run down the steps of the building and head for the coffee shop. It was a strange sort of relationship she had with him. She was thankful for the influence he'd had on Charlene, but the balance of power confused her. As a potential mother-in-law she felt she should have the upper hand, but Shaun ran the office and was Heather's right-hand man, so it seemed that she was, somehow, always deferring to him. Her aspirations for Charlene had been for someone devastatingly handsome, sensitive, charming and preferably extremely rich, who also viewed his potential mother-in-law as a fount of wisdom and beauty. Someone who would flirt harmlessly with her while adoring and being faithful to her daughter. Instead she had been faced with a series of spotty, monosyllabic youths with assorted piercings, followed by a married man in his forties and then Danny, the ghastly sleaze who Diane was sure was giving Charlene drugs. There was no doubt that Shaun was a huge improvement, but he still fell considerably short of the ideal. She watched him dodge the traffic as he crossed the street and then disappeared from sight.

Diane stood up. She hadn't seen Heather since the shooting so she should probably go and say hello to her before starting on the mailing list. Tapping lightly on the office door she opened it and stuck her head inside. Heather, her arm in a sling, glanced up, looking like death.

'Oh, Diane, hi,' she said. 'I didn't realise you were here. It's good of you to come in. How was Bali?'

'Great, gorgeous, lots of sun, lovely food, lounging round the pool . . . you know. How are *you*?'

Heather gave her a weak smile. 'Pretty grim, the shoulder, the shock and being shit scared – it's not a great combination.'

Diane thought she looked really rough, as though she were just hanging together. 'You don't look too good. Do you think you should be here?'

Heather leaned back in her chair. 'I only managed two hours yesterday and Monday, so I'm determined to survive three today,' she said. 'Are *you* sure you want to be here? You know the risks. There's no obligation for you to come in.'

Diane nodded. 'I know and I'm here, aren't I? I was wondering if you're coping okay at home. I mean, I could get you some shopping if you like, or anything else . . . '

Heather's face lit up. 'Really? That'd be great. Barbara drove me down from Morpeth and she's staying with me for a couple of days, but I think she's finding it all a bit much.'

'Well, if you want to make a list I'll nip down to Coles later and get it, and I'll put it in Shaun's car for when you're ready to leave.'

Half an hour later, Diane pulled into a parking bay outside the supermarket cursing herself. What *was* it about Heather that made her feel so inadequate? People were always running around after her. Did they all feel as she did, as though they were up in front of the headmistress? Shaun didn't, he and Heather got on well, but everyone else . . . She dragged on the handbrake with unnecessary force and got out of the car with the shopping list. Why was she doing this? Wasn't it enough that she helped in the office without dobbing herself in to do the shopping as well?

Striding irritably down the aisles with a trolley, Diane worked her way through the list: tuna, eggs, baked beans, cauliflower, tomatoes, brussels sprouts – brussels sprouts? Surely no one ate those from choice? Trust Heather to like something other people only ate on sufferance. Tea bags, washing powder, fabric conditioner. As she piled items in the trolley her resentment rose in the knowledge that she had only herself to blame. Charlene was right, the time had come for her to stop volunteering; her heart wasn't in it anymore. She cared about all the things Heather was involved in but mostly she was there because it pissed Gerry off.

Diane had been disappointed to discover that while she admired Heather she didn't much like her. Underneath the apparent niceness there was a steeliness that Diane found quite intimidating. But to leave now would be like running away. As soon as it was over, once they'd arrested someone, then it would be all right to leave. She tossed a pack of six toilet rolls into the trolley and headed for the checkout. No, she couldn't leave just yet, but she definitely wouldn't be volunteering for any more shopping.

Jill sat, legs stretched out in front of her, on Kirsty's bed, watching her stepdaughter sort clothes into two suitcases and a bin bag while from the music room, where Adam was giving a private lesson to one of his students, the bleat of a tortured cello echoed through the house. Kirsty looked so much like her father, the same fair, freckled skin and blue eyes, but she had her mother's force-fulness and energy.

'Exactly how many black t-shirts do you have?' Jill asked, staring at the bundle that Kirsty had just dumped on the foot of the bed.

'Not sure, but never enough. I mean, you never have the actual one you want, do you? It's either got the wrong neck, or wrong sleeves, too snug, too loose . . . ' She held up one with a heart shape cut out of the back. 'But I think the Salvos can have this one,' she said, dropping it into the bin bag.

'Are you absolutely sure you're doing the right thing?' Jill asked.

'Yep. It's much too girlie –'

'Not the t-shirt – moving, I mean. Moving in with Nick.'

Kirsty stopped what she was doing and looked up, raising her eyebrows. 'We've had this conversation.'

Jill sighed. 'I know, sorry. You're a perfectly rational adult and able to make your own decisions. It's just that I'll miss you. I hate the fact that you're going, and so does Adam.'

'We'll still see each other,' Kirsty said. 'I won't be staying away just to show how independent I am.' She grinned and fleetingly Jill saw the eight year old she'd met for the first time when Adam had suggested a picnic at the beach so that she and Kirsty could get to know each other. 'I might go and see Aunty Heather tomor-row,' Kirsty continued, 'maybe go to parliament. I've got the afternoon free.'

Jill raised her eyebrows and tried to iron the resentment out of her tone. 'Why parliament?'

'It'll be her first question time since the shooting. She said she was feeling a bit weird about it so I thought I'd go, be there for moral support.'

Jill gritted her teeth. It was more than six weeks since the shoot-ing and still everyone was running around after Heather.

'Maybe we should suggest she stays here for a while when she comes back to Sydney for parliament,' Adam had said.

'But she's got a lease on that place in Potts Point for when she's in Sydney,' Jill had said to him. 'Won't she go there?'

'I just thought she might feel better being with us at first. It won't be easy.'

'No, but she said she wanted to get back to normal as soon as possible.' Jill could feel her heart hardening in self-defence. 'Didn't she say Shaun was going to come to Sydney with her for the first week? He'll probably be staying nearby, and she might feel better in her own place.'

Adam, typically, had shrugged his shoulders and looked away. 'Maybe, but on the other hand –' he began.

'Look,' Jill cut in, 'let's wait and see what she wants to do, not pre-empt anything.'

He hadn't raised the subject again and a few days later it was clear that Heather planned to stay in her own place. 'So come for dinner, bring Shaun,' Jill had heard Adam say on the phone. 'Which day would suit you?' And Jill reminded herself that dinner was a whole lot better than having Heather to stay with them for a couple of weeks.

'Moral support, yes, that's really thoughtful,' Jill said now, hearing the false note in her own voice. 'Kirsty, this might seem like an odd question, but do you feel sort of exposed since the shooting?'

'Exposed?'

'Yes, like we could be part of the target . . . the wider target, if someone wants to get rid of Heather.'

Kirsty shrugged. 'Nope. Should I? Do you think we are?'

'No,' Jill said hastily, 'of course not. I . . . well, I just wondered.'

'So we could meet and go to parliament together if you like,' Kirsty said. 'I'm going to look for a new duvet cover, Nick's is falling apart. We could go shopping, have lunch and then go to question time.'

Jill shook her head. 'Busy day, meetings, stuff to finish . . . sorry.' She paused. 'Do you ever wonder why Heather doesn't have any friends? Women friends?'

Kirsty straightened up from a pile of shoes. 'Where's all this coming from, Jill? Being a target, women friends – doesn't she have friends?'

'I don't think so. She never talks about them, or seems to do anything with friends.'

'Too busy, I suppose. I'd hate to have a job that meant I couldn't have a life. Still, I'll have to find something serious now, no more making cappuccinos to earn a crust. No more uni, and I even submitted my paper ahead of time, so it's the end of an era. I have to move out now that I've finally given up on waiting for you to be an evil stepmother.'

'I *can* be evil if that's what'll keep you here.'

'You *are* being evil now, actually,' Kirsty said. 'This is emotional blackmail.'

'I know, and I think I could get really good at it. Will you still babysit?'

'Would I miss out on the chance to bully my siblings? Anyway, the TV and DVD player here are much better than Nick's.' She stopped suddenly and sat down on the bed. 'Is everything okay?'

'Apart from you moving? Yes, fine, why?'

Kirsty shrugged and looked away. 'You look a bit stressed. Sometimes I wonder if Dad . . . well, he's gorgeous and we all love him to bits, but he does seem to opt out a bit.'

Jill sighed. 'You've noticed! Yes, he does, and it pisses me off. It's not easy being the one who always has to be in charge of things getting done.'

'He adores you, you know,' Kirsty said, anxiety in her eyes.

'And I him,' Jill said, reaching out to pat her hand. 'It's nothing for you to worry about. Just work, and then Daisy and Toby are so full on, and I'm at least a century older than all the other mothers. Not that I'd change anything, but sometimes I feel a bit worn out.'

'What's worn out?' Daisy said, appearing in the bedroom doorway and bounding towards a pile of bags and shoes. 'This?' she cried, picking up a pink, heart-shaped handbag patterned with butterflies. 'Is this worn out? Can I have it *pleeeease*, Kirst, please?'

Kirsty nodded and threw her a matching belt. 'Yes you can, but don't mix up those shoes; they're all sorted. Well, at least there's one of us out of the way now,' she said, turning back to Jill. 'Less work, fewer people to look after.'

'That's not how it feels,' Jill said. 'I've loved having you here, loved *you* since that first picnic.'

Kirsty grinned and started packing again. 'Even the dope-smoking, and having to talk to me about safe sex?'

'Some moments more than others,' Jill replied. 'Remember, if it doesn't work out you can always come back.'

Kirsty, who was peering into the wardrobe, turned to face her again. 'Thanks, I do know but I'll try not to. This is the big one. I need to make my own way, stop relying on you and Dad.'

'And stop us relying on you?'

'That too,' she said, dropping two pairs of jeans into a bag and kneeling to close it.

Adam, standing by the window, his back turned to his student, could hear the low murmur of female voices coming from Kirsty's room. The comfort he derived from this reassuring background music was, he felt, like a guilty secret. He had been eleven when his father died and he spent the remainder of his childhood and adolescence in a house filled with women: his mother; Barbara; and Heather, who was two years younger than him. There had been times in his teens when he'd resented it, moaned about it to his friends, and brooded in his room, planning confrontations with one or all of them simply for the sake of it. But he was a boy who hated conflict and he usually talked himself out of it. And when, at nineteen, he moved into a share house the daily rows and noisy, abusive banter came as a shock. He longed for the serenity of home but moving back was not an option; it was the sixties, living at home was totally square.

It was Heather's campaign to leave home eighteen months later that allowed him to quit the horrors of a houseful of his con-temporaries without losing face. They could get a place together, he suggested. It worked. Heather got her independence, and Adam regained his peace of mind and kept on avoiding conflict by writing his mental scripts for imagined disputes and then dis-carding them. Now, almost forty years later, it was still working. He continued to avoid confrontations that might bring him into real conflict with the women close to him. It was so much easier to let *them* take the decision, to acquiesce, to suggest rather than insist, to compromise without their ever knowing he was doing it. And, in any case, they rarely presented him with dilemmas worthy of struggle.

Flinching now as thirteen-year-old Brad sawed at the strings of a rather nice instrument that his limited talent barely merited, Adam breathed deeply in an effort to calm the anxiety that had dogged him since Heather's shooting.

'Everything seems threatened now,' he'd confided to Stefan, the third cello, as they waited in the orchestra rehearsal studio for the arrival of the celebrated Russian guest conductor to start the rehearsal. 'Nothing seems safe anymore.'

'Sure,' Stefan said, nodding slowly, 'is very troubling.'

'More than that,' Adam went on, 'it changes everything, like cracks suddenly appearing in what you previously thought was a very safe building. Of course it can't go on forever. We'll get some security again when the police arrest someone.'

'You think?' Stefan asked. 'Is not so easy to get back, I think.'

'Well, it *will* get better.'

Stefan shrugged. In Kosovo he had survived years of civil war followed by the US bombing which killed his wife and daughter. He had fled his homeland to find a new life to help him survive his grief. 'Is a myth, I think, Adam, the security, you know? Before this happens, you think, "I am secure", then bang! It is not security that has gone, it never was there, only difference now is you know it is illusion. You don't get illusion back.'

Adam stared at him, conscious of his own insensitivity. 'I'm sorry, Stefan,' he said, shaking his head, 'how selfish of me. This is nothing to what you've been through.'

'No worry. What happens is you learning to live without feeling safe. Is life. You know?'

Adam nodded. 'I suppose so. I'm a coward, I've had a very peaceful life, and I've tried to keep it that way. I suppose I did always realise how vulnerable it was and cherished it all the more because of that.'

Heather, in contrast, seemed to relish risk and uncertainty.

'Yours is such an unsafe, volatile life,' he'd said years earlier when, having tabled a controversial report on prostitution law reform, she had been the victim of fierce and sustained parliamentary attack. 'How can you bear to wake up every morning worrying about what might happen?'

'I don't,' she'd replied, looking puzzled. 'It never occurs to me. I wake up thinking how lucky I am and wondering what I'll tackle first.'

'But stuff happens to you every day. At the very least you'll have an angry constituent hammering on the door, or the opposition hammering you in parliament.'

She'd laughed then. 'Those are just life's little challenges,' she'd said. 'They keep you on your toes. It's never boring but it's not exactly living on the edge.'

'I don't understand,' Adam had said again. 'Sometimes I think you're really reckless.'

And that had made her laugh too. 'Reckless? Heavens, Adam, it's not as though I'm climbing Everest or sailing single-handed across the Southern Ocean. You just think anything other than being shut away in a room with your music, or surrounded by the string section of the orchestra, is risky.'

At the time he had been hurt by her sarcasm, not only because it contained a significant element of truth, but because they both knew that once, when Heather had been vulnerable and very much at risk, it was he, Adam, who had seen her safely through it. Now, in the weeks since the shooting, his fear for his sister, and the sense that he should somehow have been able to protect her, were intensified by her own obvious fear and the loss of that enviable confidence, all destroyed by one bullet.

'How was that, Mr Delaney?' Brad asked as the last excruciating note faded away. 'I've been practising really, really hard.'

Adam sighed, turning away from the window. 'Too hard, maybe. Hard for you and hard on the music. You need to give some thought to what Brahms intended with this piece . . . ' And as he explained the delicacy of the prelude, everything that Adam valued seemed more fragile than it had ever been.

FOUR

Heather had left it until the last possible moment to take her place in the chamber. These days she hated question time, feeling it had been reduced to a celebration of ridiculous posturing, bullying and name-calling. And on this day more than any other, she was dreading it. She had been focused on the first parliamentary sitting as a milestone in her recovery, believing that by the time she arrived back in Sydney she would be over the worst and the police would have made an arrest. But the police seemed no wiser now than on day one, and while she was healing physically the deeper impact of the shooting still haunted her.

'You're very quiet,' Shaun had said on the drive from Newcastle two days earlier. 'Are you feeling okay?'

'It just feels a bit strange to be going back, that's all,' she said. 'Not like going back after the usual winter recess. It's as though I've been away for much longer.'

And strange it was to be back in the Parliament House office, to find herself staring with suspicion at the queue of people moving through the security checks, glancing constantly over her shoulder as she passed through the foyer and the Fountain Court.

'It's only natural,' said Brenda in the Clerk's office. 'You'll feel at home again in a day or two. We're all glad to see you back,' and she pulled a large bouquet of blue irises and white carnations from under the desk. 'The staff got you these, with our best wishes.'

'We'll look after you, Heather,' said the Clerk, appearing alongside her. 'More security here than Fort Knox. Anything worrying you, don't hesitate, we're all looking out for you.'

But she felt like a moving target, exposed wherever she went, and the physical violation was the least of it; her peace of mind was shattered. The public areas were seething with potential attackers, the closed sections scattered with doorways, alcoves, cupboards and other possible hiding places, and everything was brighter, sharper, faster-moving and more frenetic than she remembered.

Detective Alex Roussos had been to see her that morning. The police presence in the House had, he told her, been increased, and a guard assigned to her. Vince Potter, the sergeant working with him on the case, would also be there.

'So how long will you keep that up?' she'd asked.

'As long as we need to,' he replied, not looking at her.

She knew it was beyond his jurisdiction and at any time the resources might be needed elsewhere, or someone higher up the scale would decide that it was no longer necessary.

'And there's still nothing?'

He shook his head. 'But we're not giving up,' he said, and she heard his effort to sound confident and reassuring.

Heather had read enough about trauma to know that half the battle of recovery lay in placing the event in the past, but as long as the perpetrator was at large, that was impossible. No matter how many times she reconstructed that night and tried to consign it to history, back it came to overshadow the present and the future.

The Speaker was asking for ministerial statements when Heather looked up and spotted Kirsty grinning widely from the front row of the public gallery. Shaun was seated just behind her and his presence was reassuring. He had saved her life simply by being there and now they were bound together by an experience that no one else could really understand. She tried to recall a saying about saving a person's life, that they then became your responsibility – or was it the other way around? It didn't seem fair that he might feel responsible for her, but right now she was leaning on him to an unreasonable degree and that simply had to change.

Heather fidgeted in her seat, finding it hard to concentrate on the tedious jousting between the Premier and his counterpart, and she had an uncomfortable sense that she was being watched. She had expected the scrutiny of the journalists in the press gallery, who would be watching to see how she was coping, but this felt different. And as she looked back to the public gallery she saw that someone *was* staring at her, staring so intently that an intense rush of fear flooded her with sudden heat. At the far end of a row, diagonally opposite her on the lower level of the gallery, a man was leaning forward, his forearms on his knees, watching her with a steady gaze.

Heather swallowed hard and looked away, trying to distract herself by concentrating on the Leader of the Opposition, who was stabbing his finger in the direction of the Minister for Education. But her eyes were continually drawn back to the man whose gaze never wavered. Was she being ridiculous? The back of her neck prickled with fear and beads of sweat sprung out on her forehead. The chamber was closing in, threatening to crush her. Gripped by panic, she rose, squeezed past her colleagues and slipped out through the half-glass door at the side of the chamber.

'Everything all right?' the guard asked.

She shook her head, leaning back against the wall, her legs trembling. 'No. Well, I don't know . . . there's a man, over there in the gallery, the lower level near the outside door. He kept staring . . . '

The security guard spoke into his radio, and two more guards and Vince suddenly materialised beside her.

'On the end of the row,' she said again, moving towards the door to point him out, 'there by the . . . he's gone, he was in that end seat, and now he's gone. He must have left when I did.'

Her heart was pounding now and she was finding it hard to breathe. Vince steered her to a seat.

'What did he look like?'

'Grey hair, quite thick, squarish face.'

'Clean shaven?'

'Yes, and wearing a jumper, dark; navy, perhaps, or very dark grey . . . '

'How old?'

'Sixty, maybe more.'

Vince nodded to the guards, who headed for the side exit. 'Anything else? Did he do anything strange, try to attract your attention?'

She shook her head. 'No, it was just the staring, he was staring at me all the time. I'm sorry, I'm probably overreacting. I expect he's perfectly innocent and he's gone now.'

'We'll see,' Vince said. 'I'll send a uniformed constable to stay with you. Can you go to your office or do you need to go back to the chamber?'

'No.' She was feeling stupid now. 'I won't go back in, I can't, not today.' She looked up in relief to see Shaun approaching. 'I was so frightened in there, and now it seems silly,' she said. 'Maybe I'm becoming paranoid.'

'Maybe,' Vince said, 'but maybe not. I don't like the fact that he left when you did. We'll see what the boss has to say.'

'Okay, here's what I want you to do,' Alex Roussos said the following day. It was ten minutes to the start of question time and the House was crawling with police both in and out of uniform. 'Go in to the chamber as though nothing has happened. Behave normally, go to your seat and try not to look at the gallery. We want him to think you haven't noticed him.'

Heather's heart leapt into her throat.

'You mean he's there again?'

'There *is* a man who fits your description sitting in almost exactly the same place near the side door. One of my officers is sitting beside him and there's another just behind. Try to look relaxed and when you've been in there a few minutes you can glance around. Vince is with the usher on the other side of the chamber, between the Speaker and the Opposition benches. If you think it's the same man, just give Vince a nod. Then I want you to stay there for a while. Do you think you can do that?'

Heather nodded and swallowed hard. 'Be calm, take my seat, don't look round straight away, then when I do look up, if I spot him nod to Vince and stay put.'

'Right, good. It's important that he thinks you haven't noticed him. Stay there as long as you can, ten minutes if you can handle it, then get up and come out, same as you did yesterday, and we'll see what he does.' He gripped her arm. 'I've got officers in front, beside and behind him, Heather, so just take your time and stay cool. Remember, he's had to go through the x-ray machine to get in.'

Fear encased her in a cocoon, making her struggle for breath. People, voices, action in the chamber all existed in another dimension. She made her way to her seat, willing herself to relax, to smile, battling the urge to look up to the gallery from where his presence seemed to exercise a magnetic force. She fixed her attention on the mace resting on its stand on the green baize of the central table and waited. As the Speaker welcomed a group of year eleven students and an RSL club, she allowed herself to turn her head, along with the rest of her colleagues, towards the gallery in acknowledgement, and she saw him. His gaze struck her like a blow and she gasped, turned to Vince and nodded, before looking down at the order paper that was shaking furiously in her hands. Ten minutes to get through, why didn't they just take him now? Why wait to see what he'd do?

Her shoulder throbbed and she closed her eyes, trying again to visualise healing but able only to see herself, as from a distance, hurtling down the office steps on a dark, wet night. She managed seven minutes before her terror drove her stumbling out through the side door, where Roussos, mobile phone to his ear, signalled to her to move away from the line of sight.

'He's leaving now too,' he told her. 'They'll pick him up outside the door.'

'And then you'll never guess what happened,' Heather said, reaching out for her wine glass. 'They *did* apprehend him and carted him off to the police station, where it turns out he's not some mad would-be assassin but,' she turned to her brother, 'and you won't believe this, Adam – it was Ellis.'

Adam was silent for a moment, puzzled. 'Ellis?' he said finally. 'Not Ellis Hargreaves?'

Heather nodded and sipped her drink. 'Ellis Hargreaves. Isn't that amazing, after all this time? He'd heard what happened and he decided to come and see me.'

'Ellis Hargreaves?' Adam said again. 'That bastard! I wouldn't put anything past him. What's Ellis bloody Hargreaves doing showing up after all this time?'

'Don't be such a grump,' Heather said, her cheeks flushing slightly. 'It was lovely to see him again.'

'Why? Why did he want to see you? I hope Roussos is checking him out. It could be him. Bastard.'

Shaun, sitting on Jill's left, saw her head spring up in surprise. Clearly she was shocked by Adam's vehemence.

'Adam! That's a dreadful thing to say,' said Heather, clearly hurt. 'I know you never liked him but –'

'Liked that sleazy bastard? No. I never understood what you saw in him, especially in view of . . . ' He stopped and they both looked down awkwardly at their plates.

'He . . . er . . . well, he does have an alibi for the night of the shooting, Adam,' Shaun said, feeling some responsibility to support Heather in the face of this uncharacteristic attack. Since the police had apprehended Ellis that afternoon, Shaun had witnessed Heather's roller-coaster emotions as she swung from fear to relief at a possible arrest, to delight at the appearance of an old friend and back to fear that they had not, after all, found her attacker. 'Apparently he was at some retreat in the Blue Mountains at the time. A number of people can vouch for him.'

'Perhaps someone would tell me who this person is?' Jill said, passing Shaun a dish of steamed vegetables. 'He seems to be inciting some rather unusual passions in you, Adam.'

'He was a part-time law tutor when I was at uni,' Heather began, glancing sideways at her brother. 'We fell in love . . . '

'Ah! An old boyfriend.'

'Boyfriend,' snorted Adam. 'A married man with two small

children. Boyfriend, indeed. More like a vile seducer preying on young girls.'

'Heavens, Adam, what's got into you? You're sounding positively Victorian,' Jill said. 'Did he really seduce you, Heather?'

'No, well . . . maybe . . . yes, I suppose he did,' Heather said, flushing more deeply, 'but it wasn't as though I was unwilling. He was exciting, handsome and brilliant, and I was madly in love with him.'

'He took advantage of you,' Adam said. 'These days he'd never get away with it.'

'He was in love with me too,' Heather protested. 'He was. He said so today, he was always in love with me. He should never have left, he said so, it was just the situation. He was married . . . '

'Yes, he was married, he was much older, you were eighteen, and he was your tutor, for heaven's sake. He was in a position of trust and authority and he abused that and then abandoned you, and now he's stalking you.'

'He's not stalking –'

'Well,' Jill cut in, 'this *is* a surprise. A secret past. Come on, Heather, tell all.'

Adam glared at her and stabbed a baby carrot with his fork.

'It was just that, really,' Heather said, embarrassed now.

Adam grunted. 'Just what, exactly?'

Heather ignored him. 'I suppose it was doomed from the start, what with him being married, but just the same . . . '

Adam grunted again, louder this time.

Shaun studied his plate, slicing his chicken breast into small pieces, uncomfortable to find himself suddenly at the heart of some reignited family tension.

'So this appearance is quite out of the blue?' Jill asked. 'How long since you saw or heard from him?'

Heather paused. 'Oh, decades – must be almost forty years.'

'And you didn't recognise him in the gallery?'

Heather shook her head. 'No. Close up he looks almost the same – older, of course, grey hair, and he had a beard in those days. At a distance I had no idea it was him. It's not as though I was expecting to see him, or even thinking about him.'

'And so, what about his wife?'

'He's single. Divorced ages ago. He's retired to Byron Bay and apparently he has a beautiful house in the tree tops.'

'Retired from what?' Jill asked.

'When I knew him he was tutoring in law, but later he was a criminal lawyer. He was at the bar for years. Then some time ago he just gave it up and sort of reinvented himself.'

'As what, exactly?' Adam asked, his voice heavy with sarcasm.

'He's a life-coach,' Heather said, avoiding eye contact. 'Not the sort that tells you how to organise your sock drawer. I think he said it's more orientated to wellness and spirituality through discovery of the self.'

This time Adam snorted. 'Oh, please!'

From the corner of his eye, Shaun watched Heather's hand plucking at a serviette.

'So what now?' Jill asked. 'Now he's seen you and got arrested in the process, is he heading off back home to Byron Bay?'

Heather paused, sipping her wine again. 'No, he's going to be in Sydney for a couple of weeks. I'm having dinner with him on Saturday.'

Adam threw his serviette onto the table and got up. 'I don't believe I'm hearing this,' he said, pushing back his chair.

'Where are you going?' Jill asked.

'To load the dishwasher.'

'But we've only just started eating,' she protested.

'I'm certainly not going to sit here and discuss that . . . that man,' Adam said, turning to Heather. 'I can't believe you would even deign to talk to him, Heather, let alone have dinner with him,' and he disappeared into the kitchen slamming the door behind him.

'Door, Dad! Remember!' yelled Toby, who was passing through on his way to find cookies. 'No slamming doors.'

'Oh dear,' Heather said awkwardly, fiddling with the stem of her wine glass. 'That was a bit of a disaster, wasn't it? Sorry, Jill, I thought after all this time . . . ' Her voice faltered.

'It *was* very unlike Adam,' Jill said. 'Whatever's got into him? Sorry, Shaun, take no notice. Let's just finish our dinner and talk about something else.'

Shaun smiled and returned to his rapidly cooling food, wondering how long it would be before he could reasonably suggest that he should drive Heather home.

Jill signalled left and took the slip road off the freeway.

'Yay! McDonald's,' Toby yelled from the back seat, where she had banished him as punishment for constantly putting his feet on the dashboard. 'I want a Big Mac, large fries and a strawberry thickshake.'

'Chicken burger, chicken burger, chicken, chicken, chicken burger,' Daisy chanted, 'and ice cream.'

Jill readied herself for a lecture on healthy alternatives and decided it was all too hard. Slipping into a parking space outside McDonald's, she pulled a twenty-dollar note from her purse and handed it to Toby.

'This is for yours and Daisy's,' she said. 'And I *do* know how much change there should be. See if you can organise it without fighting. I'm going next door to get a decent coffee.'

It had been a spur of the moment decision to call Barbara and ask if she could pop up with the kids. In the three days since the scene at dinner, Adam had been like a bear with a sore head, growling at anyone who spoke to him. Her efforts to get him to tell her just what it was about Heather's friend that upset him so much had hit a wall.

'He's a bastard,' was all he'd say. 'He treated Heather really badly and I can't understand how she can bear to have anything to do with him.'

After a night of trying to sleep in uncomfortable proximity to his anger, Jill had called Heather in the hope of getting to the bottom of it, but Heather had been vague.

'It's just old stuff,' she hedged. 'Forget it, Jill, he'll come around.'

Jill was hurt and frustrated. When she'd admitted to Renée that she resented the attention Heather got from everyone, she had really meant from Adam. While she understood that being close in age, together with their father's long illness and early death, had brought them close as children, she still resented the way that he seemed to feel so responsible for Heather. The worst thing was, Jill knew that if she were asked to provide actual examples of this she wouldn't be able to. It was just a gut feeling, one that, had she voiced it, would simply sound petty and neurotic. But she'd always felt excluded from their mutual understanding, and now she was also excluded from their conflict. But there was one person who might be able to tell her what was going on. With Adam and the orchestra heading off on Friday evening for two concerts in Melbourne, a weekend visit to Morpeth seemed like a good idea.

'Lovely!' Barbara had said when Jill called. 'It's ages since I saw you and the children. I'll expect you about midday.'

'How much farther is it now?' Daisy whined as they pulled back onto the freeway. 'I'm bored.'

'Bor*ing*, more like,' Toby said through a mouthful of burger. 'Boring and soppy.'

'About three-quarters of an hour,' Jill said. 'And, Toby, if you don't shut up you'll sit in the back all the way home tomorrow too.'

While Jill supervised Daisy's shower, Barbara took a bottle of wine and two glasses out onto the back verandah and sat down to wait for her, the staccato soundtrack of Toby's DVD floating out from the lounge room. She poured the wine and sat back wondering whether she could remember anything about Ellis Hargreaves. Jill had started to tell her about Adam's outburst while they were out for a walk that afternoon but Daisy, tired of tormenting Toby, had decided to walk between them.

'He's not a very nice friend if he tried to shoot Aunty Heather,' she announced.

'He didn't shoot her, Daise,' Jill said, taking her daughter's hand. 'He didn't have anything to do with it.'

'So why is Daddy all grumpy?' Daisy asked, determined not to be left out.

'He's just tired and busy,' Jill said, looking across at Barbara, who changed the subject by asking Daisy how she was getting on at dancing class.

Now, facing the stillness of the darkened garden, Barbara wrapped a woollen shawl around her shoulders and wondered if there were something she'd forgotten that might provide a clue to Adam's hostility and Heather's reticence.

'Oh, delicious,' Jill said, joining her and picking up her glass. 'Cheers.'

'Cheers. Daisy okay?'

'In bed, thank goodness. So, you don't remember anything about this Ellis person?'

'Not a thing. I don't even think I've heard his name before, but then if Heather was involved with a married man I doubt she'd have told Dorothy or me about it.'

'So am I being paranoid or do you think it's odd the way Adam's behaving?'

'Oh, I do think it's odd,' Barbara said. 'Most unlike him. We all know that Adam takes the line of least resistance, often to the point of being infuriating, so to suddenly flare up like that is very strange.'

Jill swirled the wine in her glass. 'It's quite hurtful, really.'

'Because he won't talk to you about it?'

'That and the fact that Heather won't either. It feels like a conspiracy.'

'Now, that *is* paranoid,' Barbara said gently. 'This isn't about you, Jill, it's something between them that's never been resolved. You're just copping some of the delayed fallout.'

Jill sighed. 'I suppose so. The other night at dinner it was like when couples carry on their domestic hostilities at the table. The whole room is alive with tension, but no one else really knows what's happening, and everyone's embarrassed.'

'I know what you mean,' Barbara said. 'I've been trying to remember what was happening then. It must have been around the time Heather and Adam got the flat together, or just after. But I can't really say that anything else springs to mind.'

'Well, I'm clearly not going to get any answers from either of them,' Jill said.

There was a scuffle in the lantana and George's cat darted out chasing something small across the grass.

'Rusty's found a mouse,' Barbara said. 'Now he'll take it home and present it to George. He's always finding little corpses on the doorstep.' She took a deep breath. 'Adam and Heather aren't the easiest combination to cope with, Jill, but, again, this is about them, not you. Adam is devoted to you and the children. If he's going through an odd patch, you can bet your life it's not about you.'

Jill nodded. 'I hope you're right. He's a strange mix, really understanding and loving, but sometimes so cut off. He disappears into that music room and plays those Bach suites as though he's in another universe.'

'It's his compensation for putting up with the rest of it, I suppose,' Barbara said. 'That old baroque cello, the Bach preludes – compensation.'

'For putting up with the rest of what?'

'The orchestra. The disappointment.'

'What do you mean? What disappointment?'

Barbara pulled the wrap further around her shoulders. 'The ordinariness of it, the pettiness, the grinding monotony.' She sighed. 'Poor old Adam, he thought he was moving into a magical world and found it was just a job like anything else.'

'But a job doing something he loves obsessively,' Jill said.

'Mmm. He loves his cello and his music certainly, but do you really think he loves the orchestra?'

'Of course, of course he does . . . ' She hesitated. 'Doesn't he?'

'I don't know, really. Sometimes I think he hates being just another cog in that great machine.' There was silence then and although she couldn't see Jill's face in the darkness, Barbara sensed a change in her. 'That's why he plays at home, I think,' she went on. 'You see, most musicians come home from work and the last thing they want to do is play their instrument. They'd rather mow the lawn or watch cricket or make soup. But Adam goes to his second cello as though it's something different from what he's been doing all day. He can play what he wants, he can improvise, he doesn't have to play every note of Wagner or Rachmaninov, he doesn't have to play them at all. He can just play at being Adam with a cello.'

'Really? I suppose I just took it for granted that because of his passion for music and the way he loves his cello that he must love the orchestra too,' Jill said. 'I mean, he often has a grumble about work, but no more than anyone grumbles about their job. Why would he have kept doing it all these years? Long before I met him.'

Barbara laughed. 'What else would he do? It's a vicious circle for him, I think. He's ambivalent, dislikes the orchestra but can't break away. You know Adam, change is not his thing, and it would take some strong external force to make him change. And while he might dream about doing something different, security is very important to him.'

'I see,' Jill said thoughtfully. 'At least, I think I do. But he's never said anything.'

'Perhaps he thinks you know.'

'But how? How would I know?'

Barbara shrugged. 'I don't know, dear. That's between the two of you. And, of course, I may be quite wrong. But one thing I'm sure of, complicated as he is, he's devoted to you and the children, even more than he is to his cellos.' She finished the last of her wine, yawning as a wave of tiredness swept over her. She'd often reflected on her good fortune in having acquired a de facto family, even to the point of grandchildren, without having to go through the inconvenience of marriage, pregnancy and childbirth. But recently she had been feeling the emotional costs of loving them all so dearly.

'Everything's a bit of a mess at the moment,' she said. 'We seem to be at odds, fragmented. The shooting was such a shock, and then the police not catching anyone. It's the stress. Everything will sort itself out once they find who did it.'

'So, here's to us,' Ellis said, raising his glass. 'To meeting again after all this time.'

'To us,' Heather said, touching her glass against his and sipping her champagne. 'It seems quite extraordinary to be sitting here with you, like this, after all these years.'

Ellis smiled. 'Isn't it wonderful? Just like yesterday?'

Heather hesitated. She felt like a character in a film in which the narrative constantly jumped back and forth in time. 'A little,' she replied. 'I keep trying to visualise us then, who we were compared with who we've become.'

'Well, you've become a very wise and beautiful woman, Heather,' Ellis said, 'just as I anticipated.'

Heather blushed and looked down at her menu. Compliments were rare these days, and she could barely remember the last time she'd been out for dinner with a man on anything other than a professional basis. Not that it was a date exactly, but it was still a world away from her usual Saturday nights spent at some official function, or at home in her dressing gown with her feet up, dividing her attention between work and *The Bill*.

Since Ellis's appearance on Wednesday, Heather's focus had undergone a remarkable shift. His presence had insinuated itself between her twin obsessions – the shooting and its perpetrator, and her efforts to get her professional life back on track. Now, at the end of the first week back in parliament, when she had anticipated working quietly in the safety of the tiny Potts Point apartment, she was instead in one of the finest restaurants in Sydney, wearing a low-necked black dress that was rather more snug than the last time she had worn it, having dinner with the man she had once believed was the love of her life. Once believed it? She no longer knew, because sitting here like this it was easy to convince herself that this was what he had always been – after all, none of his few successors had ever quite measured up. And she was starting to feel younger, flirtatious, something she hadn't felt for a very long time, as though the girl she had once been was still around, just out of sight.

'You're sure you'll be okay if I go back to Newcastle?' Shaun had asked the previous evening. 'I can stay if you want.'

'I'll be fine,' she'd said, with more confidence than she had felt for some time. 'Honestly, you go. We need you to be there in the electorate office next week. If you don't mind driving my car back, I'll fly home at the end of the sitting.'

And that morning, after Shaun had collected the car and set off for Newcastle, she had, to her own amazement, pulled out the Yellow Pages and phoned around the beauty salons in the hope of getting a facial. Locking in a two o'clock appointment she had paused briefly to ask herself what she was doing, why seeing Ellis had created this strange sense of buoyancy and girlish anticipation. Was it simply that it had diverted, or at least diluted, her attention? Or was it that seductive opportunity to see herself again, herself as she once was? Still contemplating the question she let herself out of the apartment, strolled up the slope of Macleay Street, and spent most of the morning in a café by the Alamein Fountain, trying to read the weekend papers but more often drifting into memories as the spring sunlight scattered rainbow colours through the great puffball of sparkling water.

'I've thought of you so much over the years, Heather,' Ellis said at dinner after they had caught up on the missing years. 'I often thought of getting in touch, but I wasn't sure what sort of reception I'd get.'

She smiled. 'I'd always have been delighted to see you,' she said. 'At least, I would have after the first few . . . well, once I'd got over you ending it like that.'

Ellis pulled a wry face. 'We can do some truly reprehensible things when we're young,' he said. 'But am I forgiven?'

Heather reminded herself that it was she, not Ellis, who had been young, but she bit her tongue. 'Of course. So what made you decide to come now?'

'You really want to know? This time I felt I had something to offer. I felt that at this time it would be more than pure self-indulgence.' He took her hand across the table. 'I couldn't stop thinking about what you must be going through.' He paused briefly. 'People do sometimes need some help with –'

Heather withdrew her hand. 'I don't need a counsellor, Ellis.'

'No, no, of course not,' he said. 'I didn't mean to suggest that. I simply felt that because we love . . . loved each other all those years ago, that you might appreciate having an old friend to talk to. And, you know, now, as I say it, I realise that the desire to help is probably just another sort of self-indulgence, really. Look, Heather,

I came because I care. Despite what happened all those years ago, I did and still do care, I want to be here for you, with you; that is, if you think you have space for me – emotional space.'

Heather relaxed her hand and with it her resistance to words that sounded embarrassingly close to lines from an afternoon soap opera. She swallowed the lump that had risen in her throat. 'Emotional space?' she asked, noticing how wobbly her voice sounded.

He smiled as he topped up her champagne. 'In times like these it helps to have someone who cares about you and who's prepared to step into that emotional space with you.'

Heather was accustomed to managing her emotional life alone, trying not to burden Adam while envying the intimacy he enjoyed with Jill; trying not to rely on anyone for emotional support, even Barbara. This solitariness made her feel that she was living on the margins, as though real emotional life were happening elsewhere and that somehow she had failed to understand what it was all about. There had been times when she had poured all her emotions into relationships, when she had been deeply and desperately in love.

The first time had been with Ellis, and she wondered if he had any idea of the devastating effect his abandonment had had on her. For months he had promised that he would leave his wife, that they would be together because he couldn't live without her. And yet, in the end it was she who had been abandoned, for not only had he ended it, he had almost immediately moved away. One moment there, the focus of her life, the next moment gone, leaving a great dark void. Perhaps it was easier than seeing him constantly, sitting mute and helpless in his classes, though it hadn't seemed that way at the time. But decades had passed, they had both moved on, and she had long since recognised how hopeless the situation had been.

However, first love keeps a seductive hold on memory; it teases the wisest imagination with promises of what might have been, establishes the gold standard beside which all others are measured, and leaves a clutch of unanswered questions like scars on the self-esteem. Why did he go? Was I not good enough, clever, mature or pretty enough? What could I have done better? What's wrong with me? Heather had recovered from Ellis's desertion, but when she fell in love again she struggled to be everything she might have failed to be with him. It was a disastrous formula that left her always resenting the enormity of her effort and the failure of her partner to respond in equal measure.

'I always seem to overdo it,' she had confessed to Barbara once as she foundered on the rocks of another relationship failure. 'I keep trying so hard to be what they want me to be and in the effort I actually abandon myself.'

'What you are is perfectly good enough for any man,' Barbara had told her. 'If you have to be something else to hold on to him, then he's not worth holding on to.'

But Heather recognised that she didn't know how to do it differently. It was, in the end, simply easier to focus on her work, and to channel her passion into issues where she could make a difference. She knew that people sometimes found her cool and distant, but that distance kept her safe. Losing was as much a part of public life as winning, it was something which she knew and accepted, but private life was different, particularly private emotional life. In that respect, self-protection was her first priority. She felt Ellis watching her but could not look up, for the old fear was rising in her gut and she needed to quell it.

'I don't think I know anything about emotional space, Ellis,' she said.

'A lot of looking outwards, I suspect,' Ellis cut in. 'Looking out towards others through your job, which provides the satisfaction of interaction but protects you from the challenges of real connectedness.'

She looked up quickly now. 'What do you mean?'

'I mean, Heather, and forgive me if I'm wrong – after all, we've only just met again, and I'm guessing – but I suspect that you find it easier not to be emotionally involved.'

'Well, it's certainly true that it's years since I was in a relationship.' She had gained control of her voice now by summoning a useful coolness that she had perfected to keep people at bay.

'And your friends?'

'I'm very fortunate, lots of people care about me,' she said, looking down at the food that the waiter had just placed in front of her. 'I was so moved by all those flowers and cards, the people outside my office –'

'Oh yes, I saw all that on the news,' Ellis cut in, 'but your friends, Heather, where are your friends?'

'I don't have a lot of time,' she said. 'I'm very busy. Work is my . . . ' she hesitated, 'my . . . '

'Your way of keeping friendship and intimacy at bay?'

She blushed, feeling caught out. 'Maybe. But I'm a very independent person. I don't want to be a burden on anyone.'

Ellis leaned forward across the table. 'Real friendship is a gift, Heather. Intimate friendship is a precious gift, not a burden.'

She looked away again, stripped suddenly of her protective cover. 'Probably,' she admitted, 'but it's also intrusive, risky, all sorts of risks . . . emotional risks.'

Ellis nodded. 'Of course, that's part of life. And I wonder, Heather, what sort of life have you really been living?'

FIVE

Shaun found the tablets by chance the evening that he got back from Sydney. Charlene was going to a birthday party with friends and, knowing it would be a night of loud music and that most people would have too much to drink and then want to go on to a club, he had resisted her efforts to get him to go along.

'I just want a quiet evening at home,' he'd said, hoping against hope that she wouldn't decide to stay home with him. 'You go, have a good time. I'd just be a boring old fart anyway.'

'I would *like* to go,' she'd said, 'if you really don't mind.'

'I really don't mind. I'll drop you off, if you like, and you can get a cab home. Just take care and don't drink too much.'

''Course not,' said Charlene, who had already had three glasses of wine. 'I'll just go for a little while. It's Gemma's twenty-fifth and I really don't want to miss it.'

Shaun dropped her at the party, ordered a family-size special with double anchovies from the pizza place, and settled down in peace to watch a movie. It was his favourite sort of evening, probably a bit sad at thirty, but he'd never been much of a one for parties and he relished time at home alone.

Buying the house had been a big step for Shaun. He was cautious with money, and had weighed up the relative benefits of cash flow versus home ownership and opted for the latter. It was just a little weatherboard house in Hamilton, near the Beaumont Street shopping area and conveniently close to his favourite café. Not being adept at DIY he had found a local contractor to do the structural renovations. His father, an electrician by trade, was also handy with a paintbrush, and together he and Shaun were finishing off the rest of the work. Other than a few flashes of concern about whether he was getting middle-aged before his time, Shaun found that the pattern of life that came with the house was comfortable and satisfying.

When Charlene moved in, things changed. Her drinking made him uneasy and he wasn't entirely convinced that she didn't pop the odd pill. Together with the constant background music about settling down, her presence in the house was no longer a pleasure but a burden. Almost daily he contemplated how he might extricate himself from the relationship. There may well be fifty ways to leave your lover, but was it possible to find just one way to get her to leave him? Was there one way for him to end it without seeming a complete bastard?

Halfway through *Fight Club*, Shaun felt the pizza sitting heavily in the middle of his chest and he wrapped the remains in cling film, stashed it in the fridge and went to look for some Mylanta. He'd bought a roll of the tablets a couple of weeks earlier but there was no sign of them in the bathroom cupboard or the drawer of his bedside table. It occurred to him that Charlene might have needed them and gone searching, and it was as he was looking through the drawer on her side of the bed that he saw, tucked away behind two old pairs of sunglasses, a manicure set and several months' supply of contraceptive pills, the small plastic bag. Alarm bells went off in his head. There were half a dozen tablets – ecstasy or amphetamines? He wasn't familiar enough with drugs to know. Half a dozen: not a huge quantity, but even fewer would have been too much for Shaun's peace of mind.

Sinking down on the bed, he put the plastic bag back in its hiding place and stared at the dressing table, anxiety turning to suspicion. The dressing table was a white Queen Anne style monstrosity that Charlene had brought from home. Shaun sighed, staring at the drawers. There was a difference between finding something by chance and actually going hunting for it. On the other hand . . . He opened the right-hand drawer. It was full of cosmetics, lipsticks, eyeliners, mascara wands, bottles of nail polish and small sample-size pots and tubes of skin care products. He closed it and tried the left-hand one. It was locked. Shaun's heart beat faster as he searched for the key. Charlene's jewellery box stood on the dressing table and he hesitated once more before opening it. The lid lifted out into three pink velvet-lined tiers; there were lots of earrings, beads and other sparkly stuff, but no key. He was about to close it when he noticed a slim pocket of the same fabric along one side of the bottom tier. Seconds later he was holding the key.

There was a pile of scrunchies at the front of the drawer, and some other hair ornaments, two curling brushes and a bulky, unsealed manila envelope. Blood thumping in his temples, Shaun opened it and counted out six hundred dollars in fifties. He put the envelope back, pulled the drawer open further and reached for a sequin-embroidered jewellery roll. As soon as he touched it he could feel the slippery shifting of plastic bags. He unrolled it to reveal several small plastic bags with two, three or five tablets in each, so obviously ready to sell.

Shaun was dizzy with shock. Charlene may have stopped using but she was clearly dealing, and that meant one thing, or rather one person – Danny. Danny, who had blacked his eye over Charlene; Danny, through whose hands flowed all manner of strange substances and small electronic goods that had fallen off the backs of trucks. Had she always been dealing? Could Diane have had any idea what was going on? Shaun had had a horror of drugs since his best friend had fallen by the wayside. He and Ben had known each other since primary school but Shaun's fear of what his father would do to him if he found him using meant that while he'd certainly experimented, that was where it stopped. But nothing held Ben back, and two years after they left school he was found dead in a side alley in Winfield after a self-administered overdose of heroin cut with some poisonous substance.

Shaun retied the jewellery roll, pushed it to the back of the drawer and returned the key to its hiding place, seething with anger and resentment. He had trusted her and she had abused that trust. He had warned her that if she kept using it would all be over, and he'd warned her again when he once caught her dropping ecstasy at a party. The final warning had been delivered the day she moved in.

'No drugs, not even any dope, not yours, not anyone else's.'

'Sure, sweetheart,' she'd said, kissing him. 'You know I don't do that anymore.'

'I hope so,' he'd said, ''cos I'm serious. One strike and you're out.'

'The drugs are off. Honest, dead and gone, Shaun, I promise.'

Shaun turned off the bedroom light, went back downstairs and sat watching the remainder of the film without seeing it. Then he got up again, washed up his plate, binned his stubby, and picked up the phone.

When Ellis booked the serviced apartment in Elizabeth Bay he chose it for convenience. Discovering that he was staying a mere ten-minute walk from Heather's unit confirmed his feeling that this reunion was meant to be.

'I do have some work I need to get through today,' Heather said on the phone the morning after their first dinner, 'but would you like to meet up later this afternoon – a walk, perhaps?'

Ellis, who was in Sydney for two reasons, the main one being to re-establish his connection with Heather, said that he would love it.

The harsh afternoon sunlight had faded, parents were packing children into cars, and a few strolling couples remained on the broad, tree-lined pathways of the Domain. Ellis was attuned to the spirit of the moment, the chance it offered to take them further along his chosen course.

'I'm so glad you wanted to meet,' he said. 'I've been thinking about you nonstop. You meant so much to me all those years ago, Heather, and you still do.' He stopped walking; she turned towards him and he kissed her lightly, quickly, on the lips.

'You meant just as much to me,' she said, 'and you picked the right time to come back. That bullet didn't only rip into my shoulder, it ripped through my sense of myself as well. The past is really powerful, isn't it? Last night I realised that I'd almost forgotten the person I was with you, and now you've given me back something of her – of the girl I used to be.'

'But there are other people who knew you then,' Ellis said. 'Your brother, your aunt.'

Heather nodded. 'But somehow having always been with them makes it different,' she said. 'The changes are incremental – we look at each other and see what we expect to see from day to day. You look at me and see the person I was. You have expectations of her, I think . . . ' She paused. 'And I think I probably see a part of you that others don't see. I look in your eyes and see the Ellis of all those years ago. It's such a gift, the opportunity to see ourselves as we were. Oh dear, this probably sounds incredibly silly and New Agey. I never talk like this.'

A couple of teenagers on skateboards hustled noisily past them. Ellis took Heather's arm as she moved out of their path. He knew the first hurdle was cleared. At dinner he had shocked her, had taken a risk and challenged her, and her discomfort had been obvious. By the time the taxi drew up outside her door she had been cool and distant. She thanked him for dinner and disappeared inside without a backward glance, and he was left wondering if he had pushed her too far too soon. Driven by his desire to recapture the romance of the past, he was now determined to draw it into dramatic connection with the present. He had loved her once, and since reading about the shooting he had become convinced that he had always loved her. They were partners, Ellis now believed, in a dance performed across the decades, a dance that circled inevitably back to its starting point.

'It doesn't sound silly at all,' he said now. 'But I can see that it's unfamiliar territory for you. It was to me at first, when I left the law and did my sea change thing. But after a while I discovered the pleasure and the power of resisting cynicism and listening to my inner wisdom. Some people really can't handle it. It takes something dramatic to help them break out of their shell.'

'A shell,' Heather said, turning to him. 'Yes, I suppose that's what it is. And when it cracks, it leaves you exposed.'

'Exactly. When something terrible happens, the change that it creates provides a silver lining.'

Her expression was soft and uncertain now, so different from the chiselled lines that he had seen at the dinner table. He reached out and brushed aside a strand of hair that had blown across her face.

She laughed, embarrassed. 'So much grey, I'm getting old. Remember how much I used to hate the copper colour? Now I'd give my right arm to have it back.'

'It's softer now,' he said. 'I like it. Age robs us of many things, Heather, but beauty is not one of them, because, of course, it comes from within.'

Heather laughed again. 'Heavens, Ellis, you'll be writing verses for greeting cards next.'

Ellis was stung, but he persisted. 'It's true and you know it, you just don't know how to respond with anything other than cynicism.'

'Well . . . ' she faltered, 'that certainly put me in my place.'

'Your place? What place is that, Heather?' he asked. 'I thought we were moving towards the same place.'

She blushed deeply. 'I'm sorry,' she said. 'I was being stupid, flippant. Like I said, I'm not used to talking like this. It's a bit confronting . . . give me time.'

'You can have all the time you want,' he said, taking her hand and smiling, sensing he'd won a small battle. 'Be gentle with yourself, you've had a lot to cope with.'

She nodded. 'Being shot was awful, but not knowing who did it or why makes it so much worse. This week, when I thought they'd got someone, it was such a relief and then it turned out to be you. Strange, really; disappointment and delight hand in hand.'

Ellis nodded. 'Of course, but the answer lies with you, Heather, not with the perpetrator.'

She shook her head. 'It'll be much better when they find him.'

Ellis shrugged. 'Well, you'll stop worrying about him trying again, that specific threat will disappear. But do you think that will really be the end of it? What about the chaos he's created? Will finding him and locking him up fix all that? I think you might find that it's just the tip of the iceberg, that once he's safely under lock and key, the real challenge will begin.'

*

'But whatever's the matter?' Diane asked. Although she hadn't been asleep, the lateness of Shaun's call agitated her. 'Can't you tell me now? Why does it have to be tomorrow morning?'

'We need to sort something out,' he said, in the same tone he used with difficult constituents. 'It may take a while. Just tell me you'll meet me in the Eurobar tomorrow morning.'

She hesitated. It occurred to her that this wasn't an emergency but a surprise. They were going to tell her they were getting engaged and she warmed immediately to the prospect of meeting.

'Okay,' she said. 'That'll be lovely, I'll see you both there.'

'Just me, Diane,' Shaun said. 'Charlene's not coming. She doesn't know I'm calling. I need to talk to you alone. I'll see you at nine.'

Of course! He was actually going to ask her permission. It was the sort of odd, old-fashioned thing Shaun *would* do. She hung up smiling and lay down again thinking of engagement parties and weddings, all with a great sense of relief that Charlene's wild days were over and she was really settling down at last.

The following morning, Diane walked into the Eurobar right on time to find Shaun hunched over an espresso and looking distinctly uncomfortable. 'Hangover?' she enquired, but in what she hoped was an encouraging, even affectionate tone. And she slid into the seat opposite him.

'Not me, I stayed home,' he said dryly. 'Charlene's still sleeping hers off. She didn't come home till four.'

Diane sighed. 'Those girlfriends aren't a good influence. Can't you get her away from them?'

Shaun paused, looking at her for a moment, and then tossed back his coffee in one gulp. 'We have more than girlfriends to worry about,' he said, signalling the waiter so they could order more coffee. 'A lot more.'

'I don't believe it,' Diane said dismally when he told her about the pills. But of course she did believe it; she'd been there before and, like Shaun, had thought that Danny and the drugs were now a thing of the past. But the drugs were only a part of it.

'There's more,' Shaun said. 'When I leave here, I'm going home to tell Charlene it's over, she has to move out. I wanted you to be clear about why I'm doing it, because she'll probably turn up on your doorstep later in the day.'

'Over!' Diane said. 'What, you mean you're ending it because you found a few drugs –'

'Not a few, Diane. Far more than Charlene can afford, far more than she'd need for her own use. Maybe she's not using but my bet is that she's dealing for Danny.'

'She wouldn't,' Diane protested. 'She wouldn't do that. And, anyway, even if you're right, this is no time for you to be dumping her. She needs your support.'

'She's had that,' Shaun said, 'for more than six months, and by letting her get away with it again I'd just be enabling her to dig herself further into this mess. You realise it's possible she was dealing while she was still at your place?'

'She wouldn't, she couldn't . . . I would have known.'

'Would you? I didn't. I found most of these in her dressing table drawer. It was locked but I found the key.'

Diane clasped a hand to her mouth. 'The left-hand drawer? It was always locked. I thought she had letters or something private in there.'

'She did,' Shaun said with a wry smile. 'Look, I made her promise and she broke that promise twice. This is the third time and it's much more serious than I'd imagined. Perhaps if I'd pulled the plug earlier it would have brought her to her senses and it mightn't have got to this stage. Besides, Diane, I have some rights in this too. I don't have to put up with being lied to, with having drugs in my house – maybe sold from my house.'

Diane shrugged angrily. 'Oh, you . . . you're just thinking of yourself. Just like all men, selfish, thoughtless and incapable of being faithful.'

Shaun sat back raising both hands, his palms towards her. 'Whoa!' he said. 'Lay off. That's your stuff. I haven't been near anyone else since I started going out with Charlene. Look, I know you're upset but you have to face up to what's happening.'

'You have to put a stop to it,' Diane said, dabbing at her eyes with a tissue, 'not just ditch her when she needs you.'

'No.' Shaun shook his head. 'This is not my responsibility, and it's not yours either. It's down to Charlene; she has to make up her mind what she wants. She has to take responsibility for her own behaviour.'

Diane drove home knowing Shaun was right. She still resented what she saw as his opting out but the time had come to take a firmer line. Charlene was not a teenager, she was twenty-five, and it was time she got her act together. She would lay it out for her, no holds barred, make some rules, maybe even use Shaun's 'one strike and you're out' line. But nothing prepared her for her daughter's arrival on the doorstep later that day, surrounded by carrier bags of clothes and a large pink fake Gucci holdall.

'He turned me out,' Charlene wept as the cab pulled away from the drive, 'just like that. I went to this party without him and I came home late and he just said, it's over, it's over, just like that.'

Diane gathered up the bags from the doorstep and drew Charlene into the house. She would give her a chance to come clean voluntarily, then she could set out the rules. But Charlene was in crisis, against which all the good intentions in the world were no defence, and it didn't take Diane long to work out that the confrontation, the rules, the firmer line would all have to wait; meanwhile, she would be firm, sympathetic and stay calm.

Several days later, though, Charlene was still in denial, blaming everything on Shaun, and Diane had a sickening sense of déjà vu as she called her daughter's boss and made an excuse for her absence. How many times had she done this while Charlene slept off the previous night's excess? How often had she believed the promises that it wouldn't happen again? It seemed shocking to her now that she had been able to ignore the reality of what was happening. Shaun had provided a welcome interlude but now she and Charlene were back where they had started, only it was worse this time, because Diane could no longer pretend to herself that it wasn't happening. That was when she decided she might take Shaun's advice.

'Can't her dad help?' Shaun had asked. 'I think you need to get him in on it; otherwise, as soon as you crack down on her she'll be running to him.'

And so the next day found her sitting in a small Italian restaurant in The Junction waiting irritably for the one person she had never wanted to speak to, let alone see, ever again. Her fingers drummed nervously on the table; she was far too early but driven out of the house by anxiety. Now she wished she had timed it to make him wait. She had spent far too much of her life waiting around for Gerry. What good would it do talking to him, anyway? He had, after all, deserted them to live with this other woman; a woman she had never met but quite naturally hated, a woman whose name she couldn't bear to think of let alone speak. And now here she was, already worn out with waiting, and it was still fifteen minutes before he was due. Diane swallowed the last of her glass of water and, as she reached for the bottle to refill it, in he walked. It was the first time she had seen him since the divorce, and her initial reaction was shock. He looked younger, fitter, but softer too, more like the man she had first fallen in love with. Gerry glanced around, spotted her at the corner table and made his way across the restaurant.

'You're early,' was all she could think of to say as he smiled and pulled out a chair.

'And you're earlier,' he said. 'You sounded worried, so I didn't want to keep you waiting.'

Diane swallowed the urge to mention that it was a shame he hadn't been so thoughtful during more than thirty years of marriage. No point starting off on the wrong foot.

'Thanks,' she said. 'I *am* worried. It's about Charlene.'

'Well, I realised that,' he said, picking up the menu. 'Do you want to order or talk first?'

'Talk,' she said. 'But maybe you want to order a drink?'

Gerry shook his head. 'I've given up,' he said with a wry smile. 'Twenty-three months and counting,' and he picked up the bottle of water and filled his own glass. 'So, tell me, what's our girl been up to this time?'

SIX

Daisy was confused. Strange things were going on at home and she didn't know what to make of it. Kirsty had moved out and Daisy missed her dreadfully. She'd been back lots of times of course, but it wasn't the same as having her living in the house, turning up at bedtime to play scary games or tickle Daisy until she screamed.

'I miss you,' she'd whined when Kirsty and Nick came over to sit with her one evening. 'It makes everything different.'

'Well, you've got two of us here tonight,' Kirsty had grinned, grabbing her and cuddling her between them on the settee. 'Two for the price of one. So shut up and find the remote, cos we've got *Lemony Snicket* on DVD.'

And that was the other thing. Most times when Kirsty came over, Nick came too, so Daisy had to share her. It didn't seem fair – Nick had Kirsty all the rest of the time, after all. But the weirdest thing was that Toby had suddenly started being nice to her. It bugged Daisy at first because she thought he was setting her up for something. But then she'd discovered that Bree Adams, who was thirteen and wore fake tattoos and had four earrings in one ear, had agreed to be his girlfriend. Daisy learned this from her own best friend, Sam, who had heard it from her older sister who was Bree's best friend. Daisy thought Bree Adams must be seriously mental to let Toby be her boyfriend but, as her Aunt Barbara often said, there was no accounting for taste, and it was certainly making Daisy's life a lot easier.

But Toby's love life didn't account for her parents being weird.

Adam was distinctly grumpy and most unlike the description she'd written a few months ago in a school composition: *My Dad is called Adam, he plays the cello in a bedroom and his job is being first cello in an orchestra. He is tall and he has blue eyes and grey hare. He always tells me answers to queschuns. He is very smiley and cuddeley. Mum says he has a soft center.*

But Adam hadn't been smiley or cuddly over the last few weeks, and Daisy was more likely to get a grunt than a proper answer to a question. Jill was different too. Daisy was used to her mother being busy and tired, but she didn't seem to laugh so much now and when Daisy needed to discuss important things, like why she wasn't allowed to wear black leggings, or what rhymed with orange, Jill always seemed to be thinking about something else.

Hanging upside down in the tyre that swung from the branch of the Moreton Bay fig in the front garden, Daisy wondered what was going on. Usually her parents seemed sort of glued together. It was hard to sneak in between them if you wanted to get one to agree to something before you started trying to convince the other.

'They form a united front,' Kirsty had said once when Daisy mentioned this. 'United they stand, divided they fall.'

'Why would they fall down?' Daisy had asked, confused.

'Well, they wouldn't actually fall, not on the ground,' Kirsty said. 'It's like . . . it's a figure of speech.'

Daisy still didn't get it. Jill and Adam didn't seem cross with each other, but it was as though there was an empty space between them where anyone could just walk in. And while this had certain practical advantages, it actually didn't make Daisy feel good and she wasn't sure why. She wanted to ask questions but for once her instincts warned her that it might be best to pretend that everything was normal.

Daisy craned her neck around the curve of the tyre to see whose car had just turned into the driveway, and in doing so she fell out of the tyre and thudded down onto the grass.

'Bugger!' she cried, sitting up and rubbing her head. 'Bugger, bugger, bugger.'

'Daisy, beautiful Daisy,' a voice cried, 'did you hurt yourself?'

'Uncle Stefan,' she said, delighted to see him. 'I'm okay. Just scraped my leg. Bugger.'

'Daisy, this is not a nice word for a beautiful girl, not ladylike. You don't say bugger.'

'I think it's a good word,' Daisy said, scrambling to her feet to hug him. 'Bugger, bugger, bugger.'

Stefan shook his head and grabbed her, swinging her into the air. 'No, very bad. You say it again, I throw you in the water tank.'

Daisy squealed with delight. 'Bugger. No one told me you were coming, Uncle Stefan. Dad's not here, he's gone to get something for the car. He'll be back soon.'

'I know,' Stefan said, lowering her to the ground. 'I am coming to take him to rehearsal but your mother tells me she is making pasta and if I come early I get some. So here I am, but really I come to see you.'

'Good, cos I want to show you what I did for art this week,' Daisy said. 'We made masks. Mine is a vampire with yellow teeth with blood on them,' and she took his hand, dragging him towards the house. 'Mum's in the kitchen. I'll go and get the mask from my bedroom.'

Stefan tugged gently at one of her silky bunches, and she raced off up the stairs two at a time singing out 'bugger' with every leap. Stefan shook his head affectionately and wandered through to the kitchen, where Jill was at the sink washing lettuce and spinach for a salad.

'Stefan, how lovely, come on in.' She dried her hands and went over to kiss him on both cheeks. 'Sorry about Daisy and her buggers. She picked it up at school this week and she won't drop it. I think she's after attention, so I've decided that ignoring it might be the best thing.'

Stefan grinned. 'She will forget it in a day or two,' he said. 'Is a novelty now, soon it wears off, I think. That is children. Daisy is a darling girl, Jill, you know you are very lucky.'

'I do know,' she said, squeezing his hand. 'Adam won't be long. Like a beer?'

'Thanks.' He took the bottle she handed him and picked up the opener. 'How are you, Jill?'

'Fine, although Adam's a bit stressed at present.'

'Ah.' Stefan nodded and took a swig of his beer. 'Cheers. His sister. This shooting is very bad. He worries the police don't find no one and they come back and try again.' He shook his head. 'It is hard for you.'

Jill began to chop radishes. 'Yes. We're all feeling it,' she said. 'Things'll settle down when they catch someone.' She looked out of the window to check that Adam's car was not in the drive. 'Stefan, can I ask you something? What do you do when you get home after rehearsals?'

Stefan shrugged. 'I watch TV, do gardening, sometimes I go to the gym.'

'You don't play your cello?'

He grimaced. 'Sometimes, if I have to practise, but most days I leave it at work.'

'And you don't have another at home that you play a lot, on your own?'

Stefan laughed aloud. 'No way. I have one cello. I don't want to bring my work home. And you? You want to do the council work at home?'

'Not if I can help it.'

'So, music is no different.'

'Do you think so? I mean, is that what most musicians do, leave it behind when they go home?'

'I think yes,' Stefan nodded. 'They go in the family, or play sport, do cooking. Arthur, you know Arthur, he is second violin, yes? Arthur is painting watercolours, very beautiful. Me, I listen to jazz, sometimes country, you know, not what we play in the orchestra. Nobody wants to take work home.'

'Adam does,' Jill said, turning to him. 'He spends a lot of time in his music room.'

'But for Adam, it is a little bit different. First cello is the one who must mark up the score, organise things, he has responsibilities. For the rest of us, not so much work.'

'I know that,' Jill said. 'But Adam actually spends a lot of time playing that old baroque cello.' She felt guilty suddenly, as though she were telling tales, but she couldn't stop, compelled as she was to try to understand. 'Mostly he plays the Bach suites, the ones for unaccompanied cello.'

Stefan nodded. 'Of course, very beautiful. It is an interesting story, you know. Pablo Casals discovers this music in an old shop.' He snapped his fingers, searching for a word. 'Not antique but . . . '

'A second-hand shop?' Jill suggested.

'Yes, thank you, second-hand shop. He is only a teenager and he takes the music and practises it. For years he practises and then performs them – more than thirty years, I think, before he records them and makes them very popular.'

'I see,' Jill said. She had abandoned the salad and sat down opposite him at the table. 'So why are they so special? I mean, I enjoy music but I didn't have a musical education. Why would a cellist play these suites in particular?'

'Ah, yes, it is the emotional range, it is very large, and what we call voice interactions, the conversations . . . ' He paused and Jill saw him searching for the right words.

'Intimacy,' he said finally, grasping the word with satisfaction. 'Yes, intimacy. And they demand much from the musician technically, so these suites they are making for perfection. But intimacy most, I think, this is the special quality.'

'Intimacy,' Jill repeated, 'really? Do you like the orchestra, Stefan?'

He took another drink of his beer. 'Oh yes, they are very nice people, very friendly. When I come from Kosovo, I am a stranger, you know, I struggle with the language, but they make me very welcome.'

'No, I meant do you *love* it, do you love being the third cello in the orchestra?'

He shrugged. 'It's a job, like any other job. It's okay but you have the composers you like and then you spend weeks playing the ones you don't like, no room for improvisation. It is frustrating, boring, you must play every note, sometimes it pisses off –'

'That is *very* rude,' said Daisy from behind a hideous black, red and yellow mask. 'It's much ruder than bugger.'

'I don't think so, Daisy,' Stefan said, reaching out to draw her closer. 'But neither is nice for you, nor for this vampire. Vampires, you know, they say bad words and they lose their power. These teeth, they fall out.'

'Really?' Daisy said, impressed by the potential of her new vocabulary.

'Really,' he said. 'Better to watch out, Daisy. Now, let me have a proper look at this wonderful mask you make.'

'So,' said George from the top of the ladder, 'do you want to hear about my plan?'

'Love to,' Barbara replied, 'but preferably at ground level. I'm not at all sure you should be up a ladder at your age.'

'Rubbish,' George said, chucking down the last clump of rain-soaked leaves that had been clogging the gutter. 'And anyway, it's *our* age, not just mine.'

'Yes, yes,' Barbara said, picking up the leaves on a spade and loading them into the wheelbarrow, 'I know, but come down, please. I don't think it's safe. I wish I never told you I was going to get someone in to clean the gutters.'

'No point paying out good money when you've got an able-bodied handyman next door,' George said, stepping off the bottom rung. 'Now, that should fix you up for a while.'

'Well, I'm very grateful,' Barbara said. 'Shall I make us some coffee?'

George washed his hands in the laundry sink and wandered out into the kitchen, drying them on a towel.

'D'you want to have a guess at my plan? You'll never get it, but have a go. If you get it, I'll buy you lunch at Savannah.'

Barbara poured water into the plunger. 'All right . . . um . . . I know, you're going to take up hang-gliding.'

'Nope. You've got two more guesses.'

Barbara, who would far rather that he just told her outright, racked her brains. 'Golf then, you're going to learn golf.'

'Much better than that,' George said, a large smile spreading across his face, which was spattered with blotches of muddy water from the gutter.

'Oh,' she said, 'I don't know. Are you having milk or is it one of your black coffee days?'

'Milk, please,' he said. 'Go on, last chance, one more guess.'

'Oh, er . . . I know, China,' she said flippantly. 'You're going to take a slow boat to China.'

'How the bloody hell . . . ?' George looked affronted. 'Of all the things I could be planning to do, of all the places I could be going, how come you guessed it's China?'

'Ever since I've known you, you've wanted to go to China,' Barbara said. 'Are you really going?'

'Yes, yes I am. Dammit, I owe you lunch now.'

'Cleaning the gutter will do nicely, thanks,' Barbara said, carrying the tray out to the deck. 'Come and tell me about the slow boat . . . '

'Not a slow boat, just China,' George said. 'Have I always said I wanted to go there? I thought it was only in my head. Didn't realise I'd talked about it.'

'Constantly,' Barbara said. 'So, this is exciting. When are you going?'

'Well, not just yet,' George said, picking up a chocolate brownie. 'The plan is a bit more complicated.' His surprise that Barbara had guessed right turned to pleasure in allowing the rest of the plan to unravel slowly. It was important to get the reaction he wanted, so he took his time over the brownie, watching patiently as she poured the coffee. Barbara was the light of his life and, as he often told his son and daughter-in-law, without her friendship and her company, his life as a widower would have been a miserable affair.

George tried not to look smug. 'Complicated, but I think you'll agree it's a good plan.'

'A or B?' Barbara asked with a grin.

'What?'

'I'm joking. You know – is it plan A or plan B?'

'Ah, you see, it started as plan A, but then when I thought about it more, I developed plan B, which is infinitely preferable.'

'Go on then.'

'Well, I've always wanted to go to China –'

Barbara rolled her eyes.

'Yes, okay, you *do* know that. But the thing is, I'm not very good at holidays. I want to go and stay there for a while, a few months.'

'Can you do that?' Barbara asked. 'Visas and things, is it possible?'

'This is where plan A begins,' George said, warming to his task. 'I kept thinking to myself, if I manage to buzz off there for a while, what would I do? It's probably not the most comfortable place to live, and how will I get to know people? All that sort of stuff. And then it dawned on me – get a job!'

'A job? What sort of job? I mean, you don't speak Chinese and . . . I don't want to be rude but you *are* seventy-five. Who do you think will employ you?'

'Quite a lot of people, it seems,' George said triumphantly, picking up his mug. 'People who run language schools, and who want to employ English teachers.'

'But you're not an English teacher, you're a retired industrial chemist.'

'Right, but I am about to *become* a teacher of English as a second language, and apparently when I do that, even at seventy-five, I will be quite a valuable commodity in teaching English to Chinese industrial chemists.'

It had come as a surprise to George to discover how keen the Chinese might be to have someone of his experience. He had gone in to the language school to enquire about the course and had a very interesting conversation with Robert Sachs, the director, who had taught in China.

'Plenty of opportunities,' Sachs had said. 'Especially for someone with your experience who just wants something to do. Not full time or anything like that, and not teaching kids, but running some classes for industry. You get your teaching certificate and you bring all that industry language as well. I don't think you'd have a problem.'

'I don't speak Chinese,' George pointed out.

'You don't need it. The teaching is conducted entirely in English, and in any case your value is not in teaching beginners, but industrial chemists who already have some knowledge of the language.'

'And my age?' George had asked.

'I don't think it's a problem, you should be able to pick up a few classes, but I'll make some enquiries and get back to you, if you like.'

George did like, but he was a bit nervous about the course.

'Four weeks intensive,' Sachs had said. 'Bloody hard work; relentless, really. Grown men end up in tears and there's quite a high dropout rate. The program is very tightly packed and after the first day you learn a technique one day and you practise teaching it the next, under observation by your peers and your instructor. When you leave here after the classes you write lesson plans for the next day and work on assignments.'

'Practising on real live students?' George asked in surprise.

'Real but not fee-paying,' Sachs replied. 'Don't underestimate how hard it is, especially if it's some years since you've learned anything new.'

George had come away from the meeting thrilled by the possibilities but still anxious about the course. He could easily afford it, but could he stand the pace? Could he pass? He might be the only old fogey in a group of youngsters. On the other hand, what had he got to lose? And, as Sachs had pointed out, even if he didn't pass he would still have learned the teaching techniques, and some schools and employers in China didn't demand the formal qualification anyway.

A couple of days later, George got an email from Robert Sachs telling him that his age wouldn't be a problem.

'And so the next course starts in November,' George told Barbara, 'and I'll be on it.'

'Good on you, George,' she said, 'you're so enterprising. Of course you'll pass the course.'

'Who knows? But by the time I recover from that and get my act together, make contact with a few possible employers, I reckon I'll head off in the New Year, three months, six maybe. That should get it out of my system. It'll probably be bloody cold, uncomfortable living conditions, but what an experience, eh?'

'It sounds wonderful, and I can see you doing it really well,' she said. 'But if that's plan A, what's the infinitely preferable plan B?'

'Ah,' said George, rubbing his hands together and hoping that he had made it sound sufficiently inviting. 'Well, I just happened to mention to Sachs that I had this very good friend who had been an editor and publisher of academic books, and he got very excited about that. It seems that this is also an area where the Chinese would consider an experienced older person who can teach English very valuable. So plan A is A for *alone*, and plan B is that you come along and take this terrible course, and we pop off to China together. Plan B is *Barbara* comes too. Now, don't you think that's a much better plan?'

SEVEN

Heather had never been so tempted to wag it as she was at the end of the first parliamentary sitting. She had been in Sydney for two weeks and there was a one-week break when she really should go home to Newcastle before returning to Sydney for the following fortnight. The shooting had thrown her life into the air like a pack of cards but now, in less than a fortnight, Ellis had assumed the role of comforter and sounding board. And Heather, unaccustomed to the presence of a constant supportive companion, marvelled that when fear and grief struck, when the pain in her shoulder and the limits on the use of her arm frustrated her, and when an unfamiliar sense of loneliness threatened, he was there.

'I *could* wag it next week,' she'd said to Ellis on Saturday morning when they met for breakfast by the fountain. 'Stay on here. I'm coming back next weekend anyway.'

Ellis shook his head. 'You've got enough on your plate at the moment, Heather,' he said. He took her hand in his. 'I'm so happy that you've enjoyed our time together, but if you start ducking out now you'll feel guilty, and all that good will be undone. I'll stay on here. You'll be back next weekend and we'll talk some more. I've arranged to hold on to the apartment until the end of the next two sitting weeks. After that I really will have to get back to Byron Bay.'

Heather toyed with her yoghurt. 'I suppose you're right,' she said. 'But you don't have to stay on here for me, you know.'

'But I'd like to,' he said. 'If you want me to.'

'You know I do. You could come to Newcastle with me for the week, if you like,' she added hopefully.

'Not this time,' Ellis said. 'You get back to your electorate office, concentrate on your work. Why not come back on Friday evening instead of Monday, then we'll have the weekend before you have to go back to parliament?'

Heather's disappointment was countered by his reassurances about wanting to spend the weekend with her and by the way he looked at her. She had forgotten how it felt to be looked at in that profoundly personal way by a man. For the first time in more years than she could remember, Heather felt desire; she longed for sex with an urgency that she had never previously known. The longing gnawed at her, destroying her concentration, flooding her with heat, and as each day passed and Ellis seemed happy just to be with her, she wondered if she were misreading him. Perhaps it really was only friendship he wanted; perhaps he just wanted to help.

The following morning she flew back to Newcastle, and Shaun met her at the airport and drove her home. He looked drained and exhausted, and Heather knew immediately that it would have been grossly unfair of her to have stayed on in Sydney. For almost two months he had carried the responsibility of the electorate office, and the effect was obvious. Well, at least she had the satisfaction of having done the right thing.

She let herself in to the house, put her bag down in the hall and wandered slowly through each of the ground-floor rooms enjoying, as always, the fact that it remained as she had left it, free of any other influence. She considered her own choices of colour and style: the renovated art deco settee and armchairs, upholstered in primrose damask, a colour that was repeated in the blurry clumps of primroses that patterned the blue and cream curtains, and the matching walnut veneer dining table and chairs. She paused in front of the paintings that reflected her changing and developing tastes. The sharp modernist prints, the originals by emerging Australian artists and a group of small Aboriginal dot paintings. How would it look to Ellis? What would he learn about her from these rooms? How would he fit into them?

Upstairs in the bedroom she threw open the shutters and stepped out onto the balcony, inhaling the cold air from the ocean. Leaning forward, her arms resting on the top rail of the wrought-iron lacework, she felt a sudden and quite intense sadness about being alone. She had thought for so long that alone was what she wanted, that it was something she did well, something safe and peaceful. Now it felt different, precarious, even here in this house that she loved, in the city she loved. She had bought this house fifteen years earlier and its value had risen exponentially since then. It was now what real estate agents called a prestige property, in a highly desirable location. One of an elegant cluster of houses on The Hill, it faced a park, and from the balcony where she now stood she could see through the palms and pines to the sea, where the freighters stood at anchor waiting for entry to Newcastle port, their bulky silhouettes charcoal against the misty grey-whiteness of the horizon.

Now more than ever, she wished Ellis were there with her. So many times since the shooting she had said that she wanted to get back to normal and here she was, doing just that, first the electorate office, then parliament, and now home again. But she was restless, unwilling to move back into the old routines. Ellis had made Sydney different, made the colours richer, the air fresher, even the ordinary seemed memorable; here the usual pattern of her life loomed as dull and routine. Why had she been so desperate to return to it? 'Normal' no longer had the same appeal it had held in the hospital bed or in Barbara's cottage, and 'alone' seemed totally devoid of attraction.

She thought about Jill, whom she liked and admired but also envied. Jill's freedom seemed endless to Heather. Weekends were real weekends, free of work and full of time to spend with Adam and the children, the ability to decide something on the spur of the moment, the freedom to be herself without the need to live as a public figure weighed down by responsibilities and expectations. Yes, Jill's freedom was what she envied, that and the sense she must have of being loved, by Adam and by her children, by being the centre of their lives.

*

The following morning, Heather arrived early at the electorate office, but Shaun had beaten her to it and was at his desk sipping a large takeaway coffee and going through the morning papers. She was struck again by the strain and exhaustion that showed in his face.

'I'm okay,' he said, 'just tired. It's been a long haul since that night. And then there's personal stuff – Charlene and I have split up.'

Heather, who was moving papers from her briefcase to her desk, looked up. 'You have? Oh, Shaun, I'm sorry. I mean, I know it wasn't working out for you but just the same . . .'

'It's the best thing,' he said swiftly. 'Irreconcilable differences, as the A-listers say. It was never going to work. Anyway, Roussos called just now. He tried your mobile but you must have forgotten to switch it on. He wants you to give him a call.'

Heather's eyes lit up. 'Did he say what –'

'He just said he wanted you to call.'

Heather sat down at her desk and switched on the mobile, excitement surging as she dialled the number. After his few days in Sydney at the start of the parliamentary sitting he had handed over to the Sydney police and returned to Newcastle. This must be it, he was on to something at last.

'I just wanted to touch base, after that debacle the week before last,' Alex said. 'I was a bit shaken to discover that I was about to arrest an eminent person.'

Heather's anticipation hit the wall and slumped. 'Oh,' she said. 'I thought perhaps you rang because you . . . oh, well . . .'

'Nothing, I'm afraid. Not a dickybird. And Mr Hargreaves? Has he recovered from being wrestled to the ground by two police officers?'

'He's fine about it. He realised you were just doing your job. Is he actually eminent?'

'Sure is,' Roussos said, and she could hear the sound of a keyboard being tapped, as though he were calling up something on the computer screen. 'You should Google him sometime, some of the people he's defended make interesting reading.'

Heather put down the phone, rested her chin on her hands and stared at the list of appointments that Patsy had put on her desk. Four meetings with constituents, with half an hour allowed for each. A short break and then a visit from the state secretary, probably about pre-selections, and then she had to present an industry award to a local business, tour the factory and have lunch with the directors. Heather's heart, which had been sinking slowly since the start of her conversation with Alex Roussos, went into freefall. Sighing, she switched on the computer and went into her personal email. There was a message from Ellis at the top of her inbox, and her stomach lurched with excitement.

Good morning! Take care of yourself and have a good day. Sydney is not the same without you. Longing to see you on Friday. Love E x

She read the brief message several times and considered calling him, but didn't want to appear clingy and intrusive. On impulse she clicked on Google.

There were more than thirty thousand references to Ellis Hargreaves: academic papers, memberships of boards and committees, controversial statements, lists of trials, and articles on his defence of high-profile criminals. Heather scrolled through the first few realising that she had been so locked into the crisis in her own life that she had seen Ellis only in relation to herself. She had asked him little or nothing about his marriages, his career, his decision to leave it all behind and reinvent himself in Byron Bay. No wonder he hadn't wanted to come to Newcastle with her; he must have needed a break from her neurotic self-obsession.

She went back to his email, hit 'reply' and stared at the screen, wondering what to say, how to tell him she was sorry. Patsy stuck her head around the door.

'Mr Muir is here for his appointment, Heather. Can I bring him in now?'

'Two minutes, Patsy,' Heather said. 'I just need to reply to this message.'

You have a good day too, and thanks for everything, she wrote. *Sorry to be so self-obsessed. I'll try to behave better next time. Friday can't come soon enough. Love H x*

She hesitated, considering whether she was right to follow his lead in the sign-off. Name or initial? Initial seemed almost intimate.

One kiss or two? His one seemed natural, casual, two might be assessed for meaning, just as she was assessing his one kiss. Why did it even matter? Mr Muir's voice boomed from the outer office. He was very deaf and made up for it by bellowing at everyone else. Heather sighed, hit send and opened her office door.

'Mr Muir,' she shouted, 'so sorry to keep you waiting. Do come in . . . ' and she ushered him into a chair, contemplating as she did so why the words of a two-line email, and the number of xs to include, had suddenly assumed such importance.

It hadn't taken Barbara long to make up her mind to agree to plan B. Living a totally different life for a few months in a country where she didn't speak a word of the language was not something that, at her age, she would have considered doing alone. But to travel with a friend put a whole different complexion on it, especially a friend as dear and congenial as George. Even so it was a bit daunting to think of taking this very intensive course which, apparently, had even the young and energetic hollow-eyed and jittery within the first week.

'Will you be okay about sharing a place in Beijing?' George asked as he turned into the car park of the language school. 'Sachs said we could probably rent a small flat.'

'That'll be ideal,' Barbara said, thinking that it was infinitely preferable to being alone in a large apartment building if the electricity went out or the water was cut off. George had very civilised domestic habits. She had already made one stipulation – she wouldn't go before March.

'Winter in China is bitterly cold, and I'm not going to freeze to death in a Beijing apartment with ice on the windows.'

'Done!' George had said. 'You're right about the weather, good thinking.'

'Here we are then,' he said in the car park, switching off the engine. 'Let's get in there, hand over the money and register for the course.'

'Do you want to do the test now?' Sachs asked as he greeted them in reception.

'Test?' they responded in unison.

'Grammar, usage and so on, easy as falling off a log, but you have to pass in order to get onto the course. You won't have any trouble.' And before they knew it, they were sitting in separate booths in an otherwise empty room, and given half an hour to complete a test paper, with instructions not to talk to each other.

'You didn't tell me we had to do a test,' Barbara said as they walked back to the car later. 'It's years since I had to do a grammar test – decades!'

'I didn't tell you because I didn't *know*,' George replied irritably, searching his pockets for his car keys. 'Anyway, what are you grumbling about? You got a hundred per cent. I only got eighty-nine.'

'Yes,' she said with a smile, 'it's your bizarre use of commas that undid you, George. But you can console yourself with the knowledge that if they had asked us to provide the symbols for chemical compounds, I wouldn't have got even *one* right. Cheer up. Let's get over to Heather's office, she'll wonder where we've got to.'

George grunted and started the engine. 'We could take Heather out for a meal as we're so late,' he said. 'Have you told her about our plan?'

Barbara shook her head. 'Not yet. We can tell her while we eat. Let's go to Scratchley's, it's ages since I went there. Lend me your mobile and I'll see if they've got a table.'

'China?' Heather said. 'You're joking, aren't you? You can't be serious, you're both over seventy.'

'Aren't you the person who shamed the council into introducing a more adventurous seniors' program?' Barbara was rather enjoying Heather's astounded reaction. 'Don't look so amazed, Heather. Life after seventy isn't all lawn bowls and genealogy classes, you know.'

'Well, I know, but . . . ' Heather hesitated. 'Will you be all right? I mean, China's not the safest place.'

'Neither is Newcastle, if your experience is anything to go by,'

George chipped in, nodding toward Heather's shoulder. 'We'll be fine. It's certainly not going to be luxury, but it'll be an experience we'll never forget.'

'I suppose so,' Heather conceded. 'And you think you'll manage the course all right? I've heard it's pretty hard.'

'Really, Heather,' Barbara was irritated now, 'at what point did you decide I'd entered my dotage? I just passed the test with a mark of a hundred per cent, and Robert told me it was the first time that he'd ever known anyone get everything right. Even George got eighty-nine per cent, and he's no grammar buff.'

'Even George –' George began, but Barbara was in full swing now.

'Just because I no longer roll up every day for life in a city office, it doesn't mean I've lost my marbles.'

Heather flushed. 'No, no, of course, I never thought that. It's just that other people, much younger people, have said that it's very hard, very intensive. Do you really want to put yourself through a month of that?'

'Yes,' said Barbara decisively, more sure of it now than ever. 'Even if I didn't want to go to China, I think it would be a great thing to do. I could get involved in that English language program for the asylum seekers. I think it's very exciting.'

'I've brought some bits and pieces about China to show you, Heather,' George said, moving their wine glasses and putting some leaflets on the table. 'You don't need to worry about Barbara, you know. We've both still got our wits about us and we're tough old buzzards, really.'

'Of course you are,' Heather said. 'I'm sorry, it was just a bit of a shock. I never imagined you doing anything like this.'

'Nor did I,' Barbara said, 'but surprise is part of the attraction. It seems like a great adventure.' She poured some water into her glass and looked at Heather again.

'Anything from the police?'

'Not a thing. And, of course, the longer it is, the less likely they are to find anything. Roussos says that the more the trail cools the more difficult it becomes, not that they ever seemed to find a trail in the first place.'

George got up to speak to an acquaintance sitting at a nearby table, and Barbara grasped the opportunity of a few moments alone with Heather. 'Jill tells me that you've met up with an old flame. Is it anyone I know?'

'No. His name's Ellis Hargreaves. He was one of my uni tutors and he was married, so I kept him well away from you and Mum.'

'Obviously. But he's not married now, presumably?'

'No, and honestly, Barb, it's wonderful to see him again. He came all the way from Byron Bay to Sydney to see me because he'd been reading about the shooting and thinking about me. He says he's always wanted to get in touch with me again.'

'It sounds rather romantic.'

'Oh, I don't know. It is lovely to have Ellis around, but romance? You know me, about the most unromantic person in the world, and very set in my ways.'

Barbara, who had enjoyed being single for most of her life, had never been convinced that it was quite so satisfactory for Heather. 'Don't rule anything out,' she said. 'Extraordinary and unexpected things happen, you just never know what's around the corner. Like me going to China, for instance . . . '

'Or me getting shot. You're right, of course. Has Adam said anything to you about Ellis?'

'Nothing at all. In fact, I haven't spoken to Adam for a while. Jill says he's a bit moody at present.'

'Moody,' Heather said with a laugh. 'Bear with a sore head is more like it. But I guess he'll get over it eventually.'

'Who'll get over what?' George asked, sitting down again.

'Adam,' Heather said. 'He's annoyed with me for going out with an old boyfriend.'

'Ha! Protective older brother, eh?' George said. 'Well, you're right, he'll get over it. Now, what's happened to our meal?'

Adam lay on his own side of the bed curled in a foetal position. It was a position he seemed to be adopting with greater frequency these days. Jill had gone out to dinner with some women friends, and he had gone to bed early but had lain there, restless and unable to sleep. A few minutes earlier he'd heard Jill let herself in through the front door and come quietly up the stairs.

'Are you awake?' she whispered, putting her head around the bedroom door, and when he didn't answer she closed it again and he heard her go into the bathroom. He felt incapable of speaking. For weeks now the normal rough and tumble of work and family life had overwhelmed him. He tried to resist the urge to disappear even more frequently into his music room, because he knew it wasn't fair to Jill or the children, but despite his efforts he couldn't seem to behave normally. He even found it impossible to tell them all how much he loved them and ask them to bear with him while he went through whatever it was that had him in its grip.

It was such a contrast to the day he'd flown back from Newcastle filled with the joy of being home. The smell of cold toast in the kitchen, the stacking of the dishwasher, the pile of unopened mail on the hall table had seemed like paradise. But a few days later his spirits had crashed. The managerial part of his job in the orchestra felt exceptionally onerous, and he was awash in a dull sort of confusion that made him feel as though he were wading through mud. He thought his shattered sense of security was at the heart of it, his recognition that the people he loved most were always at risk. He wondered how, in the past, he could have lived without that constant awareness, how he could have assumed that life would go on in the same way it always had done. And then there was Ellis Hargreaves crawling out of the past like a slug from under a rock to be welcomed by Heather as though the misery he'd put her through had never happened.

The taps were turned off in the bathroom and Jill came quietly back into the bedroom. Adam tried to breathe as though he were asleep, and he heard the swish of her clothes dropping onto the chair, and another sound, softer still, as she slipped her nightdress over her head. She pulled back the duvet, slipped into bed and moved close to him, and he felt the comfort of her cool body against his back. She ran her hand lightly down the length of his spine and Adam shivered involuntarily.

'So you *are* awake,' she said.

Adam moved slightly, hoping she might think he was simply stirring in his sleep.

'Adam, I *know* you're awake,' she said in a small voice. 'I knew it before I went into the bathroom.'

He turned over onto his back and took her icy hand in his warm one. 'Cold night?' he said.

'Very.'

'Did you have a good time?' The effort of speaking seemed enormous, the intimacy of it unbearable.

'Lovely, thanks.'

The silence throbbed as they lay side by side, holding hands in the darkness.

'Can't you talk to me, Adam?' Jill asked softly, her voice heavy with hurt and confusion. 'Can't you please try to talk to me?'

He opened his mouth but no words came out.

'Is it me?' she asked.

He shook his head and forced himself to turn on his side. He raised his hand to stroke the side of her face.

'No,' he managed to say at last. 'No, darling Jill, it's not you.' He paused. 'I don't know how to explain it, but since the shooting I feel like . . . like I'm falling apart.'

'And for some reason it's worse since this Ellis person turned up?'

Adam nodded in the darkness.

'But why?' Jill asked. 'What's he got to do with it? You know he's nothing to do with the shooting?'

'I know. I can't explain, Jill . . . '

'But you know stuff . . . you and Heather know stuff that you're not telling me,' Jill said. 'Do you have any idea how it feels to be shut out like this? But I've always been shut out of your secret bloody society with your sister, haven't I? Your exclusive little club for two. Well, keep it all to yourself if that's what you want.' And she threw back the bedclothes, got up and picked up her pillow.

'Jill,' Adam struggled to say. 'Jill, please don't . . . it's not like that . . . '

But she was gone, and he heard her cross the landing to Kirsty's old room and slam the door behind her.

EIGHT

Ellis was frustrated by his lack of progress. Sitting on a seat in Hyde Park, eating a sandwich between appointments, he reflected on the uphill job of finding a PR consultant. He'd been confident that, having had time to study his proposal, someone at Markson Sparks or the Harry M Miller Group would snap him up, but he'd been met with a disappointing lack of interest. This afternoon, though, he had an appointment with Luke Scriven, principal of Scriven Communications, who sounded promising. He flicked through the material he'd downloaded from the website: *Strategic solutions for A-list clients in government, business and the entertainment sectors.* Ellis wrapped the rather dry crusts of his sandwich in a paper napkin and tossed them into a nearby bin. The whole week had been a waste of time. He might just as well have gone to Newcastle.

He was torn between the longing to re-establish the past and the confronting nature of the present. In imagining this reunion he had not allowed for the changes that four decades had wrought or the irritating practicalities. Heather was, naturally, very busy and, not having fully recovered from the shooting, she tired quickly and her emotions swung between dramatic peaks and troughs. More difficult to contend with was the fact that the sweet, impressionable young woman he remembered made only fleeting appearances. Heather circa 2006 was very different: strong-minded, often out-spoken and constantly challenging. He compared it to reaching out to stroke a cute kitten and being greeted with the hiss of a mature cat.

Not that Heather had actually been hissing, but the old (or rather, the young) Heather had been delightfully submissive and accommodating, had hung on his every word, whereas this one had a lot of words of her own and often disagreed with his. Ellis had imagined her stepping (or preferably falling) into his arms, declaring that she had always loved him. In his bed among the tree tops he had visualised the passionate lovemaking that would surely follow their reunion. But now it was harder to picture, because in imagination Heather was a lithe and beautiful girl keen to do his bidding, and in reality she was . . . well, what was she? Not lithe and not a girl, and apparently unlikely to do his bidding, but the magic of the past and the romance of recapturing it remained. Changed she might be, but Heather was still what Ellis wanted. He would just have to learn to adjust. And so, of course, would she.

The incident with the police, while unpleasant, had its advantages. It had allowed him the opportunity to be gracious; to smile and shrug and assure Detective Roussos, in front of Heather, that he was pleased to see the police were doing such a thorough job in trying to find the gunman. But nothing was really working out as he'd hoped, especially not his search for an agent.

Shortly after his return from the Blue Mountains, Ellis had offered his services to the rather elegant holistic health centre where he had been on retreat.

'Well, of course I remember you, Ellis,' Jean Carson, the director, had said. 'But I'm not clear what it is you're offering.'

'Life-coaching,' he'd explained, 'a unique type of life-coaching that enables people to find their inner wisdom, and move into genuine selfhood. Byron Bay's a fair way out from where you are but I could come down for, say, ten days at a time and you could put me up at the centre and I'd run a series of sessions. I'd be a coach in residence, so to speak.'

There was silence at the other end of the line and he wished he had mailed the proposal first and then called her. 'Jean?' he said. 'Jean, are you still there?'

'Yes, yes I am,' she replied. 'It's just that I hadn't realised you were . . . doing this sort of work. I thought you used to be a lawyer.'

'That's history,' Ellis said. 'Past life. These days I'm in the business of life-coaching.'

'I see. Well, it sounds rather vague, but perhaps you could put your proposal in writing. Send me details of what you've done, and maybe some examples of people you've worked with, and I'll think about it.'

Ellis was mildly offended at the idea of having to submit evidence as though he were applying for a job. For years in the law he'd asked the questions and demanded the evidence and others had done *his* bidding. But he'd faxed Jean Carson the same day, with a long description of the four-week course in life-coaching that he'd taken two years earlier at the Nirvana Haven in San Francisco. He wrote of the glorious sunlit studio overlooking the Bay at Sausalito, where they sat on rattan mats, reclining against piles of calico-covered cushions. He described the slow and rhythmic daily warm-ups, the group sharing sessions, and the fascinating discussions about the nature of health, mindfulness and the centre's dynamic new concept of life-coaching as a means to achieving selfhood. Each time Ellis thought of it he recalled that blissful sunlit month during which they all wore simple white cotton caftans to break down the barriers created by perceptions about dress. He remembered the discussions of Tantric sex, and the ritual dances and bodywork designed to free repression and release the true self. It was, he explained to Jean, a life-changing experience, an interlude in which everyone seemed beautiful, youthful and golden, and just so . . . well . . . Californian. Before leaving the US he'd approached Zoran, the Jesus-like director of the retreat, about the possibility of a Nirvana franchise in Australia.

'Sure,' Zoran had said, nodding thoughtfully. 'Sure thing, Ellis, that sounds like a swell idea. Franchising isn't something we've explored yet but it's certainly a possibility. The best thing might be to write a proposal and make a donation to Nirvana and I'll put the idea to the board.'

Back in Byron Bay, Ellis had developed his proposal and sent it to Zoran along with a generous cheque. For some time he assumed the lack of response indicated thoughtful consideration of his proposal. But, as time dragged on, and his emails bounced back as

110

undeliverable and the phone line seemed to be disconnected, he knew there was something seriously wrong.

'Can you do a bit of research for me?' he'd said on the phone to one of his former clerks who was now, like Ellis, retired. 'I want you to track down this company in Sausalito.'

'Sorry, Ellis,' Stan had said. 'Got a lot on at the moment. Just heading off on the grey-nomad trail.'

So Ellis had had to do the research himself and he'd hit a dead end. Nirvana Mind-Body Haven had disappeared down the drain. Too much competition probably, Ellis thought, but here in Australia it would be a different story. There was no reason why he couldn't go it alone, developing what he'd learned from Nirvana into a concept of his own. He envisaged a sophisticated clientele of professional people, the sort of clients he might himself once have been. Initially a peripatetic practice, he thought, seeing people in their homes or offices, and some residencies in existing clinics and holistic centres. His approach to the Blue Mountains retreat was his first foray into this new occupation. But, to his surprise, Jean Carson had written him a very abrupt letter saying that as he had neither formal qualifications nor experience as a counsellor or life-coach, they would not be able to take up his offer. Rather short-sighted, Ellis thought, but then, some people were simply unable to think outside the square.

The trip to Sydney to meet up with Heather had fitted well with his need to find an agent or PR consultant to target a campaign at high-flying individuals in the corporate and government sectors. Ellis was not blind to the intriguing irony of a high-profile criminal lawyer turning life-coach. It had obvious novelty value as a marketing and promotional tool, and he visualised media interviews and double-page spreads in glossy magazines, all so much more effective than mere advertising. All he needed was someone with the insight and drive to grasp and run with the concept.

In the reception area of the Pitt Street offices of Scriven Communications, Ellis admired the colour scheme and the branding: ice blue and charcoal spoke to him of drive and efficiency, and he liked the edgy artwork on the walls. He strolled back and forth; courtrooms had given him a preference for being on his feet. He was not a tall man but what he lacked in height he made up for in confidence. A journalist had once described him as leonine, and he enjoyed that sense of himself as moving with grace and power, almost magisterial in his control of situations.

'Ellis,' said Luke Scriven, welcoming him into an office in which a granite plinth supported a huge slab of glass; it was, apparently, his desk. 'What a pleasure to meet you, and to read your splendid proposal.' He steered Ellis towards a coffee table and two low couches which occupied one corner of the office. 'Please, have a seat and Lucy will bring us some tea.' He curled catlike into a corner of one of the couches, dropping Ellis's portfolio onto the table. 'I can't tell you how excited I am about this.'

He was dressed entirely in black: long-sleeved black, designer t-shirt; tight black jeans and leather boots. Rather affected, Ellis thought, as was the watery green tea in a square charcoal teapot with a cane handle, which was poured into tiny cups without handles. Ellis, who would have preferred a strong cup of English Breakfast, sipped it and smiled as though it were just what he needed. Pretentious clothes and wanker tea were easy to forgive in the warmth of Luke Scriven's enthusiasm. Ellis had lived his working life in wood panelled offices with ornately patterned Persian carpets, polished mahogany desks and library lamps, and in high-ceilinged court buildings, their entrances flanked by fluted columns. His days had been spent knowing the rules and how to manipulate them, in unpicking the detail in complex information, and structuring it into argument, rhetoric and performance. The light, modern space and design of Luke Scriven's office delighted him, just as California had done, with its difference.

Luke Scriven put down his cup and held up his two hands palms outwards, tips of his thumbs touching to form a viewfinder in which to capture Ellis's face. 'I can see it now,' he said. 'From head to heart. From the law to the spirit, from rat race to enlightenment and self-actualisation.' He dropped his hands and smiled. 'Potent, Ellis, potent! Let's talk about how we could work together on this.'

*

'Do you fancy lunch over the road?' Shaun asked, and Diane looked up in surprise. It was the first time that he had ever suggested they have lunch together. 'Stuff to talk about.'

'Okay,' she said. 'But we need to go soon. I've got an appointment later.'

He nodded. 'Right, just got a couple of calls to make and then we'll go.'

Diane had noticed a subtle change in Shaun since he had turfed Charlene out of his house. He was obviously exhausted by everything that had happened, but he was friendlier and she had warmed to him, especially since Gerry had come out solidly in favour of Shaun's view that it was time for serious confrontation with Charlene.

For two years, Diane had gone to great lengths to avoid seeing Gerry, which was helped by the fact that he had moved out of town to what she referred to derisively as his 'love nest in the valley'. But she made sure she never went anywhere near his office, the restaurants he frequented or the wine merchant where he would certainly still have an account. And she joined a different tennis club from the one where they had played together as a couple. Their social life had been as a couple too, a couple among other couples, and Diane had resisted the awkward but good-hearted attempts those couples made to straddle their loyalties. She turned down invitations to dinner parties, barbecues, tennis matches, Christmas and New Year drinks and the marriages of their friends' children.

She resented the unfairness. She had stuck with Gerry through the hard times when he was a bricklayer trying to turn himself into a registered builder and then into a property developer, and now this bimbo was reaping the benefit. But the worst part was that she still loved him. So many of their friends were together through habit or lack of alternatives, but Diane had thought that she and Gerry were together because they loved each other. She had certainly continued to love Gerry for better or worse, and worse had included his legendary drinking and the emotional switchback on which she was alternately hurt by his drunken hostility and then seduced into forgiveness by the seemingly genuine remorse and promises that it wouldn't happen again.

But since that hastily organised meeting to talk about Charlene, Diane was faced with a different problem. The moment she saw Gerry looking so much like his old pre-booze self, she felt something inside her snap like a rubber band. He had hurt her bitterly, embarrassed her, toppled her self-esteem and trampled over every emotion, but quite suddenly she realised she didn't care anymore because she no longer loved him. Perhaps she hadn't loved him for some time. She realised she didn't give a stuff about Gerry and his girlfriend, his new life and his place in the valley. She actually thought that, commendable as it was that he was losing weight and had given up drinking, it was quite pathetic that he was doing it in an attempt to hang on to a woman who was less than half his age. What's more, the style makeover was a disaster. He was a good-looking man and had aged well, but the diamond stud in his ear looked simply silly and, as she or any other decent hairdresser could have told him, while grey hair was attractive and sexy, dyed a nasty shade of tobacco it was death to style and made him look like a hamster.

Most of all, Diane realised she was tired of hating. Gerry was clearly unaffected by it, and it was poisoning her life. It was over. Thirty-one years of organising her life around Gerry, and more recently in opposition to him, were over. The realisation was shocking, like letting go of the rope in a tug-of-war: the initial relief was followed by the crash down into emptiness and failure. Hate and anger were very motivating; the loss of both left only a vacuum.

'So, how's it going?' Shaun asked when they had placed their orders. He had told her that he didn't want to discuss the Charlene problem in the office, and that he would not tell Heather about it. He felt that if it got out that her electorate officer had drugs stored in his house, it would be better if Heather could honestly say she knew nothing about it. Diane thought this might be one time when Shaun's instincts were wrong. In Heather's shoes she would have preferred to know what was going on, but it was his call.

'Hard,' Diane said. 'She's still very upset about you ending it and she's very cagey about Danny.'

'What's happened to the stuff she had at home?' Shaun asked.

'She says she's given it back to him and she won't be seeing him again but I'm not convinced. Look, you were right, I can see that now, she's scared of him.'

Shaun nodded. 'He might lay off her for a while, but he'll be back, that's for sure. She must be a nice little market for him, lots of friends who'd be popping those pills at parties and clubs. He won't want to lose that. What does Gerry think?'

'The same. He's threatened Charlene that he'll go to the police about Danny but of course he won't because he'd also be turning her in. He even talked about paying Danny off, but he knows that won't work either. I just wish we could get her away from him. I'm worried sick about her, Shaun.'

'I know. Do you think she'd go away somewhere? A long way away, I mean.'

'What – a holiday?'

'Longer than that. Another state perhaps, get a job for a while. That might break the cycle.'

Diane hesitated. It made sense but getting Charlene to do it was something else. 'It might work, I suppose, if she'd go. She's never been away from here alone, it would be hard for her, some-where strange –'

'But Charlene's not stupid,' Shaun cut in. 'She must know what a mess she's in even if she's not admitting it, and if she's fright-ened and can see a way out she might take it.'

'But where would she go? She'd need a job, somewhere to live . . . '

'I might be able to help. My cousin is assistant manager of a resort on the Gold Coast. They're always on the lookout for staff and Charlene's good with figures and on the computer. She's done payrolls too. I could ask Denise if there's anything going. Charlene's met her and they got on well. Maybe Denise'll help her find something.'

Diane had often encouraged Charlene to travel, to try some-thing new, to make the most of being young, free and single, but now her maternal instinct went into overdrive. 'The Gold Coast. I could hardly keep an eye on her there.'

'This is about giving her a chance to keep an eye on herself,' Shaun said. 'Getting her away is giving her a new start, without all the Danny baggage.'

'I suppose so.'

'It's not all that far, after all. If we could fix it and Charlene agreed, maybe you could go with her for a week or two until she settles in. That might help her and you.'

Diane felt a huge lump in her throat. She wanted to put her head on Shaun's shoulder and sob. This was a really positive suggestion, something that neither she nor Gerry had considered. 'I suppose it might work,' she said cautiously. 'Let me talk to Gerry and see what he thinks.'

'Do that,' Shaun said. 'And, meanwhile, I'll talk to Denise.'

NINE

Roger, Director of Infrastructure and Services, was a bully. Jill suspected that Renée had already carpeted him about it at least once, maybe twice, and that he was on his last warning. It didn't seem to be bothering him, though, probably because he was arrogant enough to ignore the warnings. She wondered what it would be like to be married to someone whose homecoming you feared, whose behaviour and reactions you could never predict or trust, who said they loved you but treated you with contempt. She had once met Roger's wife at a Christmas function. She was a quiet woman, simply but elegantly dressed, with a permanent smile. She blinked a lot, and nodded in agreement when her husband spoke. But when she thought no one was looking, she drew her lips together in a tight line and swallowed hard several times, as though she were trying to rid herself of the taste of something unpalatable.

Jill watched as Roger completed the presentation of the final section of his report, leaned complacently back in his chair and looked around the table in expectation of a response. The rest of them shuffled papers, crossed or uncrossed their legs and waited for Renée to move on to the next item on the agenda. There were obviously far worse things than living with someone sensitive, someone who cared too much about everything, and seemed to have an unhealthy sense of responsibility for his sister.

'He could be depressed,' Renée had said when Jill broke her self-imposed veto on discussing the situation with her.

Jill shook her head. 'He's upset certainly but not depressed in the way you mean. There was the shooting, and Kirsty leaving home, and now this thing about Heather's old flame turning up. There's stuff going on that he won't talk about.'

'Won't or can't?'

'Who knows?'

'Maybe he should get some help.'

'Last time you said it was me who needed a counsellor.'

'Yes, well, this thing with Adam hasn't just happened, it's been building up for some time. You need to talk about it. It's bound to make you feel weird.'

'I've always felt weird about Heather,' Jill said. 'Almost from day one, but the shooting sort of brought it to a head. And now there's this stand-off between them. I feel like piggy-in-the-middle. Sometimes I'd just like to bang their heads together really hard.'

'So, have you met this Ellis?' Renée asked.

'No. Heather was in Newcastle for a week and she came back here again last week. I'm obviously not going to invite them for dinner with Adam behaving like a pork chop.'

Renée closed the meeting and there was movement around the table as people gathered their files and headed back to their own offices.

'Just a moment, please, Roger,' Renée said, and Jill watched as he turned back into the room. His number was up. Renée was tough and decisive, skilled at cutting through the mind games and confronting people. Roger was not going to be easy but Renée would prevail.

Jill closed the boardroom door behind her and walked back to her own office. It was so much harder to sort things out with the people you loved, to find your way through so many layers of unspoken sadness and resentment, to risk disturbing old hurts and misunderstandings. Jill remembered how she had felt the morning following the shooting, watching the TV coverage, listening to the various views on what had happened and why. She had peered at the screen wanting to catch sight of Adam, going into the hospital perhaps, or driving away with Barbara. She'd needed to see him because she had a sinking feeling in the pit of her stomach that this crisis would penetrate much deeper than the bullet itself.

Jill gazed out of her office window. It was a full week since she had moved out of the bedroom, and neither she nor Adam had referred to it. Where did they go from here? Perhaps she should just say nothing, move back, let Adam and Heather sort out their own problems, and trust that eventually Adam would return to being the person he had always been. But then she would still be bugged by his disappearing into the music, and her own ambivalence about his relationship with Heather. Perhaps Renée was right and it would help to talk it through with someone else. But a counsellor? And then it dawned on her that there was someone else she could talk to. Someone to whom, for this and a whole lot of other reasons, she should probably have talked a long time ago. Taking a deep breath, she dialled Heather's direct line at Parliament House.

In a fitting room in the Market Street branch of David Jones, Heather was struggling with a size sixteen skirt which was stubbornly resisting her efforts to drag it up over her hips. She'd had a sixteen in this label before but the manufacturers seemed to be skimping on fabric these days, cutting things tighter. Discarding it, she reached for the eighteen she'd brought in with her just in case. It eased on all right but as she turned side-on to the mirror, it was clear that the zip was going to be a challenge. She pulled in her stomach, clenched her buttocks and tugged. The zip moved a couple of centimetres and stopped, and as she relaxed her muscles it ripped away from the fabric and stuck out at an angle as though poking fun at her. She swore silently, wriggled out of the skirt and sat down on the fitting-room bench, wearing only her bra, knickers and pantyhose. Surely she couldn't need something bigger than an eighteen? A flush began its smouldering journey from her face, down through her whole body, flooding her with its smothering, prickly heat.

Was there no end to the horrors of ageing? Extra weight, loss of concentration, hot flushes . . . Bugger this stupid thing about power surges, there was nothing less empowering than finding yourself bathed in sweat day and night. Just that morning she'd read an article about glamorous, sexy older women: Helen Mirren, Candice Bergen and Raquel Welch, all over sixty and looking forty. So being old was cool, but only if you actually looked twenty years younger. Men could go grey or bald, acquire wrinkles and paunches, their jowls could drop and hair sprout from their ears, and they were still considered sexy and attractive. But heaven help the woman who was found guilty of not attempting to hold on to youth.

'Bugger it,' Heather muttered, 'I'm so totally sick of this.'

'Are you all right in there, madam?' the sales assistant called, tapping on the door. 'Do you need any other sizes?'

'No, thanks,' Heather said, fanning herself with a sale catalogue, 'I'm fine.'

The woman's footsteps trailed away and Heather stared at the offending skirt. Suddenly she wanted to cry, to howl with disappointment at the unfairness of being fat, menopausal and having bad hair. And now she'd have to pay for a useless skirt. A very expensive useless skirt, unless . . . Cautiously she pressed her ear to the door. It was early and the store was quiet. There was no one else in the fitting rooms. She clambered up onto the bench, and over the top of the door she could just see through to the entrance to the fitting-room area – not a soul in sight. Jumping down she opened the door and, still in her underwear, ran to the end cubicle, hung the offending skirt on the wall, and fled back to her own.

Her face was blazing with the flush and with guilt about her bad behaviour, but there was enormous satisfaction in not doing the right thing. It was liberating, although not as liberating as getting into a size sixteen with room to move would have been. She struggled back into her clothes, hating the sight of herself in the mirror. She had worn her favourite olive green suit with the cream silk shirt, because she thought it made her look slim, and because she was meeting Jill, who always looked as though she had been born with the casual elegance gene. But all she could see now was an untidy, shapeless mess topped by a beetroot-coloured face. Turning away from the mirror she buttoned up her jacket and gathered up the clothes.

'Any good?' asked the sales assistant when she emerged from the fitting room.

'No thanks,' she said, gracing the woman with her most generous smile. 'All a bit on the big side. I probably need a fourteen, but I don't have time now, got to get to a meeting.'

The woman took the clothes from her and cast a surreptitious glance at her hips. 'Right,' she said. 'We do have a range for the fuller figure on the next floor. You might like to try there.'

Heather resisted the urge to punch her, and made her way down to the ground floor, surrounded by real and airbrushed images of young, slim and beautiful women. Had she looked like Helen or Candice, perhaps Ellis would have made a move by now. It was par for the course that older men fancied younger women, but presumably she was no longer young enough. And he clearly thought she was not paying him enough attention, not like she did all those years ago. Just this morning they had had an awkward conversation in which she told him that she wasn't free until the evening. She needed to go shopping, she had meetings and parliament, and Jill had called and suggested that as she was in town they should meet for lunch.

'It's important to me,' she explained to Ellis. 'I've always wanted to be closer to Jill but she seems so . . . well, complete as she is. Almost as though there's no more space for anyone else. So this is something different and I don't want to say no.' She'd felt intimidated by his curt reaction and resented it, fighting her instinct to be accommodating. She longed for tenderness and affection and, not for the first time, someone to indulge and make a fuss of her. Despite his reassuring presence and his talk of romance, Heather suspected that physical affection outside of sex was not part of Ellis's emotional repertoire.

She reached the bottom of the escalator and walked out into the street, heat prickling her armpits and beads of sweat crawling down her spine. She reminded herself that she was not necessarily the fattest person on the streets of Sydney that morning, and that menopause and trauma were bound to be a challenging combination. She knew she should walk the short distance to Parliament House but her feet hurt and her mood had sapped her energy. Ignoring her guilt she slipped into the back seat of the first taxi at the rank.

'Where to, love?' the cabbie asked.

'Parliament House, please,' she said, and began searching her bag for a cab voucher.

They pulled away from the kerb into the traffic moving down Market Street. 'Aren't you the one that got shot?' he said, looking at her in his rear-vision mirror.

'Yes,' she said. 'That's me.'

'Shocking business, that. But that's what you get, letting all these foreigners into the country.' Heather closed her eyes and took a deep breath. 'They haven't caught him yet, then?'

'No, not yet.'

'Funny, you know. I wasn't sure when you got in the cab, but when you said Parliament House I thought, yes, that's her, that's the one that got shot. Thing is, you look younger in the photographs, so I wasn't sure . . . know what I mean?'

'Yes,' said Heather. 'I know exactly what you mean.'

Jill arrived early and sat in a corner of the café in Macquarie Street, trying to look as though she were reading the paper but wondering why she'd organised this lunch. She couldn't remember a time when she had actually had a conversation alone with Heather about anything personal. They had rarely been alone at all except in the context of family functions: preparing food together in the kitchen, washing up, or walking side by side in a straggling group. They had never before met alone, never talked intimately about themselves and certainly never discussed Adam.

As Jill stirred her coffee and glanced out of the window wishing she were anywhere else, she caught sight of Heather walking towards the café, and her self-esteem took a dive. She looked, as always, smart and professional in a dark green suit and cream shirt, and Jill felt slightly in awe of her. She wished she had worn the red wool Carla Zampatti suit with the black buttons that she'd bought for less than a third of its original price in the recycling shop. She'd opted instead for the black leather bomber jacket, black skirt and leather boots (all also from the recycling shop – did she have anything apart from underwear that wasn't from there?), and she felt scruffy and suburban. Heather opened the door, looked around and smiled when she spotted Jill. No turning back now.

'This was a lovely idea,' Heather said, kissing her and pulling out a chair. 'What are you doing in this part of town?'

'Oh, just a meeting,' Jill said, 'so I thought it'd be nice to catch up.'

'We should do it more often. We never seem to get a chance to talk.'

'No. Silly really, isn't it?'

'Very silly. After all, we're family.' Heather opened the menu. 'Have you ordered?'

A waiter materialised and Jill shook her head. 'I was waiting for you.'

'Well, I'm starving. I'll have the club sandwich with chips. No, scrub the chips, just the sandwich and a salad. And a mineral water, please.'

Jill ordered a caesar salad and handed her menu back to the waiter. 'Well,' she said in the silence that followed, 'how are things? You're looking a whole lot better than when I last saw you.'

'Oh, I don't know,' Heather said with a shrug. 'Up and down. One little bullet and everything changes. I saw it, you know, the bullet, before the police took it away. It had my blood on it and I remember thinking, that's that over and done with. I had no idea, just no idea and now . . . ' Her voice trailed away.

'And now everything's a mess,' Jill said. 'Now it's changed everything and everyone.'

'You too? You and Adam?'

'All of us,' Jill replied. 'All of us, and Adam especially.'

They talked at length about the shooting, and the police investigation that seemed to have run out of steam.

'It won't let go of me,' Heather said. 'I'm waiting, waiting all the time for it to be over, for everything to be back like it was before that night.'

'I wonder,' Jill said, 'whether things ever get back to how they were. Something like this changes people. I think you can't go back, you just go on in a different way.'

'That's what Ellis says. But anyway, let's talk about something else. I'm too obsessed with what happened and why. I'm sorry, Jill. What's that line from *Beaches*? "That's enough about me, let's talk about *you* – what do *you* think about me?"'

'It's fine,' Jill said, feeling perfectly at ease at last.

'Tell me what you meant about Adam.'

Jill hesitated, wary of the track that led to her resentment of Adam's relationship with his sister. 'He's more withdrawn than ever,' she said slowly. 'But that's been going on a long time. He's spending more and more time shut in his room playing his cello.' She felt a sudden burst of anger. 'I'm so sick of those fucking Bach suites, Heather, I want to scream at him.'

'I know what you mean. He was doing that when he and I shared a flat. It's an avoidance technique, when he thinks there's an argument brewing.'

'I realise that,' Jill said, 'but he does it more and more, even when there's not a whiff of conflict to avoid. He just seems to want to cut himself off.'

'It's probably just a part of the way he is.'

'So he did it with you too?'

'Oh yes, and with Yvette. It used to drive *her* insane. I think that's part of the reason she left him. Well, probably part of the reason she had the affair and then left – eventually she couldn't cope with his withdrawal.'

'I thought it must be my fault, but he doesn't seem able or even willing to discuss it.'

Heather nodded. 'It's just him, and I think the orchestra gets him down.'

'That's what Barbara said. That he never expected the orchestra to be like an ordinary job.'

Heather nodded again. 'Yes, that sounds about right.'

'But he never mentions it.'

'No,' Heather said, 'he wouldn't. You see, he had very romantic ideas about spending his life immersed in music, and when he chucked the geology degree so that he could get into it full time, Mum and Granddad were furious. They kept telling him that if Dad were alive he'd be terribly disappointed in him, that he would have wanted Adam to have "a proper job". Granddad thought music was for dilettantes, and anything that wasn't played in chapel was a fast road to sin. Even after he died it took a long time for Mum to feel really okay about Adam's desire to be a musician, because of that. Barb was the only one who encouraged him, so I suppose he felt he was just going to keep his head down, press on and prove that music *could* be a proper job. But there is so much more than the love of music or the instrument that's involved in being in an orchestra.' She paused, pouring the last of her mineral water into a glass. 'And I suppose that once he got to be first cello, there were more of the sort of responsibilities he dislikes: the everyday running of things, organising people . . . that's not his scene.'

Jill shook her head. 'No, not at all.'

'And you think the disappearing act is getting worse?'

'It got worse quite quickly after you were shot. And now, since . . . ' she hesitated.

'Since Ellis turned up?'

'Yes. Since then he's been more uncommunicative than ever, and he's angry, I think.' She leaned forward with a sudden insight. 'In fact, it's almost as though he's in pain. Not physical pain, something more profound.' She took a deep breath and summoned all her courage. 'It's horrible, especially this thing about you and Ellis, it's as though there's something between you and Adam around this, something that excludes me. It makes me really uncomfortable.'

Heather flushed. 'Yes,' she said, looking away. 'Yes, I can see that it would, Jill. I'm sorry, it *must* be horrible, and you need to know that it isn't anything about you. It's about the past, about how Adam felt about it. He was wonderful to me, but he took it all very personally, and now, Ellis coming back like this, he's taking that very personally too.'

'But why?' Jill asked. 'It's so long ago.'

'Yes, and I've got over it, so why can't he?'

'Exactly.'

Heather shrugged. 'He's a man, they see things differently. It was a horrible mess. I suppose you could say I had a breakdown. Adam looked after me, doing all those things he hates, taking responsibility, doing the practical stuff, and holding off Mum and Barbara so they wouldn't ask questions. We both thought they'd have a fit if they found out I'd been involved with a man who had a wife and children.' She laughed, leaning back in her chair. 'Weird. I mentioned it to Barb the other week and she didn't turn a hair. Times have changed so much.'

It was something, but Jill was sure that there was more. 'And that's all?'

'Yes, it's Adam – being himself and not being able to get the past in perspective.'

Jill sighed, still unconvinced. 'Oh well, I guess I'll just have to hang in there and wait until he comes through it.'

'You could be tougher with him, about the other stuff, the opting out,' Heather said, signalling to the waiter.

'What do you mean?'

'You take on so much, you're such a tower of strength for him; I sometimes think he takes advantage of that.'

'Really?'

'Yes. You could stop doing that.'

'How do you mean?'

'Well, Adam, lovely as he is, is very indecisive and hates taking responsibility. In the orchestra he has to. At home you pick all that up, and he *doesn't* have to.'

'You mean I'm contributing to it?'

'Yes, actually, I do,' Heather said, looking embarrassed now. 'I'm not blaming you, but I know how frustrating he can be and I think you let him get away with murder. You're super responsible, so he doesn't have to be.' She hesitated, looking away and then back at Jill. 'I'm sorry, it's not my business. I shouldn't interfere.'

'Go on,' Jill said. 'I asked, just go on.'

Heather paused while they ordered cappuccinos and the waiter took away their plates. 'Adam's always had me and Mum and Barb to rely on. He always did his bit, housework, shopping and so on, never shirked that, never grumbled, but he always had to be told, or asked. He never initiated anything, just waited for things to happen or to be told what to do. And, of course, we kept on asking and telling, and so did Yvette, by the way. So he was always surrounded by women who ran his life for him. We're all the same, Mum, Barb, me, Yvette and now you. I often wonder what would have happened if one of us had stopped taking the initiative, stopped running things. If he were left to . . . to trip over reality, so to speak.'

Jill sat in silence staring at the pepper mill in the centre of the table. 'If I stopped making sure everything runs smoothly, you mean?'

'Yes. Stopped reminding him to pick up his tail suit from the cleaners, or jogging his memory about rehearsals, or reminding him to go to the dentist . . . '

'Or getting his car serviced, or doing things he promised to do with the kids.'

'Yes, all that. The thing is, of course, that it would be so hard for someone like you or me to do that. To hold back and let him, as I said . . . let him trip over reality. But who knows, it might just work.'

'You may be right,' Jill said thoughtfully.

'I suppose,' Heather continued, 'it's the sort of thing that's made me avoid getting into a relationship again. I have this horrible habit of tying myself in knots and then feeling trapped by my own behaviour.'

Jill leaned forward. 'What do you mean?'

'Well, I try to be the perfect woman, anticipate what they want, do all the looking after, take responsibility for making everything work, but in the long term it doesn't work for me and I start to resent the burden. Do you know what I mean?'

'I know exactly what you mean,' Jill said.

'I resent the fact that I have to have my head cluttered with stuff that should really be someone else's responsibility, and I end up feeling they're to blame. I resent the fact that I can't do my job properly because running the relationship occupies my headspace and uses all my energy.' She shrugged. 'But that's just me, it's probably different for you. You seem to take it all in your stride.'

Jill shook her head, thinking of her own mother. 'Not really,' she said. 'I struggle with it and spend a lot of time feeling guilty for not being able to take it all in my stride. So what about Ellis, Heather?' she asked, anxious now to take the attention away from herself. 'Is this . . . I mean, are you . . . ?'

'Are we sleeping together?'

Jill blushed. 'That's not exactly what I meant, although it had crossed my mind.'

'We're not, but I think . . . I hope . . . we might. I can't work out what he wants.'

'Sounds like you're doing what you just described, working out what he wants in order to deliver it. So the obvious question is, have *you* worked out what *you* want?'

'I'm so bad at knowing what I want from anything outside my job. And, as I said, I gave up on relationships a long time ago. But this . . . ' She stopped.

'But this is Ellis, so it's different?'

'Yes, I think it is really. Despite the decades I feel as though I still know him, and know him well. As though it would be . . . safe, I suppose. He actually makes me feel safe and that seems important right now.'

'Well, then?'

'It's still awkward, though. The terror of intimacy, sex after all this time, taking one's clothes off again, being that vulnerable. Running away seems tempting but then when I'm with him . . . ' She paused and looked straight at Jill. 'I can't believe I'm talking to you like this.'

'There's always a first time,' Jill said. 'Like you said earlier, it's shaken us all up. I wish I could meet Ellis.'

'We could have dinner,' Heather said, suddenly excited. 'I'd love you to meet him, Jill.'

Jill shook her head. 'I don't think there's any way Adam would agree to have dinner with Ellis.'

As the train pulled out of the station heading north to Chatswood and home, Jill rested her head against the window and tried to figure out how the gulf between Heather and herself had developed in the first place. Was it her fault? Today they had talked like friends. Had a phone call and a conversation over lunch been enough to eliminate the distance between them or had they needed a violent crime as the catalyst?

A crowd of teenagers in school uniform jostled each other for seats, slinging their bags onto the overhead racks. Jill closed her eyes, waiting for them to settle, remembering what Heather had said about the compulsion to do what she thought was expected, the guilt that came as one constantly fell short of the gold standard and the resentment that followed. Was this at the core of the crippling formula of love manifested as domestic and social control that had driven her own mother?

The household had been Pamela's personal domain and attempts to introduce individuality into any part of it amounted to treason. She chose everything in the house, from the polished wood floors, chintz upholstery and prints of English hunting scenes, to the powder-blue kitchen cupboards and the pale green tiles in the bathroom. Even Jill's bedroom, with its rose-covered wallpaper, frilled pink bedspread and kidney-shaped dressing table with a triple mirror, was her mother's selection. The only exception was her father's study, for which he had been allowed to choose his own desk and some Australian bush prints.

Pamela had high standards when it came to order and cleanliness, standards maintained with the help of a woman who came in for three hours on Wednesday mornings to polish the silver, clean windows and scrub the floors in the bathroom and laundry. Good wives, according to Pamela, were responsible for maintaining the family's image and managing each person's social, work and school commitments. Not an unreasonable load, of course, for someone with one very well-behaved child, paid help, plenty of money and no job.

'You need to remember this, Jill,' Pamela told her as her father drove them home after her university graduation, 'home and family are what matters. That's what you'll be judged on. You can have your fancy arts degree and your independence, but it means nothing if you can't manage a home and family.'

Jill did want to be a good wife, but it was another twenty-odd years before she met the right person. Coming to marriage so late it seemed particularly important to get it right. When she and Adam met she was living in a tiny, very neat apartment which Adam said reminded him of a rather nice hotel suite. He had just bought a small but cute Federation cottage that needed lots of work and which he thought he might renovate. It didn't take Jill long to fill it with her choice of furniture and pictures, to change the rather dark curtains and set about repainting the interior walls. Adam had thought it a big improvement and was glad to hand the house over to her. It was simple at first but with the arrival of Toby and then Daisy they needed more space. They sold the cottage and Jill's apartment and bought the house, a big house, which was a good thing because then Kirsty joined them. So they had two small children and a teenager and two full-time jobs.

Jill knew she was pushing her luck, she knew women *could* have it all, but trying to have it all at the same time was risky. But the biological clock was ticking and if she didn't have it all now she wouldn't have it ever. The nature of the plan, as she had seen it back then, was that things would get easier as the children ceased to be dependent toddlers and went to school. Where the hell did she get that idea? And why hadn't she factored in the psychological and biological effects of ageing?

The train moved off, and the teenagers whooped and punched each other and fell about over the seats in laughing heaps as it gathered speed. Perhaps Heather was right, she had colluded in the aspect of Adam's behaviour that most distressed her. Maybe she had even set it up. She had assumed that he needed her, needed her to be as she was being, as she had been from day one of their time together. Now she wondered if perhaps what he really wanted was the chance to be needed himself.

TEN

'I'm going to have a party,' Barbara said. 'A birthday party, before I go on this terrible course which may well kill me, but don't mention that to Heather, she thinks I'm mad anyway.'

'I doubt she thinks anything of the sort,' Adam said, undoing his tie and opening the top button of his dress shirt. 'She's probably just surprised. It's not something she, nor I for that matter, ever imagined you'd do.'

'Me neither, but I'm doing it.'

'And it is wonderful,' Stefan said. 'I admire this very much going to another country. The challenge, you know?' He hesitated. 'For me . . . my situation, it kept me sane. For you, I think it is a wonderful adventure.'

'Thank you, Stefan, I think so too.' She glanced at the kitchen clock. 'Now, I'll make you both some tea before you get on the road.'

The orchestra had been playing a single matinee at one of the vineyards, and Adam and Stefan had collected Barbara on the way there and brought her home again, before the drive back to Sydney. Adam opened the kitchen door and walked out onto the deck. There had been a brief shower as they drove back to Morpeth and the smell of damp grass hung on the dusky evening air.

'Going to have a quick look at the garden,' he called over his shoulder, and sauntered down the steps and along the path.

'So you'll come then, Stefan?' Barbara asked, getting the mugs out of the cupboard.

'Excuse me?'

'You'll come . . . to my party, I mean?'

'Ah, but of course, if you ask me I'm honoured. You will have all your family?'

'Yes, and a few of George's too, I hope. He's organising it. Nothing big, just family and a few friends.'

She didn't add that she was counting on Heather bringing the mysterious Ellis, whom she had so far kept hidden. If she could get both Adam and Ellis in the same place with some excellent wine and food, it might help – besides which, Barbara was dying to meet Ellis. She had a niggling feeling that she was missing something significant in all this, that she knew something about it that was simply eluding her. She must be getting more forgetful. The ESL course would be good for keeping the Alzheimer's at bay.

'Aren't we a bit old for parties?' George had said when she told him.

'You might be but I'm not,' Barbara replied. 'And frankly, if you're not too old to trek off to China, you ought to be able to survive a small birthday party. Look, everyone's been really upset by the shooting. It feels as though we're falling apart. It's weeks ago now and we need something nice to happen. And anyway, I've never had a birthday party before.'

'Never?' George said in amazement. 'Not even as a child?'

Barbara shook her head. 'My parents didn't believe in parties. I'm sure I told you. They were in a very odd and strict little religious sect, and fun wasn't part of it. No parties, no dancing, the only music was from the piano, and I was only allowed to play hymns. Roy and I had a very bleak childhood.' She paused. 'You know, Roy struggled against our parents for years, particularly Dad, and yet when he became a parent himself he seemed determined to re-enact that bleakness and austerity.'

'Probably the only way he knew how to be a father,' George said. 'We often seemed destined to repeat all the things our parents did, the things we swore we'd never do.'

Barbara shrugged. 'Probably. And of course the polio left him so weak he couldn't do much. He was very bitter. It sounds awful but I'm thankful Roy died when he did. Adam was eleven and being the eldest child and a boy he'd already copped the worst of it. How would he and Heather have turned out growing up with a father like that?'

'Hmm,' George said. 'Well, you did and you turned out all right.'

'I suppose so, but I do wonder how much of Roy's shadow has fallen across Adam's life.'

George raised his eyebrows. 'Adam seems fine to me.'

'In many ways,' Barbara said, 'Adam is wonderful and not at all like Roy or our father, but I sometimes think the darkness of his early years has had a big effect on him.'

'Can't see it myself,' George said with a shrug. 'You worry too much about him and Heather. They're fine people. Anyhow, a birthday party is one of life's special treats and you must obviously have one and I will organise it.' And since then he'd been busy on the computer designing an invitation which he was about to send out to everyone on Barbara's list.

'Jill and Adam and the children will need to stay the night,' she'd said, 'and maybe Kirsty and Nick too. That will fill up my place, so how would you feel about having Heather and her new old friend to stay with you?'

'Is that one bedroom or two?' George asked with a grin.

'Not sure yet,' Barbara said, 'but I'll find out. I'm hoping it's one.'

'You haven't even met this bloke yet,' George said. 'You might feel like Adam does.'

'I doubt it,' Barbara said. 'In fact, I'm determined to like him. He seems to be just what Heather needs at the moment. And Adam'll get over it; whatever happened was donkey's years ago. He'll come round.'

Alone at the bottom of the garden, Adam sat on the damp timber seat enjoying the stillness and the silence. Until Barbara had made her move to the country it had never occurred to him that he might want to do something similar. Now, each time he came here, he longed for his own bolthole; somewhere green and quiet, away from the city and suburbs. It wasn't on the cards yet, of course, they were both trapped by work, but when the kids grew up and left home, maybe he and Jill . . .

Adam leaned forward resting his elbows on his knees, his chin in his hands. He and Jill, what had they come to? Her move out of the bedroom was such a dramatic gesture; more dramatic, surely, than the situation warranted and so dramatic that he had no idea how to respond to it. Now it hung between them, a cone of silence that grew larger and more oppressive as each day passed. Adam sighed with frustration at his own failure; he was a useless husband and father, a useless brother, a useless musician. No wonder Jill moved out of the bedroom, presumably for the same reasons as Yvette had left him; strong women escaping from the leaden burden of his failure. And he was still awash in his own inertia, unable to claw back what was most precious to him.

When Yvette left, his sadness had been tempered with relief: the relationship had been in rapid decline and her affair had finally turned it sour. But losing Kirsty had been devastating. The one bright spot, Adam reminded himself now, was that Kirsty had chosen to come back to him, so he must have done something right. But if Jill left . . . he couldn't even bring himself to think about losing her, losing Daisy and Toby. He had to find a way out from this torpor that made him feel as though he were living under a pile of wet newspaper.

'Hey, Adam,' Stefan called from the verandah. 'Come drink your tea, we need to get going.'

Adam stood up and brushed a couple of dead leaves from his trousers. Get going. He had to get going. He straightened his back and stretched out his arms, feeling a slight stirring of energy. Get going, Adam, he murmured, get going or you will lose everything and you'll only have yourself to blame.

When Ellis called Heather to fix a time to meet for coffee in the morning, he was offended that she couldn't fit him in because she needed to go shopping and then to a meeting, after which she was having lunch with her sister-in-law. 'I could meet for an hour or so around four o'clock,' she'd said.

'And I've got a meeting at three thirty. I've only got a couple more days in Sydney,' he protested, 'and you're giving priority to shopping and your sister-in-law. You can meet her any time.'

They had finally agreed that she would cook something for dinner at her place that evening and he'd hung up, fairly ungraciously, and killed time alone before going to his meeting with Luke Scriven.

'What we need first,' Luke said, 'are some products – an inspirational CD and a book.'

'A book?' Ellis said. 'What sort of book?'

'Your book of the journey.'

'What journey?'

'The journey to selfhood, your own journey as an example. As we discussed, Ellis, Head to Heart, rat race to self-actualisation and wholeness. It doesn't need to be long, just intimate, inspirational, meaningful; and it shouldn't give away all the secrets – very important. I'm thinking,' and he raised his hands, waggling his fingers to imply quotation marks, '"an inspirational personal story of one man's journey to maximise his life potential". That's just off the top of my head, of course.'

'You don't think some leaflets –' Ellis began.

'Of course, but we need a book as well. A small, classy looking paperback. Everyone has a book these days. And the CD, some commentary, perhaps some meditations for change, that sort of thing. We'll launch the whole package with a series of inspirational talks, and market the book and CD at the same time. And you'll need a website. Themed images: you in your robes in court and you today, lots of golds and fresh greens there, implying energy and new life, relaxing on a verandah, glorious rural setting, lots of trees. We might add an eating plan – "a regime for mind and body wholeness" – that sort of thing. We can work on the details.'

'Eating? I don't think I –'

Luke waved it aside. 'We'll find someone who knows that stuff, dieticians are ten a penny. Now, none of this is cheap, of course, but we want to do it properly. I'd say we should run with this from next June.'

'That's a long way off,' Ellis said. 'I was thinking we might kick off some talks early in the New Year. After all, it's not as though I'm an unknown –'

Luke smiled. 'Ellis, you are known as a defence lawyer in Adelaide. While that's an obvious plus we are now going to build a profile, rebrand you for a much wider and rather different market. You want to be top of the range in this business and preparation is the key, as I am sure it was in the law. We don't want to go into this half cocked.' He flicked through the pages of the plan which was ring bound in elegant blue and charcoal plastic bearing the Scriven logo. 'Take this away, read it all, think about it carefully and give me a call next week,' he said. 'And, remember, at this stage it's merely a proposal and subject to your approval and alterations.'

In the cab on the way to Heather's place, Ellis sat with the folder in his lap. Top of the range was right, it was designed for people just like himself. He had hit a winner with Luke Scriven, he knew that now. As the taxi headed out towards Potts Point, he asked the driver to stop at a bottle shop where he bought a bottle of Moët.

'You're looking very pleased with yourself,' Heather said as she opened the door. 'Good meeting?'

'First class,' he said, handing her the champagne. 'Absolutely first class. Let's open this and I'll tell you all about it.'

'It looks very impressive,' Heather said as he flicked through the plan. 'I don't really know anything about this sort of thing, but Scriven seems to have done a great job, and you're the expert. If you're happy . . . '

'Ecstatic,' he said, 'and raring to go, even to write the wretched book.'

'And what about the budget?'

'I haven't gone through that yet. It'll be hefty but, as Luke says, if you want to be top of the range you have to do it properly. I'll go through it in detail when I get back to Byron Bay.'

She refilled their glasses and collected the salad from the kitchen. 'Come and eat,' she said, putting the bowl on the table.

Ellis put down his glass. 'It means a lot to be able to share this with you, Heather,' he said. 'A hell of a lot.'

'Me too,' she said, turning to him. 'Meeting you again, Ellis, that's meant a great deal to me. You've helped me more than I can tell you.' She sighed and looked away. 'I'll really miss you when you leave on Friday.'

'I'll miss you too, very much,' he said, slipping his arms around her waist and drawing her to him. 'I guess that's why I was so grumpy this morning. Sorry about that.' And as she tipped her head back to look up at him, he was transported to the past. The look in her eyes was as he remembered – trusting, loving, innocent. He laid his hand on her cheek. 'I've always loved you, Heather, you know that, don't you? Always loved you and still do.' And he bent his head to kiss her and was thrilled to feel her arms close around his neck and her mouth yield to his.

'I don't have to go *straight* back to Byron Bay,' he whispered softly into her hair. 'I could make a brief detour to Newcastle first.'

'That sounds like a very good idea,' she murmured, kissing his jawline. 'I was wondering when we might get around to this.'

'I don't like to rush things,' Ellis said, thinking that he would actually have rushed at it on day one if he'd thought he could get away with it. 'Unfortunately, it means that we've missed a number of opportunities.'

Heather ran her hand through his hair. 'Well, we don't have to miss this one,' she said.

The following morning, sitting up in bed with the coffee Heather had made for him before she left for work, Ellis laced his fingers together behind his head and leaned back. He had so often imagined how it would be to make love to Heather again after all those years. The inevitable merging of past and present, of fantasy becoming reality the previous night, had been almost surreal. There had been an awkward patch when Heather suddenly pulled away as he was about to enter her. She burst into tears and talked about penetration and bullets – for some reason she was linking the shooting with sex, god knows why, but he had made all the right noises. It had annoyed him, though, and he'd had to concentrate on not losing his erection, or figuring out how he'd get it back if he did. Anyway, she got over it, and Ellis thought he'd put up a first-rate performance for a man of his age. The purple pills certainly fulfilled their promise.

So, it was all working out; once he'd had a shower and some toast, he'd change his flight to go with her to Newcastle for a long weekend. Ellis finished the remains of his coffee, threw back the duvet and swung his legs out of bed. Fantasy was, he thought, part of a successful relationship. Last night he had closed his eyes and imagined making love to the young Heather – it was perfectly natural, he was sure all men did it. In fact, most men probably imagined they were making love to *other* women, screen goddesses, supermodels; at least he was fantasising about the same person. And it was also natural to feel disappointed when he woke expecting to see a nineteen-year-old and found he was in bed with a middle-aged woman. It was early days, it was magic, and magic was sometimes challenging.

The women's toilet at Parliament House was empty and Heather peered at her reflection in the mirror, trying to decide if she looked younger. She thought she did, rather as though she were in soft focus, glowing and slightly blurred. Ten years of celibacy and she was, once again, a sexually active person. It had begun so unexpectedly she hadn't had time to worry about her body; had she known what would happen, the anticipation would have been dominated by thoughts of cellulite, excess kilos and the fact that she hadn't shaved her legs. The urgency of Ellis's desire and the subtle light that filtered in from the sitting room had enabled her to survive nakedness. She had read somewhere that one effect of being shot was that the penetration trauma could be revived at the prospect of a foreign object entering the body; even so, the panic took her by surprise.

She smiled now, thinking how wonderful he had been, holding her reassuringly until she had weathered the storm. Eventually they had made love with a slow but passionate intensity, as though they were carefully crafting every move, every murmur, every sensation. Dragging herself out of bed and away from Ellis this morning had required a superhuman effort. He was, she had thought as she lay watching him sleep, a man who had improved with age. Confidence, maturity, an assurance of his place in the world, and indeed in her bed, were incredibly seductive. She knew she was in the grip of long forgotten symptoms of love: the heightened sensuality, the desire that destroyed concentration, the sense of having been transformed. His smell still clung to her as though he refused to be swept away in the shower. The door swung open, disrupting her reverie.

'Heather,' an Upper House colleague said, 'I was just looking for you.'

'Well, now you've found me,' Heather said, blushing slightly and turning on the tap to pretend to wash her hands. She wondered again if her changed status were noticeable.

'Yes,' the woman said. 'There's something I need to run past you, but I need to go in here first.' She opened a cubicle and stepped inside. As she turned to close the door she noticed Heather's reflection in the mirror. 'You look fantastic this morning, by the way. What is it, new hair? Make-up?'

Heather held her hands under the flow of water. 'No,' she said. 'Nothing different, same old me. Just feeling good, I suppose.'

'Excellent,' the woman said, closing the cubicle door. 'About time, after all you've been through.'

Heather smiled smugly at her reflection. 'If only you knew what I went through last night,' she murmured into the noisy blast of the automatic dryer.

'So she's gone, then?' Ed Masefield said, sitting on the step and pulling his tobacco tin out of his pocket. 'Young Charlie, she's gone?'

Shaun watched his father ease the lid off the tin and take out the packet of papers.

'Charlene? Yes, she's gone.'

'Where to?'

'She's at her mother's place now, but she's going up to the Gold Coast next week. Denise got her some temporary work in the resort.'

'That's good,' Ed said, teasing out the tobacco threads and laying them carefully on the paper. 'She'll like that, fit in well up there. Nice girl but not right for you.'

Shaun rolled his eyes. 'You always say that.'

'Because you haven't found the right one yet. You will, eventually, although the rate you're going you'll be lucky if you find her before you draw the pension.'

'Well, thanks, Dad,' Shaun said, putting down the spirit level and unscrewing a bottle of water. 'That's very encouraging.'

Ed shrugged. 'True, though. Did you give her the heave-ho or did she go of her own accord?'

Shaun turned away. 'It was a mutual decision.'

'I take it that means you kicked her out, like the last one. I could see it coming. I said to your mother not so long ago, that one's for the heave-ho, you mark my words. Wondered where she was, and then when I went in the bedroom to fix that skirting board just now I saw that bloody awful dressing table had gone.'

Shaun nodded, said nothing and swigged his water.

'When'd she go, then? Coupla weeks?'

'Four.'

Ed nodded. 'Met someone else, have you?'

'Nope.'

Ed rolled the cigarette paper and licked the edge with the tip of his tongue. 'Trouble with you, Shaun, is you're all in your head. It's all right doing up the house, yarning over politics with me and working all hours, but you need to get out more. We used to go dancing. That's how I met your mother, dancing.'

'It's different now, Dad,' Shaun said. 'Dancing is in clubs, lots of booze, drugs, very loud music. There are no ballrooms or girls in long dresses with chaperones and dance cards.'

'Get off,' Ed said, flicking his lighter without success. 'I'm not that bloody old. Rock 'n' roll, Bill Haley, "Rock Around the Clock", the twist. That's my era.'

'Just winding you up.'

'You should move on, y'know,' Ed said, finally getting a flame and drawing on his cigarette. 'You've been in Heather's office too long. You want to go somewhere where you'll meet more people. Women, I mean.'

Shaun laughed. 'I thought I was supposed to meet them dancing.'

'Yes, but you won't go dancing, will you? How'd you meet Charlene?'

'At work,' Shaun said. 'Her mother volunteers at the office, and Charlene came with her to a sundowner one night.'

Ed removed the cigarette from his mouth with his thumb and first finger, the lighted end turned inwards towards his palm. 'Well, you want to go somewhere where you'll meet women who like the same things as you. That other one, the one before Charlene – Tanya, was it . . . ?'

'Teena.'

'Yes, Teena, very nice girl, very pretty. Daft as a brush, though.'

Shaun sighed. 'Yes – apart from not getting out enough, I don't seem to be very good at picking them when I do go out.'

Ed flicked the ash off his cigarette. 'It'll happen eventually. Always does, you just need to get out more.'

Early in the evening of the day that Adam and Stefan had played in the vineyard, Jill got home and realised she had forgotten to switch on the washing machine that morning, and clothes they all needed for the next day were still unwashed. She'd had a really dreadful day at work and now she would have to stuff everything through the dryer tonight. She switched the machine on, and considered what she and Daisy could eat. Toby had gone from school to Bree Adams's house and would have to be picked up later. Adam would probably just want a sandwich when he got in. She opted for beans on toast, and then found they had run out of baked beans as well as Daisy's favourite tinned spaghetti.

'Scrambled eggs or fish fingers and oven chips?' Jill asked her.

Daisy sat at the table contemplating the options as though considering the fate of nations.

'Eggs, I think,' she said eventually. And Jill got them out of the fridge and cracked the first two into a bowl, at which point Daisy changed her mind.

'You asked for *eggs*,' Jill said irritably.

'But I didn't really *mean* it,' Daisy said in her most infuriating

141

wheedling tone of voice. 'I thought I meant it but then I found I didn't mean it. What I *really* meant to say was fish fingers and oven chips, because you see, Mum, I really do love oven chips, and the best thing in the world would be oven chips with tinned spaghetti –'

'Daisy, shut up!' Jill said. 'We're having eggs.'

'But I hate eggs,' Daisy wailed. 'I just remembered that I really hate eggs. If I have to eat them I'll probably be sick.' She pulled a face and made retching noises.

Jill put one hand on the side of the sink, closed her eyes and thought of her friends. She thought of Renée, married to a corporate executive, childless and moderately wealthy, sipping champagne at a town-twinning reception that Jill was missing because neither Adam nor Kirsty was available to babysit. She thought of Elise, the same age as her, whose children were in their late twenties and scattered at comfortable distances around the world. And Stella, a year younger than her, whose two children, although still living at home in their early twenties, were civilised grown-up university students like Kirsty. She pictured Stella and her husband, Grant, side by side on the sofa, watching SBS with a bottle of red while the students studied, emerging occasionally to have intelligent conversations in which there was no mention of tinned spaghetti, Harry Potter, or whether they were allowed to watch *Australian Idol*.

'Okay,' Jill said eventually with a sigh, unable to face an argument. 'Fish fingers and chips and that's *it*.' And she covered the eggs with cling film and put the bowl in the fridge.

'Brill,' Daisy said, 'and then after dinner –'

'After dinner we're going to collect Toby, and you are going to have a shower. You can watch TV for half an hour and then it's bed.'

'No, we have to do my insects project,' Daisy announced. 'I have to finish it for tomorrow.'

'What insect project?'

'I have to draw six insects, and write about their habitats and their feeding habits,' Daisy said. 'It's for tomorrow.'

Jill shook a packet of oven chips into a tray. 'And how long have you known about this?'

142

'Um, last week, I think,' Daisy said, 'or it might not be.'

'You mean it might be longer?'

Daisy, avoiding eye contact, opened a box of coloured pencils. 'It *could* be longer, I think. Mum, what is a habitat?'

Jill had heard experts say that when children told their parents 'I hate you', in that moment they really meant it. She wondered if the experts knew that when parents stared at their children and thought the same thing, they also really meant it. She slammed the baking tray into the oven and told Daisy to fetch the nature encyclopaedia.

When she got back from collecting Toby, there was a message on the machine from Adam to say that he and Stefan had broken down on the Pacific Highway and were waiting for the NRMA. Just after ten he called again to say the problem was fixed and they were mobile again but were stopping to get something to eat on the way home.

Toby and Daisy were in bed, and Jill flopped down in her favourite chair, hooked one leg over the arm and flicked through the TV channels with the sound on mute, thinking she'd probably just go to bed. Every night since she quit the bedroom she'd considered going back and knew it was essential if they were to re-establish any meaningful dialogue. She imagined herself walking back into the room clutching her pillow like a repentant child. How would she cope if Adam rejected her, or behaved as though he'd prevailed in some sort of battle? But Adam wouldn't be back for another hour, probably more, and the easiest thing was to be in bed when he got back. It would seem natural, reassuring, but not necessarily repentant. And maybe, just maybe, Adam would be smart enough not to say anything. He might even be smart enough to give her the very big hug that she so desperately needed.

The morning after Diane flew home from the Gold Coast dawned as grey and overcast as her own mood. Dragging herself out of bed and into the bathroom she stared at her face in the mirror. She looked really terrible. She had cried all the way home despite the efforts of the Virgin flight attendant who plied her with tissues, chocolates, magazines and the offer of aspirin. There were dark shadows under her eyes and the wretched little lines that were clustering around her mouth seemed deeper than ever.

Through her tears she had noticed a woman board the flight and sit a couple of rows in front of her. She must have been in her early seventies, and she was wearing beige cotton pants, a white shirt and a brown velvet jacket. Her hair was grey, and cut close to her head in a neat crop. She wore no make-up and had a pair of glasses slung on a cord around her neck. As the woman walked down the central aisle, Diane was so fascinated by her that she almost stopped crying. She appeared entirely happy and completely confident about being herself, being her age, untroubled by efforts to look younger or more attractive.

Diane thought about the woman several times during the flight, and observed her closely as she walked past on the way to the toilets. She had a relaxed air and seemed unconcerned by what people might think of her; as though she were saying to the world, 'Yes, I'm an old woman and if you don't like it that's your problem'. Diane wondered if, in the process of ageing, there was a cut-off point at which one stopped worrying about one's appearance, about trying to look younger, or thinner, or more attractive, and became happy just to be seen as oneself. She couldn't imagine such a minimalist approach to appearance, one which didn't factor in how others – men, mainly – would look at her.

Diane splashed her face with water and went through to the kitchen to make some tea. She had been away for two weeks and the house felt like a morgue. It had seemed big and lonely before, when Charlene moved out, but in those days she was living nearby with Shaun and so it was different. Now her daughter was really gone, gone for a long time. Gerry was gone for good, and gone too was the energy that she had drawn from her anger. She wondered if she would feel better when she got over leaving Charlene, if the place would feel more like home again, but she doubted it. What did she need with a four-bedroom, two-bathroom house anyway? There was no one to come and stay with her and she never entertained these days. The whole battle with Gerry about keeping it had just been part of her need to get back at him for hurting her. Now it seemed like a waste of time.

Diane carried her tea back to the bedroom, sat on the bed and switched on the news. Charlene would be getting ready for work now. At least she was in a safe place with nice people.

'It sounds like a good idea,' Charlene had said when Diane suggested the move to the Gold Coast. 'Although I can't imagine why you're still talking to Shaun after what he did to me.'

It was at that point that Diane knew it was time to end the denial. The conversation that followed bore no similarity to any that had gone before. She listed the drugs, the lies, the excuses, the very real dangers of Charlene's situation, and the painful truth of why the relationship with Shaun had come to an end.

'This really is your last chance, Charlene,' she'd said finally. 'It's a chance to start again, and sort your life out. And frankly, if you don't take it, I don't want to know anymore. You can move out, find a place, do what you want, but I've had enough – you're not staying here.'

And while she had known she was doing the right thing, the responsible thing, she had felt like the biggest bitch of a mother on the face of the earth. And she was relieved and amazed when her daughter acquiesced and, three weeks later, when they stepped onto the Tarmac at Coolangatta, Charlene was excited at the prospect of working in a glamorous resort. Diane, meanwhile, felt drained by the events of recent weeks. If her daughter were starting a new life, the challenge for Diane was to come to terms with the old one.

She showered, dressed, unpacked the suitcase she'd been too tired to unpack the night before, loaded the washing machine and then poured some muesli into a bowl. She always ate it dry with some yoghurt but this morning she found it hard to swallow, and she pushed the bowl away and went out the back door into the garden. The lawn man was due and it was looking messy and overgrown. She should really get out there and do some gardening, pull out some weeds, prune the roses. Diane loved gardens but loathed gardening.

'Why am I here?' she asked herself suddenly and quite loudly, and a couple of parrots who had been sitting on the low branch of the lemon tree fluttered up and away in fright. 'Why the hell am I here? This is the last place I should be.' And she turned back to the kitchen, picked up the phone and dialled Gerry's mobile.

'Me,' she said to his voicemail. 'I want to sell the house. Call me back as soon as possible, we need to talk about it.' And she put the phone down and picked up her handbag.

It was Monday and she normally went to Heather's office on Wednesdays and Thursdays, but she needed to get out of the house, and somehow tennis and shopping had lost their appeal.

'Oh, Diane, thank goodness,' Heather said as she walked in the door.

A couple of constituents were sitting in reception looking rather disgruntled, and three of the four telephone lines were ringing.

'Where's Patsy?' Diane asked, pulling off her coat.

'She's sick. Shaun's at a meeting, and the Monday volunteer still won't come in when I'm here in case he gets shot.'

Diane nodded towards the reception area. 'Have they got appointments?'

'Yes,' Heather said. 'And they've been waiting ages, because while I was seeing the person before them I also had to keep answering the phone.'

'Okay,' Diane said. 'You see them and I'll look after the phones.'

'You are a saint, Diane,' Heather said, and walked through to reception. 'Mr and Mrs Tan, I'm so sorry to keep you wait-ing. Please come on in now.' And she led them through into her office.

Diane picked up all three lines, asked two callers to wait, put them on hold and starting dealing with the third, who wanted to know if Heather could help her son with his problems with Centrelink. A vaguely familiar elderly woman came into recep-tion while she was on the phone, and then another line started to ring. The woman's expression seemed to be asking if she wanted some help, and Diane realised it was Barbara, whom she'd met a couple of times when she'd called in to see Heather.

'Please,' she whispered, holding her hand over the mouthpiece and gesturing to the other lines. 'If you could take that call, put it on hold, and then talk to one of the other two.'

Barbara walked around the counter, sat down beside her, picked up the ringing phone, and the two of them worked on side by side, until the rush seemed to be over and Heather was ushering the Tans, now smiling, out the door.

'I quite enjoyed that,' Barbara said later, when she and Diane were in the café where Shaun had dispatched them for a break when he got back from his meeting. 'I'd forgotten what it was like to be under pressure. I only popped in to say hello as I was in town.'

Diane leaned back in her chair and stretched. 'I enjoyed it too. I don't usually go in on Mondays, but I needed something to do this morning. My daughter's gone up to the Gold Coast to work and it seemed really miserable being alone in the house.'

'What about your husband?' Barbara asked.

'How long have you got?'

'All the time in the world,' Barbara said. 'And I'm a very nosy person, I love hearing about other people's lives.'

'I'll get us some more coffee,' Diane said.

'I suppose it *could* work,' Heather said. 'I mean, she's not my first choice of someone to have around, although she's nothing like as prickly as she used to be, and she does know the routine.'

'She's really much nicer when you get to know her better,' Shaun said. 'I think we should give it a try.'

'Is Charlene still living with her?'

Shaun shook his head. 'Got a job in a resort on the Gold Coast.'

Heather raised her eyebrows. 'Gone away to get over you?'

'Gone away to get a new life,' Shaun said, looking away. 'It'll suit her up there.'

The door to the outer office opened and Barbara and Diane came in laughing. 'Ah! The dream team,' Heather called. 'Come on through.'

'That's us,' Diane said, 'and we even brought you both some

coffee.' She lifted the cardboard cups out of their holder and set them on Heather's desk. 'Large flat white for you, Heather, long mach for Shaun.'

'Thanks, Diane.' Heather took the lid off her coffee. 'Look, we were just talking. Apparently, Patsy's got rheumatic fever, she's really quite sick. I was wondering –'

'Sure,' Diane cut in, 'that's fine. I can stay for the rest of the day.'

'We were thinking perhaps a bit longer,' Heather said. 'Shaun suggested that you might be willing to temp for us. We'd pay you, of course, but it would be nice to have someone who knows the office and the routine.'

Diane looked blank for a moment. 'What . . . you mean . . . are you offering me a job?'

'Well, yes, until Patsy comes back.'

Diane hesitated, her head spinning. A few weeks ago she was going to leave, but a few weeks ago she was there for different reasons – a few weeks ago lots of things were different. 'Yes,' she said, thinking her voice sounded nervous and high. 'Okay, I'd like that.'

'She might be away for a while; several weeks, a couple of months, even.'

'Even better. Would you like me to start now?'

'You already have,' Heather said.

'She's a very pleasant woman,' Barbara said as Heather walked her out to her car later. 'We got on well. She'll do a good job.'

'I suppose so,' Heather said. 'I've never liked her much but she seems to be changing.'

'She's had a lot happening recently. Anyway, I've invited her to my party, and I hope you're bringing your Ellis. We're all dying to meet him.'

Heather pulled a face. 'Not everyone.'

'I doubt Adam is going to punch his lights out at my birthday party,' Barbara said with a grin. She opened her car door and got in. 'I'll see you in a fortnight, then. Jill and Adam are coming with the children, and Kirsty and Nick. I can just about squeeze them all in. I thought you and Ellis could stay at George's place.'

'Fine,' Heather said, 'that'll be lovely, if George doesn't mind.'

'Not in the least, but he needs to know whether to make up one room or two.'

Heather laughed. 'You can tell him one will be fine. As if you hadn't already worked that out.'

ELEVEN

'I hate Nick,' Daisy said, squirming round in her seat to look back at the object of her hatred, who was driving behind them with Kirsty. 'Why does he have to come to the party?'

'Why not?' Jill asked. 'I thought you liked Nick.'

'He has to go everywhere with Kirsty and she doesn't play with me anymore,' Daisy whined.

'Don't talk rubbish,' Jill said. 'Kirsty took you rollerskating the day before yesterday, and last weekend she sat with you while we were out and you played some computer games.'

'But Nick did too *and* he came rollerskating. I liked it when Kirsty lived with us and Nick only came sometimes.'

'Well, you just have to get used to it. Nick makes Kirsty happy.'

'But he makes me miserable,' said Daisy with a huge sigh.

'Ignore it,' Adam said quietly. 'She's bored. She seems to be exceptionally demanding lately.'

'Maybe we should get her an iPod too,' Jill said, glancing back at Toby who was in another world, twitching and jerking to the music on his. 'It certainly reduces the noise levels.'

'Don't even mention it, you'll just get her started on that.'

'Started on what, Dad? What will I get started on?'

Adam sighed. 'See what I mean?' He took his eyes off the road and glanced across at Jill. 'And you can stop looking so worried. I promise I won't upset Heather and I'll be civil to Ellis. In fact, I'll stay as far away from him as possible. It's Barb's birthday and I won't do anything to spoil it.'

'I know. I just think it would mean a lot to Heather if you could be friendly.'

'Friendly is not on, civil is my best offer.'

'Maybe he's changed.'

'Maybe he has,' said Adam without conviction.

'You never know, you might find you like him.'

'And pigs might fly.'

'Well, I'm dying to meet him,' Jill said. 'So is Barb.'

'Ellis is a funny name,' Daisy chipped in. 'Is he the one that shot Aunty Heather?'

Jill sighed. 'No, Daisy, I told you, it was a mistake, the police mixed him up with someone else.'

'So is Aunty Heather going to marry him?'

'No,' Adam said. 'Definitely not.'

'You can't be absolutely sure of that,' Jill said quietly.

'Over my dead body,' Adam said, and pulled into the inside lane. 'Okay, we're stopping for a drink and the toilets.'

'McDonald's,' Daisy shouted very loudly in Toby's face. 'McDonald's, we're stopping at McDonald's.'

'Shut up, moron,' Toby said, pulling off his earphones and attempting to strangle her.

Adam changed gear and turned into the car park. 'Okay, you two,' he shouted above the din, 'cut it out or no drinks.'

'You stay here if you like,' Jill said as the kids piled out of the car, and Kirsty and Nick pulled in alongside them. 'I'll go and get the coffees.'

Adam got out and stretched his legs as he watched the children race off ahead and Jill stroll across the car park with Kirsty and Nick. He was wordlessly grateful for her attempts to reach him, especially as he could barely reach himself. The night he'd found her back in their bed his immense relief was rapidly undermined by his fear of ruining it all again. He'd slipped quietly into bed beside her, listening to her breathing, certain she must be able to hear the way his heart was thundering in his chest. Cautiously he reached for her hand, and she took it, moving closer. Instinctively he let go of the hand and put his arms around her. Adam knew that the next step was up to him.

Jill was waiting for him to talk to her, to explain to her what he couldn't really explain to himself.

He strolled back and forth parallel with the side of the car, pushing the toes of his shoes through the cigarette butts, dry leaves and gravel. What would his father think? Pointless question, because everything would have been totally different if his father had lived. For his own part, Adam knew he'd never have dropped out of geology and taken up music, Roy would have insisted that he study or train for a proper job. Resisting his grandfather had been hard enough; he wouldn't have stood a chance against his father.

When Roy died Adam had wept, but it was more from shock and confusion than grief. A dark blanket of cloud had been blown away, leaving the sky clear. Around him everyone was weeping and guilt told him that his feelings were unnatural, but even the guilt couldn't destroy his sense of freedom. But freedom was not so easily won, for his father's legacy was captured in his last words to him: 'It's up to you to look after them, son,' Roy had said, 'your mother and your sister. You're the man of the house now, it's up to you to take care of the women. Don't let me down.'

It hadn't meant much to Adam at the time. At eleven it was so obvious that even if he were occasionally needed to look after his younger sister, his mother and aunt were more than capable of taking care of themselves. Dorothy seemed happier now too, and life in the Balmain cottage with her and Barbara was bliss by comparison. But later, Adam found himself dwelling on those words and the burden of responsibility that he felt inadequate to bear. *How* was he to take care of them? As his sense of incompetence grew he turned to his music, practising his cello for hours at a time, cocooned in his own little world. And then there was his faith or, as he thought of it now, his religious practice and the rules that went with it, rules so clear and strict they eliminated moral dilemmas: you always knew what you could or couldn't do. Adam clung to the security believing that it would, eventually, show him how to carry out his father's last instructions.

He'd been questioning his religious beliefs when Heather moved out of home and they found the flat, and the events of the following year had rocked him. Even so, it was another couple of years before he finally worked out that what he needed was a spiritual life rather than a practice he followed for fear of the consequences.

'But you still hold on to vestiges of it, don't you?' Barbara had asked him once. 'I know I do. Not in any form my parents or Roy would recognise, but one that I believe God understands.'

Adam, then in his early forties, had been shocked at her mention of God as though it were something they had in common, for they had never discussed religion except in terms of the crippling effects of her upbringing, and Roy's own behaviour. He had thought that he was alone in his faith, an outsider, that God was now his secret in the family.

'I still believe, if that's what you're asking,' he'd said. 'And those beliefs are still basically Christian. But it's a lot more forgiving, more self-directed. Dad would have seen it as a total cop-out.'

But of course Roy would have seen his son's whole life as a cop-out, the unfinished degree, the orchestra, his broken marriage to Yvette and, worst of all, his failure to look after the women, particularly Heather, first as a teenager and now in middle age. If Roy were looking down on him from heaven, Adam knew he would see a complete write-off, although he suspected that God himself might be a little more forgiving.

It was, Adam thought now as he climbed back into the car, hard to be a believer when so many of those around you assumed that you shared their disbelief. He watched Jill, Kirsty and Toby heading back, their hands full of takeaway coffee, drink cans and a large bag of barbecue chips. Bringing up the rear, Daisy was being given a shoulder ride by the recently hated Nick; she was squealing with delight and splashing milkshake into his hair. Adam glanced in the mirror and rubbed his hands over his face, hoping to brighten his expression. His father would have told him that God was the answer; he would have found solace in the word and the law of his religion. How much more simple life would be, Adam thought, if he could do the same.

*

'Children!' Ellis said in horror as Heather turned into Barbara's driveway, where Toby and another boy were dragging a large Esky from the back of Adam's car. 'You didn't mention children . . .'

Toby abandoned his helper, bounded over to them and flung open Heather's car door. 'Aunty Heather, I'm making a model of the gun that shot you. It's a kit, come and see. I haven't painted it yet, but when I have I could make another one for you, if you like.'

'Really, Toby? That's very kind of you,' Heather said. 'This is Ellis.'

'Hi,' Toby said, nodding in Ellis's direction. 'And I've got a picture of the bullets for you too, I found it on the Internet. I think I'm going to start collecting bullets, so if you don't want yours could I have it, please?'

Ellis snorted and got out of the car.

'The police have it, Toby,' Heather explained. 'It's evidence.'

'When they've caught him, then?'

'I doubt it,' Heather said. 'I think they keep those things for years. Anyway, I'd like to see your model. D'you want to get my bag out of the boot for me?'

'More children,' said Ellis, flattening himself against the side of the car as Daisy raced up the path with George's grandchildren in pursuit.

'I'm in charge of Aunty Barbara's presents,' Daisy announced, looking suspiciously at Ellis. 'So you can give your present to me and I'll look after it.'

'I don't have a present,' Ellis said. 'Who are you, anyway?'

'I'm Daisy, and these are Gareth and Emily and that's Simon over there with Toby, they're Uncle George's grandchildren.'

'You didn't tell me there'd be children,' Ellis said, looking accusingly at Heather over the top of the car.

'Family party,' she smiled. 'Bound to be children. They're all quite civilised really, just excited.'

'You should've brought a present,' Daisy said. 'Everyone else has.'

'Heather's brought a present,' Ellis said. 'I just brought flowers. You can look after those, if you like, they're in the boot. My name is Ellis, by the way.'

Daisy pulled a face, clapped a hand over her mouth and rolled her eyes. 'That's a silly name,' she said. 'Poor you. I'll get the flowers. I hope they're not carnations because Aunty Barbara hates carnations.'

'They're not carnations,' Ellis said.

'Phew! That's a relief.' Daisy raced around the car, kissed Heather, grabbed the flowers from the boot and headed off to the house, followed by her entourage.

'Amazing,' said Ellis, who was not keen on children, including his own.

'When did you last see your grandchildren?' Heather asked, locking the car door.

'Never,' Ellis said. 'I told you, they live in Adelaide.'

'It's not all that far away, you must have visited –'

'No,' Ellis said. 'Never. Has the boy taken your bag or do you need me to carry it in for you?'

George was standing in the sitting room watching the children chase each other around the front lawn, and feeling a pleasant sense of anticipation. He was frequently at a loss for ways to show Barbara how much he appreciated her. How much he really loved her. He'd never said it, of course, not 'I love you, Barbara'. It seemed too difficult, as though it might be attached to all sorts of expectations. He was pretty sure that she didn't want or need him to say it, that it would embarrass her, that she would turn to him with that indulgent smile that she never gave anyone else and tell him not to be such an old fool. No, he wouldn't say it, but he hoped she knew.

'Suppose we'd met years ago,' he'd said to her one evening after a couple of glasses of wine. 'D'you think we'd have got married?'

'I've put a good bit of effort into avoiding marriage,' she'd said with a laugh. 'I expect I'd have managed to avoid it with you too.'

'I reckon we'd have been good together,' George responded. 'Right time, right circumstances, we'd have made a go of it.'

She'd turned to look at him then. 'You never know,' she said. 'Maybe I would have made an exception in your case.'

Well, he'd organised the party, her first ever, he was very happy about that and they were off to China together. So many of his old friends and colleagues had already dropped off their perches or were living half-lives alone watching daytime television with a cask of red and shaking their fists at kids on skateboards. That could have been him if fate hadn't generously decided that his retirement and his potentially lonely life as a widower should run parallel to Barbara's. What a stroke of luck that was. Sometimes it even made him think there might be a god.

'Why are you skulking in here, George?' Barbara asked, popping her head around the open door.

'I'm not skulking, just watching the kids,' George said.

She joined him at the window. 'Jill's made a beautiful birthday cake with candles. It even has my name and happy birthday written on it.'

'Thank goodness for that,' he answered. 'I'd completely forgotten about a cake.'

'You thought of everything else,' Barbara said. 'There's enough food and wine in the kitchen to feed several rugby teams.'

'Forgot to invite them too. But better too much than not enough, that's what my mother would have said.'

'Mine would have talked about greed being an offence before the Lord,' Barbara said. 'I still feel rather guilty about it but I'm embracing the concept of abundance.'

'So you should,' George said, glancing out of the window. 'You are a very generous person, time to be on the receiving end. Good lord, what the hell's Ellis Hargreaves doing here?'

Barbara peered over his shoulder. 'Oh, that must be Heather's new man, the old boyfriend I told you about. Do you know him?'

'You mean that man is going to be sleeping in my house?'

'Yes,' Barbara said, 'you suggested it.'

'You didn't tell me it was Ellis Hargreaves.'

'How was I to know you knew him?' Barbara said. 'Anyway, he looks nice, very good looking.'

'Arrogant bastard,' George said. 'Defended some pond life that tried to poison a whole batch of fertiliser on a strawberry farm. Could've killed anyone who ate the strawberries. I was an expert witness for the prosecution.'

'Oh dear,' Barbara said, watching Heather and Ellis talking to each other over the top of the car. 'Well, he was just doing his job. I'm sure he's a very nice person.'

'I doubt it,' George said, 'but for your sake, my very dear Barbara, I will be a model of civility.'

'Thank you, George,' she said, leaning over to kiss his cheek. 'And for Heather's sake too.'

'For Heather's sake too,' he repeated, 'but mostly for you,' and he returned her kiss.

'I've put the house up for sale,' Diane told Shaun on the drive to Morpeth. 'I'm going to look for somewhere smaller, somewhere just for me.'

'Sounds like a good idea,' Shaun said. 'It's a very big house.'

'Yes, but it's not just that. It's full of the past. I want to get away from that. Charlene's got a new life, it's time I got one too.'

Shaun looked at her briefly before turning back to the road. 'That sounds even better. Very positive.' He was surprised how much he liked Diane now. Women seemed to dominate his life these days – older women, especially. A couple of weeks earlier, at a conference he'd attended in place of Heather, he'd met a woman called Rosa Hartman, who was an expert in voting patterns and ran her own political consultancy. They'd had lunch together both days and Shaun had felt his old enthusiasm for the big issues returning. Working in the electorate office it was easy to get blinkered by smaller, local issues, but talking to Rosa had reminded him of his earlier ambitions and made him restless.

He slowed down for some traffic lights and looked again at Diane. 'Have you heard from Charlene?'

'This morning,' Diane said. 'She loves it up there. She's moved into a flat with a couple of other girls who work at the resort. She sounded really happy and settled. She even said something nice about you.'

Shaun raised his eyebrows. 'Things *are* looking up.'

Diane laughed. 'Yes, well, it's all thanks to you. So, tonight we'll get a look at Heather's friend. You've met him, haven't you?'

'Only once,' Shaun said. 'In Sydney, just after he'd been apprehended by the police, so it probably wasn't the best time.'

'And?'

Shaun shrugged. 'He seemed okay, bit condescending maybe
but, as I said, he probably wasn't at his best.' He slowed again as
the lights changed to red, and drew to a halt, turning towards her.
'He wasn't the sort of person I'd ever imagined Heather with,' he
said. 'Not the sort of person at all.'

'Really? Sometimes it's hard to know what people see in each
other,' Diane said. 'And it's harder still to look back on your own
relationships and wonder what you once saw in a person. I guess
we all have to kiss a few frogs before the right person comes
along, and one person's frog is another's prince. I always thought
Heather was through with frogs *and* princes, but someone from
the past has a certain magic and mystery, I suppose.'

'So I gather you're not too keen on Ellis Hargreaves?' George said,
putting a glass of his best Pinot into Adam's hand.

'You could say that, but I've promised to be discreet and
civilised.'

'Me too.'

'You mean you know him?' Adam said in surprise.

'I've met him,' George said. 'In court. And you could say I've
followed his career with interest.'

'And?'

'Well, there's no doubt he was a first-rate criminal lawyer, and
someone has to defend the criminal classes and those innocents
who somehow get on the wrong side of the system. But he does
seem to have made a habit of successfully defending people who
are later revealed to be guilty as hell.'

'I'm sure Heather would tell me that's simply because he was
good at his job,' Adam said.

'That may be so, but there's something about him that makes
me feel it was more about the Hargreaves ego than about protect-
ing the rights of the accused. I don't think we're talking principles
here.'

Adam sipped his wine and held the glass up to the fading light. 'That wouldn't surprise me at all,' he said.

'He tells me he's into something else now,' George said, gesturing to Adam to walk with him to the barbecue, where Toby and Simon were tinkering with the charcoal. 'Said he'd done a sea change thing, reassessed his values, and he's in the business of helping people find their true selves through life-coaching.'

'So I heard,' Adam said with a laugh. 'What total crap.'

'Apparently he's got a PR consultant working on it, and they're developing a marketing plan. Head to heart – rat race to mind–body something or other – something in there about setting spiritual goals, I believe.'

'Oh, for fuck's sake,' Adam said. 'If Ellis Hargreaves has a spiritual bone in his body, then I'm the Pope.'

George picked up a pair of barbecue tongs and handed them to Toby. 'You can start putting the steaks on now. Toby, and Simon, can you run inside and bring the chicken and prawns out of the fridge, please.' He paused to watch his grandson head off to the back door at a run. 'I think your chances of being Pope are slim, Adam,' he said. 'Hargreaves is about as spiritual as my arse, but I suspect he believes his own publicity and that he's developed all the right language to sell this crap to people with more money than sense.'

'He's probably selling it to Heather too,' Adam said, 'and she's in just the right state of mind to fall for it.'

'And I have to have him in my house,' George said as the first steaks sizzled on the grill. 'The things we do for those we love.'

'Are you part of the family too?' Diane asked as Stefan came over to her with a bottle to top up her glass.

He shook his head. 'Sadly, no. But I am what is called a hanging-on.' He held out his hand. 'Stefan, I am in the orchestra with Adam.'

'Diane,' she said, shaking hands. 'I'm a hanger-on too.'

'Ah! Hanger-on, yes; sorry, I am still doing the battle with English. So, where do you do the hanging-on?'

'In Heather's office,' Diane said. 'I was a volunteer but some-one's sick and so now I'm doing her job while she's away.'

Stefan sat down beside her. 'It is very pretty here,' he said, look-ing up at the trees that George had hung with fairy lights. 'George has done it very nicely, I think.' He turned to her. 'And which gentleman is your husband?'

'I don't have a husband,' Diane said. 'I'm divorced.'

'I'm sorry,' Stefan said.

'Don't be, I'm not. I was for a very long time and now I'm not. And you?'

'My wife is dead,' he said without looking up. 'She and my daughter, they are killed in Kosovo bombing. Collateral damage, it is called. This is one expression I never get wrong.'

'How terrible for you,' Diane said. 'I can't even begin to imag-ine how you must feel. But you're here, playing in the orchestra. How did you get your life together –'

'Anger,' Stefan said, looking up at her now. 'I am so angry I want to kill anyone who talks to me. So, I have to leave, to get away from places where I see them always, the house, the street, my daughter's school. It is the only way I can live again.'

'You're not angry now, though.'

'Sometimes yes, but I learn to live with it. I turn it into gratitude.'

'Gratitude?'

He shrugged. 'For their lives, for the time I had with them, for my survival, for being here in this beautiful country.'

'But what about the grief, the bitterness?'

'The grief does not go away. Seven years and each day I am grieving still, but bitterness?' Stefan sighed. 'You know, Diane, I think that I am spared and that means I must live a good life. I must not be eating it up with being angry and bitter. Do you not think?'

Diane had a sudden urge to touch him, as though some of his serenity and wisdom might rub off on her. She put her hand on his arm and he smiled, reaching up and putting his hand on top of hers. 'I think you are absolutely right,' she said. 'I haven't had to face anything like that and yet I've wasted the last two years of my life plunging around in my own sea of anger and bitterness. And now suddenly it's changed and I can see I have the chance to be different, to do what I want. I just can't work out what that is.'

Stefan laughed. 'I know this feeling,' he said. 'One minute it is full of power and opportunities, the next minute it is just confusion and emptiness.'

'Exactly.'

'Do you come sometimes to Sydney?'

'Yes, of course.'

'Then you come please to see my garden. It is my peace of mind. I make it for them, for Katya and Anna. New life, the plants, growing – you know, it helps.'

'I'd love to see it, if you're sure.'

'Come soon then, please,' he said. 'We can plant a tree for you, for you to be different.'

'I'm not really a gardener,' Diane said.

Stefan shrugged. 'I dig the hole, you put the tree, I put back the earth, you water the tree,' he said. 'It is easy, we do it together.'

Sitting on the verandah steps watching George supervising Toby and Simon at the barbecue, Jill wondered whether Adam had it in him to organise a party. He certainly had the goodwill, would even have the intent, but since talking to Barbara and Heather she had arrived at the conclusion that circumstances were draining him of much else.

'Aunty Barb's wonderful, isn't she?' Kirsty said, joining her on the steps. 'Imagine going to China at seventy-six, and that teaching course. She and George are awesome.'

'Mmm,' Jill agreed. 'They are. They're a constant reminder that energy is renewable. Most of the time it feels as though it's finite and I am about to use the last dregs of mine.'

'You should take a holiday,' Kirsty said. 'You and Dad, go off somewhere nice on your own. Nick and I could stay with Tobes and Daisy, if you like.'

'That's very generous of you,' Jill said, turning to her in surprise. 'Very generous, I hadn't thought . . . '

'Well, maybe you *should*.'

'I'd actually been thinking of something rather different.'

'Like what?'

'Like going off somewhere on my own, somewhere that I don't have to speak to anyone, where no one expects anything of me, and other people make my bed and put nice food in front of me.'

'Without Dad?'

Jill nodded.

'Good on you,' Kirsty said.

'But Adam –'

'He'd be fine.'

'He won't like it.'

Kirsty shrugged. 'So? He goes off on tour, and he went on that musical retreat thing. Why shouldn't you have a break too?'

'I don't know how he'd manage, the kids, everything, himself . . . '

'He's a grown man, Jill,' Kirsty said, taking a sip of her beer and putting the can down on the step. 'It would do him good to have to take over for a while.'

'But he's fragile at the moment . . . I'm afraid he might think it was a prelude to me leaving him, which, of course, it's not.'

Kirsty looked at her. 'He's no more fragile than you, and you can reassure him about the other stuff.'

'Well, I don't think –'

'Jill, just do it. I'll tell you this, from what I can see something needs to happen to shake Dad up a bit.'

'But that's it, he's shaken up already.'

'But not enough to change. Tough love. This might be just what it takes.'

'I didn't think it showed.'

'Jill, hello!' Kirsty said. 'Talk about the bleedin' obvious. I can see it more clearly since I moved out. Either he's depressed and needs to get some help, or something has to kick-start him out of wherever he's at.'

'But it seems unfair . . . '

'Now you're being ridiculous,' Kirsty said. 'It's only a week or two, and Nick and I will help him with the kids. What about that woman who went off to France for six months? You know, the gardening woman who wrote a book about it, we saw her on TV. And here *you* are feeling guilty about a week or two. Come on, Jill, get a life.'

'I'm so glad you came, Diane,' Barbara said. 'How are you feeling?'

'Embarrassed,' Diane said. 'I want to apologise for dumping my life on you that morning. I had no right; after all, we hardly knew each other.'

'We do now, and it was absolutely okay,' Barbara said. 'I told you, I'm a very nosy person. I always want to hear people's stories.'

'I just heard Stefan's story,' Diane said.

'That really makes you think about priorities, doesn't it? Are you going to see his garden?'

'He's invited me.'

'Then go, it's very special.'

'He's not like any other man I've met,' Diane said. 'And your friend George is lovely too. He told me you're the light of his life.'

'He does tend to say that.'

'I think he means it.'

Barbara looked at her and smiled. 'He does, and I reciprocate. It's interesting how, as you get older, you appreciate things in people that you would have shunned in the past.'

'Like what?' Diane asked.

'Steadiness, reliability, values – most of all, values.'

'And you didn't appreciate those things in the past?'

Barbara laughed. 'Not in men, I'm afraid. I always went for raciness, danger, instant sexual chemistry with men who were terrific lovers, emotional cripples and totally unreliable.'

'You're kidding?'

'Not at all. I was a thrill seeker – a reaction, I think, to a very

163

austere religious upbringing. My poor mother would have turned in her grave if she knew what I got up to when I escaped from home.'

'Well, George is pretty different,' Diane said, 'so presumably you've changed too. Are you and he . . . ?' She hesitated, realising she was on the verge of embarrassing them both.

'No,' Barbara said. 'We're the best of friends, and yes, I've changed. Celibacy suits me. And I've discovered that one can have love and intimacy without sex. It suits me down to the ground.' She turned to Diane suddenly. 'Actually, I've never said that to anyone before. You can't say that sort of thing to people who are your de facto children; it embarrasses them to even think you ever had a sex life at all.'

Diane laughed. 'But you're seventy-six today,' she said. 'Surely that entitles you to do whatever you want?'

'Maybe,' Barbara said. 'But I think I shall hold my tongue. There are already a few too many secrets causing trouble in this family.'

'You're taking it all very personally, Adam,' Heather said. They were sitting on the seat at the bottom of the garden, away from the group clustered around the barbecue. 'It's a very long time ago.'

'And I have a very long memory,' Adam said. 'Look, Heather, it's your life, your business. I've been civil to him but nothing is going to make me like Ellis, or forgive him, for that matter.'

Heather sat, looking over to where Barbara was letting Daisy open one of her birthday presents. She could barely remember a time when she and Adam had been seriously at odds about anything. She hated that she was both hurt by and hurting him. 'Isn't forgiveness part of what you believe in?'

'Yes, but certain things I find impossible to forgive and this is one of them.'

'Selective forgiveness, then.'

'I'm not claiming to be God, Heather, we all have our limits.'

'Look,' she said, 'I don't want to hurt you, really I don't. You were wonderful to me all through that time, and I'll always be grateful for that. But I loved Ellis then, that was why it was so hard, and now . . . well . . . now I think I still love him, and he loves me. I want this chance to see if it can work.'

Adam nodded. 'I know. Jill says I'm being selfish and I do want you to be happy, Heather, you know that. But this . . . ' He shook his head. 'It makes me feel . . . '

Heather swung round to face him, blazing with a sudden surge of anger. 'It's not about what *you* feel, Adam. Can you even begin to imagine how *I* feel? Someone who hates me and everything I stand for drove up in the dark and shot me, and that person is still out there somewhere, waiting to try again. Everything I do, everywhere I go, I wonder if he's round the next corner, behind the next bush, outside my window, watching me in the supermarket, in the office, at home, everywhere. And you know how that feels? Well, it's terrifying, more terrifying than you could ever imagine, and it makes me feel utterly and completely alone. And now someone comes along who just wants to help me through this; someone who loves me and makes me feel safe. And you want me to turn my back on that because of what happened in the past. You want me to throw it all away, because of the past.'

The tension strung out like fine wire between them. Adam got up.

'I'm sorry, Heather,' he said. 'I really can understand that this must all be quite terrible for you. And I can also understand how unsafe you feel and how you want to grab at anything that eases that feeling. What I simply can't get my head around is that at this really awful time in your life you are able to find safety with the one person who, in the past, put you at very great risk, a risk, I'd add, that has had lasting consequences for you. That's what I can't understand.' And he walked away from her to where Toby and one of George's grandsons were messing about with a box of matches and the burnt-out candles from Barbara's birthday cake.

TWELVE

Barbara had grown up with hard work at school and at home and with the prospect of hard work in a boring job in a shop or a factory until she married and took on the hard work of looking after a husband and children. She was a girl in training to be a good wife, and Beryl Delaney was determined that the devil would not find any opportunities between school, prayers, bible study and domesticity to get his hands on her daughter. The interesting thing, Barbara often reflected, was that it had seemed all right at the time, the way things should be. She didn't fight it, didn't argue, didn't even think about what she might be missing until just before her fourteenth birthday, when she came top in everything except arithmetic and her teacher suggested she should stay on at school.

'You could get a scholarship, Barbara,' Miss Wootton had said, 'to allow you to stay on here, and then go to university.'

Barbara's understanding of the world outside school, home and chapel was limited, but when Miss Wootton explained scholarships and opportunities and the sort of jobs for which she might be suited, Barbara was sold on the idea. Selling it to her parents was another matter.

'Who's going to pay for it?' Stan Delaney asked Miss Wootton. 'We're working people, you know, proud of it. Her brother's apprenticed to a cabinet-maker. I don't know what she wants with all that education.'

'And who'll marry her stuck with her nose in a book all day?'

Beryl said. 'It doesn't do for girls to be too clever, and we don't want her getting into trouble.'

'The scholarship will pay for her,' Miss Wootton explained. 'It'll pay the education costs, and leave something for her keep.' But she chickened out on the subject of getting into trouble. That was a battle Barbara would have to fight alone.

It took patience and persistence to convince them that her morality and godliness were, thanks to their training, invincible. Smart enough now to navigate her way around her parents, she made sure she kept up with all those things which, if abandoned, would signal moral decline. She went to every prayer meeting and bible-study class, kept her place in the chapel's cleaning roster and never shirked her share of the housework. Now, years later, it amazed her that once she had escaped she threw herself with immediate abandon into a comparatively wild life for a young woman in the fifties. But learning had been her escape route and had remained a part of her life, so the first few hours of the ESL course really didn't faze her. George, on the other hand, was having an anxiety attack after the first session on Monday morning.

'There's so much,' he whispered to her as they stretched their legs in the corridor during a break. 'I won't be able to remember it.'

'You don't have to remember it all,' Barbara told him. 'The trick is in working out what you need to remember and what you just need to know is there. You need to learn process, method and practice. *How*, that's what's important. Listen for the *how* – the *what* you can always check on later.'

'And they're all so young. No one in there is over twelve.'

'Rubbish. They're mostly in their twenties – thirties, even – and that woman in the green dress is in her fifties. So is the man with the glasses. Stop panicking.'

'But lesson plans,' George insisted. 'I've never written a lesson plan in my life.'

'Nor has anyone else, George,' Robert Sachs said, materialising beside them. 'Don't fall into the trap of thinking that the others know more than you do just because they're younger. They don't, and neither do they have the wealth of life experience you bring to it. Stay cool, you'll be fine. Worn to a frazzle, but fine.'

But by the Friday of the first week, even Barbara was feeling the strain. 'This is the most intense learning experience I've ever had,' she said as they sat on a seat in the park at lunchtime eating their sandwiches. 'Thank god it's the weekend.'

'You too?' George said. 'That's a relief. I thought I was the only one who was swamped.'

She shook her head, her mouth full of tuna and cucumber on rye. 'No way. I spoke to some of the others and we're all in the same boat. I could happily lie down under that tree for a nap.'

'We could lie on my coat,' George suggested. 'I could set the alarm on my phone so we don't miss the next class.'

'Oh, I don't know,' Barbara said, glancing around at the other people in the park. 'We're a bit old for that, aren't we? What would people think?'

'Who cares?' he said, getting up, brushing crumbs off his trousers and shaking out his raincoat.

'We'll look like tramps.'

'Couple over there are lying on the grass and they don't look like tramps.'

'But they're young,' Barbara said, 'and they're necking.'

'And we're old codgers and we're having a rest. You can sit up there if you like but I'm having a catnap,' and he started fiddling with his phone.

'My mother would be horrified.'

'Your mother,' George said, lowering himself onto the raincoat, 'is having her own afternoon nap watched over by angels. We'll be back in class before she wakes up.'

Barbara didn't hear George's phone beeping forty minutes later. She was so soundly asleep that when he shook her arm and called her name repeatedly, she felt as though she were being dragged up from the bottom of the sea.

'Come on,' George said, reaching down to give her his hand. 'Stone the crows, that ground's hard. Let's get moving or we'll be late.'

Barbara struggled to her feet and straightened her skirt. 'We should bring bedrolls on Monday,' she said, 'then we could lie about under the trees in comfort. I had the weirdest dream, about Adam and his cello –'

'Never mind that now,' George said. 'Let's get going, you can tell me about it on the way home.'

But Barbara didn't tell him about the dream because, before it evaporated under the pressure of the next class, it revived the memory of something previously forgotten.

'Are you on your own, Jill?' she asked on the phone that evening, feeling conspiratorial. 'Or is Adam there?'

'Sorry, Barb, he's out, back in about an hour. Thanks so much for the weekend. We all loved it, and the kids are still eating up the remains of your birthday cake. D'you want Adam to call you when he gets in?'

'No, it's you I want to talk to. But before I forget, what did you think of Ellis?'

'Well, he wasn't what I expected,' Jill said cautiously. 'I actually thought he was a bit up himself, but I've decided to reserve judgment. What about you?'

'The same, really,' Barbara said. 'I didn't warm to him much but I didn't dislike him either. It must have been difficult for him with all of us sizing him up, and Heather seems so happy that I'm giving him the benefit of the doubt. Anyway, what I wanted to tell you was that I remembered something today, about that time . . . you know, what we were talking about – Heather and Adam, the Ellis time?'

'Really?'

'Yes, today I realised that it was about the time that Dorothy and I went on a cruise.'

'A cruise, Barb? You?'

'Yes I know, not my sort of thing, is it, but Dorothy was dying to go, so I agreed. I got rather bored on the ship but the stops were interesting, and the final one was in Fremantle and we got off there and had a look at Perth before we came back to Sydney on another boat, so we were away for several weeks.'

'So what are you saying?' Jill said, puzzled.

'When we got back – the most extraordinary thing, Adam had pawned his cello.'

'Pawned his cello?'

'Yes, it's odd, isn't it? I can't believe I'd completely forgotten about it, but there you are. It's surprising what one forgets. He told me the day after we got back and he begged me not to tell Dorothy. He said he'd needed money and that was all he could think of to do. He asked me to lend him the money to get it back and not ask any questions.'

'So what did you do?'

'I gave him the money of course, and I didn't ask any questions, although I do remember being quite worried about it. Anyway, he retrieved it, and a couple of months later he paid me back the money.'

'How much was it?' Jill asked.

'That's what I can't remember,' Barbara said. 'I remember it seemed like quite a lot, although I suppose it wouldn't be in today's terms.'

'And you never found out what the money was for?'

'Never. Well, I never asked. In fact, I must have forgotten about it quite soon after, and I haven't thought about it for years. He didn't seem to be in any trouble and I can't remember any consequences, so I suppose I just forgot.'

'I see,' Jill said. 'I mean, I don't really see, it's such an extraordinary thing for Adam to do. You don't think there was a girl, perhaps . . . could he have got someone pregnant?'

'I was thinking about that on the way home today,' Barbara replied. 'But it doesn't make sense. Adam was still in his religious phase then. He was twenty-one, and I'm sure I've heard him say that he was a virgin until he was twenty-three.'

'That's right,' Jill said. 'He laughs about it, says he was a late developer.'

'There you are,' Barbara said. 'And, Jill, I'd rather you didn't mention this to Adam. I'd prefer to ask him about it myself sometime when we're together, when it feels right.'

'Of course,' Jill said thoughtfully, 'no, I won't mention it.' And as she hung up, Jill was already pretty sure who and what Adam might have needed the money for, and that it might have been very much to do with Ellis Hargreaves.'

Heather, surrounded by pressing tasks, felt incapable of starting on anything. She sat, shoes off, her feet resting on a pile of Hansards, staring at the desk calendar, the one that showed the parliamentary sitting weeks blocked out and highlighted in yellow: sixteen weeks, three sitting sessions since the shooting. Sixteen weeks ago she had been in the hospital bed, confident that before she was released an arrest would have been made and that by Christmas it would all be over and forgotten. If only. Alex Roussos kept assuring her that the police regarded her case as a high priority and were still working on it but it was hard to believe as weeks passed with no further developments. She had given up pointless speculation about who might have been responsible and was simply waiting for something to happen.

Outside the office window a car door slammed and Heather leapt to her feet, adrenaline pumping, heart pounding. Was there no end to it? It was easy for Ellis to talk about how catching the gunman wasn't the issue, how she had to learn to feel safe within herself. He didn't see the shadows, hear the noises, feel the sweat break out on his skin as hormones charged around his body; he hadn't been shot.

'You must try to put it in the past, Heather,' he said. 'He may *not* come back. Didn't the police say that if he was going to try again it would have happened sooner rather than later?'

Alex had, indeed, said that this was the most likely scenario but he also said, in a roundabout way which was supposed not to scare her but to make her alert, that there was always a chance that the person would try again – weeks, months, even years later.

'It's like driving,' Ellis had persisted. 'Every day we have a very high chance of getting killed or injured on the roads, yet we drive confidently to and from work, or the shops, or wherever, and don't give it a thought. You have to make it like that in your mind, awareness without a sense of persecution.'

'That's easy for you,' Heather had said. 'You can't know what this is like. Even Shaun feels it just because he was there, and they weren't shooting at him.'

'I can't help you if you resist everything I say,' he'd said irritably. 'Healing only works if you are open to the message of the healer.'

'And don't talk to me as though I'm one of your clients,' she'd snapped back. 'I told you on day one that I didn't need a counsellor.'

Heather's heart settled again, and she dropped heavily back into her chair. Why did everything have to be so hard? Why did she always seem to be struggling? The one time she had actually gone to see a therapist, years earlier in her thirties, she'd asked those very questions, and the woman had questioned her about her birth experience.

'How would I know?' Heather had responded, thinking it a stupid question. 'I wasn't there. I mean I was, but not with any sort of intellectual consciousness.'

'But what did your mother tell you about your birth?' the woman asked patiently.

'Oh, I see what you mean. Well, apparently I was in the breech position and I had to be turned and the cord was round my neck. I think Mum said they used forceps.'

'There you are then,' the therapist said with a triumphant smile. 'You were born in struggle, and you continue to repeat that. You create struggle for yourself, you choose the hardest way of doing things.'

'No I don't,' Heather had protested. 'I'd kill to find easy ways to do things.'

'But you don't *allow* yourself to find them. Struggle is part of who you are, the way you see yourself in the world. You need to let go of the birth experience, and then you can stop struggling.'

Heather paid the bill, left and never went back.

'That sounds like very good advice,' Ellis had said when she told him. 'We could do some meditation around that, if you like.' And she had shouted at him then. Shouted! She, who had never in her life shouted at anyone, had shouted at him to shut up and stop counselling her, shut up and start being her friend, her lover, anything, but stop acting like some guru. She'd surprised herself with the intensity of her anger and the abandon with which she'd let rip.

'Maybe it's because I love you so much,' she'd said later. 'Perhaps the intensity one feels for a person is reflected at all levels in the relationship. So I love you more than anyone and in consequence get madder at you than I do with anyone else.'

On the other hand, Ellis could be exceptionally infuriating, and her anger had flared again the next day when, searching for her keys on the coffee table, she'd moved some of the papers he'd been working on for his book and saw that he had noted down the thing the therapist had said about birth experience.

'It's good stuff,' he'd protested, 'I can use it.'

'Aren't you supposed to be creating your own good stuff,' she'd said, 'not nicking other people's?'

They hadn't spoken for a couple of hours after that. Heather had never experienced such extremes of emotion. Where was it all coming from? She had always been such an equable person. Now here she was shouting at Ellis one minute, and aching with love and lust the next, high as a kite or deep in gloom, losing it with Adam, revealing so much to Jill and then, at Barbara's party, bursting into tears at the sight of Daisy and Emily doing an improvised fairy dance. What was the matter with her? Was it the bullet that had unleashed this great well of emotions, or was it something to do with being in love? Whatever the cause, it simply made life more complicated, and didn't help alongside the terminal boredom she was feeling in relation to her job. For the first time ever she wished she could write a letter of resignation, give two weeks' notice and leave.

'You *could* do that,' Ellis had said at the weekend. 'It wouldn't be the wise or responsible thing to do, but you *could* do it. So maybe you need to find the wise and responsible way and think about doing that.'

'There is no wise and responsible way. Not for another year, not until after the next election.'

'That's rubbish, Heather. No one's indispensable and this is bleeding-heart crap.'

'I'm being realistic,' she'd protested. 'The party needs me, the electoral boundaries have been changed to our disadvantage and because I've been here for so long, I'm the candidate with the best chance of holding the seat. Besides, there's the constituents – look how wonderful they were when I was shot. I owe it to them.'

'You don't owe them anything, and they wouldn't hesitate to vote against you if it suited them.'

'You are so hard, Ellis,' she'd said, throwing herself on the sofa in frustration.

'I'm not hard, I'm realistic. A man would not be poncing around like this. A man would do the best thing for himself in the circumstances.'

'Some men.'

'Most men.'

'Well, I'm not a man, something for which I've always been thankful.'

'Fuck it, Heather, you are *so* argumentative. You never used to be like this.'

She'd got up then and put her arms around his neck. 'No, I used to agree with you and do as you told me all the time. And look where that got me.'

'That was a cheap shot,' he said, but he kissed her all the same and minutes later they were both half naked on the primrose damask in full view of the ground-floor windows.

'If you resigned,' Ellis said later, zipping up his fly, 'we'd have more time together. You haven't even been up to my place yet. I want you to come to Byron Bay, stay with me, see my house. But you always seem to have things on at weekends.'

And so she'd promised him she would cancel everything for the weekend after next and fly up from Sydney for a long weekend between sitting weeks. It was so tempting to dump everything, everything she'd built up here in the electorate, and retire, relax, take a long holiday, read more, exercise more and, most of all, have more time with Ellis here in Newcastle and in Byron Bay.

'And you haven't even had time to read the business plan properly,' he'd said. 'It would be nice if you could take a bit more interest in it.'

He was right, she hadn't read it yet. She kept putting it off, and not just because of the pressure of work. There was something about the whole idea of it that made her uneasy. It sounded a little too New Agey for comfort. She wished that Ellis could just go and get on with it without her ever having to know any more about it but that, of course, would be totally unfair.

There was a tap on the office door and Diane opened it. 'I thought I might go to lunch,' Diane said, 'if that's okay with you.'

'Sure,' Heather said. Diane was proving to be a real asset, and with Shaun away taking a much needed break, she was managing the office better than Patsy ever had. 'Sure, but look, why don't we just shut the office for an hour and go together?'

Diane's eyebrows shot up. 'Shut the office?'

'Why not? We're entitled to a lunch break, aren't we?'

'Shaun would have a fit.'

'He's not here,' Heather said, 'and if we don't tell him, he'll never know. Besides, I'm actually the boss, and if I say we can go, we can go.'

'So how's the house sale going?' Heather asked once they'd found an empty table. 'Any joy yet?'

'We've had an offer at the asking price,' Diane said. 'The agent rang this morning. He's bringing the paperwork over this evening so Gerry and I can sign off on it.'

'That's so quick,' Heather said. 'But maybe you should see if you can push the price up a bit.'

'I want out,' Diane said, pouring herself some water. 'And Gerry wants his share of the money freed up.'

'How long have you been there?'

'Seventeen years. And since I got back from the Gold Coast, I've been so fixated on getting out I haven't even begun to think about where I'll go.'

'What does Charlene think?'

'Charlene is too busy with her new life to be particularly interested. I guess I'll put everything into storage and rent somewhere while I look around.' Diane watched Heather cutting her focaccia into four equal parts and rearranging them on the plate. If she'd been having lunch with any other woman, she'd be asking her how her new love life was going, but Heather? What the hell. 'So what about you, Heather, how are things going with you and Ellis?'

Heather smiled. 'Good, I think. But it's hard work being in a relationship, isn't it? I've lived alone for so many years and you get used to doing your own thing without having to take anyone else into account.'

'But he's up in Byron Bay most of the time, isn't he?' Diane asked. 'It's not like he's living with you.'

'No, he's not. But it's about having someone else in your head all the time even when they're not around, having responsibilities to them, living up to their expectations. Sometimes I think I'm missing that gene, that I'm a person who's supposed to be alone. But then I think, well, I'm so lucky, not many people get a second chance.' She paused. 'Ellis is an unusual person but then, you've met him, Diane. What did you think? Did you like him?'

Diane almost choked on a rocket leaf. Heather was asking *her* what she thought, talking to *her* like a friend. 'Sorry,' she said, patting her lips with the paper napkin, 'went down the wrong way.'

'Are you okay?'

'Fine, thanks.' She drank some water.

'So, did you like him?'

Diane thought Heather sounded like Charlene when she brought home her first boyfriend – proud, triumphant almost, but also terribly vulnerable. 'Of course I liked him,' she lied. 'He's a very charming man.' Charming was the best she could manage and at least it was sort of true, because there was no doubt in her mind that Ellis went out of his way to be charming, particularly to women, but he had failed to charm her.

'Marks out of ten for Ellis?' Shaun had said on the drive home. 'I give him five.'

'On what basis?' Diane had asked.

'Well, I don't think I'm really keen on him personally, but I'm being generous because he makes Heather happy and she really deserves that. Come on, your turn.'

'Oh, a grudging two and a half, I suppose,' Diane said. 'One for good looks, one for being obviously very intelligent, and a half . . . actually, no, scrub the half, I'll stick at two.'

'So you didn't like him at all?'

'I thought he was a totally pretentious wanker,' Diane said, 'and I wouldn't trust him with my toenail clippings.'

Shaun spluttered with laughter. 'Gee, I'm glad I didn't turn out to be your son-in-law. I'm sure I'd have been subjected to much more brutal assessment.'

'You were,' she said, 'and you outrank Ellis by miles in every possible category.'

Heather was pushing her food around the plate, and Diane felt a sudden burst of empathy. The cool, professional mask had slipped, and in a fraction of a second a different woman had been exposed.

'I'm so glad you liked him,' Heather said, smiling now. 'You see, my brother can't stand him, Barbara didn't say much at all, and my sister-in-law said she really hadn't had much of a chance to form an opinion. I so much wanted them all to love him, but I suppose they're cautious because they don't want me to get hurt again. So, you see, it's good to have an honest opinion from some-one who's totally objective.'

'I –' Diane began.

'No, really,' Heather cut in, 'we're about the same age, you and I, and you've been through a lot recently and I think that makes people more perceptive. So I really trust your opinion.'

THIRTEEN

Wendy, Ellis's first wife, was an argumentative woman – at least, in his opinion. Other people described her as forthright with a strong bullshit detector, but Ellis preferred argumentative. When they first met, Wendy had been twenty, sweet and rather mousy. Ellis was seven years older than her, it was the sixties, and a few years after they were married things started to change. First of all, Wendy had her hair cut and restyled into a blunt, straight Mary Quant bob that finished halfway down her ears, and dumped her floral print dresses and bought a pair of dungarees and several short shift dresses patterned with large bold blocks of contrasting primary colours. She also threw out her stockings and lacy suspender belts and started wearing flesh-coloured tights and talking about women's rights, chauvinism and patriarchal attitudes. Ellis told her he was all for women having equal rights, but Wendy was not convinced.

'I totally support women,' he told her frequently. 'I think women do amazing things. You more than anyone, Wendy, should know that in my mind women are on a pedestal.'

'That's what I *mean*,' Wendy replied. 'When you're on a pedestal there's only one way, and that's down. Equality actually means thinking of people as equal, not on different levels. You just haven't got a clue what I'm on about, have you? You just don't get it.'

What Ellis didn't know was that Betty Friedan had spoken to Wendy and spoken clearly. In *The Feminine Mystique*, a book she'd mistaken for one on fashion and cosmetics, she had recognised her own life to date, analysed and interpreted in ways that left her gasping for breath. Wendy never told Ellis about this, instead she joined one of the early consciousness-raising groups and her consciousness shot through the roof. Ellis never really understood what had hit him.

When the marriage was over he wished he'd been the one to end it, and that he had done so a few years earlier so that he and Heather could have been together. But he had run away from Heather when the going got tough, and stayed with Wendy because it seemed easier and because of the twins, then just eighteen months old, adorable and fairly easily confined to a playpen. How was he to know that by the time they were five years old he would have discovered that children were most definitely not his thing?

Ellis was in his late forties when he married Julia. She was the daughter of a former chief justice and wouldn't have been seen dead in dungarees. She had high-level connections, a Masters degree in art history, and was part owner of an elegant gallery where most people felt compelled to speak in hushed tones, though Julia and her partner would talk in loud, confident voices with accents more English than the English, and whinny with noisy laughter like thoroughbred racehorses. Ellis enjoyed Julia. She lacked the warmth, girlishness and romantic sensibility that he sought, but she was a splendid companion who opened all the right doors, and she was fun. So he was both amazed and insulted when she fled the marital home with an odd-job man who had done bits of construction work at the house and the gallery.

'How common,' Ellis said to himself when he read Julia's farewell note. 'How very trashy. I thought better of you, Julia, I really did.' And mentioning in the note that she was sure that, as a true romantic himself, Ellis would understand her need to follow her passion, was particularly hurtful. But he had recovered and had gone on to other, transient, relationships, confident that in time he would find the right person. Now, despite the initial hiccups, he knew he was on the right track and that this could be his last chance.

'I've so much to show you,' he'd said when Heather finally

cancelled some appointments and committed to a long weekend in Byron Bay. 'I can't believe you've never been to the Bay.'

Her visit would, he believed, be a significant step forward in their relationship. At last she would be on his territory; it was his opportunity to establish his ascendance in the relationship. In Sydney and Newcastle he was a guest, Heather called the shots, and his tolerance of that situation had worn very thin. And he'd made a big effort for her: he'd suffered through the birthday party, which was a nightmare swarming with children, but felt he'd behaved impeccably, even with the surly brother and the grumpy old sod who'd once given him grief as a prosecution witness. As he sorted through the papers on his desk, he even caught himself mumbling about a few days in Byron Bay being a chance to bring Heather to heel. The term shocked him with its inappropriateness but the sentiment was spot on.

He set himself to planning the weekend carefully to establish his role in their relationship and Heather's impression of him in this environment. He also wanted to talk with her about Head to Heart. He was finding the writing of the book extraordinarily difficult. Writing had come easily to him in the past; he had drawn on his rhetorical skills and knowledge of the law to create persuasive openings, memorable closing statements and finely tuned opinions. But right now he was struggling.

'I need to get you to look at this,' he'd said to Luke on the phone. 'Go through it with me.'

'Absolutely snowed under at present, Ellis,' Luke had said. 'Carry on. I'm sure it'll be splendid.'

Clearly, although Luke would drive the marketing and promotion, the content was down to him. The prospect of another mind being brought to bear on the material was very encouraging, and it would be a chance to show Heather that they could work together. Ellis looked forward to the coming weekend with enthusiasm, confident that by the time he drove her to the airport on the Monday evening, he would have demonstrated to her that they would make an excellent partnership, personal and professional.

*

Since the day he met Rosa Hartman at the conference, Shaun's old ambitions had returned to haunt him. He had planned to spend a couple of years in Heather's electorate office while he did his Masters part time, and then maybe move to federal politics or possibly the office of a state minister. But by the time he'd finished his Masters, he'd grown comfortable. The job gave him satisfaction, a measure of authority and the gratification of knowing he was really good at what he did. But now he wondered if his father was right when he said he should get out more. It wasn't only about meeting women, it was about broadening his horizons, moving further up the career ladder. That was why, during his few days off, he had arranged to meet Rosa Hartman. His life, he reflected, seemed to operate in the orbit of older women, and now he was orbiting another. He wondered if a therapist would suggest that it was compensation for his virtually non-existent relationship with his mother, but he didn't really care. Rosa was a political animal, she knew Heather and now him, and she was familiar with the party and the political landscape. Who better to nut out the issues?

'Sure thing,' she'd said when he called to make a time to see her while he was in Sydney. 'But let's have dinner. I live just off Oxford Street. Come to my place and we'll walk to this great little Italian restaurant around the corner.'

The restaurant was small with low lighting and red-checked tablecloths. 'I love this joint,' Rosa said. 'It reminds me of a place I used to go to in London, Earls Court, back in the sixties. Look –' she pointed to a raffia-encased Chianti bottle holding a candle – 'candles in bottles. We used to think that was the personification of cool.'

Now that he was there, Shaun realised he had no idea where to begin. What did he want from her – ideas, advice, direction?

'Thanks for doing this,' he said awkwardly once they'd ordered. 'I don't really know where to start.'

Rosa raised her glass and clinked it against his. 'To frank and open discussion,' she said, taking a sip, 'presumably about your future.'

'How did you know that?'

She grinned. 'I didn't. But, irrespective of what you wanted, I planned to raise the subject. Looks like we're on the same wavelength. So, d'you want a job?'

Shaun was taken aback. 'I've . . . I've got a job,' he said. 'A job I like. A boss I like, and if we win the election, which seems likely, Heather will get a ministry and I'll be –'

'She won't,' Rosa cut in.

'Sorry?'

'Heather will not be a minister.'

'You don't know that,' Shaun said.

'Yes I do. Of course I do. I work with these people all the time. They talk.'

'Gossip.'

'Some of it, yes, but not this. Heather's not stupid, she knows it. She's been there for fifteen years. If she was going to get a ministry it would have happened by now, but it won't.'

'I don't see why not,' Shaun said, wanting to defend Heather. 'She's a terrific local member.'

'Exactly. She's a terrific local member but she's not ministerial material. She doesn't have the authority, and she doesn't have the support in the party. And really, Shaun, while you and I and many others respect the work she's done, she's not going to make it into the cabinet.'

'But I admire her and –'

'That's not the point. Look, *you know* all this, and you just don't want to face it. Whether or not the party stays in government, you'll still be working for a good solid backbencher. Time you got out and tried something new.'

Shaun remembered the night, a week or so after the shooting, when Charlene had told him to leave the job. He'd felt the same stab of anxiety, the same emotional shutdown then as he felt now. But this was different. Charlene had been talking about safety. She had understood nothing of his job or his politics. Rosa knew both, inside out and back to front.

'You're wasted in that job,' she said now, helping herself to some garlic bread. 'You do it extraordinarily well, and that's been noticed, but people wonder about your attachment to Heather.

They reckon it's lack of judgment or lack of ambition, and as they think your political judgment is pretty good, they assume it must be the latter.'

An uncomfortable prickly sweat broke out on the back of Shaun's neck. 'Does it matter?'

'Not to me, Shaun, not in the least. But in the long run, it might well matter to you. Your loyalty to Heather is admirable, but how old are you? Thirty, perhaps? Do you really want to spend the next five or ten years nursing Heather's political career?'

It stung. The job did involve a certain amount of looking after Heather, making sure she had what was needed to do her job. He didn't think she made any special demands on him, but perhaps, because she was single, he had assumed some of the support role that a partner might have played. It made him feel comfortable, needed.

'I suppose eight years as an electorate officer is quite a long time for . . . well, for . . . '

'Come on,' Rosa said, 'say it. For someone your age.'

'For someone my age.'

'It is, and that's why you and I are here now. Not because you thought I'd offer you a job, but because you needed to talk about it. And once you start talking, of course, you can't go back, you can't unthink it. This is the last meal of the condemned man, Shaun. You've blown open your comfort zone and are thinking about change. The question is, what change will you make?'

By the time he got back from his leave, Shaun was even more distracted and uneasy than when he'd left. Gathering the mail from his box he let himself into the house and dumped his stuff in the hall. Only later, when he had turned on the hot water system, checked some new plants in the garden and made himself a sandwich, did he get around to looking at the mail.

As he sorted the junk from the rest and tossed it in the bin, he noticed an envelope addressed in Charlene's handwriting and his stomach lurched. The last time he'd seen her she was screaming abuse at him as she climbed into a taxi. He was relieved for both

Charlene and Diane that the move seemed to have been a good one. He wanted her to be safe and happy, but he'd put that whole episode, the good and bad, into the past and he certainly didn't need a letter. As he stared anxiously at Charlene's envelope, he wondered what new level of confusion it was going to bring to his already addled state. He put off opening it that night, and when he remembered it the next morning, he put it in the inside pocket of his jacket and took it with him to the office.

'Mr Scolaro with the planning problem is coming in at nine to see you,' Diane said as he walked in. 'He sounded demented on the phone. He wants Heather to get the Minister to overrule the planning committee. He said if he doesn't get this through, then he'll shoot the chair of the committee and every councillor who voted against it. I pointed out that this wasn't a very smart comment in view of recent events, but I fear it went over his head. I tried to defuse him but it's you he wants. He says you understand his situation and he'll sit in this office until you fix it, because you are a man of action.'

Shaun raised his eyebrows. 'I wonder where he got that idea.'

'Who knows, but he'll be here in fifteen minutes.'

Shaun picked up the Scolaro file and walked to his office, hesitating at the door. 'Thanks, Diane,' he said. 'Have I told you how good you are at this job?'

'Three times the day before you went on leave, and once when you called in. You must be going soft. Fifteen minutes, get on with it. I'll go and get us some coffee.'

Shaun put the file on his desk and stared at it. Then he took out Charlene's envelope, laid it alongside the file and stared at them both. Finally he decided that the letter was the lesser of the two evils and slit open the envelope.

Hi Shaun

Bet you weren't keen to open this letter! I hope you're okay and enjoying life, although I know that's a tough one for you (ha ha)!!! Anyway I'm just letting you know that I'm having a great time up here. Denise is a doll, the job's brilliant, and I love working at the resort. I've moved into a unit with two other girls who work there and it's good. Nothing nasty in the dressing table drawer!!!! Thanks for sorting this out for me. I know I let you down, and I just want to say I'm sorry I messed up. Sorry you got the worst of it, you didn't deserve it. BUT you do deserve something, you're mega-smart, really cool and a very good person, so when are you going to get a life?

Take care, talk soon.
Love and xxxxxxxxs
Charlene

FOURTEEN

'Why can't we both go?' Adam asked, twisting a tea towel in his hands. 'We could go together, to that place we stayed at before, near Batemans Bay.'

Jill let the water out of the sink and shook her head. 'I need to be on my own,' she said.

'You're not –'

'I'm *not* leaving you. I just need a break, silence, solitude, some headspace. Surely you can understand, that's what you do when you disappear and play your cello for hours on end.'

Adam flushed. 'But I don't go away.'

She turned to him, dried her hands on the end of the tea towel. 'You don't go out of the house but you do go away. You go away for ages, and recently you've done it more than ever, day after day. And your presence in that room, the sound of those Bach suites, hangs over the house.' She reached out and gripped his hand. 'I need a break. I need to get out from under the shadow of whatever it is that you're dealing with. And I think *you* need a break from the feeling that I'm waiting all the time for you to talk to me.'

He looked at her hard, hesitated and then grasped her hand in both of his. 'Yes,' he said. 'Yes, I see that, it makes sense. If you're really not –'

'I'm not leaving.' She looked around the kitchen at Daisy's paintings on the fridge, school timetables, family photographs, the litter of Toby's maths homework on the table, a pile of ironing on a chair and, in one corner, a stack of old newspapers and a bag of cans and bottles waiting to be taken out to the recycling bins. 'How could I leave all this? I do love you, Adam, but I need to look after myself for a while. I'm trying to hold myself, us, all of us, and all of this, together, but I'm struggling.'

He nodded, pulling her towards him. 'Okay then, if that's what you need to do,' he said, and she was surprised by the energy in his voice. 'Take a couple of weeks off. I'll look after things here.'

'You will?'

'Of course. It's a good time for it – fairly quiet, nothing big coming up. Are two weeks enough? Three?'

She'd expected a battle, an emotional tug-of-war. 'Two would be great.'

'Okay,' he nodded. 'Book it then, somewhere nice. Have you told Renée?'

'Yes, she's fine about it. I've got plenty of leave.'

'Well, then . . . '

Jill thought there was something different in his face – relief, perhaps? Was he actually glad to get rid of her for a while? She felt a prick of victim-like hurt, but wasn't that just what she wanted too? To get rid of him, all of them, the children, the house, work, and yes, mostly Adam, just for a while, not to be needed, not to be responsible, not to have to respond to everyone else all the time. She put her hands on Adam's shoulders, and kissed him lightly.

'Thanks,' she said. 'Maybe it'll work for you too.'

He nodded, and hung the tea towel neatly on the rail, smoothing out the damp folds. 'Maybe,' he said. 'I'm sorry, Jill.'

'It's not just you,' she said. 'It's both of us, and work, and our age, and . . . ' She shrugged and went through to the computer to search for a place to stay.

They were all out on the day, a week later, when she closed the door behind her, tossed her suitcase on the back seat of the car, started the engine and reversed out of the drive. She headed south and west, dropping down to Homebush and onto the motorway, driving as fast as she dared, feeling relief with every kilometre that she put between herself and home. She had always loved the Blue Mountains and as the road started to climb, she stopped and got out. The air was sweet, even the smoky scent of a recent fire seemed delicious, and she stretched her arms above her head, trying to feel her body, to shake off the tension and guilt of leaving them all behind. The guilt she now realised was far more about Adam than the children. They would be fine, probably even enjoy the change, but Adam?

Clouds swept across the face of the sun and the first drops of rain began to fall. Back in the car again she drove on through breathtaking stands of gums, past her destination, taking side roads to places she'd never visited. Steep and rugged natural sandstone walls lined the roadside, leading her to narrow unmade tracks densely bordered by low brush and trees. At a break in the rain she stopped and got out near a fall of smooth flat rocks dotted with moss and tree ferns, where the water rushed into sparkling pools so transparent she could see through the depths to the multicoloured beds of rock and stones. The clear, moist air was filled with the smell of bracken and wet leaves, and light spilled through the trees transforming the falling water into dazzling prisms of colour. Jill sat on a jutting rock and ate her sandwich until the fine, silent rain began again and she turned back to the car, feeling the beauty and tranquillity of the landscape had somehow entered into her and driven out the tension.

'So your husband's joining you later?' asked the woman at the desk when Jill checked in at the hotel. She had introduced herself as Marcia and was obviously determined to be sociable with the clients.

Jill shook her head. 'No, it's just me.'

Marcia raised her carefully pencilled eyebrows. 'Oh well, I suppose you have friends in the area.'

'No, I'm on my own. Just having a bit of a break.'

'We don't get a lot of single people here, mostly couples. I hope you won't be lonely. There's plenty to do of course, lovely walks, the Skyway's not far away, the waterfalls, and the Rhododendron Festival is magnificent, you must make sure you see that.'

She handed Jill a leaflet. 'And you'll find our lounge and bar very friendly, I'm sure you'll find some people to keep you company.'

Jill took off her glasses and pushed the registration form back across the desk. 'I'm not looking for company,' she said, feeling the need to make a point. 'I won't be lonely. I'm here because I want to be alone.'

Marcia's eyebrows shot up again; they seemed to be extremely mobile. 'Alone? Miss Garbo, I presume,' she said with an arch smile.

There was something smug and judgmental about Marcia that made Jill want to shock her. 'I'm here to get away from my husband, my children and my job,' she said, 'to get a break from people talking to me and expecting me to do things for them.'

'Really?' Marcia looked affronted. 'Well, I hope you enjoy it. I've been married for forty-one years, had four children and I'm very happy to spend every day of my life with my husband. Perhaps if you –'

'Is there a problem, Marcia?' a tall man in a checked shirt and jeans asked as he emerged from an office behind the reception desk.

'Oh no, Stuart,' Marcia said, picking up Jill's form. 'Mrs Delaney's just checking in. She's on her own and I was just telling her –'

'I expect she'll want to get to her room,' he said. He glanced at the form and took a key from its pigeonhole. 'Hi, I'm Stuart McCabe, the owner. Let me take your bag.' And he walked around the desk, picked up Jill's suitcase and gestured towards the staircase. 'Sorry about that,' he said as they made their way up the stairs. 'Marcia doesn't always know when to stop.'

Jill smiled. 'It's okay, I'm sure she meant well. I was just a bit . . . '

'Worried she might spend the next two weeks talking to you and trying to organise your life?'

'Exactly.'

'She won't,' Stuart McCabe said, setting Jill's bag down outside a door and unlocking it. 'She's not a member of our usual staff, only comes in occasionally when we're . . . actually, when we're desperate. She's got a very good heart but she does go on a bit. We've had a couple of staff sick, but they'll be here tomorrow and we'll be back to normal.' He pushed the door open and stood aside to let Jill pass.

'Oh! It's glorious,' she said, catching her breath in delight as she crossed the room towards French doors that opened onto a small balcony and sweeping views across a wooded valley to smoky, mauve-smudged peaks beyond. 'Absolutely glorious. This is the view I saw on your website – it's what made me choose this place.'

'Good,' he said, setting her suitcase on the luggage stand. 'We like it. Well, I hope you'll be comfortable. You've got the television and DVD and we've got a reasonable selection of movies down at reception. Breakfast is in the dining room from six thirty until ten, unless you prefer it in your room. Marcia's right, there is plenty to do around here and you really should see the rhododendrons, but we'll leave you to yourself. Just let us know if there's anything you need.'

Jill turned back to the balcony. With the exception of Marcia, the place was just as she'd hoped; a beautiful Victorian build-ing, restored in keeping with the period but with every modern comfort. She felt she could happily spend the rest of her life here where no one knew her, and where lifting a phone could bring her anything she needed. She had come equipped for relaxing and walking and had packed the minimum, wanting to be free of the sense of having things to look after. Her extravagance was half a dozen books bought the previous day in anticipation of time and solitude in which to read without interruption. Hanging her clothes in the wardrobe, she stacked the books by the bed and pulled on her walking boots. There were still a couple of hours of daylight left, plenty of time for a walk.

'You'd better take this map,' Marcia said, catching sight of her heading for the door. 'Do you think you need some water?'

'I think I'll be fine, thank you, Marcia,' Jill said, taking the map and realising how easy it was to be polite now she knew the woman wouldn't be around for long. 'Absolutely fine.'

Absolutely, perfectly fine, she told herself as she strode out up the steep, tree-lined track at the side of the hotel, enjoying the pull of the climb on her leg muscles and the peaty smell of the damp early evening air. She walked on briskly, noting her turns on the map, hearing the occasional rustle of small creatures in the under-growth, the warning calls of birds and the sweeping flutter of their wings at her approach. Further up the path a roo hopped into a clearing and froze, staring at her, before disappearing back into the bush. Finally, her lungs burning with exertion and a fine sweat coating her skin, she stopped at a fork in the path and looked back to where the hotel nestled, the building with its neat lawns and garden like a small oasis in the rugged grandeur of the surround-ing landscape.

She sat down on a fallen tree trunk and listened to the perfect silence, broken only by the sounds of nature. It was almost seven. Adam and the children would be eating at the big kitchen table, Daisy deciding which bit of her meal she was going to reject and Toby, forced to unplug himself from the iPod, trying to make deals about how much TV he could watch. And Adam – his goodness had prevailed and he'd made it easier for her. When she'd handed over the list of all the things he needed to remember, the school run roster, washing and ironing school shirts, Daisy's dancing class, Toby's dental appointment, the phone and electricity bills, he'd taken it from her as she tried to go through it with him.

'It's okay, darling, I can read a list. It'll be fine,' he'd said, strok-ing her shoulder. '*We'll* be fine. We'll miss you but we'll manage, trust me.'

'Oh well,' she said softly now, her voice floating into the evening silence. 'It'll be chaos when I get back, but who cares? A couple of weeks of this and I'll be fit for anything.'

Some small creature nearby scuttled away at the sound of her voice. Would this time alone really help? Who knows, perhaps it was too much to ask, but at least she would feel more able to cope when she'd had time to think about who she used to be and who she had now become. Jill stood up, inhaled another bracing lungful of mountain air and strolled slowly back down the hill towards the hotel.

*

It was so long since she'd been in the shed that Barbara had to fetch the big screwdriver from the kitchen drawer and lever it in behind the hasp to force it free. The door was stuck too and, as she put her shoulder against it and felt it shift, a shower of dry leaves, dead insects and dust descended on her. Stepping inside she brushed the debris from her shirt and stared at what looked like a pile of rubbish that she neither needed nor wanted. She should really clean it up, sort out anything useful, deliver it to the Salvos' shop and dump the rest. But the prospect was far too daunting to take on alone, and she certainly wouldn't ask George, who'd insist on her keeping everything in case it came in handy, or else secretly shift it over to his own shed. Maybe Adam would help her with it, and Toby, he'd probably love it.

She pushed past an old Esky and two folding chairs to where, under a dusty drop sheet, her bike leaned against the back wall. Tugging off the sheet in another shower of dust, she stood back. The bike was nowhere near as bad as she'd anticipated – in fact, there didn't seem to be much wrong with it at all, but then, it had never really had much use. She'd bought it under pressure from a friend, a couple of years before she left the city. The friend was a keen cyclist and suggested they could do some long rides at week-ends to keep them fit. Barbara was half-hearted at first, but after the first few rides she started to enjoy it, at which point the friend, who had met a man through a dating agency, decided to move in with him and shot off to Cairns, taking her bike with her. Barbara never managed to muster any enthusiasm for cycling alone.

She dragged the bike out onto the grass and put down the stand. The tyres were low and dry looking, there was grime and old oil around the chain, but otherwise, she thought, it was as good as new – or rather, as good as when she'd moved to Morpeth and put it away in the shed. She ran her finger through the dust feeling a small thrill as the electric blue paint gleamed in the sunlight. She glanced towards George's house; she knew he'd be out all afternoon and had waited till then to look at the bike because she didn't want him to see it until it was roadworthy. She wheeled it up the garden to the house, dragged it up the steps onto the back verandah, and then wheeled it through the central passage to the front door.

'Whatever for?' George had said when she'd suggested they should consider doing some bike rides in China. 'I haven't ridden a bike for years.'

'China is the bicycle kingdom of the world,' Barbara said. 'Everybody rides bikes.'

'That doesn't mean we have to,' George said. 'In fact, just the other day when I was on the Internet, I read that the Chinese government is now encouraging the use of cars. You used to have to register your bike in China, but they've scrapped that. It's symbolic of the move away from bicycles as transport and the growth of the car society.'

'Really? Well, that may be so, but I don't think we'll be hiring a car in China and there are wonderful trips you can do on bikes. We could start getting into training.'

George, still somewhat frayed by the rigours of four weeks on the language course, didn't look even remotely enthusiastic.

'He will, of course,' Barbara said when Terry, who ran the bike shop, came to collect her bike. 'If you take this away and fix it up for me, you can bet your life that George will soon be in your shop looking at bikes.'

'I don't know,' Terry said dubiously. 'I don't see George as a bike person. He just might not take to the idea.'

'George has a very macho, competitive streak,' Barbara said. 'He hates not to be able to do something that someone else is doing. If he sees me riding a bike he'll want to. And he'll want to do it better, faster and wilder. You'll see, once I'm on the road you'll be selling George a bike, and he'll be looking for something noticeably better than mine, top of the range. You should probably put me on commission.'

Terry shook his head. 'If you say so, Barbara, but I've known George a long time and he's never shown even a remote interest in owning a bike.'

'Ten bucks says he'll be in your shop before Christmas,' Barbara said.

'You're on, but don't blame me if you lose your money,' Terry said, lifting the bike into the back of his van. 'This is a nice one. Doesn't look as though it needs much doing to it. I'll drop it back later in the week.'

'Thanks, Terry, and not a word to George, mind,' she said, grinning. 'I'm just going to start riding it. I shall lead by example and we'll see what happens.'

'So what'll you do now?' Gerry asked when he arrived to sign the contract for the sale of the house. 'Have you decided where to go?'

'Not yet,' Diane said, pouring boiled water into the plunger. 'Only four weeks to settlement, so I suppose I'll just store things and rent somewhere while I make up my mind.'

'There are some nice new units out near Nobby's Point,' he said. 'Might be just your sort of thing.'

'And what is that?' she asked, not looking at him. 'What is my sort of thing?'

Gerry stared at her and shrugged. 'Well, you know . . . no need to be sarky.'

'I'm not, and I'm not being funny either. I don't actually know. I have no idea what I want to do or what *my sort of thing* is. I just know I need to get out of here. We lived here so long and I've loved it, and now I don't. It's a beautiful house but it's the past and I have no idea what the future is about.'

He sat, watching as she carried the plunger and the mugs to the table. 'Do you know if you'll stay around here?'

'Gerry, I told you, I know nothing. You wouldn't understand because you've always been fired by something you wanted to do or to own. It was different for me. I was motivated by us, you and me together with Charlene, a family. That's over. I don't have that anymore.'

'You could go back to work,' Gerry suggested, and Diane saw that he didn't like this reminder of what his actions had created for her.

She poured the coffee, explaining as she did the problem of hairdressers' registration and the need for retraining. 'No way out of that and I can't get my head around being a junior again.'

'Well, what about your own place?' he said. 'Your own salon, you run it, do some of the junior work but get one of the senior staff to retrain you. Different situation altogether.'

She paused, plunger in hand. 'My own salon?'

'Yes. Take over a going concern, refit, new concept, or simply find some new premises.'

'My own salon? I'd never even considered it.'

'You could now. You can afford it and if you need refitting or renovations, I'll get that done for you. You don't want to hang around that bloody woman's office anymore, get yourself a business of your own.'

'I like Heather's office,' she said, suddenly defensive. 'I'm actually working there full time for a while, while someone's sick.'

Gerry shrugged. 'Okay, whatever. But you're not going to stay there forever, are you? That person will get better and then you'll need something else.'

'I suppose so. I suppose it's a possibility.'

A week later, Diane sat in her car outside a rather elegant looking hair salon. She'd been in there a couple of times for a cut and colour but, unimpressed, had taken her business elsewhere. It was, as far as she could remember, an interior that could easily be refitted in any one of a variety of styles. She opened the car door and got out. From this distance it looked quite attractive – a large, tastefully renovated Federation building, dark green walls with cream window frames and trims. Through the full-length windows she could see high ceilings and a dark slate floor. It had obviously had a makeover since her last visit.

Reaching back into the car she took out the information the real estate agent had given her and glanced at the figures; the turnover was good, the lease a little inflated. She stepped off the kerb to cross the road and then stepped back again. Why was she doing this? It was Gerry's idea, not hers. Did she really want to take on a business of her own? Still reading through the information on the salon, Diane stepped off the kerb again, this time into the path of a car that had just swung in to park behind her. The driver hooted, making her jump back, mouthing an apology.

'It's all right, Diane,' the driver called, letting down her window. 'I wasn't going to run you over.' She took off her large sunglasses and got out of the car. 'It's me, Lorraine. I was only thinking of you the other day, wondering when you were going to come out of hibernation.'

Diane blushed. Lorraine and Gordon had been friends, good friends, whose kindness and support she'd rejected when Gerry walked out. 'Sorry, Lorraine,' she said, surprised and embarrassed by this chance encounter. 'I must have seemed awful. I just needed . . . I don't know . . .'

'You needed time and space, darl,' Lorraine said. 'But it's lovely to see you. Why are you standing on the side of the road staring at the hairdresser's?'

'If you really want to know, I was wondering about the business. It's up for sale.'

'Thinking of taking it on now you've sold the house?'

'You know about that?'

'Gerry told Gordon last week.'

'I was thinking about it. It would make sense, sort of . . . but then, I'm not sure that I'm a businesswoman at heart.'

Lorraine slipped an arm through hers. 'I was just parking to go and get some shopping, but have you got time for a coffee? We can chew it over, and I want to hear all about Charlene.' And she steered Diane across the street and into the coffee shop next to the salon.

FIFTEEN

'What do you mean – away?' Heather said, cricking her neck to balance the phone between her ear and her good shoulder so she could rummage on the desk for her glasses. 'Jill never goes away without you.'

'Well, she has now. Toby, can you pull the sausages to the side and turn off the ring, please.'

'Work, is it? A conference or something?'

'Nope. Time out.'

Heather forced her attention away from the reason for her call and onto what Adam had said. 'Time out? From what?'

'From work, from the kids, from the house, from everything. But mainly, I think, from me.'

'Understandable.'

'Thanks.'

'I didn't mean the *you* bit, just all of it.' She paused. 'How long has she gone for?'

'Two weeks. Left a couple of days ago.'

'Two weeks! Is everything okay?'

There was silence at the other end of the line and Heather knew enough not to break it. Finally he said, 'Not perfect.'

'Presumably it's something to do with your amazing communication skills.'

'That and other stuff.'

Heather hesitated. 'Anything to do with . . . you know . . . '

'A lot to do with that,' Adam said dryly, and she heard him

move a chair across the tiled floor and pictured him sitting down, one elbow leaning on the draining board. In the background, Daisy and Toby were arguing about something, and there was the sound of the television playing in another room. 'Hey, you two, go and argue somewhere else while I talk to Aunty Heather. Tea'll be ready in five minutes.'

A door was slammed, the background noise faded, and Heather opened her mouth to say something and then changed her mind.

'So,' Adam said, 'you wanted Jill. Can I help?'

'Not really. Did you . . . did you tell her?'

'No.'

'Maybe you should.'

'You made me promise.'

'And you made me promise too, more vehemently as far as I remember. But that was a long time ago.'

Adam didn't reply.

'I could release you from your promise,' Heather went on. 'You can tell Jill.'

'So I can speak about it, but you never will. Not even . . . not even to him.'

Heather's shoulder throbbed with tension. 'It's not about Ellis.' She heard Adam give a strange sort of grunt. 'It's not. Not this thing with you and Jill. Maybe now, you . . . both of us, owe it to her. And anyway, it's not just my stuff. Part of it, a big part, is you and what you chose to make of it. I thought you'd sorted that out ages ago.'

'So did I,' Adam said, 'but things happened and I find I haven't.'

Silence again. Noisy, drumming, painful silence.

Heather cleared her throat. 'Well, I really want to speak to her. Will I get her on the mobile?'

'She's probably out of range. She's up in the Blue Mountains.'

'Can I get the number of the place she's staying?'

'She wants to be alone.'

'Adam, please.'

'The Valley Hotel,' he said, and he read out the number. 'Give her my love,' and he put the phone down.

Heather stared at the silent receiver and returned it to its cradle. She hated this stand-off with Adam. She wanted to shake him so furiously that his teeth would rattle and all the old hang-ups would come to the surface, break up and disappear. She knew he was trapped, and she knew why, but his inability to face it and sort it out infuriated her. Did he have any idea at all how responsible it made her feel? It just wasn't fair.

She smoothed out the paper she'd written the hotel number on, picked up the phone again, dialled the first three digits and then stopped. This wasn't fair either. She had only wanted someone to talk to and the day they'd had lunch, she'd realised that all this time – years, in fact – she and Jill could have been friends, real friends. They still could, but not now, not this evening, this was Jill's time. Heather put the phone down, stored Jill's number in her mobile, and looked around to make sure she had everything she needed. It was stupid, anyway; Jill would have thought she was stupid, needing to talk, needing Dutch courage before heading off to spend a weekend with the man she loved in his gorgeous treetop house. A moment of panic, that's all. She picked up the small suitcase and walked out of her office through the late afternoon quiet of the Parliament House foyer.

'You driving back to Newcastle or flying?' asked a colleague who had just summoned a taxi.

'Flying, but to Ballina, I'm spending the weekend in Byron Bay.'

'Lucky you,' he said. 'Share this cab to the airport?'

She slipped into the back seat and checked her briefcase. She absolutely had to read Ellis's business plan before she got there. It was important to him and she couldn't avoid it any longer. Thank heavens for travel; she should be able to get through it at the airport and on the flight.

'Ready, are we?' asked the driver. 'Domestic terminal?' and he pulled out into the traffic.

Adam pulled the frying pan back onto the heat, put a bowl of mashed potatoes into the microwave to reheat, and finished cooking the sausages. He liked this, deciding what they'd eat, knocking up a meal, organising the kids.

'It's ready,' he called. 'Go and wash your hands.'

'Brill, Dad, mash,' Daisy said, sliding into her seat. 'I love mash. In fact, I think it's my favourite food in the whole world.'

'Last time we had it, you told Mum it made you feel sick,' Toby said.

'That's because hers had lumps in it,' Daisy said, lifting a large forkful up to her mouth.

'This probably does too,' Adam said.

'Mmm. It does actually but they're nice lumps.'

'You're only saying that to suck up,' Toby said. 'You still have to eat some salad with it. Doesn't she, Dad?'

'She certainly does, you both do,' Adam said, pushing the bowl towards Daisy. 'And I don't want to hear another word about it.'

Daisy spooned a minute amount of salad onto her plate with the expression of one who had been asked to eat slugs. 'I hate –'

'I said not another word.'

'She always argues with Mum,' Toby said, adopting a superior tone and helping himself to larger portion of salad than normal.

'That's because Mum is always here,' Adam said.

'Why *has* Mum gone away?' Daisy asked through a mouthful of potato for what Adam thought was probably the tenth time in two days.

'I told you before. She's gone for a rest, to get away from us lot, from looking after us all.'

'I suppose I'll do that when I'm married,' Daisy said with a sigh.

'Fat chance,' Toby cut in. 'Who d'you think's going to marry *you*?'

'Cut it out, Tobes,' Adam said. 'Now, what do you think about this. Aunty Barbara wants some help cleaning up her shed, so I thought we'd go down on Friday evening and stay till Sunday afternoon.'

'Awesome,' Toby said. 'I bet she's got heaps of brilliant stuff in that shed.'

'And we'll take the bikes,' Adam said.

'We can't ride bikes *and* clean the shed,' Daisy said.

'We certainly can and, what's more, Aunty Barb is coming cycling with us. She's cleaned up her bike and she wants some company while she gets used to riding it again.'

'She's awfully old to ride a bike,' Daisy said. 'She might fall off.'

Toby sighed and shook his head the way he'd seen George do when someone said something particularly silly.

Adam poured himself another glass of wine and sat down to watch the seven o'clock news. His new routine was working well. Toby was loading the dishwasher and Daisy had just started her homework. The simplicity and practicality were wonderfully satisfying, dealing with the basics – food, washing, ferrying kids around – instead of agonising over marking up scores, organising players, and playing every single note of stuff he hated. 'Up yours, Rachmaninov,' he said aloud. 'Up yours.' He'd even given himself time off from his private students. There was something about being with the kids, despite the noise and the arguments and their infuriating habits, that brought you back to reality, out of your head and into your body. He often had time alone in the house when Jill was at work and the kids at school – that was one advantage of the job, to balance out the parts he hated. But this week having the house to himself seemed different, as though it were more his than usual, and it was okay to do the things he wanted. He hadn't played his cello for two and a half days.

'It's only like that because you don't have to do it all the time and you're not going to work as well,' Barbara had said when she'd called him that afternoon. 'I can't believe you've never done this before.'

'Nor can I, really,' he said. 'But you know Jill, she does tend to like things done her way. I feel a bit redundant.'

'Hmm,' Barbara said, 'well, I can fix that for you. Could you come over sometime and help me with my shed?'

He'd laughed when she told him about the bike, and how she was leading by example. 'You mustn't say anything to George,' she said, 'just behave as though it's the most natural thing in the world. But I'd like a bit of an escort for my first sortie on two wheels.'

Adam sipped his drink, and swung his feet up onto the sofa.

'You're supposed to take your shoes off,' Daisy said, waving her exercise book at him. 'Mum'll be cross.'

'If you don't tell her, she'll never know,' Adam said.

'That's what Mummy says,' Daisy said, nudging him with her bum to make room for her. 'Don't tell Dad and he'll never know.'

'About what, exactly?'

'Oh, heaps of stuff, everything, I can't remember. Can you read what I've written about dinosaurs?'

'Good lord!' George said, straightening up from a bucket of soapy water as they rode slowly down Barbara's path. He was washing his car in his driveway. 'Where are you lot off to?'

'G'day, George,' Adam said. 'Just a bit of a ride.'

'Thought you were the shed-cleaning crew,' George said. 'I'm barred because I'm a hoarder, but you never know when things'll come in handy.'

'So I heard,' Adam said. 'I'm no good at throwing out either, and it drives Jill crazy. Hang on, Toby,' he called. 'Aunty Barbara's not here yet.'

'Barbara walking along with you, then?' George asked, chucking his cleaning brush into the bucket. 'Or is she driving the support vehicle?'

'Oh no, she's riding too.'

'Barbara, riding?' He looked along the path to where Barbara was just emerging from the back garden, pushing her bike. 'Didn't even know you had a bike,' he said.

'I am a woman of many parts, George,' Barbara said, and she nodded towards the car. 'Didn't you tell me that you shouldn't stand about talking when you're washing a car because it goes all streaky?'

George took a step back and dragged the leather from his pocket. 'Yes,' he said. 'Quite right, better get on. Have a good ride.'

'Don't try to get on until you're off the gravel,' Adam whispered, 'then stay by me on the inside until we get round the corner out of sight, then we can reorganise. Okay, kids, off you go. We're turning left at the end of the road.'

It was strange to be on the bike again, but once around the corner and out of sight of George, Barbara began to feel more confident, and then to enjoy it. They rode steadily for more than half an hour before turning back into Morpeth to stop for coffee at the café that looked out over the river.

'I could go further,' she told Adam when Toby and Daisy, having finished their milkshakes, had raced off down the river bank.

'I'm sure you could but I don't think we should,' Adam said. 'You'll get stiff and sore and it'll put you off. Bit at a time – we can go again tomorrow. Lead by example, remember.'

'I remember,' she said. 'Actually, I remember being barely able to move the first time I went out after I bought it. I thought I'd never walk or ride again.'

'Exactly.'

'Do you still ride with Kirsty on Fridays?'

'Mostly. When we both can. I haven't really got used to her not being there. I still miss her,' he sighed. 'Just one of this year's upheavals. I'll be glad when the new year comes and I can think about things being different.'

'You think a date makes a difference?'

'It's a milestone, isn't it?' Adam said. 'You need them as markers to put things behind you.'

'I wish we could all put the shooting behind us,' Barbara said. 'I don't understand how they can't have found someone yet. It's as though we're all on hold waiting for it to be over.'

Adam bounced his helmet on his knee. 'More than four months since you and I were sitting in that hospital café, thinking that they'd pick someone up any day. Four months. Heather's coped amazingly well.'

'I'm not so sure about that,' Barbara said. 'I'm not sure that coping is what she's doing. I think she's pretending she's coping but I think she's waiting, and meanwhile she's hiding.'

'Hiding?'

'Behind this man, this Ellis. She's focusing on him to distract herself, to create something positive, because without that she can't handle the fear and the waiting.'

'She says she's in love with him,' Adam said.

'Yes, well, maybe she is, but . . . '

'Are you saying she wouldn't have got involved with Ellis again if she hadn't just been shot?'

Barbara shrugged. 'How should I know? I don't know anything about him, really. But I do think the shooting made Heather feel very lonely and then he came along and seemed to be offering something comforting. Maybe she really is in love with him or maybe she just fell into this because she needed someone.'

'You didn't like him, did you?' Adam said with satisfaction.

'I didn't *dislike* him. He just wasn't what I expected; he didn't seem to fit with the picture Heather had painted of him. But I've only met him the once. I guess we'll see him again at Christmas as we're all going to Heather's. George can't stand him. And, of course, we all know what you think, although I must say, Adam, I'm not sure why you seem to hate him with such a passion. It's unlike you to take against anyone so vehemently.'

Adam looked away, out across the river. 'We all have our blind spots, I suppose,' he said. 'Well, let's get a move on, the kids'll be ready for lunch soon.'

'Just a minute,' Barbara said, putting her hand on his arm. 'There's something I've been meaning to ask you. The year that Dorothy and I went on the cruise, remember? When we got back you borrowed some money –'

'I paid you back,' Adam said quickly, getting up.

'I know you did, dear. Oh, for heaven's sake, sit down. Toby and Daisy won't starve to death, they're having a wonderful time over there. Of course you paid me back, but what was it *for*, Adam? I know I promised not to ask but it's so long ago it can't matter now. Why did you need the money?'

SIXTEEN

'So, what do you think?' Ellis asked, watching from the kitchen as Heather wandered back in through the glass doors from the balcony.

'Gorgeous,' she said, 'it's absolutely gorgeous, Ellis, even better than I'd imagined. Paradise. The stillness out there, the moon on the water, and the little pinpoints of light from the other houses on the escarpment. Magic.'

'Wait till you see it in daylight.'

'I'm sure it's just as lovely, and I'm dying to see Byron Bay.'

Ellis smiled as he pulled the cork from a bottle of wine. 'It's taken long enough to get you here.'

'I know. You're right; it's ridiculous living in Newcastle all this time and never having come up here before.'

'I meant it's taken me long enough to get you to come to my place,' he said, walking over to her and handing her a glass. 'Anyway, let's drink to the first of many visits,' and he clinked his glass against hers.

It was enormously satisfying to have her there; enormously gratifying to see how much she loved the house. 'I've missed you,' he said. 'It's been far too long, three weeks is ridiculous. A day is too long; this is simply not good enough.'

'Well, at least there's no chance of us getting sick of each other,' she said with a laugh.

Ellis blanched. He hadn't yet got used to Heather's unerring ability to misjudge the moment, nor her failure to deliver in the romance stakes. Somehow she managed to clodhop all over his sensitivities. She was a good lover, though, and since that first cautious night interrupted by tears, she was more sexually confident. Ellis was enjoying more and more challenging and rewarding sex than he'd ever had in his life. But it had taken him time to get used to her body. He'd always been attracted to slim women, preferably ones with large breasts. Heather was certainly endowed with the latter, but she was also endowed with some rather unnecessary layers and bulges which were less than attractive and certainly not sexy. Ellis had noticed, when he was going through various profiles on an Internet dating site, that about ninety per cent of men stated they were looking for slim or very slim women, but when you read the women's profiles, a lot were quite overweight – fat, even. He couldn't understand why women let themselves go like that, especially if they wanted to find a man.

Heather also had funny skin and indentations on her thighs, which he assumed was the cellulite people seemed to talk about a lot. He preferred not to think about it. Years ago her thighs had been smooth and soft, they'd driven him crazy with desire, and long after he and Heather had split up he had still had erotic dreams in which her legs were wrapped around him. Maybe, he thought, if she could get rid of some of the excess weight, the thigh problem would sort itself out.

'I thought tomorrow morning we'd go for a long walk along the beach and a swim,' he said. 'The exercise will do you good, tone you up a bit, then we can go into town for coffee.'

'Sounds lovely,' Heather said, snuggling against him, resting her head on his shoulder. 'And I hear the shops are great, lots of little arcades. I'd like to have a wander around those, and I want to look at some galleries. But most of all I just want to be with you, veg out, sleep, lie on your lovely balcony, watch the view and read.'

'If we have time,' Ellis said, seeing his carefully planned schedule for the weekend disappearing into a chaotic mix of sightseeing, shopping and resting.

'Of course we have time. We've got three days, that's heaps of time. I am *so* looking forward to a rest and to knowing that if the phone rings it's not for me. Parliament was hell this week, I'm totally stuffed.'

Ellis bit his tongue. He'd been about to ask her what she'd thought of the business plan that she'd had for weeks, and the three chapters of the book he'd emailed her a few days earlier, but this clearly wasn't the moment. He pulled away slightly, looking down at her face. She was obviously tired, there were dark shadows under her eyes, and the way she seemed unable to get comfortable on the sofa was an indication that her shoulder was hurting.

'We'll eat soon,' he said. 'I got some fresh perch in town this morning. You can sit out there on the balcony with me while I cook it.'

'Bliss,' Heather said, stretching up to kiss his cheek. 'You are wonderful, just what I need. The job has always been tough but combined with menopause and being shot, it's really a struggle.'

Ellis wished she could have left out the menopause bit, he hated knowing about that messy side of women's lives, and he certainly didn't want to talk about it. Women these days seemed to have very little modesty about the subject. He had grown up in a time when the menstrual cycle and its distasteful effects were never discussed; at least, not with men. Women kept it to themselves, made an effort to hide it, and seemed quite happy to behave as though it didn't exist. These days you just couldn't avoid it – it was as though they wanted to force men to acknowledge that it had some sort of significance. Even when he was still in the law, women openly mentioned in evidence that they'd been menstruating or were premenstrual at the time something happened, or that their behaviour had been affected because they were going through menopause, as though it were something that should be taken into consideration. The other day he'd seen a picture in a magazine of rainbow-coloured tampons, and then a television advertisement of a man going out to buy tampons for his girlfriend and speculating on what size to get. How much more insensitive and tasteless could it all get?

Ellis extracted his arm and stood up. 'Well, I've told you the answers to that,' he said. 'You have to put the shooting behind you, and ditch this silly idea that you can't resign.' He put his glass down on the table and went through to the kitchen.

'Just like that! You make it sound simple.'

'It *is simple* – what could be *simpler*?' Ellis said.

'You know,' Heather said, 'there's something I've never understood about men. They can't just explore something, they always have to whip up a solution and slap it down in front of you and you're expected to pick it up and put it on. What would really be nice would be if you could just talk it through with me without trying to push me towards your preferred outcomes. That's the sort of thing I spend my working life resisting.'

The salon was larger than she remembered and equipped in a minimalist style that was almost clinical. A round reception desk in the centre immediately reminded Diane of the control centre of Dr Who's Tardis. Each bay was marked with a simple black slate shelf, full-length mirror and black chair, and in diagonally opposite corners two huge, shoulder-height vases stuffed with exotic silk flowers and foliage in shades of green and white provided the only softening effects. Was it the large space and the ceiling height, or just the décor that created the starkness? It would be better, of course, when there were staff and clients, but she had needed to see it empty and on Monday the salon was closed.

'What do you think?' Diane asked, crossing to the wet area, her heels clipping across the African slate tiles. 'A little austere, perhaps?'

'Austere?' Barbara said. 'Intimidating, I think. You'd have to be feeling very confident and self-assured to come in here, especially if your hair was a mess.'

'She has a very upmarket clientele,' the agent said, casting a disapproving look at Barbara's navy blue cotton pants and crumpled white linen shirt. 'She ran a salon in LA for a while.'

'So what's she doing in Newcastle?' Barbara asked.

'She has family here.'

Diane strolled back into the middle of the room, her attention to the salon distracted somewhat by her dislike of the agent, a sharp-faced woman in a black suit and white blouse, and too much make-up. She obviously hadn't read Charlene's advice on dark lipstick for the over fifties. 'I think I've seen enough, thanks,' she said.

'If you want to make an offer . . . '

'I need to think about it. I'm interested and I like the building and the location, but I'm not sure it's right for me.'

'You could reconceptualise the interior, although, of course, it was only remodelled fifteen months ago.'

'So you said earlier.' Diane was flexing the assertiveness muscle that had gone into hibernation when Gerry left but was now reviving. 'Thanks for letting us in. I'll get back to you.'

'My advice is don't take too long. We've had a lot of enquiries. If you leave it too long you may miss the boat.'

Diane put on her sweetest smile. 'That's the way of things, I suppose,' she said. And she steered Barbara out of the door and into the street.

'Strewth,' Barbara said. 'What a pain in the arse. It's a wonder she sells anything. She looked at me as though I just crawled out of a wheelie bin. For all she knew I could have been the one with the money.'

'Let's go next door and have some lunch,' Diane said. The office had been quiet and with Heather going straight from Byron Bay back to Sydney, it would be a slow week. Shaun had been very laidback, telling her not to rush the appointment with the real estate agent, and she'd been heading out of the office door when Barbara showed up unexpectedly after a visit to the dentist. 'Come with me?' Diane had asked. 'I could do with a second opinion.'

'Well, what did *you* think?' Barbara asked when they'd ordered coffee and toasted sandwiches..

'It's beautifully done, not my style, but all the same . . . but intimidating, like you said, unfriendly. I can't imagine that even when it's open and there are clients that it would feel much different. It lacks warmth.'

'You could create that if you do as she said and *reconceptualise* – what a ridiculous word. Why do people think that creating stupid new expressions will make it sound as though they're saying something significant? Maybe I'm just a grumpy old woman.'

Diane shook her head. 'I don't think so. You know, probably ten, fifteen years ago I'd have gone for something like that but it doesn't work for me anymore.'

'I'll tell you a secret every hairdresser should know,' Barbara said, leaning forward conspiratorially. 'Those mirrors that go right down to the floor are a killer. Not only do you go in there with your hair a mess when all around you are gorgeous, but you have to sit for an hour contemplating the fact that the trousers that made you look slim in the mirror at home make you look hideously fat when you're sitting, and your shoes are all wrong. Don't have floor-length mirrors.'

'I'll remember that,' Diane said, laughing. '*If* I do it.'

'Is it really what you want to do?'

'I don't know. I suppose that's the thing – apart from anything about that particular salon, I just don't know. It makes sense but I'm not at all sure that it's what I want.'

She looked around the café, the tables mostly occupied by women, and thought how pleasant and relaxing it was to be sitting here with Barbara, talking as though they were old friends. A few days earlier she'd sat here with Lorraine, wondering then why she had made that sudden decision to cut herself off from well-meaning people. She had brought her life to an embarrassing halt in response to Gerry's desertion. If she'd really wanted to get back at him she should have been seen everywhere, looking her best, socialising, getting in his way, spending heaps of money. As it was, she'd wasted two whole years bristling with anger, determined to be a victim. Even Charlene had been desperate to escape from her when she got the chance to move in with Shaun.

'I wish I *knew* what I wanted,' she said now. 'All I've managed so far is to know what I don't want. And after all that drinking and then buggering off, now Gerry's friendly and seems to want to help . . . well, to sort of manage me, I think. *He* thinks this is the right thing, not necessarily this salon, but having my own business.'

'Does it matter what he thinks?' Barbara asked. 'It sounds rather as though things might be a bit dodgy with his new partner and he's looking for someone to lean on.'

'That had crossed my mind. But no, it doesn't matter. It's over for me, totally over, and the relief is enormous.'

'You have plenty of time,' Barbara said. 'I think if you wait, if you're patient, something will emerge and you'll know because it'll feel right. Ouch!' she said, twisting on her chair. 'I went bike riding with Adam and the children twice at the weekend and I'm really stiff. I'm a novice in training for China.'

'Really?' Diane said. 'That sounds like fun. It's ages since I rode my bike. Gerry and I used to ride together on Sunday mornings and then go for breakfast.'

'Why don't you get it out?' Barbara said. 'Bring it to Morpeth one Saturday, stay the night and on Sunday we'll go riding and I'll take you to breakfast at a nice café by the river. Stop worrying about what you're going to do – it'll all work out in the end, things always do. You should go and see Stefan's garden. After all, he's the role model for reinvention.'

Some weeks earlier, unable to sleep one night, Heather had sat up in the Potts Point bedroom, switched on the television, surfed the channels for something to watch and settled on an old black-and-white movie with James Mason as a ruthless, manipulative husband bent on his wife's destruction. Her three sisters tried to warn her but she was determined to be a good wife and, as her mental and physical health broke down, the sisters attempted in vain to rescue her. Watching it, Heather wished that she had sisters, three at least; not that she needed warning or rescuing, but just so that she could talk things through with them. Ellis, of course, was not remotely like the Mason character any more than she was like the hopeless, cowering wife, but there was something that struck a chord; whatever happened the wife was always in the wrong. As the aircraft roared down the Ballina runway, Heather reflected on the fact that she had spent much of the weekend being in the wrong.

Admittedly she had started badly, biting Ellis's head off just as he was about to cook the fish. But the candlelit dinner had restored the mood, and she had entered as fully into the romance of the occasion as she knew how, savouring the moment, the beautiful house, the warmth and stillness of the night air, the full moon reflected on the glassy surface of the water. But the whole romantic thing was a problem for her, something she tried to engage with for Ellis's sake but which frequently eluded her. She knew that his coming back into her life like this *was* romantic, she even called it that, but romance was something for which she had no flair. She understood friendship, desire, lust and the longing for a deep, intimate connection and companionship with another person – this she felt was real love, the love she felt for Ellis. But romance seemed like artifice. She just didn't get it.

And she didn't really get what Ellis meant by it either, apart from that great gesture of coming to find her. What was it that made him describe himself as a great romantic? He insisted that forty years ago she had been a true romantic, and that all that was needed now was a leap of imagination on her part. But a leap into what? What would she actually have to do to *be* romantic? And wasn't physical affection *outside* the bedroom part of romance? Words seemed inadequate proof of this magic ingredient. But that Friday night, she did appreciate the romance of the occasion and the setting, as well as her great good fortune in being there with the man she loved constantly declaring his love for her. She relished her meal, sipped her wine and ignored the niggling feeling that she needed to stay alert. After a long and particularly unpleasant week in parliament, a tiring day and several glasses of wine, her alert switch flipped to off.

'So,' Ellis had said as they stacked the dishes in the dishwasher, 'tomorrow morning, a swim and a walk, coffee, and then you can give me your feedback on the plan and my first three chapters.'

'You forgot a look around the town and a siesta on the balcony,' said Heather, by now quite light-headed. 'And then I'll read the stuff and we can talk about it.'

Ellis slammed the salad bowl into the machine and straightened up. 'You haven't read it yet?'

Heather stopped short. She'd meant to read it on the flight but exhaustion beat her. She'd fallen asleep minutes after take-off and woke as they were landing at Ballina.

'Whoops,' she said, in a manner more cavalier than she would have adopted three glasses of wine ago. 'Sorry, darling, no, actually, I haven't. I know it's bad of me but, honestly, I've been up to my ears in work. I *intended* to read it on the way here but it didn't quite work out –'

'Obviously,' Ellis said.

He was standing with his back to her, putting unused cutlery into a drawer, and she went up behind him, slipped her arms around his waist and rested her cheek against his shoulderblade. 'I'm *sooooo* sorry, Ellis, really. You can't imagine how hectic it's been this week.'

'How long would it have taken?' he asked, not turning around. 'An hour? Two at the most. And anyway, you've had the business plan for weeks.'

She lifted her face from his back. 'I know, it's ridiculous, isn't it? But that's how it's been, my headspace is overflowing, I couldn't cram anything else in.'

'It *is* ridiculous,' he said, turning to her and removing her arms. 'Totally ridiculous. *You* are ridiculous.' And he walked past her, out on to the balcony to collect the empty wine bottle and snuff out the candles.

In other circumstances, Heather thought, she would have given him heaps for that last remark, but knowing he was hurt she let it go. It took well over an hour to defuse the situation and by the time they eventually got to bed they were both too tired to do anything but sleep.

She woke early next morning to the sound of cockatoos arguing outside the open window, Ellis's hands exploring her breasts and his erect penis nudging her bottom. Heather had never enjoyed sex in the morning, her hormones simply weren't on duty at that time of day, but even in the haze of waking she knew that refusal would be disastrous.

Later, sitting on the balcony with a cup of coffee while Ellis was in the shower, she reflected on the fake orgasm and felt it had been an admirable effort; it had certainly convinced Ellis. Years earlier when her last, albeit brief, relationship had ended, Heather had vowed that despite her proven skills she would never again fake an orgasm. But that was like taking a vow against wearing a lifejacket when you were on dry land – it was a different thing altogether when you were out at sea facing ten-metre waves. Early in the morning after the night they'd first made love, Heather had broken her vow and summoned the fake orgasm back into service. Women were, she thought, damned if they did and damned if they didn't. What was the point of adopting the moral high ground on fake orgasms when its alternatives were so unappealing? You either struggled to achieve a real one at a time when you'd rather have been sleeping or reading a good book, or you spent the rest of the day copping the fallout from a bruised ego. Orgasms were great, but how many does one woman need? Faking at least got it sorted and out of the way.

Ellis was a worry, though, because for a man of almost seventy he seemed to have very frequent erections. Heather thought that if he were, as she suspected, taking something, he might be exceeding the stated dose. Not for the first time she considered how strange it must be to live with a part of your anatomy that constantly demonstrated inappropriate behaviour and over which you had very little control. No wonder men could close their minds to the possibilities of orgasmic deception; it must make them feel that for a while at least they'd gained control and achieved a result. That was something else she'd never understood: so many men were focused on outcomes, when for women it was usually process that was more important.

In the centre of town later that day, a couple of Ellis's acquaintances wandered into the coffee shop and joined them at the table.

'You mean you've never been here before?' Leah asked while her husband, James, talked investments with Ellis. 'Then I have to take you through the arcade and show you this wonderful little shop. Come on, it won't take long.' She got up, gesturing to Heather to follow her.

'Where are you two off to?' James asked, glancing up.

'Just want to show Heather something,' Leah said.

Heather stood up and patted Ellis's shoulder. 'Won't be long, darling,' she said, and followed Leah down through the narrow arcade to a tiny shop full of beads, sarongs and sequinned cushions, feeling a stab of regret that it was so long since she'd last been shopping with a woman friend. On impulse she bought a turquoise sarong for herself, another in shades of yellow and burnt orange for Jill, and some wooden beads for Barbara.

'What exactly was all that about?' Ellis asked tight-lipped as they walked back to his car.

'What?'

'Since when do you abandon the person you're with and disappear for hours?'

'Hours?' Heather said, laughing. 'It was about ten minutes, and I didn't abandon you. You knew where we were.'

'But you're supposed to be with me.'

'I was, I am. For heaven's sake, Ellis, you were having a conversation exclusively with James and you were still engrossed in it when we got back. You don't need me to be an audience.'

Ellis's mouth tightened, but he didn't respond.

The trouble, she realised, was that she was simply too accustomed to being single and liking it. She must try to think of herself as part of a couple in future and this afternoon she absolutely had to read his Head to Heart stuff and make a real effort to get involved.

'Straight after lunch,' she promised him as she laid the table. 'And it's much better reading it here where I can really concentrate without distractions.' And an hour or so later they were both ensconced in the deep cane armchairs on the balcony, Ellis with the weekend papers, and Heather with the business plan and the draft chapters, four of them now, on her lap. Although Ellis had talked her through it the day he'd collected it from Luke Scriven, she'd promptly forgotten most of it.

Now, as she opened the glossy document, its cover and first pages scattered with aphorisms, Heather felt her chest and bowels tighten. She loathed the whole concept of lifestyle and the associated marketing. Lifestyle! Now everyone had to have a life-style. Wasn't it enough to simply have a life anymore? Heather had inherited a taste for moderation from her mother and Barbara, and it led her to resist glossy magazines featuring exotic locations, luxury watches or promises of youth and beauty. And she had no time at all for anything with a scent of New Age.

'But you've done yoga, meditation and naturopathy, Heather,' Kirsty had said one day after returning from something called deep crystal rebalancing.

'They are ancient wisdom,' Heather replied. 'It's all this hippie-hyped stuff that infuriates me.'

Before Ellis's unexpected arrival she'd viewed life-coaching as something which combined the worst of consumer-driven life-style rubbish and New Age psychobabble. Why people would need someone to coach them in how to live their lives was a mystery to her. But Ellis was a highly intelligent man, accustomed to sifting evidence and flushing out charlatans, so presumably he knew what he was talking about, and she was therefore prepared to revise her judgment.

'It was that time with Nirvana that set me on this new course,' Ellis had told her during their first days together. 'An experience like that changes you, takes you to a level from which you can only look down in dismay at the place you've come from. It makes you want to take others with you along the same track.'

And Heather, enchanted as she was by the unexpected gift of this second chance at love and its promise of escape from the aftermath of the shooting, wanted to believe him.

The business plan was written in contemporary business and management jargon spiced with New Age and lifestyle language. And it was obviously aimed at people with more money than sense. The budget took her breath away. Scriven's fee for the plan alone ran into thousands and she could hardly bear to look at the extraordinary figures for management of the marketing and promotion. And the suggested scale of charges for consultations was mind-blowing. But it was the idea of Ellis as life-coach and counsellor that triggered an increase in Heather's heart rate. She felt physically sick at the prospect of having to provide the long-awaited feedback.

To her relief, a panel van pulled into the driveway and Ellis left the balcony to help unload some rocks and a pump for his proposed water garden. Breathing space. Heather turned in desperation to his first draft chapter – perhaps there was something in his own work that she could latch on to. But it was not to be; try as she might she could see nothing but vacuity masquerading as wisdom, fatuousness as integrity, and the slick contemporary superficiality that promised redemption and rebirth through reorganising everything from the linen press to faith. Heather closed her eyes and rested her head on the chair back. Did he really believe all this? If he did, or indeed if he didn't, what did it say about him? And any minute now he would be settling back in the chair alongside her waiting for her feedback.

Questions, she reminded herself. Questions were the weapons of choice when asked for an opinion on the impossible or unreasonable. Ask questions, and in the travail of analysis and interpretation the cracks would appear without her having to pass an unpalatable opinion. She had done it often, and had had it done to her. Grabbing a pencil she jotted down some questions for Ellis. It was risky. This was how lawyers worked, and he would know what she was doing. She would have to phrase her questions in the spirit of genuine enquiry, to appear constructive rather than critical. She would stall him with questions, force him to rethink, leave him something to grapple with and then, when he could see it all more clearly, perhaps help him to find another way to channel his desire to help others. Ellis had fallen into a black New Age hole, and rescuing him before he made a fool of himself was not going to be easy. There might have to be a few more fake orgasms before the weekend was over.

But now that it *was* over, and she was bound once again for Sydney, Heather wasn't entirely sure that even fake orgasms and legal-style interrogations were going to prove sufficient to steer Ellis from his chosen path.

SEVENTEEN

Alex Roussos ducked under the crime-scene tape, walked up the path to the house and nodded a greeting to the uniformed officer on duty at the front door.

'Contamination, Alex!' a voice called from within, and a plastic bag containing shoe covers and sterile white overalls flew out of the door and hit him in the chest.

'Shit,' he said, blinking. 'Manners, Andy, manners,' and he picked the bag up off the ground.

'Sorry, mate, but uniform have already had a party in here,' Andy Weaver, the forensic pathologist, said. 'We don't need anything else to confuse us.'

Alex struggled into the overalls, covered his shoes, pulled on thin latex gloves and stepped through the hallway into a large, expensively furnished room from which a wall of glass overlooked a swimming pool. In the centre of the room, Weaver was crouched over the body of man who lay face down, his blood spattered across the beige carpet and onto the pale green fabric of the nearby sofa.

'Okay,' Alex said, 'what've we got?'

'Male, thirtyish, shot three times, presumably with the gun over there but I can't confirm that yet,' Weaver said.

'And one male witness, shot once in the pelvic region and scared shitless,' said Vince, appearing from a door at the end of the room. 'He's in an ambulance on his way to emergency right now.'

'Any ID?'

'For him, yes,' Vince said, handing him the witness's wallet and a mobile phone in an evidence bag. 'For this guy, not yet. Can't get into his pockets until Andy lets me turn him over.'

'Who owns the house?'

'I've got someone finding out right now.'

Alex stood up, took a slow look around the room and then turned back to the body on the floor. 'This guy looks vaguely familiar,' he said, 'but the hole in his head might be confusing me. How long before we can have a look at him?'

'Patience, my son,' Weaver said, picking up a bloodstained fibre and dropping it into a bag. 'We'll get to that in a minute. Give a bloke a bit of space, can't you?'

'I thought I might join you if that's okay,' George said, as Barbara wheeled her bike down the path. She had taken a ride at the same time each morning for the two weeks since that first outing with Adam and the children. George was standing at her gate, wearing a bike helmet and holding an impressive looking red mountain bike with black trim.

'You've bought a bike!' Barbara said, feigning amazement. 'And what a beast it is. Well done, you.' How satisfying it was to know someone well enough to predict their behaviour, and to love them enough to find their idiosyncrasies endearing. How lucky she was to have this precious friendship at a time in her life when she had least expected it.

'Yes, it is rather good,' George said, looking proudly at the bike. 'I had a secret little run on it yesterday evening. Seems I still know how to ride.' He reached in the pocket of his shorts and handed her a ten-dollar note. 'Terry asked me to give you this. He said you'd know what it's for.'

'I do indeed,' Barbara said, slipping Terry's betting loss into her pocket. 'Well, this is excellent, George, we can get into training for China.'

'That's what I thought,' he replied. 'Not such a bad idea after all, and rather more fun than the language course.'

'I liked the language course, though,' Barbara said as they ped-alled away. 'It was terribly tiring, so much to take in, but I enjoyed it. It's a good thing to have done. When we come back, I'm going to help out with the asylum seeker classes. Even if we weren't going to China, it would have been worth doing that course.'

'Yes, well, we *are* going to China,' George said. 'I made the bookings yesterday when I went into Maitland to pick up the bike. First of March we're on our way. *And* yesterday evening I got an email from Robert with the contact details for a bloke in Beijing to email about classes – very interested, apparently.'

'Really?' Barbara said, swerving slightly to look at him. She'd always thought that the chance of either of them getting any work was remote. 'Classes for you?'

'For both of us. Come back home with me afterwards and we'll compose an email together. Do we get to go for coffee at the end of the ride?'

'Naturally,' Barbara said. 'My shout, as this is your maiden voyage.'

The whole China plan had been a godsend for Barbara. It dis-tracted her attention away from the feeling that everyone she loved was in a mess; that their lives were either stalled or fracturing. Worry had destroyed her concentration, bringing her writing to a halt and interrupting her reading. She thought it was the sort of anxiety that parents must feel observing the lives of their adult chil-dren, knowing that intrusion or interference was the best they had to offer. But China, and all its possibilities, allowed her to surf the Internet reading short, easy-to-digest pieces on its history, culture, politics, tourism and much more without too much concentration.

Barbara had stopped believing that once the police made an arrest everything would be back to normal. What she now knew was that while the shooting in itself was terrible, it was the peripheral damage that could prove fatal. Probably all families had their secrets, the old hurts and simmering discontents that ran so deep you could blunder into something without even realising it. When she had asked Adam about pawning his cello, it simply hadn't occurred to her that she might be treading on such sensi-tive ground.

'I can't really talk about it,' he'd said at first, his gaze fixed firmly on Daisy and Toby, who were stalking something down by the water's edge. 'I'd be breaking a confidence. Letting someone down.'

'But, Adam, it's forty years ago. It can't matter now.'

'It does matter. To me it does,' he'd said, and he picked up his bike helmet, pulled his wallet from his pocket and handed it to her. 'Let's get going. Can you take this and pay, and I'll round up the kids.'

That evening, exhausted by cycling, shed clearing and all the noise and activity that went with having two children in the house, Barbara was sitting quietly reading the paper with the TV sound turned down when Adam, who had been supervising Toby and Daisy's bedtime, came down the stairs.

'I thought of making some tea,' Barbara said. 'D'you want some?' She folded the paper and glanced up to see Adam framed in the doorway. His face was a deathly white, the hand resting on the doorjamb shaking. 'Good heavens, Adam, whatever's the matter? Are you sick?' she asked, dropping the paper and getting up to take his arm. 'Come and sit down. Can I get you something?' He shook his head and allowed her to lead him to the sofa, and sat ghostlike beside her, his hands clenched between his knees, tears running down his cheeks in fast and silent streams.

Barbara reached for the box of tissues and pulled out a handful. She wanted to dry his tears as she had so often done when he was a small boy, but she suspected it was demeaning to dry the eyes of a grown man, so she pressed the tissues into his hands. Adam wiped his eyes, holding the wad of tissues over his face now as his body rocked with silent sobs.

'I've done a terrible thing, Barb,' he'd said when he was finally able to speak. 'A really terrible thing, and I've let everyone down.'

The memory of Adam's grief that night brought a lump to Barbara's throat. Ahead of her she saw George turn into the main street, heading for the same café. She followed him slowly, dismounted and wheeled her bike to the rack.

'I suppose one gets used to the bum ache,' George said, holding out his hand to take hers. 'My muscles are feeling a bit elderly; not bad, though, starting again at seventy-five.'

'I'll treat you to a chocolate muffin,' Barbara said, taking his hand. 'That'll take your mind off it. By the time we get to China you'll be riding like a teenager again.'

'Whatever are you doing *here*?' Jill asked when she saw Heather getting out of a cab in the hotel car park. 'Oh my god, there's been an accident. Is it Adam? The children?'

Heather took her arm, 'Everyone's absolutely fine, Jill, honestly. Sorry, I should've phoned. Really, there's nothing to worry about.'

Jill sighed with relief. 'Thank goodness, so why –'

'Look, this is an awful cheek. I'm taking advantage of your good nature, abusing our overdue friendship, and imposing on your privacy,' Heather said, 'but I . . . well, I need to talk and . . . '

'And you came all this way?'

'I should've rung, but parliament rose early and I'm not flying back to Newcastle till tomorrow. I've wanted to talk all week, ever since Byron Bay, so I just walked out, got a train and then a cab and here I am.'

'Just in time for a shower and some dinner,' Jill said. 'And I'm really pleased to see you. I thought of ringing you. I've been dying to know about your weekend.'

Heather rolled her eyes. 'That's what I need to talk about,' she said. 'Debrief. Can you bear it?'

'I'd love it,' Jill said, taking her arm. 'Are you staying the night? My room is vast and has two double beds. Good thing you didn't get here earlier. I only just got back from the Rhododendron Festival.'

The rhododendrons had been magnificent and Jill had even felt a tremor of warmth for Marcia, without whom she might never have known about them. More than halfway through her precious time in the mountains, the things that had oppressed her at home now seemed infinitely more manageable and she was convinced she'd be a nicer person by the time she got back there. She pictured Adam surrounded by the usual chaos and at the beck and call of the children, and she felt ever so slightly guilty, but only ever so slightly. It would show him what she coped with all the time, it was the trip-up on reality he needed. When she got back she would talk to him about the burden of being responsible, and how desperately she needed him to share it.

'So, tell me all about it,' Jill said as they waited for their meal. 'Did you have a wonderful romantic weekend? Is the house gorgeous?'

'The house is truly gorgeous,' Heather said, looking calmer now, less fraught than when they had met in the car park. 'I took some photos – they're in my camera. I'll show you when we go back to the room. And Byron Bay is really lovely. I can see why people rave about it and . . . ' Her voice trailed away.

'And?'

She sighed. 'And I had a very difficult weekend which, of course, is why I'm here. Oh, Jill, I do love Ellis so much, and I desperately want this to work, but sometimes it's so hard, and I seem to be so bad at it, I wonder if it's just too late to start all over again.'

'Of course it's not too late,' Jill said. 'And bad at what, exactly?'

'At being in a relationship. Perhaps I've been single too long.'

'It's bound to be difficult at first, Heather,' Jill said. 'Relationships always are, all that sizzling sex and bliss and then you hit the reality check. And I'm sure it must be harder as one gets older. We all get stuck in our ways, and it gets harder to change, to adapt to someone else.'

'I know, but I keep getting it wrong. I keep stuffing up.' Heather paused, looking around the half-empty restaurant and lowering her voice. 'And I keep thinking Ellis just wants me to be nineteen again.'

Jill smiled. 'He probably does. Wouldn't most men like us to be like we were? Younger, slimmer, sexier and more willing to do their bidding? But the men who live with us go through the process of change with us, they get used to it. Ellis probably came back with the dream of how you were, and now he has to get to know you as you are. Didn't you expect him to be the same as all those years ago?'

Heather propped her chin on her hand and thought about it. 'Well, not really, but then I was just presented with him as he is, totally out of the blue. It was different for him. He says he'd been thinking about it, dreaming it, for a very long time, so yes, I suppose all that would have been about how I was, not how I am.'

'There you are, then,' Jill said. 'The dreams were based on the old Heather. Now he's coping with the new one and it must –'

'Be a shock to his system,' Heather cut in. 'I see what you mean.'

'But he loves you, and you obviously love him.'

'Yes,' Heather said hesitantly. 'And there are times when I feel he knows me and understands me completely, when he makes me absolutely melt with love and desire. But there are others when I could happily strangle him.'

Jill laughed. 'Sounds pretty normal to me.'

'But is it?' Heather asked insistently. 'Is it really? I mean, the dramatic reverses, the plunge from love to . . . not hate, but exasperation and a sort of fury. Is that really normal?'

'I'm sure it is for lots of people,' Jill said, 'probably for most of us at times.'

'You and Adam?'

'Oh well, I do know how lucky I am, Adam is such a wonderful person. But, as I told you the other day, sometimes he drives me right up the wall. Why do you think I'm here now?'

Heather nodded. 'He more or less told me that himself when I called. Perhaps I'm overreacting, but Ellis, he has a very short fuse and he seems to be so easily rattled. If I disagree with him it's always very personal, as though he's affronted that I have a view that's different from his. Emotionally he's high maintenance.'

Jill shrugged. 'It's still early days. You haven't been able to spend much time together yet. Perhaps he just wants a bit more of your attention.'

'You're probably right,' Heather said, leaning back in her chair. 'The time thing is part of the problem. He's got heaps and I've got very little.'

'Let's go for a walk,' Jill suggested when they had finished their meal. The sun was close to setting but it was still light and she loved the dusk here in the mountains. 'Just a stroll before the light goes?' There was a path that had become her favourite; it meandered through tall trees up a steep slope towards a small clearing with a bench made from roughly hewn tree trunks, and a stunning view of the distant peaks.

'There's something else I need to tell you, Jill,' Heather said as they walked. 'About what you asked me earlier, about me and Adam. Before I went to Byron Bay I called to talk to you. Adam gave me your number, and we talked. Well, *he* didn't say much, of course –' she rolled her eyes – 'when does he ever? But when he told me you were away I got the feeling that . . . that part of the trouble between you was about what happened with Ellis all those years ago.'

Jill nodded, holding her breath in anticipation.

'It's pretty simple, really,' Heather said, 'but the longer you keep a secret, the deeper you lock it inside you, the harder it seems to talk about it. Your head tells you that it's not that awful or extraordinary, that it's something that happens to a lot of people, but you can't really convince yourself that the world won't fall apart if you start to talk about it. Anyway, that's what Adam and I did when Ellis left. I . . . well, I . . . '

'You were pregnant, and Adam helped you to terminate it and pawned his cello to pay for it,' Jill said.

Heather stopped walking and turned to face her. 'You know? How do you know?'

'I worked it out for myself,' Jill replied. 'It wasn't that difficult. What happened when Ellis left was obviously something that both of you wanted to keep hidden. Then Barb mentioned that when she and your mother got back from their cruise, Adam had pawned his cello because he needed a large sum of money. As soon as Barbara told me that, and added that he'd asked her not to tell your mother, and not to ask any questions, it was pretty obvious. Who or what mattered enough to Adam to make him pawn his cello? Only you, his mother and Barbara, and it wasn't about either of them. It didn't need a genius to work it out.'

They were in the clearing now and Heather brushed some leaves off the bench and sat down. 'So you know. Why didn't you tell Adam?'

'Because he needs to be able to tell me himself,' Jill said, sitting beside her. 'Not just about what happened, but why it was so significant to him that he wasn't only silenced by your promise, but by something within himself.'

Heather shivered slightly in the evening air, pushed her arms into the sweater that had been draped over her shoulders and pulled it on over her shirt. 'It was his religion, of course. He was still doing battle with all Dad's stuff. He'd had sin, hellfire and damnation hammered into him. I escaped most of it because I was a girl and younger, but it took Adam a long time and a great deal of heart searching to break free of it. The termination was devastating – illegal, of course, and shonkily done. There *were* some doctors doing abortions in those days, but Adam wasn't able to find one, so it was a backyard job.

'Mum and Barb were away for ages, thank goodness. We'd never have been able to keep it from them. So I was a mess, and Adam was too, because he'd had to organise it and find the money, all under relentless pressure from me, and then look after me. I was pretty sick. I got an infection and we had to get a doctor, and lie to him. I'm sure the doctor knew but he treated me anyway. It was really only much later that I understood how the religious conflict affected Adam. When you're young, you don't realise that everything you do has consequences, not just for you but for other people, and that even if you get away with it at the time, some day you'll have to pay.'

'Are you saying you wish you hadn't had the abortion?' Jill asked.

Heather shook her head. 'No, but I'm saying I wish I hadn't been stupid enough to get pregnant. And I wish it had been safe and legal for me to have a termination. Because as well as making the decision and actually going through with it, which was bad enough, there was this backyard business that left me feeling like a criminal. It takes a long time to recover from that, to get back some self-esteem, and there were physical consequences for me too.'

'What sort of consequences?'

'Years later I was having some gynaecological problems, and my doctor did some tests and found that the abortion and the infection had caused the sort of damage that meant I'd never be able to have children.'

'Oh, Heather, I'm so sorry,' Jill said.

Heather shrugged. 'In the end, of course, it didn't make that much difference because I never got into a relationship where I might have wanted to have children. There was a time in my late thirties, though, when I went through a lot of grief about it. But there were other things happening in my life, and I made myself focus on those and eventually the grief passed.'

They sat silently side by side for a few moments listening to the sound of the breeze in the tree tops, watching the last vestiges of dusk fade into darkness.

'Did you ever consider talking about your own experience?' Jill asked. 'Talking publicly, I mean?'

'Of course,' Heather said, 'many times. But how could I? Adam and I had promised each other that we'd never tell anyone, and when I got to the stage where I felt I *could* talk about it, he was still stuck in it. I couldn't do that to him, not after everything he'd gone through for me.' She stopped and turned to Jill. 'That's the bond, Jill, the connection you sense between us as more than the brother–sister thing. You go through something awful with someone and it ties you together. When I got shot, Shaun was there and he took care of me, and because of that I feel a real bond with him. We shared that dreadful experience and it'll always be there, something only we can fully understand. It's much deeper with Adam of course, not just because we're brother and sister, but because of all the guilt, and the illegality of it. It never goes away but you learn to live with it. I've come to terms with it but Adam never did. He's been stuck in it all these years and who knows what it'll take to shake him out of it?'

Smoke from bushfires drifted south towards the city as Jill drove home a few days later. It hung in a yellow-tinged grey blanket, blocking the sun, and it reminded her of how she'd felt as she set out on this journey – as though she were in danger of being smothered. She remembered that the French had a word for this act of taking time out: *dépaysement* was the purposeful self-removal that brought clarity and improved sensitivity to one's own surroundings. As she pulled into the drive and switched off the engine, Jill felt that clarity and freshness. Home looked remarkably good. Adam had cut the grass, and there were a couple of new citrus trees in big pots near the front door, something she'd been planning to do for ages. Whatever chaos lurked within she'd sort it out over the next few days before she went back to work. The front door opened as she got out of the car and Adam came towards her. He was barefoot, wearing long shorts and an old t-shirt and he looked different, looser, more upright; the way he moved seemed both more relaxed and more assertive.

'I missed you,' he said simply, wrapping his arms around her. 'I missed you a lot, and I'm so glad you're back.'

EIGHTEEN

Shaun thought that there had been no time in the eight years plus that he'd been working for Heather that he'd done his job so badly. In fact, had it not been for Diane, who seemed to be growing more confident and more efficient every day, he didn't know how they'd be managing. She'd brought a warmth and professionalism to the office, and had developed a polite scepticism that could deter time wasters. He, meanwhile, was a mess. He had simply fallen out of love with his job. Each morning he woke to the knowledge that he no longer wanted to be there and that he would have to do something about it, and do it soon.

'There are plenty of opportunities for someone like you,' Rosa had said over dinner in Sydney. 'There are several ministers who would grab you like a shot. And I wasn't joking earlier when I asked you if you wanted a job.'

Shaun looked up in surprise. 'You mean . . . ?'

'I mean I would grab you too if you were interested.'

'But you hardly know me,' he said, both confused and embarrassed by this sudden change in the conversation.

'I know enough. You'd probably be surprised by how much I know. We move in small circles, Shaun, people's reputations precede them, or,' she laughed, 'sometimes they trip them up. I'm prepared to take the chance. What about you?'

The more Shaun thought about it, the more the idea grew on him. Rosa had talked to him about some of the projects she was working on, the ways she wanted to take the business. The next day she'd shown him around her office, introduced him to some people, suggested areas that might be of interest to him. It meant a move to Sydney, of course, but he could rent out his house. The idea grew more attractive by the day and he began making notes about the sort of things he'd like to work on, ideas that had come into his head over the years and been squeezed aside by the pressure of running the electorate office.

The one thing he couldn't think about, though, was Heather. Heather who relied on him. Heather who had been shot. Heather who, right after the coming Christmas break, would have to gear up for an election campaign for which she'd be counting on him. So his days had become an unsatisfying mishmash of urgent electorate stuff that he absolutely had to deal with, a lot of agonising about what to do and when to do it, and some fascinating speculation about the sort of things he could do working with Rosa. It was the latter that was occupying his attention on Friday afternoon when he heard the door of the outer office open and someone come in to reception. Diane had gone to the printers and he was alone in the office. He went out to find Alex Roussos and Vince, about to ring the bell on the reception desk.

'Alex, Vince, hi. Is this business or social?'

'G'day, Shaun, it's business,' Alex said. 'Is Heather in?'

'Sorry, mate, at a meeting. I don't expect her back until about five. Have you got some news?'

'Maybe. Can we go and sit down?'

Shaun led them through to his office. 'So what's this about?'

'It's about this guy,' Alex said, pushing a colour photograph across the desk. 'Have you seen him before? D'you or Heather know him?'

Shaun picked up the photograph and felt his stomach lurch. It was a typical police mug shot, full face and two profiles. 'Danny Muswell,' he said, sure that his face had turned a fiery red. 'I doubt that Heather knows him, but yes, I've met him a couple of times. Why?'

'How come?' Alex asked, and Shaun noticed Vince taking out his notebook. 'Where did you meet him?'

230

Shaun's mouth went dry. He wasn't a person who lied convincingly, besides which he had no more desire to lie to Alex than he had to implicate Charlene in whatever Danny was up to. 'He used to go out with my ex-girlfriend,' Shaun said. 'I met him once in a club, and then a few weeks later, outside Barney's Bar.'

'That's all?' Alex asked, obviously waiting for more information.

'Yes. The first time, in the club, he was pretty much out of it – drunk or tripping, maybe. He tried to cut in on us but she told him to get lost.'

'And the second time?'

Shaun took a deep breath. 'The second time, we'd been for a drink. It was quite late on a Friday evening. He was way out of it again, leaning against the wall outside the pub with a couple of mates. When he saw us come out he started yelling abuse, so I just grabbed Charlene's arm and we headed for the car park. He came after us and grabbed me by the shoulder. He was yelling and swearing, blaming me for Charlene dumping him, and then up comes his fist and he smashes me in the face.'

'Did you retaliate?'

Shaun shook his head. 'Mate, I'm no street fighter. I sort of staggered back against the wall, and I've got blood streaming out of my nose. I'd just put my arms up to protect myself, and his mates grabbed him. They dragged him off and shoved him into a car. That was the last I saw of him.'

'And you didn't report it?'

'No. Don't know why, not really, now I come to think of it. Didn't want to upset Charlene, I suppose.'

Alex nodded, sliding the photograph back across the desk and then putting it in his pocket. 'And that was the last you saw of him?'

'Yes,' Shaun said, feeling calmer now and glancing up at Vince. 'He never bothered me again. I reckon he must've got himself another girlfriend. What's going on, Alex?'

'We found Danny Muswell – or rather, his body – this morning,' Alex said. 'In a big house up near the baths. He'd been shot three times, once in the back of the head and twice in the abdomen. We won't be sure until we hear from the lab but we think he may have been shot with the same gun that was used to shoot Heather.'

'No!' Diane said, sinking her head into her hands. 'Oh no, this can't be happening, not just when we got her sorted out, not now.'

Shaun put a cup of tea in front of her. 'Look,' he said, 'it might not be too bad. I was shitting myself when they were here, but I've had time to think about it since then.'

'It's bad, it's really bad,' Diane said. 'They'll find out about Danny, and they'll work out what Charlene was doing and she'll go to jail. I can't believe this is happening. And the gun . . . why would the person who shot Heather shoot Danny as well?'

'No idea,' Shaun said, 'not yet. Unless perhaps it's some sort of hit man. Christ, I'm talking like something out of *Law & Order*.'

'Does Heather know yet?'

'No, she's still at the meeting in Port Stephens, and Alex and Vince only left about ten minutes before you got back. Listen, Diane, here's what I think. They'll want to talk to you but not yet; maybe not for a day or two, even. There's no point lying, you have to tell the truth but you don't have to tell them everything. Danny's dead, he's already on their records, it's not as if they need evidence to convict him. They'll be focusing on who shot him and why, and they already know it's likely to be drug related. Charlene is only a tiny part of the stuff Danny was involved in.'

'I see, yes,' Diane said, nodding. 'So what are you . . . ?'

'I told them about the times I met Danny with Charlene, and that he had a go at me because of her. But I didn't say anything about what she was up to and you mustn't either. We just keep quiet until we see how things are going and then I'll talk to Alex on my own, without Vince around, see if there's a way of dealing with it without dragging Charlene back into it again.'

'D'you think it *could* be a hit man?'

Shaun shrugged. 'It was just something that occurred to me because I can't see any connection. But suppose it was, who would have hired him? I mean, there's probably a lot of people who would be glad to see the end of Danny, but what's the connection to Heather? It doesn't make sense.'

Diane took a very deep breath and sipped her tea. 'No,' she said, thinking that it absolutely made sense to her, and that someone close to her would be very happy to see the end of both Danny and Heather, and hoping that that knowledge didn't show in her face. 'You're right, it doesn't.'

'Alex is coming back at five to talk to Heather,' Shaun said. 'It might be better if you're not here.'

She nodded and got up. 'Much better,' she said. 'Give me time to calm down.'

'Will you be all right on your own?'

'I'll be okay, but I'd like time to get my head around this before I have to talk to them. Should we warn Charlene?'

'Not yet,' Shaun said. 'Let's give it a bit longer. I'll call you when they've talked to Heather. And you call me if you're worried. I'll come over.'

Diane headed along the coast road towards Nobby's Point, deliberately avoiding home in case the police were planning to pay her a visit. She felt like a person on the run, her eyes constantly on the rear-view mirror, her skin prickling with anxiety when she spotted a police patrol car pulling out of a side turning. It was a relief to park the car and get out in the fresh air. The sun was brilliant but the wind off the sea was surprisingly cool and she started walking briskly towards the lighthouse. Was Gerry capable of something like this? Six months ago in her anger and bitterness she would have said an unequivocal yes, but now? He'd always been self-opinionated and ruthlessly ambitious, and it was that hard edge that had first attracted her to him. Gerry had done some dodgy deals in the past, of that she was sure, but nothing like this, nothing violent, nothing criminal. But if you were asking who would want to see the back of Danny, he would have to be high on the list. He'd actually threatened to finish him off when Diane told him about Charlene. Could he have meant it? Could he have thought that now that Charlene was safely out of the way he could get rid of Danny so that she could come back home?

And Heather? He'd been insanely angry when the protest

against his high-rise development was in full swing. Diane had even heard him say that he'd like to kill Heather, but surely that was just something people said? She'd said things like that herself, probably about Gerry, but it didn't mean she would act on it.

Diane sat down on a seat and closed her eyes behind her dark glasses, feeling the cool wind on her face, listening to the sound of waves breaking. It was ridiculous. But she did remember him telling her that he was surprised how cheap it was to take out a contract. He'd come home late from a rugby club dinner, where someone had been talking about it. Not that anyone had ever thought about doing it, he'd said, that was just what they'd heard.

Gerry had the motive, the connections and the money, but did he really have what it took to wipe people out? How could she have lived with him for more than thirty years and not be able to absolutely rule it out?

Diane got up and strode back to the car. She needed to talk to someone, someone who would understand how terrifying it was, how utterly ridiculous, but at the same time so obviously possible. She punched the numbers into her mobile and waited anxiously, listening to the ringing tone.

'Of course you can come over, dear,' Barbara said. 'Come whenever you like, stay the night if you want.'

'Thanks,' she said. 'That would be a big help. I'll see you soon.' And she hung up, put the phone back in her bag, drove out of the car park and headed towards town and the highway.

Ellis picked up his towel and sunglasses, ran down the steps and took the path to the beach. It was early, the air still and warm, the sea calm with small swells breaking on the sand in flurries of white foam – perfect for a swim, then coffee and the newspaper and back to work. Despite the rocky start, Ellis felt his weekend with Heather had been a success. In future, he told himself, he must be more tolerant, not expect everything to happen the way he wanted it quite so quickly. Heather was still unused to him and his way of life and the things that were important to him, but they were getting there.

Naturally it was taking her time to come to terms with the idea of giving up her job; she had been doing it a long time, and doing it well. It had been the same for him and he might not have done it even then had it not been for that life-changing time at Nirvana. Now he could be the catalyst for Heather, but she had to do it in her own way and he knew it would be soon. He was confident that after all that had happened in the last few months, she would not go into the new year kicking off an election campaign with all its implications for the future.

Her lack of enthusiasm for Head to Heart had been disappointing but of course it was all new to her, and in the end her response had been useful. 'You should've been a lawyer, Heather,' he'd said when she started interrogating him. 'You'd do a splendid job in court.'

She'd blushed then and put aside the paperwork. 'I didn't mean to interrogate you,' she'd said. 'But this is all so new to me, it's not an area I know anything about. I'm just raising the questions that come up for me, as a total outsider, reading the plan and these early chapters.'

'I'm teasing you, darling,' he'd said. 'This is just the sort of help I need, because these are the questions a prospective client would ask. I need to come at it much more from that angle. What people *need* to know, rather than just what I want to tell them. I can get on to that once they've signed on the dotted line. You've given me plenty to think about.'

'It's an awful lot of money,' she'd said then. 'Even the initial fee for preparing the plan is astronomical.'

'I do have a lot of money,' he'd said, trying to sound modest. 'And I'll have a lot more when this gets off the ground.'

She'd nodded. 'Yes, the client fee structure Luke has suggested is astronomical too. Do you really think people will pay this much?'

'People pay ridiculous sums for far less,' Ellis said. 'The clients I'm aiming for can afford it.'

'And you're confident you can deliver value for those fees?'

Ellis was stung but he laughed it off. 'So now you're questioning my integrity?'

'Of course not,' Heather said, blushing again. 'It's just that . . . well, it's another world, really. Sorry.'

'I should think so too,' he said, still smiling. 'I'm not some sort of shonky New Age hippie, you know.'

'No, no I realise that,' Heather said, then she'd paused and looked out to the vista of the sea framed by the branches of bougainvillea that clung to the balcony. 'Does it matter to you, having a lot of money?'

'I'd rather have money than be without it, and I'd rather have a lot than a little,' he'd said. 'What a funny question.'

'I was just thinking, what if you lost it all?'

'That won't happen.'

'But just suppose, for a moment, that it did. You know, like my shooting. If I'd been asked about it I would have said, no, it could never happen. But it did. So just imagine this happening, that you suddenly, for whatever reason, lose everything – the house, your capital, your investments, whatever else you own, gone, just like that.'

'Okay, I'm imagining,' Ellis had said, leaning back and closing his eyes. There was no harm in indulging her.

'So how does it feel?'

'Impossible.' He heard her sigh of frustration and opened his eyes again, 'Sorry, I'm trying but it's not working.'

'You mean you can't make that leap to imagine how you would feel? Can you imagine how someone else would feel in that situation?'

He shook his head. 'Not really, and I don't particularly want to.'

Heather leaned forward. She looked tense and alert, and was peering quite closely into his face. 'Didn't you have to do that to defend your clients? Put yourself in their position, know what it was like to be where they were, why they might or might not have done it? How they would be feeling?'

'No way,' he'd said then, laughing. He stood up and pulled her to her feet. 'It was a work of imagination, certainly, but my imagining of what I could create to defend them. Certainly no leap into their situation. Good heavens, if I'd tried that I'd probably have convinced myself they were guilty.' He kissed her lightly on the lips. 'Thank you, Heather, you've given me plenty to be going on with.'

Ellis dropped his towel on the sand, kicked off his thongs and padded down to the water. Behind him the familiar steep sweep of the hillside with its dense green foliage enclosing the houses and the narrow roads that led upwards to the lighthouse gave him a secure sense of the rightness of his presence in this glorious place. If he turned he would be able to see the smooth green slope of his own roof, the bougainvillea with its cascade of purple blossom and, beneath it, the creamy white and shell-pink blossoms of the frangipani trees. In front of him the ocean lapped in sparkling ripples at his feet. Paradise. Yes, he would certainly rather have a lot of money than a little. And he'd rather have Heather, with all her complexities and contradictions, than not have her at all – far rather. 'You're a very lucky man, Ellis,' he told himself, 'very lucky. But you also deserve this, you really do.'

'Deserve what, Ellis?' a voice asked behind him, and he turned to see Leah, a sarong tied over her bathers, sandals in her hand. 'Are you talking to yourself?'

'Leah!' he said, wishing she hadn't heard him. 'You're out early this morning.'

'I am indeed. My new regime is to walk every morning, and this is really the best time of the day. Heather still asleep?'

'Oh, she's gone back to parliament, so I've been alone since then.'

'That's a shame. I was planning on asking you both over for dinner. Next time she's here, perhaps? James and I liked her a lot.'

Ellis nodded and it didn't escape his notice that, although he'd known James and Leah for several years, he'd never before been asked to dinner and he wasn't actually being asked now, only in the company of Heather, when she was available. But at the same time he felt a pleasant glow at the thought of going there with her as a couple. 'She's a very special person,' he said with a smile. 'Very special.'

'So, come on then,' Leah persisted. 'What were you thinking

about, standing here in the water at six in the morning talking to yourself? What is it that you deserve?'

'Heather,' he said, surprised that he felt quite an emotional lump in his throat as he said her name. 'I was thinking how lucky I am to have found her again. And then I thought I deserve it, I must deserve it or it wouldn't have happened.'

Leah laughed and reached out her hand to touch his arm. 'I'm very happy for you, for you both,' she said. 'But it's no good her being stuck in parliament or her office. You'll have to persuade her to come here, Ellis.'

Ellis kicked his foot in the water and watched the droplets scatter in a sparkling arc. 'I have every intention of doing that,' he said, 'preferably as soon as possible.'

The meeting had run longer than Heather had anticipated and had proved exceptionally boring. She wished she'd asked Shaun or Diane to come with her because at one point she simply lost concentration and wasn't sure whether she'd missed something essential. It was past five thirty and she felt like going home, having a shower and curling up on the settee with a drink and a good book. But she needed to pick up some work for the weekend. As if to confirm her decision, her phone bleeped and, steering with one hand and with one eye still on the road, she read the text from Shaun: *Are you on your way?*

Less than ten minutes later, as she let herself in, her heart leapt at the sight of Alex and Vince sitting in Shaun's office. It means nothing, she told herself, calm down, Heather, don't get carried away again. 'Hi,' she said, 'are you waiting for me?'

'We are,' Alex said, and Heather noticed that this time he looked different. Not as though he were dreading having to tell her there was nothing new. As if it might, after all, be okay to ask the question again.

'You mean . . . do you have . . . ?' she began, her heart thumping against her ribs, her face flushing with anticipation.

'We might be getting somewhere,' Alex said with a smile. 'If we can go into your office?'

She led them through and saw Shaun turn and head back to his own room. 'Come on, Shaun,' she called.

'We talked with Shaun earlier,' Alex said. 'Now we need to talk to you.'

Heather shrugged and closed the door, gesturing to them to sit down. 'So what is it? What have you got?' she asked, barely able to contain her excitement.

'First off,' Alex said, putting a photograph on the desk in front of her, 'can you tell me if you know this man?'

Heather looked carefully at the picture and shook her head. 'I've never seen him before. Who is he? Is this the man who shot me? Have you arrested him?'

'Whoa!' Alex replied, holding up his hands. 'We're not there yet. You're absolutely sure you've never seen him or had anything to do with him?'

'Positive,' Heather said. 'For heaven's sake, Alex, just tell me what's going on.'

'Well,' he said, 'this morning . . . '

She'd heard about Charlene's former boyfriend before, of course, on the day that Shaun had come into the office with a hugely swollen and weeping eye and the side of his face turning various shades of purple. And so now he was dead, but she couldn't see what it had to do with her.

Alex held up two evidence bags. 'This one,' he said, 'is the bullet they took out of your shoulder. And this one was taken by our pathologist from the body of Danny Muswell this morning. Forensics have just confirmed that they were both fired from the same gun.'

Heather clapped her hand over her mouth in shock. 'The same gun! But why . . . I mean, how . . . what does it mean?'

'We're not sure yet, Heather,' Alex said. 'But it *does* mean that we now have something to go on. We have another bullet, the weapon, a man who's been shot and we know who he is. And we have, in the hospital, a witness to this morning's shooting who, when he comes around from the anaesthetic, may be able to tell us something. It's a hundred per cent more than we've had at any time since the night you were shot.'

'So,' Heather said, walking into Shaun's office when she'd shown them out, 'progress at last, thank god. I was beginning to think this would never happen, that it was just going to be one of those unsolved crimes that goes on so long that everyone forgets about it. Everyone except me. What do you think? It's a great breakthrough, isn't it?'

'It is,' Shaun said. 'It's the breakthrough we've all been waiting for. But, Heather, as you know, I do, or rather did, know Danny Muswell, so did Charlene and, of course, Diane. And there's some stuff I need to tell you that maybe I should have told you before.'

NINETEEN

Adam woke early and lay for a while, watching Jill sleeping soundly beside him as the morning light seeped through the blinds, casting horizontal stripes across the bed. He leaned over and kissed her lightly, and she murmured, shifted her position and slept on. Moving cautiously so as not to disturb her, he got up, went through to the back of the house and sat down on the back doorstep. The garden smelled of newly cut grass and the huge clump of sweet peas that Jill had planted weeks earlier now swarmed against the side of the house in a mass of rainbow colours.

What a difference a couple of weeks could make, he thought. He had sat here alone the morning that Jill left, wondering anxiously where they were heading and whether this time apart would help sort out the mess he'd created. On the second day, feeling a little more energised, he began to flex his muscles in the house, to take advantage of the fact that he had the place to himself and could do what he wanted.

Jill, just like his mother and Yvette, and to a lesser extent Heather, was a domestic diva. She liked things done her own way. Similar, Adam thought, to conductors with their highly individual interpretations and expectations that no member of the orchestra would ever question in their presence. Adam admired this sort of organisational masterminding, as well as the speed and skill with which it was executed, but it left him feeling surplus to requirements – as though his contributions to domestic life were unnecessary. The best plan was to withdraw, stay out of the way and let them get on with it. In a practical sense it made life easy, but at another level it was limiting – like eating a good meal but regretting that you'd had no choice about the menu.

He'd begun, that second day, by sorting the old newspapers, bottles and cans for recycling and then started on the kitchen, cleaning and tidying cupboards, chucking away out-of-date items from the pantry and freezer. By lunch time he was in full swing and by the time Daisy and Toby got home from school, the living areas looked as though they had been attacked by a team of flying domestics.

'You can have something to eat and then it's room cleaning,' Adam said, brooking no arguments and promising a choice of takeaway in return for a complete overhaul.

Ignoring Toby's disgruntled silence and Daisy's tears and whining, he worked with them liberating a rotten apple, a couple of fossilised sandwiches and a selection of socks that smelled like dead animals from the bottom of Toby's wardrobe. Despite Daisy's protests, a collection of Jill's discarded cosmetics, covered in dust and scattered with a few ancient sticky M & Ms went in the bin, along with a vast collection of pictures torn from magazines, old drawings, and junk mail that she'd hoarded from the letterbox.

The next day he started on the windows, the laundry and the bathrooms, relishing the physicality of it, the satisfaction of immediate results, and most of all the feeling that he was reclaiming something, exercising a part of himself that had been lost. It was only at the end of the first week that it occurred to him that Jill might be offended, that she might see this domestic blitz as some sort of criticism, but it was done now and he felt better for it.

'But why?' she'd asked him, looking around in amazement as he led her back into the house.

'Because I wanted . . . no, I needed to,' he'd explained. 'I need to have a part in this.'

'I'm a control freak, aren't I?' she'd said, sighing.

'Well . . . ' he started, and then decided to abandon caution. 'Yes, you are a bit. And, of course, it's wonderful that you take everything on, but at the same time I see you struggling, and I see things not getting done, things I could do, but you won't let me near them. We need to work out a division of responsibility and then get out of each other's way.'

'I thought I'd be coming home to chaos,' Jill said. 'I was dreading that part but this, it's weird, like I don't own it anymore.'

'You don't,' Adam said abruptly, and he saw her start. 'We own it together. I'm just exercising my share of ownership. I haven't done that before.'

Adam got up from the step and strolled across the cool grass to break a couple of dead heads from the roses. So they were over the domestic hurdle. Reclaiming a role in the house had given him a new sense of himself and his place in all their lives. But there was still a way to go.

The night he had sat on Barbara's sofa and wept, Adam had felt as though some ancient rusty coil were unwinding inside him. The confession that he had vowed he would never make to another person had forced its way out of him, triggered by her innocent question about pawning his cello. For the rest of that day he had struggled to hold himself in check, to organise the shed cleaning, to share a glass of wine with George, then dinner and finally to get the kids to bed. But all the time he had felt the unwinding, felt it cranking and shifting, and finally he couldn't hold on to it any longer. As the words spilled out in pools at his feet he could hear his father's rhetoric, the horrors of sin, the threats of damnation, of hellfire and the impossibility of redemption. And as they dropped away he heard himself as if he were an outsider, heard himself and was shocked by the punishing, unforgiving, blind intensity of something he no longer believed and had not believed for a long time.

'It's the past, Adam,' Barbara said. 'It's not a part of what you believe now. Don't let it ruin your life and your relationships just because you and Heather made a pact not to talk about it.'

'I know,' he'd said. 'It's the stumbling block that constantly trips me. It's not just the promises Heather and I made, it's because I let Dad down, and all of you – you, Mum, Heather, I let you all down. I was supposed to look after you, it was the last thing he ever said to me. It was my responsibility and I failed miserably. I let Heather convince me that it was what she had to do, but I was dying inside. And when it was over I was terrified, I thought she would die and we'd both go to hell. The one thing he asked me to do and I failed him and let everyone down.'

'But you *did* look after Heather. How would she have coped without you? You looked after her at great emotional and spiritual cost to yourself. Not in the way Roy would have wanted but in the way that *she needed*. Roy laid a really unfair burden on you, but he loved you and it was his way of trying to make you strong. It really is time to put that burden down.'

Adam tossed the dead rose heads onto the ground and with his bare foot pushed the earth over to cover them. It was inexplicable to him now that he hadn't talked about it before, that he hadn't been able to see the unreasonableness of his father's words, the old men's rules of manhood that had gripped him. For decades he had worn his own crippling badge of failure, binding himself to the past, to something he thought he had long ago rejected, and when Heather was shot he had added another layer of guilt and shame, as though he could somehow have prevented it. He reminded himself of his distaste for the formal act of confession; how he had despised it, called it a 'get out of jail free' card. How superficial that seemed now, now that he knew that confession was one of the hardest and the most liberating of acts. Rather than offering a free pass out of guilt it opened up the chance of forgiveness, the chance to forgive himself, the chance to know himself in a different way.

There was a faint sound from inside the house, and he saw that Jill was up and opening the blinds at the bedroom window. She waved to him, and he waved back and strolled up the garden to the house. He had made a great leap while she was away and now he must make another; somehow he must find a way to tell her about the past, and the strange and crippling hold it had had on him for decades.

Shaun was watering the garden when the phone rang.

'What are you doing?' Heather asked, and he immediately felt guilty, because he'd been standing there with the hose, thinking that if Alex made an arrest in the next few days, it might make it easier for him to do the dastardly thing and tell her he was going to resign. She had been amazing when he told her about Charlene and the drugs.

'I do wish you'd told me earlier,' she'd said. 'But at the same time I can see why you didn't. Anyway, it looks as though you and Diane came up with an excellent solution. Poor Diane, she must have been worried sick.'

They'd talked then about Charlene, and how well she seemed to be doing and agreed that it was best to say nothing about it to the police. At least, not yet.

'I'm watering,' he said now. 'Woke up early and couldn't go back to sleep, too restless.'

'Me too,' Heather said. 'I'm walking. Have been for nearly an hour and don't know what to do when I stop. I suppose you haven't heard anything from Alex?'

'No, but I think it'd be you he'd call first.'

'I suppose so. I thought we might have heard something last night, after he got to talk to the witness.'

'Maybe he didn't,' Shaun said. 'You know what hospitals are like, and the bloke might still be sedated.' He paused. 'Look, I was thinking of having a shower and then distracting myself with a large breakfast. We could go together, if you like.'

'Oh yes! A lot of bacon could make a big difference to my state of mind. Where do you want to go?'

Shaun turned off the outside tap, wound the hose onto its reel and went through the house to the bathroom. It was strange, he thought, that Heather hadn't started talking about revving up after Christmas, nor about who they should get to do what on the campaign committee. It made it easier for him, of course; he would have felt terrible having to talk about that while still trying to decide when and how he should go.

The least he could do, he thought as he finished shaving, was to find someone decent to take over, but he couldn't start asking around for possibilities until he'd told Heather. The minute he started putting out feelers she'd hear something and he needed it to come from him. Christmas was the time, he decided. Sometime over the Christmas break he'd pick the moment and tell her.

'This was a brilliant idea,' Heather said, looking with relish at the large plate of scrambled eggs and crispy bacon. She picked up a golden rasher in her fingers and sampled it. 'Oh my god, this is to die for. Taste it, Shaun.'

He shook his head. 'No thanks, I've got this thing about dead pig. Can't handle it.'

'But you've got sausages,' she said.

'Chicken sausages.'

'So dead bird is okay?'

'I never claimed to be logical,' he said with a grin. 'I'm just rather fond of pigs. I once had a holiday job on a pig farm.' The waiter put their coffee and a large plate of toast on the table and took away the menu. 'Maybe a huge quantity of food will have a settling effect,' Shaun said, picking up his cutlery.

'Settling straight on my hips, I suspect,' Heather said. 'But who cares? Have you spoken to Diane?'

Shaun nodded. 'Last night, and then again this morning. She's very agitated, more even than I imagined she'd be. I think she's very worried about Charlene. She's in Morpeth with Barbara.'

'With Barbara?'

'They've been seeing a bit of each other since the party.'

'Really? I didn't realise. That's nice for Barb. Diane's turned out well, hasn't she? Not so long ago I thought she was a pain, but now I really like her and she's doing a great job.'

Shaun kept his head down and concentrated on his breakfast, intent on avoiding any discussion about the office. He was saved by his mobile ringing; they exchanged looks across the table.

'Alex?' Heather said.

'He'd be calling you if he had anything new,' Shaun said, opening his phone. His eyebrows shot up. 'It *is* him. Hi, Alex.'

'Need to have a word, Shaun,' Alex said, and Shaun felt the same wave of nausea he'd experienced when he knew he had to tell Heather about Charlene and the drugs. 'Where are you?' Alex asked.

'Having breakfast with Heather in Beaumont Street.'

'Good. Mind if I join you so I can talk to you both together?'

'He's on his way here,' Shaun said, hanging up.

Heather's eyes widened. 'That's it, he's talked to the witness and he knows something. This is the end of it, isn't it, at last. Oh my god, I hope he hurries up.'

'Hang on, Heather, he might just have more questions, or maybe the witness told him what Charlene was up to.'

'I suppose so, but on the other hand . . . '

'Let's just cross our fingers and eat our breakfast,' Shaun said. 'Eat up – he won't be long and he might take a fancy to your bacon.'

She laughed and Shaun wished that he felt even a little bit as relaxed as he was trying to sound.

There is no right way to do this, Jill thought, no perfect time or place, I just have to tell him I know and see what happens. They were walking, at Adam's suggestion, along a path that followed the line of the lake, close to the cycle route that he and Kirsty took each week. Toby had gone skateboarding, and then on to Bree Adams's house, and they had been suddenly and unexpectedly relieved of Daisy's company, by virtue of an impromptu invitation from the mother of her new friend.

'Let's do something together,' Adam said when he got back from delivering Daisy. 'Like you said on the phone, the way we used to do.'

'I was just going to make a cake,' she'd said, reaching up for the flour which was, surprisingly, in its proper place, where it hadn't been for a long time. 'We don't have any.'

He came over to her, picked up the flour jar and put it back on the shelf. 'Jill,' he repeated, 'let's do something together.' It was disconcerting, this new-old assertiveness that she vaguely recalled from their early, child-free days. 'Let's go for a walk.'

The narrow path was bordered by steep grassy banks dense

with trees. The afternoon sun sent light dancing in corkscrews through the branches. Adam walked a few steps ahead, holding back the occasional overhanging branch for her.

'Adam,' she said, catching her breath in the tension. 'I know what happened, I know about the abortion.'

He stopped and turned to her, shock written across his face.

'Heather told me. She came to see me while I was away. She told me all about it.'

Adam swayed slightly and sat down abruptly on the grassy edge of the bank. 'I was trying to think of a way to tell you.'

'Well, now you don't have to.' Jill sat down beside him and he moved along to make room for her. 'Heather told me everything,' she went on. 'She knew the silence was a problem for us, you and me, and that you didn't want to break your promise to her.'

Adam leaned forward, resting his forearms on his thighs, clasping his hands between his knees. 'How much did she tell you?'

'Everything,' Jill said. 'How she leaned on you to help her against your better judgment, how you got the money, how you looked after her; and how terribly hard it was for you because at the time it was the absolute antithesis of everything you believed in.'

He nodded, seeming unable to speak or look at her.

'Can I ask you something about it?' Jill ventured. 'I do understand why it was so hard for you. You were there for Heather when she was in the worst possible trouble and you stood by her and did what she asked, although you believed it was unforgivable. What I don't understand is why, when you did all that sort of religious housecleaning a few years later, you weren't able to get this whole thing into some different sort of perspective.'

He nodded, still not speaking, staring at the ground, and she saw him swallow hard several times before he straightened up and looked at her, and began to explain about his father.

'That was a cruel thing he did to you,' she said later, 'a cruel burden to put on a little boy's shoulders.'

'Perhaps, but it was all he knew, the same stuff he'd got from Granddad. While you were away I talked to Barbara, I told her. She asked me something . . . '

'Why you pawned the cello?'

'Yes. It was like she'd pushed the release button. I don't think she knew what hit her that weekend.'

'She would have been glad,' Jill said. 'Glad to see you release yourself from all that. Heather too, it releases her as well.'

They got up and walked on, hand in hand now the path was wider, past the marshy edge of the lake where tall rushes brushed their arms and a pair of ibis stalked through the shallow, muddy water.

'So I suppose the fact that Heather talked to you means she's confronted Ellis about it,' Adam said.

'Confronted Ellis?' Jill asked. 'What do you mean?'

'Exactly what I said. She must have dealt with all this with Ellis, or is she still putting that off?'

Jill hesitated. 'I don't know. She didn't say anything much about Ellis. Does he even know? I sort of assumed he'd already left by the time she realised she was pregnant.'

Adam shook his head. 'So she didn't tell you everything, after all. She gave you the edited version.'

'What do you mean?'

Adam turned to face her. 'Ellis was there, Jill. He didn't dump her before she realised she was pregnant, he did it *because* she told him she was pregnant. She needed his help and support and he'd promised her many times that he'd leave his wife, but of course there was always a reason why the time wasn't right. When she told him about the pregnancy she thought it might be the thing that would make him keep his promise. She certainly thought he would be there for her. But when she told him, he . . . ' Adam paused, as though, Jill thought, it made him feel physically sick to say it. 'He asked what proof she had that it was his child. Heather was nineteen – eighteen, when she met him – it was her first sexual relationship. She was in love, or infatuated, with Ellis, who knows which? He told her that he wasn't going to be caught out by the oldest trick in the book, and he sent her away.'

Adam stopped, drawing breath, shaking his head again. 'She was a total emotional wreck even before she had the termination. Ellis never called, never wrote, he never spoke to her or saw her again, and three weeks later she heard he was taking a job in Adelaide and moving there with his family. He'd known about it for several months and never told her. That's why I hate Ellis Hargreaves, Jill, hate him with a passion. And it's why I still can't understand why Heather would consider speaking to him, let alone getting into this relationship with him. That's why I find it so hard to be civil to him, and it's why this is going to cripple my relationship with my sister if it goes on.'

Shaun had just brought up his breakfast. Grasping the toilet bowl to steady himself, he dragged himself to his feet and grabbed the doorjamb, edging his way out of the cubicle, his body pressed against the wall to keep himself upright. The white tiled walls of the men's room swayed and undulated, and the sweat that he'd broken into as he thrust his way between the tables to get there crawled down his neck and dripped from his eyebrows. The door swung open.

'You all right, Shaun?' Alex called. 'Christ, mate, you look bloody awful.' He tried to steer Shaun to a slatted bench but Shaun shook off his hand, grasped the side of the washbasin and turned on the tap. Gripping the basin with both hands he pushed his head under the stream of cold water, letting it cascade over his face and neck. Alex handed him a handful of rough paper towels and he buried his face in them, holding on to them over his closed eyes until the dizziness eased.

'Are you absolutely sure?' he asked.

'We've got a signed statement from one Kevin James, associate of Danny Muswell, who was ready to tell us everything in the hope that I'll put in a word with the judge.'

Shaun leaned back against the wall, closed his eyes and slid slowly down to sit on the tiled floor. 'Let me get this straight,' he said, as Alex joined him on the floor. 'Danny was shot with his own weapon by some dealer further up the food chain who he'd been ripping off?'

'Right,' Alex said.

'Can I come in?' Heather asked, sticking her head around the door.

'Sure,' Alex nodded, 'there's only us in here and I don't think Shaun can move yet.'

She crossed the tiles and sat down on the other side of Shaun. 'Are you okay?'

'I'm getting there. So,' he began again, 'Danny and this Kevin ran into Charlene in the pub, and Danny started hassling her?'

'Yep. Kevin says she told him to get lost, that she was waiting for you but you were still at the office. He'd been using and was totally off the planet, and so Kevin and another mate got him out of the pub and into the back of the car, and Danny insisted on paying you a visit. Kevin insists they didn't know he had a weapon but I'm not sure I believe that.'

Shaun rested his head against the wall. 'So they drove to the office and parked, and that's when Danny stuck the gun in the back of Kevin's neck?'

'That's right. They saw a few people come out of the office and drive off, and then you and Heather came out and you were messing about with the door.'

'I set the alarm and then locked it.'

'Yes, and Heather was waiting for you and so was Danny. He lined you up at the top of the steps but, just as he fired, Heather moved in front of you.'

'I tripped,' Heather said, 'I remember it clearly. I caught my shoe on an irregular tile at the edge of the top step, and I grabbed your arm to save myself.'

'Exactly,' Alex cut in. 'And in the split second you did that you caught the bullet that was meant for Shaun, and Kevin put his foot down and they took off out of the car park.'

Shaun turned to look at Heather. 'Remember I said that night that I didn't think anyone was trying to kill you? But I thought it was random, I never imagined . . . '

She put her hand on his arm. 'Of course not, Shaun, how could you.'

'Apparently, Danny was saying later that he just wanted to scare you but who knows?' Alex said. 'Ice is deadly, Danny was psychotic. But that bullet had your name on it, Shaun, and if Heather hadn't tripped on the steps you could be pushing up the daisies right now.'

'So you didn't tell him about Charlene?' Diane asked, hugely relieved that her suspicions about Gerry were unfounded, although knowing that Shaun had been the target intensified her fears for her daughter.

Heather shook her head. 'No, Shaun and I discussed this on the way here. We still feel it's best to keep quiet. They have a lot of evidence on Danny anyway, and now they're getting together a case that will pin down the guy that shot him. They're treating the shooting as macho stuff, jealousy fuelled by drugs.'

'Like I said before,' Shaun said, 'I'll talk to Alex alone if it looks dodgy. He won't be happy but I think he'll understand.'

Heather and Shaun had turned up at Barbara's place an hour or so earlier and at the sight of them in the open doorway, Diane had felt faint with shock, and with the anticipation that they were bringing really bad news.

'It's okay,' Heather had reassured her, taking her arm and steering her into Barbara's lounge room. 'It's fine, that's why we're here, but we need to look after Shaun. He wanted to come with me but he's not feeling too good.'

Diane thought he looked like death, grey-faced and distraught, and it was soon clear why. 'I don't know what to say to either of you,' she said. 'Sorry sounds ridiculous but you're both in this situation because of my daughter –'

'Don't, Diane,' Heather said. 'For heaven's sake, don't start feeling guilty for the actions of a small-time drug dealer who was off his head.'

'She's right,' Shaun said. He was clutching a mug of very strong tea that Barbara had given him, and looked marginally better than when he'd arrived. 'Absolutely right. It's just so hard to get your head around it, isn't it? After all this time.'

'I don't understand why the police didn't think about it before,' Diane said. 'Did they even consider the possibility that Heather wasn't the target?'

252

'No,' Heather said. 'As Alex said – with some embarrassment, I might add – if it had been two other people coming out of an office they would naturally think it might be either, but one being a fairly controversial member of parliament they went for the obvious.'

'They did have a look at me, apparently,' Shaun said, 'checked my record in case I might have been involved. But of course they didn't find anything suspicious. Somehow, although they seem to have known about Danny for months, they didn't actually make the connection to Charlene and then to me. Alex's boss is apparently not impressed.'

'It's a terrible shock for you, Shaun,' Barbara said, 'but what about you, Heather? It must be such a relief.'

'At the moment I don't feel anything,' Heather said. 'I was beside myself waiting for Alex to arrive, and then when he told us I just felt flat – and, of course, worried about Shaun. I keep telling myself it's over, that it was never about me, but I can't actually feel that yet. Not relief, not happiness, not anything, just flat.' She saw them looking at her and knew how strange it must sound. For months she had been saying that everything would be all right once they had found the perpetrator, and now here she was discussing it almost as though she weren't involved.

George got up and walked to the door. 'I'm going next door to get my bottle of brandy,' he said. 'You two both look as though you need something stronger than tea.'

Heather lay on the settee watching the SBS news but not listening to it. She wasn't listening to anything else either. She was just there, or at least that's how it felt, just there wondering what it all meant, why she wasn't out celebrating, what she was supposed to feel. Everything had changed so suddenly. She'd been waiting for Alex, unable to eat her breakfast because of the anticipation, and then nothing, absolutely nothing at all, except amazement and a feeling that something had been taken away from her, something that had become a part of her. She had so often imagined how it would feel to know that it was all over – the relief, the liberation of it – but it didn't feel that way at all.

Ellis had been wonderful when she'd called to tell him. He alone seemed to understand why rather than celebrating she felt more as though she were in mourning.

'There's a sort of nobility to being attacked for your beliefs,' he said, 'especially attacked in such a cowardly and brutal way. You could feel proud of it, although you may not have been aware of that. That's what's been taken away. Now you know you were shot by mistake it's as though you went through all the pain and fear for no real purpose, no cause that you can be proud of. Of course you feel terrible.'

He was right. Remembering that first morning in the hospital when she watched herself on television, listened to her colleagues, gazed in amazement at the cards and flowers that kept coming, she saw a brief cameo as a heroic survivor. She was headlines until another story came along. But it had given meaning to what had happened and now that meaning had been ripped away. Ellis had cut to the heart of it in a way that no one else had done, just as he had in their first few days together. She could see now that her own prejudice had closed her mind to his remarkable talent for understanding and made her sceptical of his plans for life-coaching.

'I'm going to hang up now and see if I can find a flight down tonight from Ballina or maybe the Gold Coast, so I can be with you soon,' Ellis had said. 'I'll call you back in a few minutes.'

Heather divided her gaze between the television screen and the telephone, wishing he were with her now. She envied Shaun, who had not had to live with the injury, and who knew the attacker was dead, while she was stuck with the appalling reality that tripping on a step could make you the victim of violent crime. She knew it now in a way that no one who had not experienced it could ever know.

Diane had taken Shaun home with her. Heather suspected she needed to mother him to expiate the guilt she seemed to feel about the fact that he'd been targeted because of Charlene. Perhaps they needed each other. But Heather needed time alone, although now, more than at any time since the shooting, alone seemed agonisingly lonely. How ironic that she had so often told herself that it was okay to live without someone for whom you came first, had even joked about her own ability to piss off potential candidates. Well, now she did have someone but he was miles away, and so often when he *was* close, she was on the defensive, never really willing to take that final dangerous step towards real intimacy.

'There's nothing,' Ellis said when he called back. 'Nothing until just before midday tomorrow.' Heather's heart sank, and she felt the tears welling in her eyes, like a child who has been promised a toy and then had the promise withdrawn. 'But listen,' he went on, 'I want to be there with you, Heather. I was planning to drive down at the end of the week anyway, so we'd have more time together over Christmas. So how about I put some things in a bag and head down there now? I can be with you in a few hours. Leave a key for me. I'm going to look after you. We'll have two weeks together, darling, or as long as you need. Trust me, Heather, I'll be with you before you know it and everything is going to be absolutely fine.'

TWENTY

Daisy was making Christmas cards on the kitchen table. She had her paint box, glue, coloured pencils and felt tips, glitter, even some ribbons and sequins that Jill had discovered when, inspired by Adam's recent blitz, she had sorted out her sewing cupboard. And she had a pile of old magazines from which she was cutting pictures to stick on the cards. Each card would also be a bookmark with a piece of ribbon attached to it, so that it would drape over the top of the book. Daisy had designed each one to reflect something special about the person. It was a big job because she was determined that everyone who was to be at Heather's place for Christmas would have one.

She'd thought at first that it would just be the family, and then she kept discovering that various other people were going to be there. Shaun she'd met a few times, and she thought she'd do guns on his because he was the one who was supposed to have been shot. Then there was Diane, whom she'd met at the party. She'd told Daisy she used to be a hairdresser, so perhaps she would draw some scissors and a comb and put glue on the drawing and sprinkle glitter, so they were all sparkly. Barbara and George were easy, they had pictures of bicycles, and George had a Chinese mandarin, and Barbara a picture of a Chinese man wearing a khaki cap with a red star on it and holding a tiny red book. It had the words Mao Tse Tung underneath. Heather had the Houses of Parliament in England and a drawing of a gun with a big red cross through it to show that it wasn't meant for her. For Adam, of course, Daisy had drawn a cello with musical notes coming out of it, and for Jill a picture of a woman peeling potatoes in the kitchen. She was left now with Ellis, the only problem.

'I haven't a clue, darling,' Jill had said. 'But he does live in Byron Bay if that's any help.'

It wasn't. Daisy slumped over the table. Too many cards, she wanted this last one out of the way. The worst thing was she didn't even like Ellis. She thought he was rude and sulky. He'd mostly ignored her at the party and he sounded really horrible when he was talking to Adam or George. It was confusing that old people could get away with stuff that children got into trouble for. But Daisy was a great believer in fairness and she knew that Ellis had to have a card. She yawned a few times, folded her arms on the table and rested her head on them, chewing the end of a felt-tip pen. She'd have to find something, any sort of man's thing would do – a car, perhaps; a dog; a cricket bat? And then she remembered: a couple of days ago she had been lying on her bedroom floor reading *Girlfriend* with the door open, when she'd heard Jill and Adam talking next door in their own room.

Daisy sat up. Of course, that's what she could put on Ellis's card, and she knew just where to find the picture. Reaching for the magazine she flicked through until she found the advertisement, and cut carefully around the picture. Then she stuck it onto the already made card below Ellis's name and attached a blue ribbon to the top.

'Mum,' she shouted, 'can you come and look at this picture for Aunty Heather's friend?'

'Later, darling,' Jill called from the laundry. 'You just go ahead, I'm sure it'll be lovely.'

Daisy sighed. Parents never did what you wanted. It had been easier when they had that funny gap between them. Now they were stuck together again. It left very little room for a person to worm her way in between and get what she wanted. The only thing was that it did feel better without the gap, although she wasn't sure why. Daisy took a final look at Ellis's card and thought it looked very pretty. She tucked it in among the others and then put the lot in the plastic folder that Jill had given her to take to Heather's house on Christmas morning.

Adam had ruffled Jill's feathers with his household blitz. Her relief at not walking into chaos was eclipsed by a feeling a child might experience coming home to find that someone had messed with her toys. To respond with anything less than gratitude seemed churlish, but her immediate reaction was defensive: it seemed like a monumental act of criticism. But more shocking still was when she had said it seemed as though she didn't own it anymore and he'd said, 'No, you don't, we own it together.' Jill couldn't have been more shaken if Adam had punched her. Indeed, that was rather how it felt, except in that case she could have punched him back. The children's rooms were war zones which she'd constantly shied away from tackling; now they were reasonably tidy and showed signs of logical organisation. It was hard not to see this as some vast takeover in response to her own shortcomings as a housekeeper. What would her mother have thought if she'd been alive to see it?

Daisy had come rocketing in from school as Jill emerged from her survey of the bedrooms.

'It was terrible,' Daisy said, relating the drama of the last two weeks. 'Dad made us do *housework*.'

'So I see,' Jill said, 'quite a lot of housework.'

'I had to do dusting, and tidying, and Toby did vacuuming, and taking the bin out, and we had to take turns to load the dishwasher and then unload it. So I'm *really* glad you're back.'

Jill knew a watershed when she was faced with one. She glanced up at Adam and saw his jaw tighten, saw him looking at her, challenging her.

'Well, that's wonderful,' she said, stroking Daisy's hair. 'Now we can all share in looking after the house.'

'No way,' Daisy said, slinging her schoolbag onto the floor. 'I don't like it *at all*.'

'That's a shame, Daisy, because I don't like it much either but Daddy's right – everyone who lives in the house should do something to help look after it.' She saw Adam turn back to the tea he had been about to make when Daisy came in, and then he looked over his shoulder and smiled at her.

Now, two weeks later, Jill was still adjusting to the fact that Adam had not tripped up on reality, he had simply grasped it. She was the one who was tripping, who kept stubbing her toe on her old habits. She had been home for five days when it dawned on her that she hadn't heard the Bach suites coming from the music room. Realisation swept over her like a hot flush: it wasn't just the state of the house that had changed.

The day Jill went back to work after her stint in the mountains she learned that her position had been reviewed. She was to be promoted with an increased budget and wider responsibilities.

'Community Development Director,' Renée had said, 'congratulations. Here are the details of your new salary and benefits. You need to go and see the salary packaging people.'

'That's wonderful, darling,' Adam said when she told him. 'Congratulations, you clever thing.'

The two weeks before Christmas were particularly busy for Adam. There were Christmas concerts, carols by candlelight, and rehearsals for a special series of concerts early in the new year. As Jill contemplated the benefits of her promotion, she also watched as Adam's job began to take its toll. She watched as the bright edge of energy and enthusiasm that she'd seen the day she got home began to fade. These concerts mostly featured music he really enjoyed, but even so his manner was more subdued, and his energy level dropped. She listened nervously for the return of the Bach suites. The orchestra was casting its shadow once again and Jill started to feel guilty about enjoying her own good fortune.

On the Friday evening of the weekend before Christmas, they were hiding in the bedroom wrapping presents for the children when the phone rang. The fourth cello had had a car accident and wouldn't be able to make any of the pre-Christmas or New Year concerts. Adam sank down onto the edge of the bed and put his face in his hands for a moment, then went through to the music room to make the calls to find a replacement.

Jill tied red ribbon around a parcel and dragged the scissors along the ends to make them curl.

'Do you hate your job?' she asked jokingly when Adam returned, trying to keep it light.

Adam glanced up at her. 'What if I do?' he said bluntly, and Jill sensed this wasn't the moment to take it further. 'I got hold of Sandy,' he went on. 'She can do it, glad to have the work. She's on her way over to pick up the scores. Have to leave the rest of the wrapping to you, I'm afraid.'

It was almost midnight by the time they got to bed and a perfect new moon, clear and sharp in the darkness, was framed in the window space.

'Look at that,' Jill said. 'Isn't it beautiful? Do you remember that night on our honeymoon when we made wishes?'

Adam nodded. 'I do. I wished that we'd live happily ever after.'

Jill laughed. 'Let's do it again,' she said.

'But I'd have to get out of bed and find coins.'

'I've got coins here,' Jill said, reaching towards her bedside table. 'Come on, grumpy.'

Adam pushed back the bedclothes. 'You are such a bully.'

'I know. Here you are.' She put some coins into his hand. 'Okay, ready? Bow three times, turn your money over and make a wish.'

Side by side they bowed to the moon and the coins chinked in their hands.

'What did you wish for?' Jill asked as Adam handed her the money and got back into bed.

'I wished that we would live happily ever after again,' he said, 'like we have, like we are. What about you?'

'I wished for something that would make that even better,' she said.

'You can't have better than happy ever after,' Adam said. 'That's just silly.'

Jill climbed into bed beside him and thumped him on the arm. 'No it's not. I wished for something that would make it easier.'

'Go on then,' he said. 'What?'

'I wished that you would think about resigning from the orchestra.'

Ellis's noble offer to drive through the night from Byron Bay to Newcastle had been made on the spur of the moment. Since the first couple of weeks in Sydney, Heather's commitments and her infernal independence had left him feeling confined to the edges of her life. But that Saturday evening it was clear that she needed him and he responded with the grand gesture. It was after nine by the time he left and by ten thirty he was fighting sleep and wishing he'd waited until the morning. It was a long drive and frequent stops at petrol stations for cardboard cups of coffee that tasted like drain cleaner made it seem endless. It was almost daylight before he arrived, and Heather got up to make coffee and cook him a substantial breakfast. He then retired to bed and slept until midday, by which time Heather was on her way out to open a Christmas bazaar.

'Tell them you can't go,' Ellis said, 'it's Sunday, for heaven's sake.'

'It's a charity and I've promised,' she said. 'This is not a nine-to-five job, Ellis, you know that. Have a shower and come and meet me about two thirty. I've got some Christmas shopping to do, we can go together.'

Ellis grunted; he gave her a grudging kiss, then had a sulky shower, unpacked the rest of his things, and read the Sunday paper until his irritability wore off. Temporarily.

As they made their way through the Christmas shoppers he started to enjoy the feeling of being a couple, walking hand in hand, being stopped occasionally by Heather's constituents wishing them happy Christmas, but by the time Heather had found gifts for three of the thirteen people on her list, he was getting bored.

'Can't you get the rest in the week?' he asked.

'It's a busy week, I've got meetings most days and –'

'You mean you're going to work?'

Heather stopped and looked at him. 'Of course.'

'But I've come to be with you,' Ellis said. 'I drove all this way, all night.'

'I know, darling, and it's wonderful of you. I feel so much better having you here with me, but I still have to go to work.'

Shoppers pushed past irritably as they faced each other in the narrow space between lead-cut crystal wine glasses and sleek Swedish vases. Ellis sighed theatrically and gave an exaggerated shrug.

'So the job comes first again,' he said, 'even when you're in such a state that I have to race down here to look after you.'

'Well,' said Heather, pausing, 'actually, yes, it does; it has to. But your being here makes everything easier to cope with, especially right now. Come on, you know what it's like to have a demanding job with big responsibilities.'

Ellis gritted his teeth. 'But I was so looking forward to spending time together.'

'And we will,' Heather said, taking his hand again. 'Look, let's go home now. I'll try to sort out the shopping during the week.'

He'd won this round, and now that yesterday's news made history of the shooting, his time was coming; time to change the rules. Heather couldn't expect him to go on taking second place to a whole constituency of people about whom he didn't give a shit.

Heather was profoundly moved by Ellis's willingness to rush to her side. The mere fact that he had dropped everything to drive to Newcastle had soothed the rawness of discovering she'd been shot for all the wrong reasons. The sound of Ellis's key in the door, his footsteps on the stairs and then the feel of his arms around her restored her confidence and her spirit. After he'd eaten scrambled eggs and toast and retired to bed, Heather had made his favourite carrot cake with a tangy lemon frosting, and cut some sandwiches for his lunch. The knowledge that he was sleeping peacefully in her bed had assuaged her loneliness, but she still felt a sadness and confusion akin to grief.

'I still can't get my head around it either,' Shaun said when she called him. 'It's not just the deed itself, it's everything we talked about, took for granted. It even had you questioning yourself. And all for nothing.'

'I know,' Heather said. 'I could never have imagined that I'd feel so weird finding out that it wasn't meant for me.'

'No relief, then? Not even the relief of knowing that there's no one waiting to try again?'

'No, and this must sound ridiculous, but being shot by mistake is such a smack in the face with reality. A reminder that the present is all we've got. You can protect yourself all you want but certainty and safety are just myths. We're all on borrowed time.'

'You *are* the cheery philosopher this morning,' Shaun said. 'But I see what you mean.'

The phone rang immediately she put it down and she snatched it up in case it woke Ellis.

'Just wondering how you are today,' Jill said, and Heather dropped down onto the settee, wishing that Jill lived close by, so that she could see her and talk to her face to face.

'Confused, and sort of grieving,' she said, 'but Ellis drove down last night to be with me. He says he's going to look after me.'

'That's lovely of him,' Jill said. 'I actually rang to suggest you should come here rather than being stuck there on your own. And listen,' she said, lowering her voice, 'I must tell you, things have changed dramatically since I got home, and for the better. I'll call you on Monday; it'll be easier to chat then.'

Heather was almost ready to leave for the bazaar when Ellis emerged from the bedroom. He looked vulnerable in his boxers and t-shirt, still half asleep, yawning and rubbing his eyes. She felt such tenderness for him that it brought a lump to her throat and she put her arms around him, inhaling the warm scent of sleep, enjoying the feel of his body against hers.

'I won't be long . . . ' she'd started to say, but by the time she did leave the house, that moment had evaporated and she knew she was, once again, in the wrong. That night, curled against Ellis's back as she waited for sleep, she told herself that the next few weeks were a sort of test. A chance to see how it felt to spend a longer time together under the same roof, and a time for her to make some decisions. She could hardly expect Ellis to accommodate her job constantly if she wasn't even sure she wanted to accommodate it herself.

'Aren't you glad you're old?' Barbara asked as they chained their bikes outside the coffee shop. They had started riding early in the mornings before the heat built up.

'Not particularly,' George said, looking startled. 'Should I be? My memory is dodgy, agility is a thing of the past and when I look at attractive young women they look back at me as though I'm a pervert or just pitiful.'

Barbara unbuckled her helmet. 'Well, I suppose there *are* negatives,' she said, 'although I don't have the slightest interest in looking at young men, but there's something so free about it. I can be as scruffy as I like, be totally unfashionable, not turn up to boring functions because no one even notices I'm not there. I can be myself now in a way I was never able to be when I was younger.'

George grinned. 'You women make everything so complicated,' he said. 'I would still like women to look at me and fancy me, crave my body, try to seduce me. No chance of it happening, of course, and if it did I'd probably have enough performance anxiety to bring on a heart attack.' He put his helmet on a chair. 'I'll go and order. Same as usual?'

Barbara watched affectionately as he made his way through to the counter. A week ago they had collected their certificates from the language school.

'An A is really unusual, Barbara,' Robert had said, handing her the envelope. 'We don't get many – maybe five a year. Congratulations, you're a star!'

'I'm always telling her that,' George said proudly, planting a kiss on her cheek. He had a B, which Robert said was very good, and was what most people got.

They had come home elated to find that the other good news was a reply to their joint email to Robert's contact in Beijing, offering them both two classes a week in the same company. George would work with the chemists, Barbara with a group of managers. And George had promptly turned his rarely used dining room into a workroom where they could sit at the table to write lesson plans and make some teaching aids.

'It's devious of me,' he'd told her. 'This way I get you to work with me because you're far better at it than I am.'

'Sure you don't want to compete to find out who's really best?' Barbara teased.

'No,' he said. 'I graciously acknowledge your superiority in this area. When it comes to bike riding, however . . .'

'When it comes to bike riding, some of the things you do are totally ridiculous. All that freewheeling down hills, and the other day you were trying to let go of the handlebars. You're just a big kid.'

'A boy's gotta do what a boy's gotta do,' George said. 'It's wonderfully exhilarating. And this is big-kid stuff too,' he added as they cut pictures from magazines, stuck them on coloured cards and printed up word cards to go with them. 'We'll be making paper chains next.'

Barbara looked out from the balcony to the river and thought about paper chains, something she'd never made as a child: they would have signalled frivolity. She'd been lucky, she thought, incredibly lucky to escape into a life that opened doors into so many different worlds, so that even now, at seventy-six, she was planning a new adventure. She wondered what Roy's old age would have been like had he lived to see it, and she thought that perhaps it was a blessing that he hadn't.

'I suppose it is pretty pleasant,' George said, coming back to the table now with their coffee. 'Getting older, pleasing oneself.' He put the cups on the table and sat down. 'The Chinese, of course, have great respect for the elderly, so we'll be a hit there.'

'Life is so much simpler,' Barbara said. 'I used to think I needed so many things. Now, unless I'm sure something is going to contribute to my long-term health and happiness, I don't buy it. The things one appreciates with age are rarely bought with money.'

George nodded, raising his cup as if in a toast. 'Like the company of a beloved friend.'

'Indeed,' Barbara said, raising her own cup. 'Just like that.'

TWENTY-ONE

Diane was wrapping a present to post to Charlene. She'd left it as late as possible in the hope that her daughter would manage to hold back from opening it until Christmas Day. It was a handbag that Charlene had been ogling when they went shopping together and Diane had filled it with some of Charlene's favourite Kylie underwear, and added a David Jones gift voucher. She wished she could watch her open it but she was also thankful that her daughter had decided to stay on at the Gold Coast with her new friends for Christmas.

The task of packing up the house was more or less complete and the place felt bleak, but the last thing she needed was to start unpacking to find fairy lights and decorations. She would be moving out in the first week of the New Year and the holiday period seemed like a tiresome interruption to the process of leaving. She would go into the New Year homeless and probably jobless, but working with some of Heather's constituents had made her aware of how fortunate she was to have enough money to make choices about the future. She was on the brink of a new life, which was both scary and exciting, and she was impatient to get on with it.

This would be her third Christmas without Gerry, her first without Charlene, and she was about to get a taste of being on the fringes of someone else's celebrations rather than at the heart of her own.

'Why don't you come to Heather's Christmas Day? I know she's invited you,' Shaun had suggested as she drove him home from

Morpeth. He was still looking horribly shaken by the ordeal of discovering he'd been the target of the shooting and he'd jumped at her invitation to go home with her and stay overnight. He had laughed when she told him her fears about Gerry, fears that now seemed simply foolish. 'But it was because you were so worried about Charlene,' he said. 'Are you going to call and let her know about Danny?'

Charlene was devastated to learn the truth about the shooting and had asked to speak to Shaun. While they talked, Diane made up the spare bed, contemplating the irony that Shaun now looked like a highly desirable son-in-law but was never likely to be *her* son-in-law.

'You have to tell Heather soon,' she said later that night when he told her that he was planning to resign. 'You can't leave it much longer.'

'After Christmas,' he'd said, 'and before New Year. I'm dreading it. You realise she might ask you to stay on?'

'Really?' Diane said, surprised. 'But what about Patsy?'

'Heather will still need to replace me.'

'But I couldn't do your job. I don't know enough about it, about the party, politics, any of it.'

'You know much more than I did when I started, and you're heaps better at it than Patsy, who's been there three years. Maturity is a big plus in this job.'

Diane laughed. 'Well, thank goodness ageing has something going for it.'

'Would you take the job?'

'I don't know, I'm enjoying it but . . . ' she hesitated. 'Oh, I don't know. Anyway she probably won't ask.'

Diane tied Charlene's parcel with gold ribbon, put some bubblewrap around it and packed it into an Australia Post box. Then she started on the gifts she'd bought for Barbara, Heather and Shaun. How strange that this time last year she wouldn't have dreamed of giving Heather or Shaun a present, and she didn't even know Barbara. She laid sheets of gift wrapping on the table and tossed the fragments of paper from Charlene's parcel into the bin. Was this how her mother had felt when Diane and her sister left home? Free to become someone different? Free to please herself? It seemed unlikely; her mother had been a disappointed woman, disappointed by her marriage and her daughters, and disappointed by widowhood and old age. As she cut the sheet of gift wrap in half, Diane realised that she couldn't remember a time when her mother seemed truly delighted or excited about anything. She had lived life regretting the past and talking about what might have been. Even when she boarded the plane to fly to Arizona to live with Diane's older sister, she had looked bored and disappointed. 'So it all comes down to who you are and what you make of it,' Diane said aloud. 'And I intend to make the most of it.'

She stacked the wrapped gifts on the table and went to the kitchen to make a sandwich. A magnet fell off the fridge door as she opened it and the slip of paper it was holding fluttered to the ground. It was the paper Stefan had given her with his phone number. She had promised to call and make a time to see his garden, but somehow she'd never got around to it. Diane looked at the paper, turned it over in her hand and put the magnet back on the fridge. 'But what sort of person wants to live in a memorial garden?' she said aloud. 'Only someone who's still trapped in the past, and I don't need that.' And she screwed up the paper, chucked it in the bin, made a toasted cheese and tomato sandwich and a cup of tea and settled down to watch the news.

'So what do you think?' Adam asked, knowing his indecision would be inexplicable to many, but that he would get an intelligent response from Stefan.

'You are asking me?' Stefan said. 'If I have a beautiful wife who loves me and tells me to give up my job, I do it like the shot. Why even do you have to ask?'

Adam sighed. 'It seems like such a big step, and as though . . . well, as though I'm opting out of my responsibilities.'

'Huh? You say you leave the orchestra but keep working, take more students, do sometimes emergency fill-in. You take on looking after the house. These are all responsibilities.' He threw his hands in the air. 'I am killing to be so lucky.'

'I *would kill*,' Adam corrected him automatically. 'But it doesn't feel like . . . like a proper job.'

'Adam, my dear friend, remember the day we are flying to Canberra to play Dvořák to politicians? And you tell me about your father, and how he will think the orchestra is not a proper job? And now you think about proper jobs too? What is it, this *proper job*? What is so special?'

They were sitting on the steps at the back of the concert hall killing time before going inside to change into their dress suits to play *The Messiah*. Adam tossed his phone nervously from one hand to the other and dropped it on the ground. When Jill had suggested that his leaving the orchestra might be the key to a better life for them both, and the children, his immediate reaction was that it was impossible – not because he didn't want to, but because it would be irresponsible to give up a secure job at his age.

'Let's work out the finances,' she'd said, 'see how it looks.' And when they did, it was obvious that as long as he kept his students and acquired a few more, which would not be difficult as he already had a substantial waiting list, they could manage.

'You see,' Jill said, 'it is perfectly possible. 'We don't have to look after Kirsty anymore, we both have good super, and we own our home. All we have to do is live a little more carefully.'

'More clothes from the recycling shop?' Adam had said in an attempt to lighten up. 'Don't you want to escape from that?'

'I've almost grown to enjoy the satisfaction of finding treasures there,' Jill said. 'We'd be fine, Adam. We have lots more than most people, we're really lucky. I love my job and I can keep working for another ten years at least, if that's what we need. I think it's just your need for security that's holding you back. But if there's something we should all have learned from Heather getting shot, it's that there is no certainty. There's only the present and we need to make the most of it.'

Adam could imagine himself saying the same thing to someone else in this situation, it all made sense, but his nights were disturbed by muddled, scary dreams in which he could recognise almost nothing except the sense that his life was collapsing around him. By day, when not at work, he fought off the urge to hide in the music room with his baroque cello and the Bach suites. But then Jill fired her final bullet.

'Look,' she said, 'I promise to shut up about it if you tell me this. Do you look forward to going to work or do you dread it? Do you like being with the orchestra or is it devouring your life one discontented day at a time?'

Adam felt as though the breath had been punched out of him. He feared he might start crying as he had done the night he was with Barbara.

'I hate it,' he said finally, getting control of his voice. 'I hate what it does to me, how it strips away my joy in music and makes it into a burden.' He heard the chink of his own chains loosening. 'When we're rehearsing and playing, I loathe it. At the end of a performance I can't believe that the audience applauds. It's only later if I hear a recording that I know we've done something beautiful. Sometimes I think I must be completely mad.'

'Yes, you are,' Jill said, putting her arms around him and looking up, smiling into his face, 'completely mad to have gone on with it for so long without saying anything. But you don't have to do it anymore. You can escape, you can have your music the way you love it, and you can own your share of how we live. It's easy.'

But Adam still felt it was a pathetic way to end the career for which he'd fought both his mother and grandfather.

'But it is *not* a career ending,' Stefan said now, getting up and pointing at his watch to indicate that it was time that they went inside to change. 'It is just different. You are still a musician, a brilliant cellist. You know Dennis? He needs a cellist for the quartet, Belinda's husband is posted to Perth. Dennis will jump to have you in the quartet. Then you play the chamber music you love, you negotiate about interpretation, and you get paid too.'

Later, when he was alone in the dressing room, Adam stood in front of the mirror, straightened his white tie and smoothed down his shirt front. He loved playing Handel, but he didn't particularly like the way this visiting conductor wanted them to play *The*

Messiah. He had spent so many years of his life playing beautiful music under pressure and resenting it. It wasn't anything terrible, just the sort of frustration and powerlessness that at least half the population would experience at work. But, despite his fears, he knew he didn't want it anymore.

'So many people!' Ellis had said when Heather told him who she had invited for Christmas Day. 'I thought we'd be having a quiet Christmas together, exchanging our presents and eating chocolate and drinking champagne in bed. Lounge around, go for a walk or swim, then a lovely meal.'

'We can do all of that,' Heather said. 'Everyone's organised to bring food. All I have to do is cook the turkey. Jill's done the cake and mince pies; Barbara, the pudding; Diane is making brandy butter and homemade ice cream; Nick and Kirsty –'

'Okay, okay, I give in,' Ellis said, leaning over in the bed to kiss her. 'You are a terrific organiser and an absolute wonder woman. I just want you to organise me a bit more, give me your full attention.'

'Easy,' she said, wrapping her leg around his. 'I am entirely at your service.'

'Yes,' he said, kissing her again, reaching down to stroke her leg, 'for about two minutes and then you'll be up and gone.'

'Right. But I'll be back early. We're closing the office at midday, and meanwhile you can go to the bottle shop and find some excellent wine, and pick up the beer and soft drinks.'

'Sometimes,' he said, 'you remind me of Margaret Thatcher.'

'No!' Heather cried, throwing back the sheet and leaping out of bed. 'Don't say that. Wash your mouth out. I am *not* like Margaret Thatcher.'

Ellis laughed and leaned on his elbow, watching her pull on the soft cotton kimono that she had, apparently, bought years ago on a trip to Japan. He had bought her something much nicer for Christmas: a short, scarlet negligée trimmed with frills of black lace. That old cotton thing absolutely had to go. He'd bought more too – expensive lingerie, lacy French knickers in black and red, matching bras, a suspender belt and black stockings. And he had done it all from the comfort of his laptop through a website that specialised in extra large lingerie – 'beautiful gifts for big and beautiful women' their advertisements said, 'slinky, sensuous, sexy'. He'd had enough of Cottontails. Glamour was coming to an underwear drawer near him soon, and he could hardly wait.

Ellis lay back in the bed planning his day. He hadn't heard from Luke in ages but knew he was waiting to see some chapters of the book. But Ellis wanted Heather to read them first and that clearly wasn't going to happen until after Christmas Day. He would finish chapter five and then get her to look at it – Boxing Day, perhaps – she'd have plenty of time then. He would be generous and reasonable about her commitments – it was, after all, only for the short term. He got up and went into the shower, singing his own discordant and muddled Cole Porter compilation. Then, pulling on his jeans and a t-shirt, he ran downstairs towards the promise of toast and coffee.

'I'm off now,' Heather said when they had had their breakfast and she'd stacked the plates and cups in the dishwasher. 'I'll see you later.'

She kissed him and he held on to her hand. 'I'll go and get the booze and then come over to the office, take you somewhere nice for lunch.'

She dropped a second kiss, this time on the top of his head as she stood up. 'Thanks, darling, that's lovely of you,' she said, 'but I'm going to take Shaun and Diane out to lunch. Just as a thank-you for all they've done.'

Ellis forgot that he was being generous and reasonable. 'Second place again, Ellis,' he said. 'Second place again.'

Heather flushed. 'That's not fair,' she said. 'You know how important you are to me, but you seem determined to make me feel guilty about meeting my responsibilities to other people.'

'It's hard to see what responsibilities you have to someone who's responsible for getting you shot, and to a woman who's really only been working for you for a few weeks. Anyway, if that's what you want, I won't interfere with it. When will you be back?'

'Probably two thirty or three,' Heather said, picking up her handbag. 'And I'm going to ignore what you just said because I don't believe you can really mean it. I'll see you later,' she called and closed the front door behind her.

Shaun thought that this might be one time in his life when he really did need to get some counselling. Learning that the bullet had been meant for him had left him with a strange mix of emotions, many of which he couldn't identify. There was guilt, of course; he could at least work that one out. Guilt about Heather and all that she'd gone through because of him; guilt exacerbated by the knowledge that he was about to resign. There was guilt too about not having come clean with Alex Roussos, with whom he had recently become quite friendly. There was worry about Charlene and whether it really was possible to keep her clear of it all, and about Diane, whose anxiety was contagious. But there was other stuff, vague, dark, shadowy stuff about knowing that it really was supposed to be him, that floated in and around the other emotions like fog, confusing, muddled and chilling.

'It'll take time,' Ed had said when they met for a beer. 'Bound to. Your mother's in a bad enough state about it and she's several stages removed from it. It's bound to stir up a whole lot of stuff for you.'

'I know I should just be relieved, thankful that I got off so lightly,' Shaun said, finishing his first drink. 'But I can't even feel that. Knowing the bloke is dead and not likely to come after me again is something Heather never had. I think I'm being a bit of a wanker.'

Ed shook his head. 'No, mate. This is big stuff, like I said, bound to take time. And changing your job, that's big too. You'll feel better when you've got that off your chest.'

'You do think I'm doing the right thing then?'

'And what if I don't?'

'I suppose I'd still do it.'

'There you are then, what I think isn't important. It's your life, your decision. But, just for the record, I think it's the right one. You need to branch out and it sounds like this Rosa woman has her head screwed on.' He emptied his glass and signalled to the bartender for refills. 'Get this stuff off your chest with Heather and it'll all get a lot clearer.'

Shaun nodded and pushed his empty glass across the bar. 'Straight after Christmas,' he said. 'Don't want her worrying about it over the holiday. Straight after Christmas.' And his stomach churned at the thought of it.

'Bloody Ellis isn't coming to lunch with us, is he?' Diane asked. 'Every time he comes in here he gets up my nose. If I see him again I may have to punch him right between the eyes.'

'Bad as that?' Shaun asked. 'How are you going to cope with Christmas Day? I'll have to put you into a straitjacket when I pick you up.'

'Wouldn't be a bad idea,' Diane said with a laugh. 'But I think there'll be enough people at Heather's that day to dilute the Ellis effect. What *is* it with her? Can't she see it, or is she so desperate to have a man in her life that she's prepared to ignore it?'

'Which particular aspect of him are we talking about?' Shaun asked. 'I mean, I know we agreed that he's arrogant and pretentious, but lots of women fall for men like that. Maybe he's not that way with her.'

'He is,' Diane said, glancing out through Shaun's open office door to make sure that Heather was still out of earshot. 'He *is* arrogant and pretentious with her; you're just too involved in your own stuff to notice. So here's the full rundown. She keeps saying he's some sort of saint because he raced through the night to be at her side and he's here to look after her. But *she's* looking after him, and she's flat out trying to do that and get ready for Christmas and finish up here before we close.'

'You don't know that,' Shaun said.

'I do. I know it from heaps of things she's let slip. And this morning she's on about how wonderful he is because he's going to pick up the wine. Oh, please!'

Shaun laughed. 'We all have our blind spots when we're in love.'

'Tell me about it,' Diane said. 'I suffered from extended periods of blindness while I was with Gerry. But I'll tell you this. Gerry did some lousy stuff drunk, and sometimes sober, but he did at least have some respect for women.'

'And Ellis doesn't?'

'Oh, come on, Shaun, you must be able to see it. Ellis is contemptuous of women. That's what all that slimy charm is about. As far as he's concerned, women are a lesser species that you control with a mixture of charm and emotional bullying. He thinks we're all here to boost his ego and serve his needs. And if you don't believe me, just stop contemplating your own navel for a while and *look* at Heather. Her confidence is stuffed. She's behaving like a headless chook because whatever she does it's never quite right for his lordship. She's a mess, and she thinks it's all about the shooting, but I'll bet you there's a big dose of Ellis in there stirring the pot. Maybe you can't see it, but Barbara and Jill will see it at Christmas. Women can always see another woman dancing as fast as she can to please a man. Especially when the man isn't worth it.'

Shaun sat in his office contemplating Diane's diatribe while she went across the road to collect some proper coffee. Maybe she was right. Heather was certainly different with Ellis than anyone he'd seen her with before. But then, he'd never seen her in love before. Wasn't everyone different when they were in love? But if Diane were right, then it made him feel even worse about his plan to desert her. He surveyed the work on his desk, work he really had to finish before they closed. You can think about Heather later, he told himself, for now you just have to pull your finger out and clear your desk.

'I've left your coffee in Heather's office,' Diane told him a few minutes later. 'She asked me to tell you she wants a chat.'

'Now?'

'Now.'

Shaun sighed and got up. This was what he'd been trying to avoid. The end-of-year chat about setting up for the campaign. The chat he could not, in all fairness, have without coming clean about his intentions. He got up and made his way to Heather's office with a heavy heart.

*

'So, has Adam actually resigned,' Renée asked, 'or is he still think-ing about it?'

'He's resigned,' Jill said with a smile. 'Did it on Monday. He said he'd do it before Christmas because it would mean he'd enjoy it more.'

'And you're sure you're happy about it?'

'I am ecstatic,' Jill said, glancing around and realising that they had sat together at this same table a few months earlier on the day she'd spilled the beans to Renée. 'It changes everything. Adam says that he's felt for ages that he was living under a pile of wet newspaper and now it's gone. And that's exactly how it feels for me too. You wouldn't believe the difference in him, Renée, since he started to take over the house, and now since Monday. He's a different person.'

'Not a saint anymore then?' Renée asked, laughing.

'No, thank god, he's almost bossy, and I haven't heard those Bach suites for ages. I know they're wonderful, and I do now understand why they've been the background music to life for so long, but if I never hear them again I will be a very happy woman. When I got home last night, Adam was making pasta and playing my Diana Krall CD. I can't really explain how significant that is.'

Waiting for Adam to make up his mind had been an exquisite sort of torture and Jill had feared his courage might fail him. She wanted this for him, for the children, but also for herself, for its potential to help her to change. Her own cautious abandonment of the old habits had made her spirits soar so that this seemed like the final liberating hurdle. She watched for signs, poised to take advantage of any opportunity to encourage him. And then, just when she'd thought he was backing off the idea altogether, he had come home late from *The Messiah* and slipped quietly into bed beside her. She pretended to be asleep, fearing that he was once again burdened by her vigilance, by the feeling that she was wait-ing for him to talk to her.

'This time it's *me* who knows *you're* not asleep,' he'd said, mov-ing closer to her, sliding his arms around her.

'Guilty,' she'd said, turning towards him. 'How was *The Messiah*?'

'Handel is one of my favourites,' he said. 'It was magnificent, which is very good because it's probably the last time I'll play that with the orchestra.'

Jill sat up, leaning on one elbow. 'You mean . . . ?'

'I mean tomorrow I'm going to resign.'

'Really?' she said. 'Really, Adam? Are you sure it's what you want? I haven't bullied you into it?'

'Of course you've bullied me,' he said, pulling her back down to lie with him. 'You are a terrible bully, but I needed it.'

'But . . .'

'But yes, I'm sure it's what I want. And frankly, I just can't wait to write that letter and deliver it to the general manager's office.'

Renée raised her glass. 'That's just brilliant,' she said. 'Here's to Adam doing his own thing, and you abandoning the domestic Madonna.'

Jill laughed. 'It is an amazing relief, especially coming in a year when I don't have to have everyone for Christmas. We're waiting to tell the rest of the family at Heather's on Christmas Day. This is going to be the best Christmas in a very long time.'

Heather had originally planned to have her conversation with Shaun when they reopened the office after the holiday. But she feared he might get wind of it on Christmas Day. Ellis could be unpredictable and he might just let something slip. She couldn't allow that to happen. Shaun had been totally committed and loyal all the time he'd worked for her, often going above and beyond any reasonable expectations, but he needed to think about his own career, especially as she was contemplating ditching her own.

She got up from behind her desk, carrying both their coffees, and indicated the armchairs by the coffee table. She thought he looked awful: exhausted, nervous and on edge. Clearly, the news about Danny and the shooting was taking its toll.

'Come and sit down, Shaun,' she said. 'You don't look too good.'

He took his coffee and dropped into the chair, lifting the plastic lid from the cardboard beaker. 'Just tired, and trying to get used to the idea of what's happened,' he said.

He seemed to be having difficulty making eye contact with her and she wondered whether he was still feeling the initial guilt he'd expressed about the fact that she'd been shot because of him.

'Look,' she said, 'there's something we need to talk about before we close down and go to lunch.'

'Yes,' he said, 'I know. Next year, the campaign and so on.'

'Well, yes,' Heather said, sipping her coffee. 'But there's something I need to tell you first, and it's quite difficult.' She paused, feeling guilty herself now. Here he was ready to talk about the campaign, ready to throw himself heart and soul into working for her re-election . . . 'I don't know quite how to say this,' she said, 'but I don't really want to talk about the campaign at this stage. You see, Shaun, I'm having serious doubts about running again. I'm going to decide over the next week or so, but I think the time may have come for me to turn it in.'

'Not run?'

'It's a shock, I know, and I'm sorry. Even if I do run, I'll probably only stay for another year. Either way, you need to think about your own future. You've been brilliant, Shaun, but you came here with big plans and they're long overdue.'

Shaun felt the tension slowly leaving his body. He ran a hand over his closely cropped head. 'Not run, that never occurred to me,' he said.

'I know, and look, I haven't decided yet, but Ellis and I have talked about it and he wants me to resign. I didn't want you to get wind of it without my having told you.'

Shaun nodded and took a long drink of his coffee. 'The party will have a fit,' he said. 'It's very short notice to pre-select and announce a new candidate.'

'Yes, the goodwill that emerged over the shooting will be a thing of the past. I'll be the she-devil. But it might be better than a by-election at a later stage. It's you I'm concerned about, though; if you give it some thought we can start talking to the right people.'

Shaun leaned forward, resting his forearms on his knees. Heather thought some colour had come back into his face.

'Well,' he said, smiling, 'the thing is, Heather, I've already spoken to the right person.'

TWENTY-TWO

'But *why* do we have to wait so long for our presents?' Daisy wailed miserably from the back seat. 'Why can't we just have them when we get there?'

Jill sighed. 'Because we're having lunch first, then presents afterwards.'

'We could have lunch straight away when we get there,' Daisy pleaded. 'I'm hungry already.'

Adam caught her eye in the rear-vision mirror and shook his head. 'Lunch will be a while, Daise,' he said. 'It'll only be midday when we get there. We'll probably eat at about two.'

Daisy let out a huge sigh. 'That's hours. It's not fair! I want to have my presents.'

'You're a greedy pig,' Toby said. 'Isn't she, Dad? She already had her stocking this morning.'

'All right, Tobes,' Adam said, 'you're happy to wait, are you?'

Toby sized up his father's expression in the mirror to see if a change were on the cards, but Adam's jaw was set. 'If that's what's happening, it's okay with me,' he said, and looked straight out of the window, missing the twitch of Adam's suppressed grin.

'It does seem a bit unfair, doesn't it?' Jill said softly. 'Do you think it's a habit first introduced to torture children, or parents?'

'God knows,' Adam said, 'but I think people who don't have children really haven't a clue how difficult the waiting is for them and, because of that, for us.'

280

'I like it better having Christmas at home or at Aunty Barb's because we always have our presents in the morning.'

'Stop whining, Daisy,' Jill said.

'I bet that Ellis man made it up.'

'Maybe he did but we're not arguing about it,' Jill said. 'We're guests at Aunty Heather's house and I want you to remember to be nice and polite. Both of you.' There was a grumpy silence from the back seat. Toby had disappeared into his iPod. 'You too,' she said softly to Adam, patting his leg.

'Same as before,' he said, turning his head to smile at her. 'Civil. In my new benign state, the only thing Ellis has to fear from me is being ignored.'

'That's –'

'I know, darling, I'm only joking. Civil, remember? George and I will both be civil to him. We agreed to it on the phone.'

'You were talking to George?'

'Yep. We had a chat. He and Barb have been making lesson plans for China and he had this idea of how they could use music.'

'Even I do sort of wish that Ellis wasn't going to be there,' Jill said quietly. 'I didn't like him much.'

'That's because you are a woman of wisdom and good taste,' Adam said, smiling at her again.

'So what does that say for Heather?'

Adam's smiled faded. 'I'm trying to think of it as an aberration on her part,' he said. 'An aberration brought on by the trauma of the shooting, exhaustion and being a bit lonely. That's what Barb thinks.'

'Hmm. Well, you may be right,' Jill said, 'but I probably talk to her more than either of you do these days and I think she's really into him. She's enjoying having someone of her own. It must be lonely, in your late fifties, single, with a really demanding job. He might turn out to be a lot of support for her. And if he does, in the end you're going to have to unbend a bit and be more than just civil.'

'Let's not even go there,' Adam said. 'Civil is all I'm promising at present and, as you so eloquently pointed out to me recently, the present is all we've got.'

*

'A quick glass of champagne before your hordes of friends and relatives arrive,' Ellis said, popping the cork and pouring two glasses. He handed one to Heather and leaned forward to kiss her. 'To us,' he said, raising his glass. 'The first of many Christmases together.'

Heather clinked her glass against his. 'To us,' she said. 'To lots of Christmases and lots of other wonderful celebrations.' They sipped the champagne, and Heather took a long breath and sat down. 'I haven't done Christmas at my place for years. We usually go to Barbara's or to Jill and Adam. It means a lot to me to have them all here with you.' She'd had a horribly busy week; squeezing all the shopping, preparations and several essential social events into the last few days had wiped her out. And, on top of that, there was Ellis's persistent sex drive to deal with.

'I don't quite know how to put this,' she'd said a couple of nights earlier, 'but I wondered . . . are you taking anything?' She was longing for sleep and recalling it now she could see that exhaustion had made her phrase it more bluntly than she might otherwise have done – and from there it went from bad to worse.

'What do you mean, "taking anything"?' Ellis asked.

'Well,' she said, 'you know, Viagra or something.'

'Why ever would you think that?' he asked, looking in the opposite direction. 'I may be considerably older than you, Heather, but I can still get it up.'

Heather blushed with embarrassment. 'Sorry, darling; oh, please don't be offended. I just wondered because you do seem to want to do it a lot and you never have any problem with erections, which I think is probably quite unusual for someone . . . someone . . . ' Her voice trailed away.

'For someone my age, you mean?'

'Well, yes.'

Ellis stretched his legs out in the bed and turned to her. 'And suppose I *was* taking something?'

Heather groaned inwardly at the emergence of the barrister. 'That's *fine*, or I mean it *would* be fine, if that's what you *were* doing.' A burning blush suffused her as she struggled to dig herself out of the situation. 'I wouldn't want you to think that I minded if you were. You *could* tell me.' His silence was arctic and, feeling now like a manic Lucille Ball confronting a stony-faced Desi, she heard her words tumbling out too fast. 'I mean, it would be fine with me if . . . well, if we didn't do it so often.'

'So you don't enjoy our lovemaking?'

Heather plunged, lemming-like, ever deeper. 'Heavens no, Ellis, it's not that. No, it's wonderful, really wonderful, and you're a terrific lover, it's just that if you *were* taking something and didn't like to tell me, then I wanted you to know that you *could* tell me. And if you were concerned about taking it too often, there are heaps of other ways . . . ' She'd always found it difficult to talk openly about sex. 'I mean, different things we could do that would mean you wouldn't have to take so much.'

'I see,' Ellis said eventually. 'It's very thoughtful of you, Heather, but you don't need to worry, it's all my own work, I'm pleased to say. But, of course, if you're finding it too much . . . '

'Oh no,' Heather leapt in, anxious to put things right. 'Not in the least, as I said, it's wonderful. I was just trying to . . . well, trying to be thoughtful. You know, I just love being with you whatever we do – I mean, however we do it.'

'There's no need to worry about me, Heather,' Ellis said, leaning over to kiss her. 'No need at all.'

But she still wasn't sure that she believed him, and she hadn't abandoned the idea of searching his toilet bag or his briefcase for evidence. She hadn't a clue what she'd do if she found it but it would be proof of vulnerability, and for some reason that would be endearing. Heather looked up at him now, standing by the fireplace, champagne glass in hand; he was a fine looking man with a commanding presence that had been there even in his youth. The young Ellis was still there, just as the young Heather was still within her, and they were together again because of that early love. That was what mattered, the rest was all incidental.

'To you, my darling,' she said, smiling and raising her glass. 'Merry Christmas, and here's to a very special year ahead.'

'Looks like we're first to arrive,' George said, pulling into the drive and handing Barbara the car keys. 'You're in charge from now on.'

The deal was that he would drive there and Barbara, who rarely drank more than one glass of wine, would drive home.

She put the keys in her bag. 'Thank god you're not a roaring drunk,' she said, 'or I'd have to drop you off in a ditch somewhere.'

'Wouldn't put it past you, anyway,' George said with a grin, 'you in your new schoolmarm mode.'

Barbara put her hand on his arm to stop him getting out of the car. 'Isn't it exciting? China. I can't believe we're doing it. I just want Christmas to be over and then it's only a few weeks and we're off.'

George took hold of her hand. 'I can't believe it either, and I don't know why I waited so long. All my life I wanted to see China, to stand on the Great Wall, and now it's really going to happen. Bloody hell,' he added, pointing down the drive, 'Ellis is waiting for us at the door, playing mine host, I presume. Pity we can't ship him out to China to get his balls frozen off right now.'

'George!' Barbara said. 'Be nice. Heather's in love with him. Don't spoil it for her.'

''Course not. I shall be the soul of diplomacy and avoid him as much as possible. Here we go then.'

They struggled out of the car and Ellis strode up the drive to meet them.

'Barbara, George,' he said. 'Merry Christmas, how lovely to see you again. Do you need a hand to bring anything in from the car?'

'Merry Christmas, Ellis,' Barbara said as he bent to kiss her. 'There are presents and a pudding in the boot.'

'At your service,' Ellis said with a mock salute before turning to George and extending a hand.

'G'day, Ellis,' George grunted. 'Greetings and all that,' and he flipped open the boot and lifted out a large basket of red and gold wrapped parcels and handed them to him. 'Give those to Heather, will you? Ask her to stick 'em under the tree.'

Daisy was lying on the patio paving underneath the table, hoping someone would notice she was missing and try to find her.

If they were worried about her they might bring forward the present-opening time. She loved that part of Christmas, not just because of getting her presents, but because she and Toby were always allowed to crawl under the tree and distribute the parcels. It wasn't easy because everyone had to have a present to open at the same time so that no one would feel left out, and as some people got lots of presents and others only a few, you had to be really careful.

'Ouch!' she cried as a foot landed on her fingers. 'You trod on me.' She sat up and clutched the tablecloth, rattling the crockery.

'Whoops – sorry, darling,' Heather said. 'Didn't see you there, but don't pull on the cloth or everything will collapse.' She bent down and lifted the edge of it. 'What are you doing down there?'

'I'm bored,' Daisy said. 'Can't we have our presents *before* Christmas dinner?'

Heather sat down on the ground beside her. 'No, not this year,' she said. 'Ellis thought it might be nice to do it the way his family always did it and that means presents later.'

'But it's such a long time,' Daisy sighed. 'I'm not being self-ish or anything, Aunty Heather, but I made all these lovely cards for everyone and I want to give them out, and there's dinner and pudding, and then the grown-ups always have to have coffee and talk for hours.'

Heather took her hand and drew her out from under the table. 'Well, I tell you what,' she said, as they both got to their feet. 'Why don't we make a special ceremony just for your cards? The dinner's practically ready, so when we've had that, I'll bring out the pudding and you can give out your cards while we eat it.'

Daisy recognised a win when she saw one. 'Yes,' she cried. 'Can we, can I, do that?'

'Of course, and we'll have our coffee at the same time as we have our presents,' Heather said, hugging her. 'And I'm just dying to see my card, I'm sure it's gorgeous. Now, do you want to go inside and tell everyone that we're eating in five minutes?'

*

285

'It's brilliant,' Kirsty said. 'Honestly, Dad, you look like a different person. And Jill looks really happy.'

'She is, we both are, but it was her idea. She loves her job and I hate mine, so it makes sense. It just took me a while to convince myself it was really okay,' Adam said.

'And you've joined the quartet?'

'I have.'

Kirsty hugged him. 'I'm so pleased. And, guess what, I've got news too. On Friday I got a job. A proper job, as you would say.'

Adam laughed. 'Really? What, full time, no more casual shifts at the café?'

'No more casual shifts. I'm going to work for the Greens. The money's okay, not brilliant but okay. I'll be writing and editing the newsletter, and it's just the sort of thing I wanted. The journalism degree was great but I never wanted to be a news reporter.'

'That's wonderful, I'm so proud of you,' Adam said. 'The Greens – have you told Heather?'

'I haven't told anyone yet except Nick and you,' Kirsty said. 'Like you, I've been saving my news for today. Do you think she'll berate me about it being the wrong party?'

'I doubt it,' Adam replied. 'I think she'll be as pleased about it as I am, and as Jill will be when you tell her.'

Kirsty smiled and threaded her arm through his. 'And we can still go cycling. You don't even miss me anymore, do you?'

Adam gasped in mock horror. 'When did you get to be so manipulative? Of course I miss you, but it's okay. A lot's happened in the last few months. And look, you picked the right time, you avoided being on my housework roster. I'm sure Daisy's told you about it.'

'In detail,' Kirsty said. 'But Toby seems to quite like it. I think he's relishing the chance to appear more grown-up than Daisy. By the way, on the subject of domestic stuff, who do you think made the place cards? I bet it was Ellis. Anyway, I've moved mine and Nick's so we can sit near Shaun.'

Barbara was stirring the gravy. She was the only person allowed in the kitchen while Heather organised the turkey onto the carving dish and made sure the vegetables were really done.

'My own gravy always has lumps,' Barbara said.

'Mine too,' Heather said, red-faced from peering in the oven. 'But who cares?'

Barbara laughed. 'By the way, whose idea was it to have place cards?'

'Ellis's,' Heather said, sticking the point of a knife into the potatoes. 'He wrote them himself – he even bought a special pen.'

'You know everybody's been out there moving them around?'

'Really?' Heather looked up. 'Oh dear, I hope he won't be upset.'

'Upset? This is your home, Heather, these are your family and friends, surely he'll be happy to fit in with us?'

'I hope so. You do like him, Barb, don't you? It's so important to me, but I feel people don't take to him straight away. Perhaps they just need more time to get to know him.'

Barbara peered down into the gravy. 'Don't worry about it,' she said. 'It's what *you* feel that's important. Just give them time.'

'But you,' Heather persisted. 'You really do like him, don't you? You've always been such a good judge of character.'

'Of course I do, dear,' Barbara said, suspecting that she might yet regret this lie. 'And most of all, it's wonderful to see you looking so happy.'

'You didn't call,' Stefan said with a smile. 'I hoped you would come to see my garden.'

Diane blushed. 'I meant to,' she lied, 'really I did, but I lost your number.'

Stefan nodded. 'I would lose my number too,' he said, 'if I was to be you.'

'I'm sorry?'

He laughed. 'If I am you, I think this man is morbid. He wants to live like in a cemetery.'

'No, not at all,' Diane said, her blush deepening. 'It wasn't like that.'

Stefan raised his eyebrows. 'I think so.'

'I'm sorry,' she said. 'I lied. That *was* the reason I didn't call. I just felt I'd spent too long dwelling on the past. I didn't mean to offend you.'

'And I am not offended,' he said. 'I agree with you. But the garden *is* for looking forward. Something dies but always, at the same time, something new is growing. The cycle of life and death, it's a reminder there is always something new to live for.'

'Now I feel really silly. I made a lot of assumptions, I suppose, based on my own behaviour. May I change my mind and come?'

Stefan put his hand on her arm and she felt a shiver of pleasure at being touched.

'Please,' he said. 'I would like it so much. When will you come? Soon, I hope.'

'Yes, soon,' she said. 'I'm moving out of my house after New Year, and it feels very strange waiting to go.'

'And you have found another place?'

'I'm going to house-sit for some old friends, Lorraine and Gordon. They're going to Europe for a few months. It'll give me time to decide what I want to do.'

'So, this week perhaps, you come while you are waiting? I am very pushy.'

'This week,' she nodded, 'if that's all right.'

'That will be wonderful. I might just manage to wait that long. I must tell you I have done a terrible thing. I went to look at the table and there are cards where we are to sit. So I moved my card beside yours. I think Ellis will not be pleased, he likes to decide these things.'

'I think you're right,' Diane laughed, 'and I'm so glad you did it. I'd love to sit with you and we will not be moved.' And once again she felt a thrill of pleasure as he drew her arm through his and led her out to the table.

TWENTY-THREE

It was like a scene from a movie, Jill thought later; family and friends around a table, laughing, talking, drinking toasts, pulling crackers and abandoning dignity in favour of paper hats. It was a scene you watch on the edge of your seat, knowing that something awful is going to happen, wondering how the characters haven't guessed what's coming, why they can't see that this is a stage set for disaster. And yet, none of them *had* seen it coming. Even those, herself among them, who harboured the odd, niggling concern about the occasion, could not have predicted anything like this.

Jill was quite relaxed despite having witnessed Ellis's dummy-spit to Heather in the kitchen about someone moving his place cards. She'd been on her way to the patio from the bathroom and heard him through the open kitchen door, but everyone else was at the table by then. In a contrary sort of way she'd found it reassuring, as though something awkward *had* happened and so surely it must be the worst that *could* happen.

There was a break after everyone had had their fill of the main course. Diane and Stefan seemed to be getting along particularly well, the children were behaving beautifully, it was all so pleasant and relaxed. So when she got up to help clear the plates the only thing that concerned Jill was Heather, who was doing a better and more frenetic impersonation of a good wife than she herself had ever done. She had dismissed all offers of help to fetch the pudding, bringing it triumphantly to the table with blue brandy flames licking the glossy sides. And that was when it started.

'Now,' Heather said, 'just before I serve the pudding, we're having a special ceremony.' Daisy had been glued to her side since the meal began and Heather put an arm around her shoulders. 'Daisy has made everyone a very special card, isn't that right?'

Daisy nodded, embarrassed now, shifting from one foot to the other as she clutched her plastic folder. 'Everyone has a card with pictures I found specially for them,' she said.

'And Daisy's going to give them to you now.'

'Sicko!' Toby murmured, but it was lost in the ripple of conversation.

Jill felt a little shiver of pride as Daisy, slowly and with great care, began to hand out the cards.

'A bicycle *and* Chairman Mao, Daisy,' Barbara cried, kissing her. 'How clever of you, darling, thank you.'

'And I've got a mandarin,' George said, showing it to Barbara. 'Now, wherever did you find that picture, Daisy?'

Diane's glittery picture of a comb and scissors elicited great admiration, and Shaun graciously said he was delighted with the picture of guns; they were some of the finest he'd seen. Daisy was only halfway around the table when she handed Ellis his card and moved on to Nick, and that was when it happened. There was a strange snorting sound from Ellis, and Jill noticed that the colour had drained from his face.

'And what the fuck is this supposed to be?' he shouted, jumping to his feet, knocking against the table and sending two glasses and a bread plate flying to the ground. 'Hey, you,' he yelled at Daisy, taking two strides towards her, grabbing her arm and shaking her. 'Is this some kind of joke?'

Adam was on his feet in an instant. 'Let go of her,' he shouted, and in two bounds he was at the end of the table, dragging a terrified Daisy away from Ellis and pushing her towards Jill. 'What the hell do you think you're doing? Don't you dare touch my daughter, and don't speak to her like that.'

'I might've known it would be you,' Ellis shouted in his face, brandishing the offending card. 'Your idea, I suppose. Typical! You roll the bullets and get a child to fire them.'

'What's all this about?' Adam said, grabbing the card from

Ellis's hand. And Jill watched a smile spread across his face as he looked up at Ellis. 'Well, well, well,' he said slowly, shaking his head. 'No, Ellis, this was not my idea but frankly, seeing how much it's upset you, I wish it had been. This is a work of total innocence on Daisy's part. As for me getting back at you? Here's the start of it.' And he swung his fist into Ellis's jaw with a sickening thump that sent him flying backwards to land with a crash on the paving.

Jill could see and hear it again now, as though it were happening in slow motion. The gasps from around the table, the sound of chairs scraping on the tiles as people got to their feet, a circle of shocked, wide-eyed faces as she thrust Daisy towards Kirsty and went to grab Adam, who was clearly in the mood to finish what he had started. But Shaun had beaten her to it. He dragged Adam into the centre of the lawn as Heather, stumbling on a chair leg and then righting herself, ran to Ellis's side, calling his name.

'Whatever was on the card?' someone asked and Kirsty, still clutching the weeping Daisy, bent to pick it up.

'A baby,' she said, holding it up. 'A baby. And it says *Merry Christmas, I hope you find out what happened to your baby. Love Daisy.*'

'But what does it *mean*?' Nick asked, walking through the park with Diane, Stefan and Shaun, who had suggested it might be a good idea for them to leave the family alone to sort things out. Toby had joined them too, glad that for once he was not part of the problem.

'I think we could all hazard a rough guess,' Diane said, aware that Toby's ears were flapping, 'but this might not be the right time.'

'It is very bad,' Stefan said, 'the way he speaks to Daisy. She is a little girl, how can he speak to her like this? I do not like this man and I am glad Adam punches him. I like to punch him myself.'

'But Adam, of all people,' Nick said, 'it's just so unlike him. He's a really cruisy guy. I never would have thought he had it in him.'

'Me neither,' Shaun said, 'but Ellis certainly does have a knack of offending people.'

'So what are we going to do?' Diane asked, sitting down in the shade of some pines. 'What next?'

The others joined her on the grass. 'Give them a bit of time, I think,' Shaun said, 'and then go back inside and try to behave as though nothing's happened.'

'We can't leave,' Diane said. 'You put your keys in my bag, Shaun, and it's inside the house.'

'And my car is blocked by Adam's,' Stefan said. 'None of us can leave, I think, without going into the house. We just wait here, as you say, Shaun, give them some time.'

'I still think I should take him up to the hospital,' Heather said, while Ellis was upstairs washing his face and changing his bloody shirt. 'Adam's probably broken his jaw.'

'Don't be ridiculous, Heather,' Barbara said, pushing her down into a chair and handing her a mug of tea. 'Ellis's jaw is not broken. If it were, he'd be in agony. He's bruised and his lip is split, that's where the blood's coming from. It's his pride that's hurting him most.'

'You could have killed him,' Heather said, looking accusingly at Adam.

'I wish I had,' he replied.

'Stop it, you two,' Jill said. 'Stop behaving like children. Heather, we're all really sorry this has happened, but Barbara's right, it's –'

'*I'm* not sorry,' Adam said, flexing the fingers of his right hand, curling them into a fist and punching his left hand. 'I'm not a bit sorry, and if he comes anywhere near me or Jill or my children, I'll punch him again.'

George rolled his eyes at Barbara and took Adam by the arm. 'Why don't we go and sit down outside and cool off, old chap,' he said, steering him out into the garden.

'I can't believe Adam's behaving like this,' Heather said.

'Well, Ellis *was* very nasty to Daisy,' Jill said. 'She's only ten years old and she was frightened.'

292

'Where *is* Daisy?' Barbara asked.

'Upstairs in Heather's spare room,' Jill said. 'Kirsty's reading her a story.'

'How did she even *know*?' Heather asked, sipping the tea. 'Who told her?'

'No one told her,' Jill replied. 'Apparently, she overheard Adam and me talking in the bedroom, about you and Ellis. We'd talked about it before, about whether you'd actually discussed it with him – the way he behaved at the time.' Jill saw Heather's mouth tighten. 'Daisy heard me say that I felt you must have done, because Ellis would have wanted to find out what had happened to his baby. Of course, we didn't know she could hear us and, of course, Heather, I'm sorry that she did, and that I was just too busy to go through the cards.'

'Heather!' Ellis called. 'Heather, come up here, please; I need to speak to you.'

Heather leapt up, splashing tea on her dress. She put her cup on the coffee table and raced out of the room and up the stairs.

Jill raised her eyebrows at Barbara and they sank down side by side on the sofa.

'This is dreadful,' Jill said. 'Can you believe Adam behaving like that!'

Barbara grinned and leaned towards her. 'Worried that you've created a monster?' she asked softly.

'Well, you've got to admit it was a shock.'

'It certainly was. But if it weren't for poor Daisy and Heather both being so upset, I'd have to say I rather enjoyed it. Ellis was appalling from the moment we arrived, so condescending and full of himself. And he has a weird effect on Heather – she's been racing around like a fart in a colander all day. I would have liked to punch him myself.'

Jill rested her head on the sofa back and closed her eyes. 'I know what you mean. But whatever do we do now?'

'Wait for Heather to come back down, either with or without Ellis. There's nothing else we can do.'

They didn't have to wait long. Moments later, they heard a door open upstairs.

'I won't be back until they've gone,' Ellis shouted, slamming the door behind him. He ran down the stairs, casting a furious glance at Jill and Barbara. 'I believe George's car is parked behind mine,' he said coldly to Barbara. 'Please move it. I need to get out.'

Barbara looked around for her bag.

'I'll do it, Barb,' Jill said, handing her the bag and getting up. 'Just give me the keys,' and she stalked out of the front door ahead of Ellis without giving him a sideways glance.

'I can't believe I did that,' Adam said later, 'but I'm really glad I did.'

'It fell a little short of your promise of civility,' Jill said, 'but Ellis did ask for it. I couldn't believe it was happening. Are you turning into the Incredible Hulk?'

Adam shrugged. 'One change leads to another, I suppose. Perhaps this is what happens to me when I start doing housework.'

'Well, I like it,' Jill said. 'Keep it up. I just wish Heather wasn't so upset. I wish I could have talked to her properly. I feel a bit as though we've abandoned her.' They were driving to Morpeth as planned, to spend the rest of the holiday with Barbara. Daisy and Toby had gone on ahead in George's car, and Kirsty and Nick had returned to Sydney to spend Boxing Day with his parents. 'She was weird all day, and Diane says she's been like it ever since Ellis turned up on his mercy dash from Byron Bay.'

'I don't know why she can't see what he's really like,' Adam said. 'He's so manipulative and transparent. When I went out to the park to find the others, they all let out a big cheer, which was nice for me but it just made it so clear that no one else can stand the sight of him.'

Jill sighed. 'Maybe she'll see it now,' she said.

'I doubt it. She's furious with me and wants me to apologise to him. I've apologised to her and to everyone else, but there's no way I'm apologising to Ellis. No way at all.'

Jill shook her head. 'Well, we can only wait and see what happens next, I suppose. I'll call her in the morning, see how it's all going. Meanwhile, let's try to forget it and give the kids a good time at Barb's. Where do you think Ellis went?'

'I don't know and I don't really care,' Adam said. 'Probably found a bar open somewhere to drown his sorrows and, frankly, I hope they choke him.'

'It's lovely of you to drive me home,' Diane said. 'It's been such a weird day, it would have felt very strange coming home alone. It's this house here on the left.'

Stefan turned the car into the drive and switched off the engine. 'It leaves the bad taste,' he said.

Diane hoped he was not just going to drop her and then head straight off back to Sydney. 'Would you like to come in for a coffee or something? I don't have any Christmas pudding but I do have some lovely chocolate ice cream.'

They ate the ice cream on the deck as the light began to fade.

'It's beautiful out here,' Stefan said. 'You will be sorry to go.'

Diane stretched her arms above her head and looked around her. 'Only because it's an ending,' she said. 'I *have* loved this place, and for years I put a lot of myself into it because of what it meant to us as a family. But I'm over it now. Leaving must have been so much harder for you; you left your village and your country.'

Stefan nodded. 'Oh yes, it is hard, but not, I think, as hard as to stay. There is one way out of anger and bitterness, so I have to take it.'

'But it must have been terrible to leave, with your wife and daughter buried there?'

'It is only their bodies,' he said, turning to her. 'Their spirits are free. I can find them anywhere.'

She looked away, so moved by the simplicity of his words that she was unable to respond. They sat in a comfortable silence as the sun turned from gold to orange.

'I offered to stay with Heather until Ellis came back,' Diane said, 'but she said she needs to be alone.'

'So perhaps she takes this time to change her mind about him,' Stefan said, helping himself to more ice cream.

'I doubt it. I think she's going to be outraged on his behalf, and she'll be defending him and making excuses. I don't think this relationship has run its course yet. Relationships are such hard work sometimes.'

'Indeed,' Stefan said, 'but it is the best way we find out about ourselves, so we must struggle on to the end, until we learn what we must learn. Heather has perhaps not reached that point yet.' He paused, putting his dish back on the table. 'So, Diane,' he said, 'which day will you come to Sydney?'

Ellis wasn't even sure where he was. He had roared out of Heather's driveway and driven off in such a rage that he couldn't remember which direction he'd taken. He didn't know his way around Newcastle and had swooped up and down suburban streets, extricating himself from turning circles, finding the sea where he least expected it, and the railway line in what seemed to be the wrong place. His rage almost blinded him. The urge to stride out to the garden and flatten Adam had been overwhelming, but the lawyer within had reminded him that, while he hadn't handled the wretched child very well, as long as he didn't lay a finger on anyone else he still had the moral high ground. He was physically shaken too. The side of his face was swollen and throbbed painfully, his head felt tight and his body was on high alert, prickling, twitching and aching. Worst of all, Heather had been such a disappointment.

'Ellis, darling!' she'd cried at first, rushing to his side, asking someone to call an ambulance. But the appalling old aunt who'd done a first aid course said it wasn't necessary. When he was finally back on his feet, Heather had helped him upstairs to clean up and then left him to go back and talk to the rest of her family. She should have stayed with him, but at least he'd been confident that she would be insisting on an apology and sending that half-wit brother and his wife and kids on their way. Ellis washed his face, changed his bloody shirt and lay down on the bed, expecting Heather to arrive any minute with a soothing cup of tea or preferably a double brandy, but there was no sign of her.

There was a low mumble of conversation from downstairs but, much as he strained, he couldn't hear what was being said. It was surprisingly quiet, and he closed his eyes and tried to relax. When the child in the spare room laughed out loud, his eyes shot open and he realised he must have dozed off for a few minutes. The muted voices mumbled on. Ellis was appalled: here he was, the injured party, alone and neglected while they behaved as though nothing had happened. For all they knew, he could be concussed, in a coma and not wake again for days, perhaps never. How would they all feel then? How would Heather feel about that? He got up quickly, feeling slightly dizzy, flung open the bedroom door and summoned Heather.

'How are you, darling?' she said solicitously, peering closely at his bruised face. 'A bit better now?'

'Apart from the fact that I'm in a lot of pain,' Ellis said, 'I am also deeply hurt and offended at the way I've been treated.'

Heather sat down on the edge of the bed. 'It was very hot-headed of Adam, and most unlike him,' she said, 'but you were rather rough on poor Daisy. She's only a little girl and it wasn't her fault.'

'That's hardly the point,' Ellis said. 'I was insulted and then assaulted in your home by a member of your family. Are you telling me you think that's acceptable behaviour?'

'Of course not,' she said, 'but I suppose it's understandable. Adam's her father and –'

'I want you to tell your brother that he has to apologise to me in front of everyone who witnessed this brutal attack, and then tell him and his wife to leave immediately,' Ellis said. 'This has totally ruined Christmas for me and, of course, for you too.'

Heather shook her head. 'Adam won't apologise, Ellis – at least, not to you. He wants *you* to apologise for the way you treated Daisy.'

Ellis snorted in disgust. 'Then just tell them to leave now,' he said. 'Right now. And you can tell him I'll have him charged for this.'

Heather put her hand on his arm. 'Ellis, please calm down. We're all upset, but it's Christmas. Let's just try to enjoy the rest of the day. The children haven't even had their presents yet.'

Ellis tugged his arm away from her. 'Either he leaves right now, Heather, or I do. I will not stay under the same roof as that man. So they go – *now*.'

'I can't do that, Ellis,' she said. 'I don't suppose they want to hang about for long either after this, but I am not going to turn my own family out of my house.'

Ellis picked up his jacket. Taking his wallet and car keys from the dresser, he stuffed them in his pocket. 'Well then, you are effectively turning *me* out,' he said, opening the bedroom door. 'And I warn you, Heather, I won't be back until they've gone.'

Once out of town, he'd stopped driving and tried to work out where he was. He saw a sign for a hotel and restaurant two kilometres ahead. It was just what he needed: a place to sit, have a drink and contemplate how to handle the situation from here on.

He drove into the car park of a beautiful estate which had been converted into a rather elegant hotel. Through the windows of the restaurant he could see people celebrating, eating and drinking, and a small band with a vocalist in a white dinner jacket singing 'White Christmas'. Ellis's spirits lifted and he locked the car, went inside, headed for the bar and ordered the double brandy Heather had failed to deliver. The liquor made its way into his bloodstream with extraordinary speed, flooding his body with warmth and, to his own surprise, a sense of success. He took his glass to a side table from where he could watch the activity in the restaurant, and sat gently rubbing his aching face. Every cloud has a silver lining, Ellis, he told himself now, testing to see how painful it was to smile: if you play your cards right, Heather will be eating out of your hand by tomorrow morning.

Heather waited until Stefan's car had disappeared around the corner, then she closed the front door and wandered back through the house. She had been longing for everyone to leave, but Adam had gone out to apologise to those who had fled to the park, brought them back and, in an awkward silence broken by occasional bursts of stilted conversation, they had insisted on clearing up and washing the dishes. Daisy and Toby's excitement in distributing the presents restored some Christmas spirit, but Heather felt as though a circle had been drawn around her, a moat which no one wanted to cross. It was easiest to pretend that nothing had happened, but she could sense the glances cast to assess how she was coping, the care with which they chose their words. The day had deteriorated into anxious pretence and they were all waiting for the moment they could escape from the masquerade. And where was Ellis now?

She was relieved when first Kirsty and Nick, then Barbara and George, got up to leave. Barbara kissed her and said she would call tomorrow, Jill and Diane both offered to stay with her until Ellis came home, Shaun told her to call him if there was anything she needed, and Adam hugged her awkwardly and apologised again for upsetting her. And, in the end, it was all because of something that happened decades ago and which was no one else's business.

Should she have confronted Ellis about the way he'd treated her back then? Adam and Jill both thought so but that didn't mean they were right. It had been a terrible time and his callous rejection had devastated her, as much or even more than the abortion itself, but it was *her* life and that part of it was in the past. Adam's obsessive guilt and his hatred of Ellis complicated the situation and kept pulling her back. Why did everything have to be discussed, dissected? Just because Adam had brooded on it for decades didn't mean she was obliged to.

Silence and relief had descended on the empty house, and Heather walked through the rooms and out into the garden where the fading light and the sweet scent of honeysuckle revived a nostalgia for childhood, when life had been simpler. She hated being trapped in this emotional quicksand between Adam and Ellis, but most of all she felt utterly exhausted. Trying to shield Ellis from the demands of her job was stressful in itself, and too often she found herself cutting corners in her efforts to please him.

Turning from the garden she went slowly back into the house, up the stairs and flopped down wearily on the bed, wishing that Ellis were there to hold her, to provide the reassurance of their first weeks together, longing to harvest the support of being a couple. How reckless she'd been to toy with it, to try to have everything. How often had she felt she was living on the margins, as though relationships were where real life happened? All she had to do was to grasp this second chance, knowing that it involved compromise. Heather rolled over onto her side and picked up the phone. The call went to Ellis's voicemail and she left a message asking him to call her and to come home. Then she lay back against the pillows, her arm over her eyes, and drifted into a deep, exhausted sleep full of people shouting and crying and the repeating sound of Adam's fist crunching into Ellis's jaw.

Ellis listened to Heather's message but stayed put. He even considered taking a room for the night to make his return more dramatic, but the hotel was fully booked. Perhaps it was for the best – after all, they hadn't exchanged Christmas presents yet and there was the promise of the lingerie. Signalling to a waiter he ordered a turkey sandwich and a pot of strong coffee, and checked his inside pocket for the blister pack of purple pills. Making up would be absolutely spectacular.

As the bar staff called for last orders he enquired about the best route back to Newcastle, only to learn that he must have been driving around in circles earlier because he was just fifteen minutes from home. As he pulled in to the drive it was almost midnight and Ellis was gratified to see that the lights were still on, so Heather was obviously waiting up for him. But when he let himself in through the front door there was no sign of her.

'Heather?' he called, walking through the hall and the sitting room to the kitchen and out onto the patio, puzzled by her absence. 'Heather, where are you?' The remains of Christmas lunch had been cleared away, and the place was spotless. He found her in the bedroom fast asleep, fully dressed on top of the bed and with the light on. Looking down at her he felt a pang of tenderness at the exhaustion and sadness in her face, and he sat down gently on the edge of the bed and stroked her cheek. The whole day must have been difficult for her too, and he understood that it was divided loyalties that caused her to get it wrong. He leaned forward and kissed her forehead and she stirred, opening her eyes, blinking at the light.

Ellis jumped up, switched it off and sat down on the bed again.

'You're back!' she said, smiling, rubbing her eyes. 'I'm sorry, I fell asleep.'

'You're exhausted,' Ellis said. 'You need to sleep. Get undressed and get into bed. Shall I bring you a cup of tea?'

'Oh, please,' she said, 'that would be wonderful.' She hauled herself up onto one elbow. 'I'm so glad you're back, Ellis, and I'm so sorry about today –'

Ellis put a finger on her lips. 'Shh,' he said. 'Don't apologise, it's over. I'm back, we're together, and that's what matters.'

Heather nodded. 'I know. That's what I was thinking. I haven't been fair to you, and you've been so patient. I've decided to resign. I'll call the Premier the day after tomorrow. To be honest, I think I've just been scared of making the commitment, but I'm ready to make it now.'

Downstairs in the kitchen, making a pot of tea and putting it on a tray with mugs and a jug of milk, Ellis couldn't stop smiling. The lingerie could wait. Right now he would deliver a tray of tea and whatever else was needed to ensure she made that phone call.

'I have a really special gift for you, Heather,' he said next morning when she had made tea and brought it back to bed. He leaned over and pulled the beautiful silver box from its hiding place under the bed. 'It's probably a good thing we didn't exchange our presents while everyone else was here.'

'How exciting,' Heather said, and Ellis saw the anticipation on her face as she untied the satin ribbon. 'What a glamorous looking present.' She put the box lid aside and folded back the silver tissue paper.

'Oh!' she said, and Ellis thought she looked rather more stunned than delighted, but then, she wouldn't have been expecting something so exotic.

'Try them on,' he'd urged as she carefully took out each item and laid it on the bed.

'Later, I'd rather have a shower first,' she said.

It wasn't the ecstatic reaction Ellis had hoped for but as he drank his tea he reminded himself that Heather didn't have the knack of responding to romantic gestures. He would have to work on that. Surreptitiously he swallowed a pill in readiness for the erotic fashion parade that was still to come.

'My enormous size seems to have made a huge impression on you,' Heather said later, emerging from the bathroom with the scarlet bra in one hand.

'What do you mean?' Ellis asked. 'Aren't you going to try them on?'

'Ellis, these are all size twenty-four.'

'And that's too big?'

'I'm a sixteen, occasionally an eighteen, depending on the label,' she said, laying the red bra back in the box amid the folds of tissue.

'But they might still be okay,' he said, trying to hide his disappointment. 'Just try the bra.'

'I did,' Heather said, taking some of her usual underwear from the drawer. 'My tits fell straight through.'

'How silly of me, I should have checked,' Ellis said, 'but I wanted it to be a surprise.'

'Well, it certainly was,' Heather said, doing up her own bra.

'I can change it all,' Ellis said. 'I bought it on the Internet. It's easy, you can pack it up today and we'll look at the website together so you can choose what you want.'

Heather pulled a linen dress over her head, and Ellis was grateful for the way she hid her disappointment. He, meanwhile, was finding that his own disappointment, plus a mild hangover and an aching jaw, had won out over the usually reliable pills. But his day improved when he went downstairs to the smell of coffee and bacon, and heard her talking to her sister-in-law on the phone, telling her everything was fine, and that she'd decided to resign. The ratbag brother had done him a favour: the debacle of Christmas Day had presented Heather with a challenge and she had responded to it by jumping in his direction.

'I'm resigning the seat but I'm not retiring,' she had told him over breakfast. 'There are lots of things I'd like to do, but nothing that will take over my life.'

Ellis half listened as she talked about the campaign and finding a new candidate, the timescale, the way it would have to be managed, and then about all the things she would have time to do, things she'd wanted to do for so long. The satisfaction was enormous, his former irritation floating out of the open windows. He decided he would give her something wonderful, and he knew exactly what it would be – something that would demonstrate his own commitment. A better gift even than the lingerie, and he'd soon have the latter sorted out too.

TWENTY-FOUR

Jill put down the phone and walked back into the kitchen.

'Well?' Barbara said, looking up from the toaster. 'How is she? Did Ellis come back?'

Jill gave an all-embracing shrug and sat down at the table. 'She's fine, or so she says, although I must say she sounds incredibly hyper. Ellis came back. Ellis is wonderful, verging on sainthood. And she's resigning.'

'What?' Adam said, dropping his spoon into his muesli.

'She's resigning,' Jill repeated. 'Apparently, she's been thinking about it for some time. She mentioned it to Shaun just before Christmas, and last night she made up her mind. She's inspired by you leaving the orchestra, Adam. She's been given a wonderful second chance with Ellis and she's going to take it.'

'What, live with him? Marry him?' Adam asked in horror.

Jill shrugged. 'I didn't ask, I was too stunned. She just said she'd call the Premier and the party secretary tomorrow and meet them later in the week. But we mustn't talk about it, because they won't want it to leak before they're ready.'

Barbara, who had allowed the toast to burn, tossed the charred remains in the bin and slipped two more slices into the toaster. 'I'm glad she's decided to get out, but not if it's for Ellis's sake rather than her own.'

'The party will flay her alive,' Adam said. 'The election's not far off, her name will be more than mud. After everything she's done, all those years of commitment, and the shooting as well.

She's going to go out with this big black mark against her.' He pushed back his chair and got up. 'I'm going to call her now –'

'No!' Barbara and Jill chorused.

'You can only make it worse, Adam,' Jill said. 'She says she's forgiven you, she wants to put it all behind her and move on into a new life.'

'Jill's right,' Barbara said. 'You mustn't call, Adam. What you say is right, but it's also good news. She's exhausted, she needs a break, and you can't tell me that, even besotted as she is with Ellis, she's going to disappear into some domestic arrangement with him. No way. There are heaps of other things she'll want to do, but it'll mean she has a life as well as a job.'

'A life with him,' Adam growled.

'Well, if that's what she wants . . . '

Adam tossed his serviette on the table and stalked out to the deck, where Daisy and Toby were arguing about who got the best presents.

'I didn't know what to say to her,' Jill said, looking up at Barbara.

'There's nothing much you can say, dear,' Barbara said. 'She has to find her own way through this. But my gut instinct tells me that this is a good decision. It's Heather looking after herself, and if she's doing that she's eventually going to see that being with Ellis may not be the best thing for her.'

Jill took a piece of toast and reached for the butter and Vegemite. 'I really hope you're right,' she said, 'because the way she sounds this morning, Pollyanna simply isn't in it.'

Heather walked out of the conference room into the corridor and leaned against the wall. It was over, she'd done it. They'd shredded her but she'd survived. Her legs trembled with relief as she took the lift down to the ground floor and stepped outside to dial Shaun's number. He had offered to come with her to Sydney when he learned she was going alone, and she had welcomed his company and the prospect of debriefing with someone who would understand every complicated nuance of what had happened.

'I'm at your favourite café at The Rocks,' he said when he answered.

'Great,' Heather said. 'Stay there and I'll be with you shortly. We can have lunch and I'll tell you everything.'

'The candidate?' he asked.

'Sorted,' she said. 'Mary Fraser, as we'd hoped. They'll push that through as soon as possible and we'll make the announcement soon. Won't be long, I'm starving.'

The city centre was teeming with shoppers heading into the post-Christmas sales or out of them loaded with carrier bags. What fun it would be, Heather thought, to have time to shop at leisure, rather than racing somewhere between meetings. It would be just one of the many things she'd have time for, and not just time but energy too. Energy to go to the theatre, to have a holiday, take up painting or dancing or rock climbing or reviving her long-forgotten attempts at the piano. There would be time to read books, watch movies, relax over long lazy lunches with the friends she'd neglected, all against the background of her relationship with Ellis. Her sense of freedom was growing by the minute and she headed swiftly for The Rocks, feeling lighthearted and almost light-headed.

It was nearly six by the time Heather had dropped Shaun off and arrived home, and Ellis was working diligently at his laptop on the patio table. Her heart sank a little at the sight of him so engrossed in what he was doing. That was the next hurdle, the dreadful Head to Heart. She was going to have to confront that before long. She could see now that he might be able to help some people with this idea, but the business plan was hideous, such an obvious rip-off. Luke Scriven with his huge fees was probably at the bottom of it, but easing Ellis out of it should be easier now, now that he knew how fully committed she was to him. She might be able to involve him in something of genuine value – working with asylum seekers, perhaps. His legal background could be really useful there.

Sometimes Heather felt Ellis lived in a fantasy world, what with his Head to Heart stuff and the hideous underwear. It was years since she'd received a gift from a man and she'd been thrilled by the promise of the silver box with its red and silver ribbon, but she had almost choked when she saw the contents. What was he thinking? She was paralysed by his failure to understand that it was all so entirely at odds with her sense of herself. There were suspender belts and black stockings – even a thong, of all things! All she could see as she carefully unpacked each item was how utterly ridiculous she would look and, worse still, *feel*. She imagined her cellulite-ridden thighs against the scarlet lace, her stomach bulging over the low waistband of the French knickers, rolls of fat on her back billowing over the bra. She was both shocked and hurt by a gift that seemed to demonstrate how little Ellis knew about her. Did he really think she would appreciate this or was this for his own gratification? Neither prospect was particularly palatable.

And yet . . . and yet she'd felt incapable of disappointing him and had dissembled to please him; his blunder over the sizes had been a godsend. But Heather knew that the lingerie, like the spectre of Head to Heart, would haunt her until she could be honest with Ellis, until she could remind him who she really was, not who she used to be or might be in his fantasies. The prospect of that confrontation made this morning's meeting with the Premier and the party power brokers seem like child's play.

'You're very late,' Ellis called. 'I expected you hours ago.'

From the kitchen window she saw him save what was on his screen and get up.

'I was worried about you,' he said, walking into the kitchen. 'You could've let me know.'

'Sorry, darling,' Heather said. 'We went to . . . ' She hesitated, quickly editing out lunch at The Rocks and the subsequent browse around the nearby shops and a gallery. 'We went to great lengths to get everything organised. It's pretty messy, as you can imagine.'

'Well, you should have rung to let me know what was happening,' Ellis said, still looking rather stern but kissing her forehead. 'It was hard to concentrate while I was so worried about you.'

It was a reminder that while the charmed circle of a relationship had an awful lot going for it, there were also distinct disadvantages, among them the fact that one was always responsible to someone else. She *should* have called, but on the other hand if he were really so worried, wouldn't *he* have called *her*? She went upstairs to change her clothes, checking as she did so whether there were any missed calls on her mobile. There were none. But she *was* in the wrong again, no getting away from that. She must try to remember that she was one half of a couple and to make this second chance work, she needed to be more considerate.

Diane found the street quite easily and drew up in front of a tiny weatherboard cottage which was almost hidden by two rambling old lemon trees. Beyond the white picket fence were great clumps of lavender, and purple and white bougainvillea careered up the verandah posts and over the side fences. It was the humblest of the lovely old houses in this quiet suburban street, but undoubtedly the most appealing.

She took a deep breath to calm her nerves, opened the gate and strolled up the brick-paved path. She had been in this state of nervous anticipation since Christmas Day, since Stefan had finally said goodnight, kissed her cheek and reminded her that she had promised to visit him on Thursday. It was years – no, decades, since she'd felt like this. Loyalty had always been important to her and although she had sometimes been attracted to other men while she was married to Gerry, she had never acted on it, and since he left she had felt sexless; immune to both the idea and the reality of being drawn to a man. Only a couple of weeks earlier she had thrown away Stefan's number, and now she felt like a teenager on her first date.

'I am so happy,' Stefan said, opening the screen door and drawing her through into the cool, dim hallway. 'I think perhaps you find some excuse not to come.'

'I've been looking forward to it,' she said in an understatement so massive it made her blush.

'Then I am even more happy. But it's a long drive. Would you like some tea, coffee, perhaps a cool drink?'

She opted for green tea and Stefan led her through to the back of the house, to a minute kitchen with an old Metters stove under the arch of the chimney piece, and curved-edge cupboards picked out in deep blue and white.

'It's perfect,' she cried, taking in the white jug filled with blue cornflowers, the pots of African violets on the sunny window ledge and the framed photographs of Glebe dating back to the turn of the twentieth century. 'It looks like a feature from a homes and gardens magazine.'

Stefan laughed. 'It is pretty but it is also cluttered. I collect too much, fill every space.'

She sat at the small, scrubbed pine table while he made the tea and told her that the cottage belonged to his widowed aunt who had lived in Australia for most of her adult life. He had stayed here with her when he first arrived from Kosovo and within a few months she had suffered a stroke and was now in a nursing home.

'So I am very fortunate she lets me stay here,' Stefan said. 'I pay rent and she is happy to know it is cared for. I pick her up and bring her here for the day sometimes, and she can sit on the deck and enjoy the garden.'

'What if something happens to her?' Diane asked. 'Will you have to leave?'

'Who knows?' he said with a shrug. 'She and I are all that is left of the family, but the house – I don't know. I don't need to know. I have learned to be in the present, it is the present that interests me, not so much the future, and so I just enjoy it.'

As they walked out to the deck, Diane gasped at the beauty of the garden. 'It's nothing like I expected,' she said.

'What *did* you expect?'

'Something formal, I suppose,' she said, unsure really what she *had* expected. 'Beds of colour-coordinated flowers, a manicured lawn, nothing like this.'

'The olive tree, the orange and grapefruit, they were all in place a long time,' Stefan said, putting their tea onto two old milking stools that stood alongside a couple of wide-backed cane chairs. 'They make the structure for the garden.'

Diane went down the steps from the deck and followed a path that curved between clumps of lavender, cornflowers, white daisies and wax plants, to a corner where, in the shade of two frangipanis, water trickled over tiers of flat stone speckled with moss and bordered with vivid blue lobelia. 'I suppose that, in spite of what you said, I still expected it to be like a cemetery,' she said, 'but the colours, the greenness, the abundance – it really *is* all about life and celebration.'

Stefan, standing behind her, put a hand on her shoulder. 'I made the garden to remind me that, although I lost so much, there is still so much to live for.'

Diane felt dizzy at his touch. 'And your cello?' she asked, having seen the case standing in the hall. 'Is that a celebration of life too?'

'Sometimes,' Stefan said with a small shrug, 'but a lot of the time it is just my job. It is the finest instrument because it mirrors all the range and subtleties of the human voice, but I am not the cello tragic person like Adam.' He paused and reached for her hand. 'You realise that the garden is a trick?'

'A trick?'

'To get you here. When we are in Barbara's garden I am so much wanting to see you again but I think if I ask you, you say no.'

Diane laughed. 'So you use the garden to lure women to your home?'

'It is a good idea, no?' he said with a smile. 'And you see it worked. But it is not a habit, only this one time I have this feeling . . . ' His voice faded and he seemed to run out of words.

Diane squeezed his hand. 'It feels very special for me too,' she said, and she slipped her hand into his as they walked together back up the path and settled on the deck to drink their tea.

TWENTY-FIVE

In the first week of the New Year, Barbara was clearing out the jumbled top cupboard in her spare room. It was a horrible job that involved much going up and down on the kitchen steps, and packing long outworn clothes and household clutter into plastic bags to take to the charity shop. She hated jobs like this but there was enough of her mother left in her to compel her to get everything in order before she went away, and this was first on a list of jobs to be done over the next few weeks.

The compulsion annoyed her. It was, after all, no more risky to fly to China than it was to drive down the Pacific Highway to Sydney, or even, as George had pointed out, to step outside your own office on a rainy evening in Newcastle. But there was something about embarking on a trip like this that made her feel she shouldn't leave a mess behind her. And then there was the added incentive that it was something to do while she felt so restless. Barbara understood that most people find it possible to live with a level of cognitive dissonance, but the more she thought about Heather, particularly her behaviour on Christmas Day, the more she worried, so that she had now reached the same level of concern that Adam had expressed when he heard the news.

'And you're sure this is right for you, Heather?' she had asked her on the phone, 'the right time, and most of all the right reasons?'

'Absolutely right,' Heather had said. 'I can't tell you how

liberated I feel by this decision. You were right, I should have done it ages ago. And Ellis is being wonderful, so supportive.'

In any other circumstances, Barbara would have got straight in the car and gone to Newcastle to see Heather, to quiz her about her plans. But Ellis was still there and apparently likely to be for the next week or two, and Barbara didn't want to risk being drawn into a three-cornered conversation.

'We could nip up to Byron and saw through one of the stilts holding his house up,' George said. 'Then he'd get an urgent message summoning him home. Should keep him out of the way for a while.'

'I believe they're brick stilts,' Barbara said. She pulled a rather smart winter coat, a throwback to her city days, from the cupboard and shook it out. She hadn't worn it for years, and wouldn't wear it again, so she stuffed it into a bag with some shoes and a handbag. What she needed was a new warm anorak, or perhaps a polar fleece which was very light to pack.

'I do have a sledgehammer,' George volunteered. 'But try to think of it this way. Adam and Jill have sorted out their problems. Kirsty has a job. The little kids are fine. You and I are about to have the adventure of a lifetime. You can't have everything go right all at once. By the time we get home, Heather might have kicked the bastard out of her life and got herself a toyboy.'

The day Barbara watched Heather on the morning news with the Premier and the new candidate, she'd looked happy, but hyped up, and not really like herself. George might be right but Barbara hoped Heather would come to her senses soon, then she could set off for China with an easy mind. From the top of the ladder she could hear George calling her from the kitchen door. Cautiously she came down the steps one more time.

'We could go for a ride,' he called. 'It's quite nice and cool now. What do you think?'

'Okay,' she said. 'Good idea, I'm sick of this. I'll meet you outside in ten minutes.' A bike ride was just what she needed and there were still a couple of hours of daylight left.

They chose a new route that took them parallel to the river and then branched away from Morpeth.

'Lovely riding in the evening,' George said. 'Thank heavens for daylight saving. We should do this more often.'

Barbara looked across at him riding as he always did with an energy that made her struggle to keep up. 'In China,' she said, 'we'll need to pace ourselves. Some of those rides are very long.'

'Right,' he said, hunched forward as they pedalled hard towards the brow of a hill. 'You can set the pace then, but right now I'm freewheeling. See you at the bottom,' and he pedalled fiercely on until he reached the downward slope and then straightened up, resting one hand on the point at which the handlebars joined.

Barbara watched him affectionately as he bowled on down the hill, the unbuckled straps of his helmet flying out behind him. He was halfway down when he hit the pothole. Did he misjudge it or just not see it? She saw him wobble dangerously and swerve towards the edge of the road and, as his wheels sank into the deep gravel and locked, she watched in horror as he was hurled clear of the bike and crashed onto the Tarmac, his helmet bouncing away.

George's accident didn't rate highly on Ellis's register of interest. Everything seemed to be going his way. He was steaming ahead with his writing, and Heather's decision to resign had made him more confident and focused. He was in the flow, the words pouring from his head through his fingers to the keyboard; finally, he seemed to be getting the hang of it. He had decided to defer Heather's reading of the manuscript until he had finished the section dealing with the Nirvana experience and he was almost at that point. He would take a break the following day, meet with Luke Scriven and talk through the new possibilities for Head to Heart.

'Come with me,' he suggested to Heather. 'You can go shopping or something while I see Luke.'

'I told you, I'm going to Morpeth tomorrow to pick up Barb,' Heather said. She was making up the spare room bed at the time. 'They're moving George from Maitland to Newcastle so she'll need to stay here to be near him.' She smoothed the quilt and picked up another set of sheets. 'I'm making up the other bed too. Adam and Jill are going to take turns to stay a couple of days at a time. We're going to work out a plan so there's always someone around to be with Barb. It could be a long haul.'

Ellis tried to curb his irritation. 'Wouldn't they be happier in a hotel?' he asked. 'It'll make the place rather crowded.'

Heather put the sheets down on the second bed and turned to him. 'You want me to send my aunt, who's been like a mother to me, to stay in a hotel while her partner might be dying?'

Ellis knew he was on dodgy ground. 'Well, no,' he conceded, 'but your brother . . .'

'They're staying here, Ellis,' Heather said, turning away to shake out a sheet. 'End of conversation.'

It was so long since Ellis had been reprimanded that he'd almost forgotten how it felt. It had happened in court, of course, but only when he had deliberately stuck his neck out and engineered the reprimand for effect. This was different. Heather was clearly upset and things had been going so nicely that he didn't want to lose ground; sometimes backing off was a good strategy.

'What I think I might do,' he suggested later, 'is leave the car in Sydney tomorrow and fly home for a few days to sort things out there. I'll come back next week, by which time you'll probably be back to normal.' He thought he saw a look of relief cross Heather's face, and he knew that he had won this round. She must feel bad having allowed her family to stay at the house after the way they'd treated him, so his gracious withdrawal would make it easier for her.

'I'll miss you,' she said, snuggling closer to him in bed later that night. 'Poor Barb, watching her with George makes me so sad. It makes me realise how lucky I am.'

'It's not for long,' Ellis said. 'You'll be busy, I'll be back in a few days, and we can get down to planning the future. It's a whole new start for both of us, Heather.'

'Mmm,' she murmured, pressing her face against his shoulder. 'It's going to be a wonderful, exciting year.'

'Where's Ellis?' Jill asked when she arrived three days later.

'Gone back to Byron for a few days,' Heather said. 'He had

some stuff to do. And it's easier without him around.' Jill's eyebrows shot up in surprise. 'Diane's being terrific. She and Barb get on well, so she's helping out too. How long are you here for?'

'Until Monday,' Jill said. 'Adam's got concerts over the weekend – he's still working out his notice. But if you can manage Tuesday and Wednesday, he'll come on Thursday. Is everything okay with you and Ellis?'

'Of course it is,' Heather said sharply, 'why wouldn't it be?'

'Whoops! Sorry,' Jill replied, 'just asking. I mean, Christmas Day can't have been easy for either of you.'

Heather's defensiveness dropped away. 'It was awful, wasn't it? And I know Ellis behaved very badly with Daisy, but Adam –'

Jill tilted her head to one side. 'It *was* so unlike him.'

Heather nodded. 'Totally. I was furious with him, but later I thought perhaps it's good that he's changing like that. Not going around punching people, I don't mean that, but actually confronting stuff instead of hiding.'

'I think so,' Jill said. 'He's changing dramatically.' She paused, debating whether or not to push on. 'And so are you,' she finally said.

'Me? I don't think so. But I've made a good decision about the job. Knowing the end is in sight is a relief. I really have had enough.'

'It's more than that, surely,' Jill answered, wondering how far she dared to go. 'More than the job. I mean, it's the way you are with Ellis.'

'I'm determined to make this relationship work, Jill,' Heather said. 'Not everyone gets a second chance, especially at a time in life when you don't really expect to fall in love again.'

Jill nodded. 'Of course,' she said, 'it must be very special. It's just that you *are* different when Ellis is around, very different, and you did say –'

'That's natural,' Heather cut in. 'Obviously, being in a relationship changes you, you have to adapt and compromise, don't you? It's give and take and –'

'And sometimes if you really want it, you can end up giving too much,' Jill rushed in, feeling she should run and hide under the table, but hoping Heather would remember the conversation they'd had over lunch a few weeks earlier.

There was a pause. 'I suppose that's a risk,' Heather said, 'but I'm sure I'll be able to resist *that* temptation.'

'Mmm. And so you feel you're doing things differently this time?'

'Oh, entirely,' Heather said. 'This time I'm really clear and centred, not twisting myself out of shape.'

Faced with Heather's self-delusion, Jill felt like a goldfish tossed out of its bowl and left panting on the carpet. She opened her mouth, shut it again, gulped for air and wondered if the shock showed in her face. 'Good,' she murmured, fumbling for something else to say. 'That's very good news. I've been finding it hard to ditch some of *my* old habits, especially around the house, but I think I'm getting there. It's fun, actually, discovering that it's possible to be different.'

'Exactly,' Heather said. 'It's a whole new adventure,' and she picked up Jill's bag. 'Come on up,' she said. 'We'll stick your stuff in the bedroom and then we can go over to the hospital to collect Barb. I'm so thankful you can spend time with her tomorrow. I simply have to get back to work.'

George lay connected to a battery of monitors that beeped and flashed, registering the fact that he was still alive, as haemorrhages from the damaged white matter surrounding his brain slowly diminished its ability to function. Day after day, Barbara sat beside him. She held his hand and talked to him about China and the things he was going to teach to Chinese chemists. She told him about Beijing and Shanghai, and read extracts from travel guides and books.

'Terry's repairing your bike,' she told him. 'He says it'll be fine, and Andy, that nice young boy next door, is looking after Rusty until we get back. He'll do it when we go to China too, although we might have to postpone that for a few weeks. Nothing to worry about, we can easily rebook, go later in the year – June, perhaps. It'll be warmer then, anyway.'

She played him the music he loved: The Supremes, Peggy Lee, The Four Tops and Mel Tormé, and over and over again the full score of *South Pacific*, and each day she read aloud the poems of his beloved Dylan Thomas.

'You do know how much I love you, George, don't you?' she asked him every day. 'How much you mean to me? I'm sorry, I'm not much good at saying it, neither of us is, I suppose. But you must know. Can you try and squeeze my hand if you know?'

She left his side only to sleep, or to make space for his son and daughter-in-law, or when pressured by Heather, Jill, Adam or Diane to take a walk with them in the fresh air through the hospital grounds, or to sit in the café dazed and anxious, drinking endless cups of tea.

But nothing drew a response from George, who had not spoken since moments after his accident when Barbara had pedalled furiously down the hill and jumped from her bike to kneel beside him.

'Silly old bugger,' he'd murmured then, looking up at her. 'Shouldn't've been going so fast. Silly old bugger.' He'd grasped her hand and held it against his cheek. 'My Barbara,' he said, kissing it. 'I love you so very much. You really are the light of my life.' He'd spluttered then, as though something were stuck in his throat, and blood began to trickle from the side of his mouth. 'You must still go, for me, for both of us . . . ' Although his eyes remained open they were empty suddenly, as though part of him had left, and Barbara heard a motorist who had stopped to help urgently summoning an ambulance on his mobile phone.

'You're worn out, Barb. Come on home and have a meal and a good sleep,' Adam urged her one evening.

'But what if I leave and he . . . ' She couldn't bear to finish the sentence and so, just as she did when Heather or Jill insisted, she got up and took Adam's arm.

'Barb,' he began, 'you know the doctors said that George can't hear you.'

'They *say* that,' she said, 'but how can they *know*?'

'I think they can see reactions in the brain,' Adam said.

Barbara shrugged. 'I don't know what they can and can't

see, and I don't care.' She turned at the door, looking back at the motionless body in the bed.

Adam, who had been delegated by Heather and Jill to handle the delicate task of ensuring that Barbara understood it was just a matter of time before the control centre in George's brain shut down, decided that it was much easier to punch someone in the face than it was to dispel hope in someone you love, and said no more.

'I can't take the risk, you see, Adam,' Barbara said. 'People *have* come back from . . . from where he is. And you know George, he's like a kid in the playground – he absolutely hates to be beaten. I have to believe in that, his stubbornness . . . you know, the rage against the dying of the light.'

But the days dragged on with no sign of change, until one morning, Heather, who had dropped Barbara at the hospital on her way to the office, called in again just before midday with the intention of forcing her out for lunch. She parked the car and walked along the corridor, wondering how Barbara would cope without George. She was self-sufficient and accustomed to living alone, but would that self-sufficiency waver now?

Heather stopped suddenly and leant against the wall, thinking of her own recent confrontations with the darker side of being alone, and remorse cast a long shadow. She had invested so much in looking after her electorate, now it seemed obvious that in doing that she had robbed Barbara of what she had the right to expect from her, and robbed herself of some of the potential riches of that relationship. And wasn't it also true of her relationship with Adam and Jill, her nieces and nephew? And where were the women friends from years ago? Had those friendships died from lack of nourishment? She struggled to get a grip on herself, to resist the urge to burst in on Barbara, to pour out apologies, explanations and promises for the future. The best thing she could do right now was simply to be there with Barbara to see her through whatever lay ahead.

The door of George's room was propped half open and Heather paused to gather her thoughts before going in. For once the corridor was silent and, as she stepped into the shadow of the open doorway, she could hear Barbara reading, her voice low and soft but compelling.

Sensing someone in the doorway, Barbara looked up. 'Heather,' she said, 'I didn't expect you so soon.' She looked at George on the bed. 'I think he's better today, come and see. Just now I thought he squeezed my hand a bit.'

Heather walked to the other side of the bed. George looked just as he had every day for the last two weeks.

'There!' Barbara said, triumphantly. 'His eyelid, did you see it? It moved, I'm sure I saw it –'

But she was interrupted by a sudden change in the reassuring beep of the monitor – a missed beat and then another, and finally a relentless and chilling monotone.

George was cremated in the first week of February on a grey and overcast day when the temperature had climbed past forty degrees and the flowers wilted in front of the eyes of the mourners. It was a simple ceremony during which Adam experienced a more profound sense of grief and sadness than he had at the funerals of his parents. He and Heather sat on either side of Barbara holding her hands, with Jill and Kirsty on either side of Toby and Daisy, who were both determined to behave perfectly at their first funeral.

Adam stroked his thumb across the back of Barbara's hand, noting with shock the prominent veins and the liver spots that freckled the loose skin. Time passed so quickly even while it seemed to drag, and as one battled from day to day, month to month and year to year through the rapids of confusion, it was so easy to lose sight of the way it carved its mark on those you loved. He had taken charge of cancelling the travel bookings, claiming refunds and advising the Chinese company that the English teachers they were expecting in a few weeks would not, after all, be arriving.

'It's my fault,' Barbara had said to Adam a few days earlier. 'My fault, all of it. I said we had to wait until the warmer weather and it was me who manipulated him into getting a bike. He'd still be alive today if it weren't for me.'

'You don't know that,' Adam replied. 'And George loved riding that bike, he loved the whole idea of getting back on two wheels at nearly seventy-six. He had you to thank for that, he told me so himself.'

'But it still feels like my fault,' Barbara said. 'I feel as though I killed him.'

The wake was a gentle affair which Barbara had offered to host in her own house to take the pressure off George's daughter-in-law. Heather, Jill and Diane prepared and served food and Adam looked after the drinks, all of them watching Barbara, who seemed to have aged ten years in the last month.

'You have to stop watching me,' she told them later when the guests had left. 'I can't handle this vigilance. I know you all mean well but it's as though you're waiting for me to collapse and I'm not going to.'

They exchanged embarrassed glances.

'I'm *not* going to,' she repeated, more forcefully this time. 'I'm exhausted and terribly sad. George was my soul mate and now he's gone, but he's still with me, here,' she said, patting her chest, 'here in my heart. And he'd never forgive me if I fell apart now. You've all been a wonderful support at the hospital and now here, and I love you dearly, but I feel as though every moment you're waiting for me to crack up.'

'Okay,' Adam said, 'we'll stop watching and worrying, but only if you promise to get hold of us the minute you need anything, or if you just want company.'

Barbara nodded. 'I promise,' she said. 'I'm lucky to have you all looking out for me. But I need to be alone, to rest and grieve, and I can't do that while you watch and hold your breath.'

TWENTY-SIX

Ellis was satisfied with his own performance. He had made a supreme effort to be reasonable and accommodating. It was good to be home and he spent several productive days tidying the garden, mowing, pruning, answering his mail and considering ways in which the house could be extended to accommodate another person living there full time. There was a second bedroom that he used as a study, but he felt Heather would probably like a study of her own, and life would generally be more relaxed with a second bathroom. He drew some rough plans and dropped them off to the architect who had designed the original building.

'I want it to blend in with the rest of the house, Barry,' he said, 'same materials, same brick piers. I don't want it to look like an extension, but as though it was always meant to be there. And there's this extra plan too, a small separate building lower down on the block – you'll see what I mean.'

'Aha!' Barry said with a knowing grin. 'You have plans for cohabitation – or is it marriage?'

'Both, I hope,' Ellis said. 'And can you get it done fast? I'm going back to Newcastle in a few days and want to take it with me.'

Barry sucked his breath in through his teeth and shook his head. 'Difficult,' he said, 'we've got a lot on. But I'll see what I can do.'

It took two weeks to get the drawings back but it didn't matter because Ellis was at home far longer than he'd anticipated. When

Heather had described George's injuries he assumed it would all be over in a couple of days, so he'd planned for time to avoid the funeral. He'd done the aunt's party and then Christmas and that, surely, was sufficient contribution to the family rituals he loathed. But he hadn't expected George to hang around so long. None of it was very convenient. His car was in Sydney and being without it irritated him, so he got out the motorbike he'd bought when he first retired.

'Nice to have the wind in my hair,' he said to Leah when he ran into her in town.

'Aren't you supposed to wear a crash helmet?' she asked straight-faced.

'A joke,' Ellis explained. 'I mean, that's the way a bike makes you feel.' It felt so good, in fact, that he did some longish runs for the sheer pleasure and freedom of it. He felt that he cut a striking profile riding into town, strolling in his leather jacket to the coffee shop. He saw himself as a sort of Marlon Brando figure, not the sad, sick and obese old man of recent years, but the *Waterfront* Marlon, young, supple and broodingly sexy. It was yet another angle for Head to Heart, the dynamic, sexy older man reunited with his one true love, riding a motorbike and starting a new business and not far off his seventieth birthday, although maybe it was better not to actually mention his age – have to talk to Luke about that.

They would have to spice up Heather's image to bring it more in line with his own. Obviously she'd need to lose some weight. Had she ever ridden a motorbike? Probably not, but she'd look good in photographs poised behind him on the pillion. At some stage, and it needed to be quite soon, they could talk it through with Luke and see if he had some suggestions for packaging her.

'When are you coming back?' Heather had asked him the day after the funeral.

'I was thinking of flying down on Friday, seeing Luke and then driving back to your place in the evening,' he said.

'It seems ages,' she said. 'So much has happened. I've really missed you.'

'It *is* too long, *again*,' Ellis said. 'But it's all over now. We can get on with our plans, and I've got a wonderful surprise for you – two surprises, in fact. I'll see you Friday evening. Put some champagne in the fridge.'

'You two seem to be getting on really well,' Jill said as she and Diane walked out into the dusky garden while Adam and Stefan cleared the table and made coffee. 'This is the first time Stefan's ever brought anyone over for dinner.'

'And he's the first man I've been out with since Gerry,' Diane said. 'And I mean, since I *met* Gerry, not just since he left.'

Jill stopped and turned to face her. 'Really? But Gerry wasn't your first boyfriend, was he?'

Diane flushed and lowered her voice. 'Well, not my first *boyfriend*, but the first man I slept with. The *only* one I've slept with.'

'No! Not really?'

Diane smiled. 'You married late, Jill! I married young and my mother put the fear of god in me about sex and at the same time failed to give me any information. You know what it was like back then. People talk as though everyone was doing it all the time, but I was really ignorant and terrified of ending up pregnant.'

Jill laughed suddenly. 'Me too. I knew nothing and was frightened of everything. My mother gave me a booklet that explained it all with drawings of rabbits. It took me a long time to translate it to human beings. I'd never seen a penis and wasn't sure what you did with them but one night I was out with a boy, sitting kissing on a seat in the park, and quite suddenly he undid his fly and put his penis in my hand and made me hold it. I was terrified. I honestly thought I might get pregnant just from holding it.'

'It *was* scary, all that stuff,' Diane said. 'A similar thing happened to me, only it was in the dark foyer of a rather dingy block of flats. I remember thinking, so *that's* what it's like, what am I supposed to do now?' They laughed, and Diane felt a sudden sense of relief at being able to talk like this. 'I never saw that boy again, and the next penis I saw was Gerry's. But what I remember from that night in the flats was a sort of confusion, that all the stories and speculation came down to this strange thing that was lying in my hand twitching like a dying puppy.'

Their laughter floated out on the still evening air in the darkening garden. 'So, I guess this must all seem pretty scary,' Jill said, 'starting again after so long?'

Diane nodded. 'I really like Stefan, and I don't want to stuff this up, but I feel incompetent. I've forgotten how to read the signs, if I *ever* knew how to read them. And he's such an unusual person. I don't just mean his cultural background, but as an individual – he's unlike any other man I've met before.'

Jill smiled. 'I probably shouldn't break a confidence, but it might help you to know that Stefan called in here this morning and was agonising about his own lack of confidence. It's strange for him too, Diane. Take it slowly and trust him. He's a good man.'

Diane hadn't intended to confide in Jill but the evening had been so entirely different from any she had ever spent with Gerry and their friends that it seemed perfectly natural. Stefan lacked the hard edge that had so attracted her to Gerry, and his friendship with Adam was different from the way Gerry had related to his friends.

'Barbara says that Stefan is a true grown-up, and that Adam's reached that stage too with a lot of help from you.'

'That does sound like Barb,' Jill said, breaking off a twig of lavender and squeezing it between her fingers. 'Adam's had a hard time recently, we both have. His friendship with Stefan helped, and they're pretty comfortable with who they are. They don't need to push and shove each other to see who's in the ascendant.' She indicated a wooden bench and they walked to it, moving aside the remnants of a game Daisy and her friend had been playing with plastic cups and a couple of dolls who had seen better days. 'Speaking of people in the ascendant,' Jill went on, sitting down, 'Ellis is far too much in the ascendant for my liking.'

'It's horrible, isn't it?' Diane said. 'Heather's a different person when he's around, like she's doing some weird dance to please him. It's embarrassing. I think he intimidates her. I keep hoping she'll catch sight of herself and be as shocked as we are.'

'With the exception of Adam, we've all fallen into the trap

of letting her think we like him just because we want her to be happy,' Jill said.

'I'm certainly guilty of that,' Diane said. 'And although Heather's become a friend, she's also my employer, and frankly I don't feel right telling her that I think the love of her life is a pain in the bum.'

'Maybe we could get together, you, me and Barb. Talk to her. What do you think?'

'Ooh! I don't know,' Diane said cautiously. 'I don't think I'm close enough to Heather to know how she'd take that. I mean, wouldn't she just feel she needed to defend him?'

'Who's defending whom?' Adam asked as he and Stefan emerged from the shadows.

'Heather defending Ellis if Diane, Barb and I tried to knock some sense into her,' Jill said.

Adam shook his head. 'Bad idea. Very bad idea. My sister is extremely stubborn and I've already made the situation worse, although it's hard for me to get over the satisfaction I got from punching him. All we can do now is stand back and wait for her to recognise what she's doing.'

Stefan nodded, sitting down beside Diane and taking her hand as though it were the most natural thing in the world. 'Adam's right,' he said. 'Ellis is too full of himself, flying too close to the sun. I don't think you have to wait very long before his wings catch fire.'

Barbara sat on the end of her bed staring at the small pile of George's belongings that she'd gathered from around the house. There was an old cotton hat that he'd left hanging on the back of a chair on the deck; several battered tobacco tins full of various sizes of screws; one of his collection of corkscrews – an old-fashioned one with a little brush on the end for cleaning fragments of cork from the bottle top; some notes and lesson plans he'd brought in to show her; and an ancient, hand-knitted, bottle-green sweater that he kept there because he always complained her house was too cold in winter. She picked up the sweater and held it against her face. It smelt of George, of autumn leaves and grass, and the Old Spice she always smelled on his face and neck when he hugged her.

'You are so conventional,' she'd teased him once. 'You smell like forty years ago.'

'And who were you hugging forty years ago?'

'None of your business,' she'd said. 'A woman must have her secrets.'

The sweater was old and much washed, the wool soft against her skin. Barbara pressed it closer to her face and rocked gently back and forth.

'Do you have any idea how much I miss you, George?' she said. 'How hard it is to be without you?' She wished she could be angry. People often were when a loved one died, angry about being abandoned. Would anger be easier, she wondered, easier than this grinding sadness and emptiness that manifested at times as panic and at others as desolation?

She had told them she wasn't going to crack up, and she wouldn't, but there were things about George's death, what it had shown her and what it meant for the future, that were unexpected and very hard to contemplate. She had been given no say in the funeral arrangements, and although George's son and daughter-in-law had accepted her offer to have the wake in her home, she knew that their acceptance was about a responsibility they didn't want rather than an acknowledgement of her place in his life and his death. She remembered a colleague who, in her late thirties, had an affair with a married man. The hardest thing, she'd said, was that if he'd died no one would let her know, she couldn't even go to his funeral and no one would legitimate her grief. In George's death, as in his life, his family had treated Barbara as one of his friends, but they had never managed to get a grip on what they had meant to each other. Unlike her own family, they didn't seem to understand that friendship could be as profoundly rooted in love and commitment as any marriage might be.

'You mean they'd take it more seriously if we shared a bed?' she'd laughed one day when he had railed about his son's failure to comprehend.

'God no, they'd probably be horrified and embarrassed. They're far more conventional than our generation. No, I think the only thing that would do it would be if we got married.'

'And still lived in separate houses?'

He'd shrugged then. 'Who knows? I certainly don't.'

'But it doesn't really matter, you know,' she'd said. '*We* know what it means and so in the end it doesn't really matter.'

But now that George was gone, it seemed to matter quite a lot. It made Barbara feel that she had less right to grieve, that her loss was, in their eyes, less than it would have been if she and George had put a more conventional seal on their relationship. Perhaps it was petty to feel like this – after all, she was the one charged with collecting his ashes and sorting out the contents of his house – but again these were rights awarded for reasons of convenience.

Barbara took a final long draw on the scent of George's sweater and then leaned over the bed and tucked it under the quilt alongside her pillow. There was something else too, something that generated an unfamiliar sense of fear. For most of her life she had thought of herself as self-contained and alone, but she had not been alone since she and George had met. For several years now they had grown old together and ageing had not bothered her, she had enjoyed its rewards and satisfactions. But now she was fearful of her ability to cope with the challenges of everyday life: the mysteries of her computer, the servicing of her car, driving to unfamiliar places, learning to use new appliances – things she had always handled competently while George was alive seemed monumentally confusing, possibly even hazardous, now that he was gone.

Only a few weeks earlier she had been planning to travel to a strange country where she didn't speak a word of the language, to do a job she had never done before. It had seemed like a wonderful adventure. But when George took his last breath, the breath of her confidence had also been extinguished, and now she questioned her ability to cope with the comparatively trivial demands of an ordinary life. 'You must still go, for me, for both of us,' George had said as she knelt at his side. But the task was beyond her now and she knew she must let him down, that she could not see China for herself, let alone for both of them.

Barbara took the small bundle of possessions off the bed and placed them tenderly on the dresser, standing briefly with her hand resting on top of them before turning away. As she walked out of the room and down the stairs to the kitchen, she wondered, for the first time since she had made her move from the city, just how many years of independent living lay ahead, and she felt the icy chill of being alone. Ageing no longer seemed like a challenge to be met with enthusiasm, but like a long dark road full of potholes and boulders, a road she must negotiate without even a torch to light her way. A road that led nowhere.

TWENTY-SEVEN

Heather sprinkled cinnamon across the top of the custard tart and put it in the oven. By the time they were ready to eat it, after the pasta and salad, it would be cooked and still warm, the pastry sweet and short, the custard softly set and creamy, just as Ellis liked it. He had called to say that he would be there by seven and she had been determined to have everything ready so that she could relax, give time to him, and think about the future. The chaos of Christmas, her resignation, the drama of George's accident and death, her own grief and concern for Barbara, had all left her in turmoil. This weekend with Ellis would restore her. At last they would have peaceful time together.

'It's really quiet today,' Shaun had said earlier. 'Why don't you make the most of it and go home?'

Heather knew that he was trying to get everything in the office, including her, running smoothly before he left in a few weeks' time. He would do well with Rosa Hartman, but she dreaded his actual leaving. Patsy had resigned, they had found a new part-timer and Diane had agreed to stay on full time until the election. She would rent Shaun's house when he moved to Sydney. 'I'm very grateful,' Heather had told her. 'I thought you might be rushing off to Sydney too, to be near Stefan.'

'It's tempting,' Diane admitted, 'but I think we both need to take things slowly. The pace seems ideal at present – we have all the time in the world.'

Heather felt slightly in awe of Diane these days. Less than a year ago, brittleness and anger had made her irritating and exhausting, but now she had an enviable serenity, taking each day as it came, focusing on the present without worrying at the past or struggling to shape the future.

'You make it sound easy,' Heather said, 'embarking on this new relationship. But for me it seems like a constant battle to balance time and commitments and try to keep Ellis happy.'

'It *is* easy,' Diane said. 'Once I got over worrying about whether Stefan would still love me if he knew what I was really like, it became easy. The morning I woke up next to him for the first time I realised that it *could* be easy with him, because his ego doesn't get in the way.' She'd turned away slightly, stopping abruptly and blushing, as though she wished she hadn't said it. Heather got the feeling that she should have asked Diane exactly what she meant, but she hadn't liked to.

Despite her preparations and her impatience to see Ellis, Heather still felt nervous and empty, still questioned her ability to retain her sense of herself within the charmed circle. Sometimes she even felt she was teetering on the edge of a disaster she couldn't define. She poured herself a glass of wine and sat on the deck drawing lines with her finger through the condensation on the glass, thinking of things she needed to sort out with him. Head to Heart was number one. It wouldn't be easy, but it had to be done. And she needed him to understand that giving up her job didn't mean that she wanted to take on the job of looking after him. They were two intelligent adults who would care for each other. She wasn't about to become a doormat. But not tonight, she didn't have the energy for any of this tonight.

She heard a car purr to a halt outside and she finished her wine, got up and walked through the house to the front door. Ellis, who was unloading some things from the car, looked up and saw her framed in the doorway.

'Heather, darling,' he said, straightening up. 'How wonderful,' and he put down the files and boxes he was holding, walked over and drew her into his arms. She leaned against him, seeking the magic ingredient that everyone else seemed to have found.

Together they carried Ellis's things into the house and piled them onto the settee. 'I'll sort them out later,' he said, taking the glass she handed him. 'To you, my darling, to us,' and they sat together talking, until Ellis said he was famished and Heather lit the tall lemon-scented candles on the table and went to the kitchen to put the finishing touches to the pasta.

'I've missed you so much,' Ellis said, following her and slipping his arms around her waist, turning her to face him. 'In fact, I'm sure you can feel how much I've missed you, how glad I am to see you,' he said, sliding his hands down onto her bottom, pressing her closer. 'Maybe we should eat later,' he said, reaching up with one hand to unbutton her blouse.

Heather felt a sudden, quite shocking revulsion, and stopped his hand. She kissed him lightly and turned back to the stove. 'Let's wait,' she said, 'anticipation is part of the pleasure,' and she stirred the pasta, hoping he would not sense the tension in her body, the lack of conviction in her voice. 'Why don't you open another bottle of wine and we'll eat straight away.'

Slowly, methodically, she tilted the saucepan and tipped the pasta into a serving dish, scraping the last fragments away with a wooden spoon and sprinkling it with chopped parsley. She was watching herself, her every movement, as if from a distance and in slow motion, wondering what on earth she was doing. She was empty, drained of feeling, almost as she had been the morning after the shooting: an empty shell, doing things, saying things, but feeling nothing. As she carried the pasta out to the table she caught sight of herself in the hall mirror and paused, surprised at how calm she looked compared with the way she was trembling inside.

As they ate their pasta, Ellis described the rockery in the garden at Byron Bay that a local man had completed the previous day. 'I think you'll agree it looks excellent,' he said, breaking off a piece of warm Turkish bread and popping it into his mouth. 'It'll be better when the plants grow up a bit, but it's made a wonderful feature of that area of the garden.' He had overcome his initial disappointment at Heather's lack of interest in sex before dinner. He'd timed that erection perfectly, taking a tablet when he was twenty minutes away from Newcastle. He was familiar now with the time the medication took to work and how long the effect could be sustained. It was always a bit of a gamble, of course – sometimes it waned before he had the chance to take advantage of it, and he had to take another rather quickly to avoid an embarrassing loss of function. Managing the medication was difficult, as difficult as keeping the secret, but it was a cross he had to bear.

'Custard tart!' he exclaimed in delight as Heather put the dish on the table. 'My favourite, and it looks so perfect too.' He took a small piece on his spoon and tasted it, closing his eyes in pleasure. 'And it tastes even better. This is truly to die for, Heather. And I have a surprise for you – a couple of surprises, actually. Why don't we take our dessert outside, and I'll make some coffee and show you everything.'

Heather sat in the darkness, her eyes closed, trying to work out what had happened to her, why the light inside her had been extinguished, why, suddenly, even walking from the dining room to the garden seemed a huge effort. And why, after all the time alone when she had longed for Ellis's presence, she now felt weak and lost and longed to be alone.

'Here we are,' Ellis said, putting the tray on the table. 'I'll have to put the light on so you can see what I have to show you.'

Heather blinked in the sudden brightness, and felt a sharp twinge of pain in her shoulder as she straightened up and looked at the papers he was spreading across the table.

'First of all, though,' Ellis said, settling down opposite her, 'I guess we should talk about a timetable.'

'A timetable?' she said, wondering if she sounded obtuse but feeling simply confused.

'Yes.' He drew a year planner from his files and placed it between them. 'By now you must have decided when to close the office. Another month, perhaps; or maybe you feel you need to go on until Easter?'

'Close the office?' she said. 'What do you mean, close the office at Easter? It has to stay open until the election,' and she stabbed her finger onto the planner. 'This would be the earliest.'

Ellis looked up in shock. 'But I thought . . . ' he began, and as he opened his mouth he realised that although he understood very well the complexities of resigning from a parliamentary seat, he'd completely ignored them.

'I announced that I wouldn't be recontesting the seat,' Heather said. 'Until then I'm still the elected representative, and until then the office stays open.'

Ellis hesitated. 'Maybe you . . . '

'I told you before, Ellis, I talked to you about it on Boxing Day. I explained that the only way I could go earlier would be by creating a by-election, and there is no way I could do that with the state election only a few months away.' She paused. 'I've told you all this, and it was on the news and in the papers. Didn't you listen to anything I said?'

'Of course,' he said, 'of course I did. You did tell me and, anyway, I know the situation. It's my fault entirely, I got carried away by my enthusiasm to be with you. Setting my own agenda. I'm so sorry, Heather.' His shoulders drooped and he waited for Heather to apologise to him. She always apologised whether or not it was her fault. There was something reassuring about it, especially when it *wasn't* her fault. But there was no apology this time – in fact, she didn't actually say *anything* and Ellis was left to wallow in his own embarrassment.

'So, what did you want to show me?' Heather asked briskly, leaning forward to pick up the plunger and pour the coffee.

Ellis revived. 'Ah yes, the plans . . . well, a little delayed now, of course, only myself to blame for that.'

Heather pushed a cup across the table to him and waited.

'Ah, here it is,' he said. 'Now, I'm going to show you two things, this is the first.' He unrolled the drawing, showing the new floor plan of the house and two elevations.

'You're extending?' Heather said, pulling her glasses from where they hung tucked into the top of her shirt. 'It's going to look lovely. What's this extra room for?'

'For you,' Ellis said proudly. 'It's a study for you, and here, this one is a second bathroom, for you too. It's fine right now for me but with both of us living there, we'll need more space.'

'Living there?' Heather looked up sharply. 'Who said anything about living there?'

Ellis was determined to regain ground but his patience was being sorely tested. 'Well, we have to live somewhere and what better place than Byron? You loved the house.'

'It's a beautiful house,' Heather said, 'but I never said I wanted to live there. In fact, I never said anything about living with you, Ellis. I have my own house, my own life here.'

'But you'll sell this place,' Ellis replied. 'We don't need two houses and once you finish working, there's nothing to keep you here.'

Heather felt as though she had been gripped by a terrible disease; her throat was dry, her face burning. 'What do you mean, nothing to keep me?' she demanded. 'I love this house, this town, this part of the coast. Of course we'll have more time together but I never said anything about moving. There are things I'm planning to do here, lots of things. I want to spend time with Barbara, help the women's refuge find new premises, pin down some funding for the language classes, catch up with friends, heaps of stuff.'

Ellis understood it now; this was the natural panic of someone giving up an important and demanding job.

'Look, darling,' he said, 'I know the prospect of no longer being the honourable member is pretty scary, I felt it myself when the prospect of no longer being learned counsel was hovering, but we have each other and we have this.' He unrolled the second sheet. 'See this down here,' he said, showing her the outline of a new building located in a far corner of his block of land, 'this is the office, our office. We can run the business from here, heaps of space, air-conditioned, and although it's lower down the escarpment it still captures the view through the trees.'

'Run what business?'

'That's my second surprise,' Ellis said, reaching across in front of her for the revised business plan Luke had given him earlier that day. 'Head to Heart,' he said proudly, putting it in front of her so that she could see their two photographs side by side on the front page, their names as joint proprietors underneath. 'I'm making you an equal partner. It's my gift to you, Heather. You can run it, do the correspondence and the bookings; oh, and the accounts too. I know you have a real feel for it . . . '

The disease had Heather by the throat now. Her head was spinning and the inner void that had flummoxed her earlier had become a cauldron of rage. It seethed and churned within her and she rose to her feet, pushing back her chair, stepping away from the table, facing the garden in an effort to get control of herself.

'Now, of course you may feel you want to get into the coaching side too,' Ellis went on, moved to see that she was now overcome with emotion at his generosity, 'no reason why you wouldn't be able to do that once I've got you up to speed. And we'll talk to Luke about branding, how we can package you and me together.'

Heather's fever burned bright, melting the ice that encased decades of hurt and resentment, ripping through suppressed emotions and reigniting the spirit so effectively extinguished by Danny's bullet. Dizzy with shock and anger, she turned to face Ellis with the issue that her anxiety about and avoidance of Head to Heart had silenced until now.

'Tell me, Ellis,' she said, with a look on her face that he'd never seen before, 'I know you've been busy since we met, and you've been working on the book, but I don't really know anything about what you did before then, the clients you worked with, who they were, how you were able to help them.'

Ellis straightened the papers on the table. 'Well, as you said yourself, I haven't had time since we met to see any clients. There's been stuff to prepare for Luke, I've been looking after you, going back and forth between home and Sydney and here – it's hardly conducive to maintaining a practice.'

'Of course not,' she said. 'But previous clients, the case histories Luke asked you for as part of the marketing strategy – have you given them to him yet? Have you contacted the former clients and got permission to use their stories?'

'Not yet,' Ellis said, seemingly engrossed in searching for something amongst the paperwork.

'And that's because?'

'Well,' he said expansively, taking his time, tipping backwards in his chair and locking his fingers behind his head, 'it's not quite as easy as it sounds –'

'No, I'm sure it's not, because you've never really worked with anyone at all, have you? You've never actually *life-coached* anyone. All you've done is take some dodgy four-week course in California, and now you think you're qualified to tell other people how to live.'

Ellis rocked forward so hard in his chair he almost fell on his face across the table. 'Now, look here –'

'No,' Heather said, moving back to the table, planting her hands on it and staring him full in the face, 'no, Ellis, *you* look here. This Head to Heart stuff is a con, a very expensive con designed to rip off people who have inflated opinions of their own importance and more money than is good for them. Just what do you have to offer? What is it that's different about you now from the person you were at the bar, or the person who abandoned me all those years ago? You talk about achieving selfhood, but you can't define what you mean. You go on about building an inner life, but your inner life is a fantasy. Just as I was your fantasy. No wonder you found the reality so difficult to cope with.'

'Really . . . ' Ellis began struggling to his feet, his face a fiery red.

'Yes, really,' Heather went on with the same fluency and passion that had won her debates in parliament. 'You're a sham, Ellis, and the worst thing about it is that I don't think you even realise it. I fell for this because I fell for you, for your grand romantic gesture in coming back and claiming to rescue me from the effects of the shooting. I fell for you because of the past and because I was lonely and frightened, so I deluded myself into thinking that you loved me and, worse still, that I loved you. I fell for you so completely that I even forgave you for the past. I forgave you without question when I should have rubbed your nose in it until you begged for mercy. But you pressed all my buttons and I responded like one of Pavlov's dogs.'

'But I love you, Heather,' Ellis said now, moving towards her. 'You know I do, I love you, I want you to live with me, marry me –'

'Don't come near me,' she said, holding up a hand. She felt like Medusa, snakes hissing and flailing around her head. 'You don't know what love is, Ellis, and maybe I don't either or I would have recognised earlier that this is not it. You love only yourself, and you use everyone else to feed your fantasies. I may be confused about love, Ellis, but I believe you are incapable of it.'

Ellis took a couple of staggering steps backwards. 'You surely can't believe that I came to find you just to take advantage of you?'

Heather shrugged. 'Maybe you did, or perhaps you are so self-deluding that you convinced yourself that you had other motives. Either way, I let myself be drawn into your madness and colluded with it to an extent that I now find breathtaking. But whichever it was it's over now, totally and completely over. Pack up your architect's drawings and your business plans, and that ridiculous box of underwear. Go back to your treetop house. And if the reality of no longer being an eminent person is too much for you, find yourself a fantasy that doesn't mess with other people's heads. I don't ever want to see or hear from you again.'

It was well after midnight and Adam still couldn't get to sleep. He lay on his side trying not to disturb Jill but he was itching to move. His legs were restless, his brain buzzing in that pointless, unfocused way that threatens hours of sleeplessness ahead. Perhaps it would be best to get up, go downstairs, make some tea and see if there were some mind-numbing, sleep-inducing rubbish on television. In nine minutes it would be half past one; if he were still awake then, he would get up. Tonight he had played his final concert as a permanent member of the orchestra. There had been drinks afterwards, and his colleagues had presented him with a large and beautiful hardback book on the history of the cello, and there had been the standard gold watch as the formal gift for early retirement.

'The first time we get you in to play as a casual, you have to give it back,' the general manager had joked as he handed it over. 'It may be easiest if I just hang on to it.'

And, amid the laughter, Adam felt the joy of nostalgia; by releasing himself from the orchestra he could now relish the good times, the artistic and social satisfactions that had been swamped by his former discontent. Jill and Diane had come to the concert and the presentation, and when they'd got home they'd opened more champagne. Too much emotion, too much talk and too much champagne . . . he probably wouldn't get any sleep. One twenty-seven; if he were still awake in three minutes, he'd get up. When the phone rang at quarter to two he was soundly asleep. Fumbling for the receiver, heart pounding with shock, he dragged himself up in the bed, expecting disaster. Beside him, Jill was hauling herself into a sitting position.

'Sorry,' said a shaky voice at the end of the line. 'So sorry to wake you . . . '

'Heather?' Adam asked. 'Are you okay? Has something happened?'

'Yes and no,' she said. 'I am okay, but then I suppose I'm not or I wouldn't be ringing at this time of night.'

'What is it?' Adam said, half turning the receiver from his ear so that Jill could hear.

'It's over,' Heather said. 'I've ended it with Ellis. He's gone. I tore him to shreds, and myself too. But it's over, Adam, it's all over, and he won't be back.'

Adam felt his heart and his gut begin to stabilise. 'Would you like me to drive up there now?'

There was a pause at the other end of the line. 'No,' Heather said, 'thank you, it's lovely of you to offer, far more than I deserve, but no. I just needed to tell someone, to make it real, confirm it to someone else, and for obvious reasons that person had to be you.'

'I see,' Adam said, aware that the sadness in her voice was underlined with a strength he hadn't heard for a very long time. 'And you're sure this is the right decision?'

'Absolutely sure. I'm so sorry, I accused you of not letting go of the past, when all the time I hadn't let go of it myself. I'd buried all that anger and hurt and pretended it didn't matter, so that when Ellis came back I was able to fool myself into believing it. I was so

338

sceptical about all the stuff he said about how romantic it was, but all the time I'd really fallen in love with just that – the idea of having him back, the romance of a second chance. It was his fantasy, him and me together, and I couldn't wait to join in.'

'It's understandable,' Adam said. 'You would never have taken him back if it hadn't been for the shooting, what it did to you.'

Heather gave a dry laugh. 'Well, that's my excuse too,' she said, 'and I'm going to stick to it. Anyway,' she went on, 'I'm sorry to wake you, and Jill too, tell her I'm sorry, for this and for behaving like a lunatic for the past few months.'

'Stop apologising, Heather,' Adam said. 'What matters is that it's over, and you're okay. We'll be there with you in the morning, we'll go and have lunch somewhere and talk it all through.'

'Thanks,' she said, 'that would be lovely. And, Adam? Thanks for . . . for loving me enough to never pretend that it was all okay.'

TWENTY-EIGHT

'You're awake, then?' Barbara said, peering across at Heather as she stretched and rubbed her eyes. 'Did you sleep well?'

'Not bad,' Heather said, looking at her watch. 'Not long now.' She took a drink from her bottle of water and looked back at Barbara. 'Excited?'

'Very,' Barbara said. 'I still don't really understand how you managed to organise this.'

'Shaun agreeing to stay on for an extra month, Rosa not complaining about it, and Diane being an incredibly efficient electorate officer.'

'But the party!'

Heather shrugged. 'I'd already sacrificed my reputation and goodwill as far as most of my colleagues were concerned, so there wasn't anything to lose. And taking a month off now is not too bad. I couldn't have done it any closer to the election. Does it matter to you very much that you're not doing the teaching?'

Barbara shook her head. 'No. I'm going to volunteer to teach classes for migrant women when we get back.' She let down the tray on the back of the seat in front of her. 'They're bringing lunch,' she said. 'It'll probably be rubbery chicken but I'm going to eat it anyway. Helps pass the time.'

Heather let down her own table. 'Me too. Why don't you put your bag on the spare seat? You've been clutching it to your chest since take-off.' She reached out to take the bag but Barbara twisted away from her.

'No,' she said, 'I need to hold it.'

'Whatever for? I've never known you be fussy about a bag. Anyone would think you'd brought all your valuables with you.'

'Well,' Barbara said, lowering her voice, 'I have, actually. Not valuables in the way you mean, but valuable to me.' She glanced around and unzipped the leather handbag. 'It's George,' she said, drawing out a battered tobacco tin. 'I've got him in here.'

'What?' Heather exclaimed. 'What do you mean, George . . . ?'

'Shush!' Barbara said, looking around nervously. 'If you want to transport human remains you have to fill out all sorts of forms and get permission from the next of kin. Well, that's for bodies, I'm not sure about ashes, but I didn't ask.'

'You mean you've got George's ashes in a tobacco tin?'

'Yes, it's his favourite tin. Golden Virginia. He liked the pattern and the colours, green and gold.'

'But I thought you collected the ashes and gave them to his family?'

'I did,' Barbara said, blushing, 'most of them. But I liberated a bit of George for myself, and for him too. I opened the container and took some out, and then I resealed it and gave it to his son.' Heather's mouth had dropped open. 'Don't look at me like that,' Barbara hissed, 'I only took a little. They're going to bury the ashes in the grave with his wife and I know he wouldn't want that. She'd *wanted* to be buried but George could never stand the thought of being underground himself. That's why he chose cremation; he thought scattering the ashes was a way to free the spirit.'

'So you . . . ?'

'Stole some of George, yes,' Barbara said defiantly. 'In fact, I like to think that what I've got here is George himself, and what's under the ground is his clothes and the coffin. I scattered a little in his garden, and a little in my own, and then I rode over to our favourite café by the river and scattered some from the balcony; only a tiny bit, of course. And the rest of him is in here to scatter somewhere off the Great Wall. He so wanted to see it, had done all his life, and then . . . ' She swallowed and rubbed her eyes with the hand that wasn't holding the tobacco tin. 'And then just when he was going to see it he . . . he . . . '

Heather leaned across and put an arm around her shoulders.

'He told me to go, you know, the day of the accident, before he . . . before he sort of disappeared from himself, that day by the road. "You go," he said, "go for both of us", but I thought I couldn't. Not alone, I couldn't, and then a couple of weeks later you turned up with the tickets and . . . '

'And you thought you'd keep some of the ashes for China.'

'Yes. I'm sorry, Heather, I should have told you. Goodness knows what they'll say if they inspect my bag at the airport and then want me to open the tin.'

Heather was having trouble restraining her own tears. 'They won't,' she said, 'they don't apprehend respectable elderly ladies. Just try to pretend you *are* one, for a change. This is one time when being seventy-six is a big advantage.'

'You think?'

'I do. But they're also unlikely to apprehend an Australian member of parliament, so I'll put George in my bag if you like.'

Barbara hesitated and then shook her head. 'Thanks, but no, I want him with me. You're not mad at me, not telling you?'

Heather laughed. 'It's wonderful. I'm proud of you, proud to be with you and with George. Of course we'll take him to a high point on the Wall and set him free.' She paused, looking down at the tobacco tin in Barbara's hand. 'You know, Barb, all the time with Ellis I kept thinking of what you and George had and how special it was. I kidded myself that *we* could have that, that I could get him to change and then it would work. But Ellis would have had to become a different person for that to happen. It's the ultimate arrogance, isn't it, believing you can change someone?'

'Yes, but most of us are guilty of it at some time or other,' Barbara said.

'I can't believe it took me so long to come to my senses.'

'Well, you did, that's what matters, and next time –'

'I doubt there'll be a next time,' Heather cut in. 'The sort of relationship I wanted – that combination of separateness and attachment – it's hard to find.'

'But not impossible. I searched for a long time and eventually found it with George when I least expected it. Maybe you will too.'

'Maybe.'

'In the end what matters is what you make of it.'

'Sorry?'

'Like with the shooting, you had a choice. You could see yourself as a victim or a survivor, and it was clear, very early on, that you chose to be a survivor. Same with the Ellis saga. What will you choose to make of it?'

'Um . . . I'm hopeless relationship material?'

Barbara rolled her eyes. 'Or?'

'Or what?'

'Or, you're a woman who's not scared of being alone.'

'I see,' Heather said. 'I like that. It sounds like someone I know, like a woman who puts the man she loves in a tobacco tin and takes him to China.'

'To set him free.'

'Exactly,' Heather said. 'That's it, then. That's what I choose: to be a woman exactly like that.'

ACKNOWLEDGMENTS

Many thanks to my son, Mark Bennett, and his fiancée, Sarah Leaton, for introducing me to Newcastle and the Hunter Valley, and for their valuable help in finding locations where my characters could feel at home. The research trip was enormous fun and your local knowledge saved me hours of tedious work.

Special thanks also to Peter Grayling and Robyn Johnston, who spent time talking with me about the qualities of the cello, the life of a cellist, the work of an orchestra and the qualities of the Bach Preludes. I am most grateful.

And I am indebted to Gail Bell's fine and fascinating book *Shot* for an insight into the immediate psychological effects of being shot.

It is, as always, a huge pleasure to work with the terrific team at Pan Macmillan, and I thank Cate Paterson and Sarina Rowell for their wisdom and patience. If there is an award for keeping writers on track during crises of confidence, they would have to be the winners. Jo Jarrah is a brilliant editor, and her creative and thoughtful contribution is always so valuable. And Jane Novak gets the award for being publicity manager of the year, and for always knowing when it is time to eat and top up the caffeine levels. Many thanks, too, to my agent, Sheila Drummond.

It goes without saying (but I'll say it anyway) that events like those depicted in *Trip of a Lifetime* do happen in the world, but this is entirely a work of fiction and any mistakes in it are my own.

ALSO AVAILABLE FROM PAN MACMILLAN

Liz Byrski
Gang of Four

She had a husband, children and grandchildren who loved her, a beautiful home, enough money. What sort of person was she to feel so overwhelmed with gloom and resentment on Christmas morning?

They have been close friends for almost two decades, supporting each other through personal and professional crises – parents dying, children leaving home, house moves, job changes, political activism, diets and really bad haircuts.

Now the 'gang of four', Isabel, Sally, Robin and Grace, are all fifty-something, successful . . . and restless.

'Finally. A coming of age novel for the rest of us.'
SUSAN MAUSHART, author of WIFEWORK

'A mature, relevant and entertaining first novel . . . subversive, GANG OF FOUR will ignite more than plum puddings.'
WEEKEND AUSTRALIAN

'This is not a book about mid-life crisis so much as mid-life opportunity. The characters are like people you know – and there will be people you know who could learn something from them.'
SYDNEY MORNING HERALD

Liz Byrski
Food, Sex & Money

It's almost forty years since the three ex-convent girls left school and went their separate ways, but finally they meet again.

Bonnie, rocked by the death of her husband, is back in Australia after decades in Europe, and is discovering that financial security doesn't guarantee a fulfilling life. Fran, long divorced, is a freelance food writer, battling with her diet, her bank balance and her relationship with her adult children. And Sylvia, marooned in a passionless marriage, is facing a crisis that will crack her world wide open.

Together again, Bonnie, Fran and Sylvia embark on a venture that will challenge everything they thought they knew about themselves – and give them more second chances than they could ever have imagined.

'*Food, Sex & Money* is an entertaining, ultimately optimistic, novel'
WEST AUSTRALIAN

'The issues of financial security, emotional independence, career, diet, motherhood and sexuality transcend age, making this a relevant, enjoyable read for all women, and for men who seek to understand them.'
GOOD READING

Liz Byrski
Belly Dancing for Beginners

Gayle and Sonya are complete opposites: one reserved and cautious, the other confident and outspoken. But their lives will be turned upside down when they impulsively join a belly dancing class.

Marissa, their teacher, is sixty, sexy, and very much her own person, and as Gayle and Sonya learn about the origins and the meaning of dance, much more than their muscle tone begins to change.

'A very funny book yet one with a serious point – women in their 50s and beyond can still have challenging, rewarding and hugely enjoyable lives.'
SUNDAY TASMANIAN

'Byrski's women have something of the wisdom of age but still grapple with the complexities of relationships with husbands, children, parents and friends. They are also still intrigued by romantic possibilities and the search for love.'
WEST AUSTRALIAN